# Hailbringer

HAILBRINGER
Copyright © 2024 by Daniel Alexandrescu.

All rights reserved. No part of this book may be used or reproduced in any manner whatsoever without written permission except in the case of brief quotations embodied in critical articles or reviews.
This book is a work of fiction. Names, characters, businesses, organizations, places, events, and incidents either are the product of the author's imagination or are used fictitiously. Any resemblance to actual persons, living or dead, events, or locales is entirely coincidental.

For information contact: www.hailbringer.com

Book and Cover design by Thea Magerand
Editing & Formatting by Daniel Alexandrescu

ISBN: 979-88-70408-80-4
First Edition: January 2024
Revised First Edition: June 2024

9 8 7 6 5 4 3 2 1

# Hailbringer

### Daniel Alexandrescu

#### A Romanian Folktale

# DISCLAIMER

The names of places in this book reflect those first mentioned in historical records, and not their current names. For example, places such as *Kruhnen*, *Härmeschtat*, *Braylan* or *Dlăgopole* are known today as *Brașov*, *Sibiu*, *Brăila* and *Câmpulung* respectively. Specific objects, characters, and certain expressions are italicized and explained in the **Glossary** upon their first mention for clarity. Many of these elements are unique to Romanian culture, so I have chosen to present them in their original form as a means of cultural promotion. Years are indicated using both the current calendar and the old Byzantine calendar, used in old local chronicles, aligning with the book's historical setting, for authenticity. This book is inspired by a rich tapestry of Romanian myths, legends, traditions, folktales, folklore, and historical events. Some elements have been altered or are entirely fictitious to enhance the narrative, and although it follows historical events, it may also include anachronisms. Any phrases that may appear discriminatory, sexist, racially, or xenophobically charged are used solely to reflect the historical context of the book and for authenticity and do not represent my personal views or beliefs. This book does not endorse or glorify suicide, violence, or abuse in any form. While such elements may be present in the narrative, they are included solely for the purpose of historical accuracy and storytelling and are not reflective of any promotion of such actions.

# CONTENTS

*PROLOGUE* ................................................................. 1
CHAPTER I ................................................................... 7
CHAPTER II ................................................................ 19
CHAPTER III ............................................................... 39
CHAPTER IV ............................................................... 53
CHAPTER V ................................................................ 75
CHAPTER VI ............................................................... 95
CHAPTER VII ............................................................ 119
CHAPTER VIII .......................................................... 137
CHAPTER IX ............................................................. 157
CHAPTER X .............................................................. 179
CHAPTER XI ............................................................. 197
CHAPTER XII ............................................................ 221
CHAPTER XIII ........................................................... 243
CHAPTER XIV ........................................................... 259
CHAPTER XV ............................................................ 287
CHAPTER XVI ........................................................... 311
CHAPTER XVII .......................................................... 327
*EPILOGUE* .............................................................. 343

# PROLOGUE

*Wallachia, April 1431 (6939)*

He was old. He was so old that he had forgotten to count his winters. Many of his memories were swimming through his head as figments of his imagination. Have they ever happened?

And he was alone. His kind, they all likely disappeared, if they ever existed. For as long as he's lived, he's never met anyone like himself. He could have been the only one who ever lived for all he knew.

When he was just a boy, his Master told him that his forefathers had been many, but with the passage of time and the wars festering the lands, there were only a few of them now, scattered across the land, fulfilling their lives missions, as he was. But he never met them.

As he was now slogging up the hill, his breath was not on his side anymore. His longtime friend, the oak cane, was merely keeping his knees from cracking under the weight of his torso. He had to cease his journey to the hill's summit several times.

While resting on a big rock to catch his breath, he encountered a family, all gathered in a horse-pulled, covered wagon, coming from the opposite direction. The mother was on foot, besides the horse, restraining it carefully so that the cart wouldn't crash as they were rushing down the hill.

But the Old-Man saw their faces. They were both scared—the

horse and the mother. Her skirt was covered in mud, ash, and blood. Her children were crying in the wagon, but the man couldn't see them. And their father was nowhere in sight either.

He would've asked the woman for some rye or even a drop of water to ease his journey to the top. She may have noticed the white-bearded stranger's tattoo carved on his forehead, a mark of his guild. And he knew that if he asked her, she would've stopped and certainly pulled out a piece of bread from somewhere and given it to him.

'Here,' she would've said. 'Take this, Master-Mason, and may you keep our harvest safe as the Lord may keep you!'

But he kept his tongue between his teeth when his misty grey eyes met her sombre, red eyes. He let the family pass without saying a word, and as they did, he could see a man's body lying in the wagon and her two dirty, snot-over-their-chest children sobbing and calling out for their father. The Old-Man sighed.

As the sun was still yet to strike the middle of the sky, he continued to put one foot in front of the other through the mushy bottle grass. Over his hooded hemp rags that he was wearing, he carried a small leather knapsack where he was usually keeping some food, his birch-tree scripture, herbs, and a waterskin, which was now dried out.

Propped on his stick, the man pulled out a small pouch from his bag. He grabbed some dry herbs between his fingers and smelled them. Some flakes snowed on his white and dirty moustache as he let the strong and minty aroma reinvigorate him, enough to keep him going.

The closer he got to the summit, the more he could hear the sorrowful laments of the village echoing in the distance.

The imposing mountains were rising like a giant wall, ready to fall over his left side as he was turning right, finding a path towards the settlement. A stench of burnt wood and flesh hit his nostrils and made him cough his lungs out, getting stuck in his throat. He mumbled. The smell wouldn't go away, but the Old-Man started to ignore it as he could finally stand straight and see the village unfolding in front of him.

He has witnessed what war can turn a man into. But the scene he was now gazing at, like an infected wound on the sacred earth's skin, was overwhelming, even for him. He breathed deeply, his eyes scouting across the sky, while his long, oily hair unreeled over his humped back. *Moșii*, the ancient Gods of these lands, were no longer listening; this land was forever forsaken and cursed.

Twisted strings of dark, choking smoke were rising from the ruins of what was until recently the home of many peaceful, field working Wallachians. The wind carried ash through the air, bringing with it the scent of death. On the horizon, even the clouds seemed stained by innocent blood.

The grass on which the Elder was walking was darkened and crisp, turning to dust under his feet. The need to pull a rag from his waist to cover his mouth and nose became more and more grave as he entered the village. The cries were louder. He saw an old woman on her knees, thrown over the body of a man lying in the puddle, with his face slashed open by a blade. Her house had been burned down, and her cattle were killed, with their throats slit.

The young boys and girls had all been taken away as blood-tribute, leaving behind only the dead and the old. But the time-worn wanderer knew that within the heart of the war-plagued thorp there was the reason he left his den weeks ago, even before the pillaging happened.

He was old, indeed, and he not only sensed his winters on this realm were numbered. But his powers had yet to leave him. He could also feel, deep within himself, that an heir to the legacy he amassed during his century on this earth was hidden somewhere in this nightmare. A bud of hope that started to bloom right when he not only lost all hope but had forgotten what hope really was, while the only thing he was then waiting for was to embark on his eternal *Otherworld* journey.

And then he heard it.

Through the echoes of the many old maids' dirges, his ear, still sharp, caught a trace of another sound, perhaps a dozen steps away, in front of him. A whimper. A child's cry. A boy mistakenly left behind by the predators during their rabid slaughter. The man took a few steps to get closer to the source, with his withered fingers pressed on the cane. The cry became louder and louder.

Right around the demolished corner of what days before someone's abode was, his eyes met the cremated courtyard, with ash scattered to all corners while embers were still fuming.

A man was lying on the ground with half of his face buried in the dirt. His free eye was still open, forever frozen in time, and his mouth was filled with mud and flies. His back was covered in blood, and he had three pokes in his shirt. His white, stiff hand was still wrapped around the handle of a steel axe.

The Old-Man could almost see how the man tried to make a stand against the intruders but was eventually overwhelmed and brought to his knees by spears cowardly dug in his back. The wanderer whispered a short prayer as he passed by the corpse on his way to the tumbled-down house's entrance, from where the cries were getting closer.

On the floor, next to the stove, he saw the body of a young woman propped against the wall. Her *ie*, the white linen shirt she was wearing, has been ripped off her chest, revealing her body covered in dry blood that ran down from her sliced throat. The mother.

Cruel marauders must have desecrated her body and ended her days when they were done. Next to her, a little boy was crying his eyes out, his voice slowly cracking. Sitting naked in the ashes of his once home, dirty, starved, and alone, he was pulling at his mother's dress, trying to wake her up and feed him.

Stuck in the doorway with one hand on his cane and the other on the door frame, the man clenched his teeth, his eyes resting on the boy. He found him—his promised heir.

He came closer to him and his mother, kneeling next to them. The boy turned and looked at him, with his snot dried out on his lips and chin, covering his nose so that he could barely breathe. His sobbing turned into rhythmic sighs. The Old-Man covered the boy's little fist with his husky palm and unclenched his little fingers off the woman's skirt.

'Easy, easy...' he whispered, then released his hand.

The boy looked at him with curiosity. His clear, blue-grey eyes met the stranger's cloudy-ashen ones. Silky, copper-chestnut hair was covering his head. The wanderer knew that it was only once in a few generations that a child like the boy he just found was born. A boy like him was destined for great things. The blood of the long-forgotten Fire-Knights must have run through his veins.

The child was never going to grow up in the village. A cruel tragedy has happened to his people, his home, and his family. But it was only fate that made it so that he would be left orphaned, forgotten by the killers, and eventually found by the stranger.

The Old-Man took off his hooded hemp cloak and covered the woman's body to hide her shame. He touched his tongue with his finger, then the floor, coating it in dust and ash. Then he swiftly murmured *rebo'ditas*, in his ancestors' tongue while drawing a dotted circle in the middle of the woman's forehead, like the one he was bearing, wishing her to follow the light.

He then stood up, grunting, and relying heavily on the stick, catching his breath. He knew that soon the Voivode's Hunters' militia would arrive in the village, so he had to go. He turned to the boy and slid his hands under his small armpits, raising him up in the air and sitting him on his right arm, close to his chest and shoulder. The boy started to cry, looking down at his mother, sensing it was goodbye.

'The Gods will care for her now, boy!' the Old-Man mumbled. 'And I'll care for you.'

He turned towards the door, scratching the floor with his stick, and as soon as he was out, his eyes lay on the boy's father once more. In the sun's warm light, with its rays struggling to crack through the smoke and ash floating in the air, the blade of the man's axe caught the wanderer's eye. He understood. The Gods were always asking for a sacrifice, even a humble one.

He used his stick to slowly get on one knee next to the corpse and then discarded his trusty oak cane. His hand unwrapped the man's fingers off the axe's handle, and then he took the tool in his own hand. When the time would come, the Elder knew that the boy raised from the ashes would need his father's arm beside him, at the ready.

'*Rebo'ditas!*' he once more released from his lips, wishing the man a smooth journey alongside his woman.

Then, pushing the axe into the ground, the wanderer used every ounce of strength he had left to get back on his shaking feet. The boy was crying, hungry, and raising his hands towards the home they were leaving behind. A few drops of sweat rolled on the man's temples, weltering down in his scratchy beard as he grunted and tried to breathe. They had a long journey ahead.

Rain clouds started to gather out of nowhere in the sky as the Old-Man, carrying the boy, made his way out of the village. Storm-promising thunder was intertwining with the child's moans, and a heavy rug of clouds seemingly smouldered the village in their dark, milky embrace.

The man looked back at it for one last time, then turned his face to the sky, and finally, as he turned his eyes ahead, resuming his path, an otherworldly flood unleashed over the boy's once-home, swallowing the embers, the smoke, the elderly, and the dead, purging the massacre off the face of the earth.

# CHAPTER I

*Mehadia Citadel, April 1459 (6967)*

'GET IN THERE!' THE MAN BLASTED, LOCKING the gateway shut behind him while spitting a well-crafted phlegm on the stone floor.

'Not so brave without your axe now, are we?' he hazed him. 'We'll see how unwilling you are to talk, come morning!' And then the man turned around, his sabatons clattering as he stepped up the stairs.

As soon as the guard disappeared, the prisoner threw himself against the iron bars the door was made of, like a rabid dog. He first tested their resistance by grabbing them with his hands and frantically shaking them off.

'*Sturdy, too sturdy...*' he thought to himself. He then took a few steps back. He poked around briefly, measuring the bleak dungeon he found himself trapped in. It was dark and suffocating, the stench of mold and gods-know-what other warm and heavy filth filling up his lungs. This hog pen's stingy, earthy whiff was overwhelming. He couldn't be here all night. He wouldn't have it. He had to get out.

The only light was coming from upstairs, where the guardian left an anaemic torch flickering in a bracket. But it was more than enough for the hostage to see his surroundings as clear as day. Walking behind, away from the entrance, his back touched the cold, wet, and sticky stone wall, covered in lichens. He pressed his palms against it and pushed, gaining a good swing.

When he knocked on the door, crumbs of plaster fell from the cracked ceiling, absorbing the impact while making a muffled sound. He cursed as his broad shoulder took a great hit too, his bones hurting and his sore muscles deforming. He repeated the attack, throwing himself against the solid bars again. And again. Like a wild cat trapped in a cage. He roared, knowing that even he couldn't take down that cell gate.

According to the dark carvings of the cross he saw outside on the walls, the Teutons might have been around this place at one point or another. While passing through the garrison's gates as he was brought in shackled, he looked at everything, as he was trained to observe. And if these knights were the ones who built this fortress, they built it to stand against time. And his shoulders.

There wasn't any other choice but to wait for the sunrise. He let himself slide down with his back against the door, rubbing his swollen muscles and setting his bones in place through the shirt, and he realized he was cold. The captors relieved him of his cloak and his belongings before they threw him into the jail wagon on their way to the citadel.

A familiar, stabbing pain embraced his temples, like two knives twisting his brains in.

'*Not now...*' he whimpered, standing up in panic and grabbing his head in his palms. He started trying to soothe the pain by rubbing his temples through the mane of his auburn hair, which turned dirty crimson in the dull dungeon. His heart started galloping, knowing very well that his migraines would never come alone.

As he was pressing on his temples, he began portioning the air he was breathing, filling up his lungs with the tainted air surrounding him, keeping it in for longer than usual, then letting it out at a snail's pace, attempting to regain his composure. As he was once told. With his eyes closed, he tried in vain to find peace.

However, the more he tried to clear his mind, the more clarity slipped away from him.

'*You've broken your oath!*' the master's sombre, trouncing voice hissed in his eardrums.

'*You have dishonoured the gifts that the Gods have offered you...!*' the Old-Man's words continued to reverberate.

'*...My legacy!*'

Other voices overlapped.
*'You are a disgrace!'* they were saying.
*'You should've never come back!'*
*'You are a disgrace!'*
*'YOU ARE A DISGRACE!'*

He found himself screaming. The wall he just hit burst his skin open on his knuckles. But his mind turned quiet suddenly, his brows pulsating like thunder dispersing in the distance. Pain replaces pain.

Thin, swift rivers of blood ran on the back of his fist, and as he watched them slow down, he thought to himself that the man—his teacher—was right. He should have never returned to these lands. Whatever has been done can never be undone.

He should have lived the rest of his cursed days on the forested shores of *Scodra*, where he'd taken his freeman's name, doing what he knew. Earning his devil's coin, he made the most of the avarice of the sly Venetian lords, who wanted their rivals dead for power and wealth.

He was born into murder, and so he became it. He has been on the run all his life, either isolated from the world, living in the shadows, or thrown into the fighting pit with the beasts. He survived them all, as he turned into one of them. His home was either a prison or the road.

And he was yearning for peace. He once knew it, many moons ago, and he knew it existed. It was the only time in his whole damned existence that his mind was clear and not poisoned by demons and nightmares. He missed it.

For him, peace had a face that he turned to again and again. He could still see glimpses of it during his few good days when closing his eyes. But that face was slipping away from him each day.

His despair was showing its claws through the cracks of his thoughts, in his dreams, or while losing himself, like he just did now before punch the solid and sharp wall of his cell. It was this despair that pushed him enough to want to leave behind his days as a soldier of fortune and take the path to the Banat, which the Hungarians called Temesköz, and its inhabitants—Temişana. From there He wanted to return to the only place that ever resembled a home—The Hollow Mountain.

The bleeding stopped shortly after he licked his knuckles, the metallic taste flooding his tongue. He was mad at himself. It was foolish to have almost broken his hand, as he knew he needed it in the next few hours, when the guard was going to come to take him up for inquisition. He had no intention to be a part of it. And he knew that he could find a way out of it, if he was prepared, not as he was when the bloody knights captured him at the crossroads, as he was leaving these lands.

Hours that felt like weeks passed. When he heard again the guard's sheet-metal shoes on the stairs, his head raised off the cold stone floor, where he spent the rest of the night with his eyes glued on the old, arched ceiling and his mind in all corners. The torch's blaze came closer, its warm light casting shaking shadows on the filthy walls. The man hit the gate's iron bars with his gloved fist.

'Stand up!' he ordered; his guttural voice filled with disdain. 'Right away, I said! You hear me?'

The prisoner cursed him just by looking at him. He was going to follow the orders for now. He knew his time would come, and this fool of a man was going to get his. And so, he stood up, getting close to the door.

When the torch's light fell on his face, the guardian involuntarily took a step back. The devilish insignia cast on the prisoner's forehead reminded the poor knight why he and his fellows imprisoned the stranger to begin with. And how much they struggled to do so. He tried to quickly come back to his senses. He cleared his throat and came closer to the door, with his free hand resting on the belt near his sword's hilt.

'Your hands, you bastard!' he mumbled.

The hostage looked at him through the straggly strands of rusty hair falling on his forehead and temples. He kept his wits about him while the headache was still floating through his brain. He passed his arms through the mid-door opening, where the prisoners were getting their food through. Next to his sword, dangling from his belt, the guardian kept his shackles. He fixed the torch on the wall, and then he took the shackles and unskilfully wrapped them around the stranger's wrists. The stranger wouldn't take his eyes off him the whole time, smelling the guard's fear and contempt and studying him in silence.

'*Patience...*' he said to himself.

'Step back!'

He followed the order, and then the chains keeping the door locked fell to the floor as his captor opened it wide. With his hand squeezing his sword's hilt, the man spit another phlegm and barked:

'Out with you, turd!'

The prisoner stepped out, and the man wrapped his hand almost instantly around the chain of his shackles, standing behind him and keeping his other hand tight around the hostage's arm.

As he was pushed up the stairs, his leather boots sounded like muffled hammers hitting wood. The arched entrance to the dungeon—a thick, reinforced wooden door—was revealed in front of him. The knight unwrapped his hand from his arm for only a few moments, enough to knock his fist into the wood twice. And then twice again.

The prisoner heard a key turning in the lock, and then the door opened, sunlight pouring through it unexpectedly. With his eyes caught by surprise, the prisoner turned his head away from it, trying to shield them from the light. But the guard had neither patience nor sympathy for it, as he hastened to keep going, helping himself with a knee poke to nudge the hostage in the right direction.

Once his eyes adjusted, he quickly looked around, scouting the space for ways out while the man was dragging him towards the exit.

They entered the courtyard of the settlement, leaving the dungeon tower behind. His boots sank into the mud, sliding, and stumbling as the stones arranged here and there to avoid turning the place into a cesspool were not covering enough of the ground. It was sunny right now, but it must have poured the whole time he was in the tower's basement. And it wasn't as cold as he felt all night.

From the walls of the massive, two-levelled tower, tall stone walls were built to the left and right, closing the court into a big square. Sentries were posted on them, patrolling in the corner areas. Some of them threw a quick eye to the guard and the foreigner as they were almost sliding on the uneven court towards its middle.

Tents were raised in the spaces between the courtyard's walls and the sloping trail they were walking on. The prisoner kept moving, waiting for an opportunity, noticing the bigger tent and the campfire towards where his 'friend' seemed to have been directing him. Unarmoured, dark-clothed soldiers were approaching, some curious, some just thrusting their heads out of their tents.

'Look at his wicked mug!' the stranger heard some of them mumbling.

'His sort dwells with *Necurat*, the Demon; there are no doubts about it.'

In front of the big tent, around the fire built for cooking, five men were sitting on fallen, large wooden logs that seemed to have been there for ages, rising from the dirt, with the grass starting to swallow them. Their eyes were locked on him as he was brought closer to them.

Unlike the other soldiers, these few had their grey gambesons covering their black undergarments, which were visible only through the empty spaces between the armour plates. The sign of a dark raven's head was knitted on their chests, while on their backs, two black spread wings completed the tapestry, with each wing placed where the men's shoulder blades were. Their helmets were lying on the ground next to their feet.

'Unchain him, Grigore!' the voice of one of them sounded. It was gruff, monotone, and descriptive of the way the Ravens' leader appeared. He had big, grey, and wavy hair, gleaming with dried-up sweat. His short beard had crumbs of bread in it, which he wiped away with the back of his sleeve when he stood up and gave the order.

The guard hesitated.

'Are you certain, captain?' he said. 'This devil would jump at us at the first chance, by the looks of it.'

'We're six grown men; he's got no weapons,' the captain grumbled. 'If we're afraid of his kind, we have no place to be here at the Citadel in the first place.'

'Besides,' he continued. 'An honourable man deserves to eat with his own hands. If he's an honourable man, that is.'

The hostage was surprised. He agreed with the guard. Knowing himself and his ways, it did seem like a poor decision to be uncuffed. He would've traded each of these men's lives if that brought him freedom. But the captain was right too. They had armour, swords, and crossbows. He had nothing.

He let Grigore take off his shackles peacefully, his eyes looking right into his liberator's. He rubbed his wrists, peeking at each of his new companions' faces. Robust men over forty winters, scarred and surely hardened by battles.

Their leader bent slowly, grabbed a wooden bowl, and handed it to the man to his left without taking his black, squinty eyes off their guest. This other knight, a younger, ashen blonde-haired mountain of a man, understood. He took the bowl and then dipped it into the large, darkened tin kettle resting on the fire in the middle, scooping out some broth. The captain then pointed his chin towards the stranger.

He was hungry, but when the man handed him the bowl, he didn't even look at it.

'Take the gruel!' the captain urged him between his teeth. 'Eat, you mule!'

But the stranger didn't take his eyes off him.

'Do you speak *Rumân* or Magyar? You understand the tongue?'

He did. He could also talk in Old Greek, Ottoman, Venetian, and Latin. And he could tell the Ravens' captain where to put his bowl of gruel in all of them.

'So be it!' the leader said, while the knight poured the broth back into the cauldron and threw the bowl into a wooden bucket filled with water.

'What are they calling you, red one?' he asked, measuring the stranger from head to toe and from under his eyebrows.

He went by many names, none of which he felt any sort of duty to share with his captor. His teacher called him *per'skrumb*, or Alidor, when he felt like calling him so. They were both names he had given him. The Ottomans mockingly called him Kir-Yüz, or *Dirtface*, due to his pagan face tattoo. Whispers of *La Ombra Cremesin*, or The Crimson-Shadow, were spoken almost as an omen in the dark alleys of Venice. He didn't care for any of them.

He sometimes wished he remembered the name his parents had gifted him with, but that was a vain wish to have, so he wasn't thinking of it much. And so, he chose his own name, which very few knew of and even fewer wanted to hear of—Codru.

'Cat ate your tongue?' his guard, Grigore, sniffed. 'Maybe he's a monk too!' He laughed, and so did two others, except the one who handed the food and another, skinny one, with an odd-looking crossbow hanging on his shoulder.

The captain chose to take a seat, expecting that this encounter might take longer than he anticipated. He shook his head at the prisoner, inviting him to follow his example and rest on the wooden log, but Codru didn't flinch. And neither did the others.

'Tell me at least where you are coming from and why you are wandering about these parts of the world,' the chief urged him.

After a few moments, Grigore interfered once more:

'He won't talk, captain,' he said. 'He had a whole night of rest in the tower, and he didn't say a word. He ought to be mute. I say we take him to the gallows.'

'I say you shut your damned hole' his leader cut him off. The soldier swallowed his last words, while the captain turned again to Codru.

'Unless you talk,' he said, 'there's not much I can do for you, red one!'

'As you can see, the dogs are out to get you,' he continued, looking at Grigore. 'We don't know who you are or why you crossed our land, and, to your misfortune, our path. You wear foreign clothes, and your face asks for trouble. You could easily be a mercenary, a scout for the Ottomans, or a vagabond praying to the devil. So, which one are you?'

Codru looked at the captain, frowning and clenching his teeth. His blood was boiling, but deep down, he knew the man was right. Wandering these lands while the war was brewing wasn't the best decision he made. But he couldn't stand the position he was in. And he was too proud to grant fulfilment to the ones who put him in chains. He kept quiet.

'Our Brotherhood's mission is way greater than bringing random bandits and spies to the Voivode,' the Ravens' captain said. 'But if you don't defend yourself, we'll have no other choice but to take you to Hunyadvár, may you be innocent or not.'

'And I promise you, stranger, with your way of being, the crows will be tickling your eye sockets by tomorrow at noon. People were hanged for less.'

Codru understood he was dead meat if he didn't react somehow. And so, for the first time, he decided to speak, even if those were going to be his last words. He raised his chin, puffed his chest, and said in a low, yet defiant voice:

'Then, I'll laugh.'

The knights were surprised to hear the stranger's voice and even more surprised to hear this wicked man spitting his arrogance in their speech. They turned almost together towards the captain, who shook his head, vaguely disappointed. He then looked at Grigore and ordered.

'May God have mercy on his soul!' he said, sighing. 'Take him away!'

As he turned, a strange light caught Codru's eye. Next to the captain's great sword, teetering on his belt, another weapon was showing its cold and deadly edge. A hatchet. His father's old hatchet. Taken from his belongings and worn, apparently, as a trophy. And that was all that it took to lose it.

Grigore's nose cracked with a gut-wrenching sound when Codru's elbow shook the guard's head as he took his hand off the stranger's arm to prepare the shackles. Before anyone had time to blink, the prisoner's boot overturned the cauldron with a kick, spilling all the broth over the embers and on some of his enemies' legs, burning their skin. Shocked, they screamed and jumped to the sides, trying to dodge the boiling gruel as the smoke, bursts of sparks, and steam coming out of the fire blinded them.

In the confusion, Codru flung himself over the campfire, his shoulder and elbow clashing in an instant with the captain's chest. The man was knocked out over the wooden log, falling on his back like a sack of potatoes. Codru's hand met the axe's handle as he was on top of his captor. His fingers grasped it, and he violently pulled it, releasing his old weapon from its clutch.

Through the men's shouting and the curses, he could hear a swoosh with just enough time before he could see a short arrow thrifting through the mist. But that noise gave him enough time to duck, and as he did, he rolled onto the ground, pulling away from the captain.

'The bastard!' the Ravens' leader yelled.

*Swoosh!*

Codru dragged himself through the mud as the arrows flew violently above his head.

*Swoosh!*

A hand grabbed his boot. He turned, and as he did, he saw his guard's bloody face plastered with clay and with his nose cracked, revealing bone.

'You cursed maggot!' he grunted while his hands were reaching out further to Codru's breeches. His own surge of anger and his survival instincts made him twist, and his axe roared through the air, striking the ground. Rain started suddenly pouring out, with thunder simmering in the distance. He missed his mark, but the knight released him from his clench when he tumbled on his side, avoiding Codru's fatal blow.

He heard men bursting out of their tents and metal rattling as they grabbed their swords, ready for combat. He jumped to his feet as the arrows stopped swirling, but not for long, as a blow to his side cast him back to the ground, taking his breath away. Lying on his back, through the rain whipping his face, he saw the captain himself standing on top of him with his sword above his head, ready to land it. He dodged it, and he quickly stood up, pulling away a few steps.

'Where are you going to run?' his foe belched out. 'Look around you...'

The Ravens gathered around the two of them in a large circle, slowly squeezing them in the middle. Codru saw them ready for battle, while their faces grimaced with rage and disgust. They were catching their breath, ready to lay their hands on the prisoner.

The walls around the camp were further threatening him with hopelessness that, even in his rabid turmoil to escape, was almost begging him to see reason and give up. He knew his odds were against him, but little did he care. He wanted to get away. He was not an innocent man, but rather than being executed for crimes they would find him guilty of, he'd better die fighting.

'Don't!' the captain ordered the scrawny, hooded knight, pointing from Codru's right side, who was preparing to release another bolt off his crossbow.

'Drop the axe!' Codru was told, but he refused.

'We shall fight then! You and me, stranger, if that's your wish!' the man turned to Codru, lowering his arm, and then twisting his gloves around his sword's hilt, strengthening his grip. Codru stood his ground, looking at his enemy stepping slowly around him with the rain swelling on their heads and with the knights ready to jump in.

'But if I defeat you, you'll willingly accept your fate and follow us to Hunyadvár to face your punishment...'

'For what crimes?' the stranger barked. 'I haven't done any wrong.'

'We're all sinners, and today your sin was pride!'

'What if I defeat you?' Codru almost shouted.

The captain hesitated, but after not too long, he answered:

'If God isn't on my side today, I'll give you another chance at telling us your story. And if what I hear is to my liking, you might just live the rest of your days here, in prison.'

The captain barely finished his words when Codru's axe stroke first, meeting his sword in a lightning clench. The man quickly rejected it with a skilful twist, making his enemy turn, changing the weapon instantly to his other arm, and hitting him once again with a more powerful blow. The captain blocked the second hit too, but it made him lose his balance and stumbled back two steps to regain it.

While Codru was ready to jump his enemy once more, with his axe glimmering with threat in his hand, the knight's eyes seemed to notice this wasn't an ordinary foe. His weapon wasn't just an object; it was an extension of his arm. His odd, blue-grey eyes were like steel, and he could cut through his movements as easily as his axe could cut through his chest plate.

Codru saw the captain's reaction, and he didn't allow it to settle. He jumped towards him like a storm, with ravenous strikes cutting through the air as his enemy was shifting and avoiding them, sliding through the mud. There wasn't even a swing of the sword attacking him, as all the knights could do was defend himself against the stranger.

This wasn't a fair fight. To gain an advantage, the captain raised his sword once again, as if his aim was to cut his enemy in half, starting with his head. A shoulder in his chest took his air. Codru swiftly rolled one of his enemy's arms under his armpit, like a giant snake twisting his prey in its deadly embrace. Whatever air he had left in his lungs got stuck in there when Codru's axe's handle hit him under the chin. Codru's forehead crushed his teeth, making the captain's eyes roll in his head.

He fell on his back in a puddle. His sword abandoned his grip and was cast to his side a few steps further.

As the Raven was coughing on the ground, trying at the same time to steer away from the feral prisoner and catch his breath, Codru stepped closer to him like a feline before capturing its prey. He never left a man breathing after swinging their sword at him. He kneeled on his chest and raised his arm in the sky, with his weapon's steel seemingly being one with the clouds.

He was ready to split the captain's head in two when a cold blade raised his own chin, waking him up from his frenzy and letting cold shivers roll down his spine.

'Enough! Drop the axe!' the voice demanded.

He turned his eyes towards the man, who slid his sword at his neck while his arm was still raised. It was the blonde-haired man who handed him the bowl of food.

Seeing that Codru was still hesitant, he continued in a calm yet threatening voice:

'I promise you; my sword would peel your neck quicker than your hatchet would reach the man's head.'

Codru looked at the man on the ground one more time and at

the man holding his edge at his throat. Then his weapon splashed into the puddle.

# CHAPTER II

*Northern Wallachia, December 1440 (6948)*

THE WINTERS ON THIS DOMAIN WERE CRUEL and harsh. The frost was making the stones crack, and sometimes they could be heard in the still silence of the woods, even from afar. The muffled hoot of the wind was whistling in the distance, threatening to break through the wall of tall and thick tree trunks.

But the trees were always there, and they've always been. Everlasting, towering guardians that protected the people from gods, enemies, and nature's own wrath for millennia.

It was now protecting the two travellers, who were wandering through the forest under its favour. The hunchbacked Elder was toilsomely pushing his feet, covered in leather *opinci* and thick woollen *iţari*, through the steep and knee-high blanket of snow. On his back, he was wearing his hemp cloak, with its hood covering like a shroud, his white head and shrunken mouth. There were only a few strips of fur patched here and there to barely keep the cold from blessing him with frostbite, and a crooked, dark stick to keep him from slithering down the valley.

There was the boy following obediently behind him, struggling to swim through the snow as he followed in his guide's footsteps left behind, shivering, and clenching his teeth. Similar rags and patches of wool and hemp were covering his small body, barely keeping it alive as the cold already bit his flesh and his nose. But there was no tear wetting his dusk-tinted eyes, and there was no whimper either. The Old-Man always told him that tears were only there to remind him what not to be.

*'Your forefathers were laughing as they were dying,'* his teacher told him. *'Pain is your sister, and you shall not fight her! Embrace her, per'skrumb, for it's only then that her claws unwind off your heart.'*

Another time, he was told:

*'If you pull the arrow from your flesh, you bleed and you die, but if you leave the arrow there, you'll hurt, but you may live.'*

Taught to endure since he learned how to walk, the boy wasn't saying a word, not even when he was feeling his head split in half or whenever his eyes were tricking him, showing him shadows and ghosts that weren't there.

The Old-Man stopped on his track for just enough time to catch his breath. He turned his head to see if the boy still followed him. The apprentice saw his master's beard covered in icicles looming through his dirty scarf. The man then raised his head, scouting the surrounding forest and breathing in the crisp, stingy air through the rag.

'Do you hear that?' he asked.

The boy's ear heard many things, but not right then. The solemn silence of the woods was broken only by his stifled breaths.

'I don't hear it, *Uncheaș*.'

The man grunted.

'Listen closely and better!'

'Stay with me, boy!' he then mumbled, resuming his scuffle with the snowbanks.

Days were short, and the silent darkness was slowly swallowing the trees and the earth, bringing with it a more sombre, sinister cold. The kind that freezes the blood in its veins. As his teacher was heading further through the snow, twigs and frozen leaves cracking under his feet, a gut-wrenching howl echoed in the woods' heart.

The boy heard it and felt his feet turn to stone, unable to unstick them from the ground. The man raised his white head again, keeping up the pace, but then he turned as he was scouting the distance around him and saw the boy getting stuck. He sniffed and turned around, slipping into his own footsteps.

'What's the matter? You were not told to rest!'

The boy didn't answer. A second howl resonated, even more heartrending than the first. His eyes turned to his master's, who looked at him from under his puffed and frowning eyebrows.

'Now then!' he rushed to his apprentice. 'Move your feet!'

Pulled out of his wistfulness, the boy unclenched from the ground, and as soon as the man saw him able enough to keep himself straight, he turned and speeded up his pace on his track. Soon, as the evening was beginning to set, they reached a clear spring that was cutting their path like a border to another realm. Its rocks and edges were covered with thin, glassy ice, while the water was still flowing fearfully, but unyieldingly, down to the valley.

'Here's where we steer sunward,' the Elder said, panting. 'The rocks will be our stepstones down. Step heavily and stay clear from the ice, boy!'

The man put his stick forward, measuring the depth and checking the rocks' safety. Then he fit his knapsack better on his shoulder and signalled the boy to follow him into the spring's bed.

'Move, before the night gets us!' the man urged.

The boy was almost jumping from one rock to another, the water starting to make its way through his opinci at his feet. His hands were almost blue from the cold, as he was grabbing any rotten vines and roots, he could get his hands on to keep himself from sliding. At his waist, the hatchet given to him by the Old-Man was just another burden, swinging freely and poking his knee.

The closer they got to the howling's source, the further away it sounded, as if it were slowly extinguishing. Once they reached the bottom of the valley, the Old-Man told him to get out of the spring. Like a dark snake, the twisted string of water was making its own way through the earth further down, but this was where they parted ways. The master stood in one place for a moment, waiting to see if the boy could find his balance and the ground beneath. Then, as soon as he did, it turned his eyes the other way, piercing the twilight with his pewter eyes.

'Look,' he whispered to the apprentice. 'Tell me what you see!'

The boy followed the man's rigid hand wrapped in rags, with his gnarled finger sticking out like a dry wooden branch. He stood beside him and looked at the horizon through the pines lying everywhere in front of them. At first, he didn't see much, but he wouldn't let the teacher know. He fixed his eyes further on the snow-covered bushes and boulders. In their midst, a fickle movement, which he could've easily missed if he changed his focus too quickly, let itself be uncovered.

'I see it!' he hailed. Then he looked up to his guide. 'There! That mound over there; it's moving!'

'Show me the way; what are you waiting for?'

The boy shook his head and took the lead, biting his lower lip and limping as his feet were now in pain, the water turning to ice in his loafers.

'*My good sister...*' he moaned to himself as the teacher followed him closely.

By the time they reached the mound, the howling had diminished to yelping. In front of the two travellers, lying there in the snow, a wolf raised its head and growled, showing its teeth as a warning. It was enough to make the boy freeze. Half of one of the beast's legs was almost pulled from its place, and the blood had melted the snow around it. The iron trap surrounding its limb wouldn't have done all the damage, but the animal trying in vain to earn back its freedom certainly did.

'His flame is fading, Uncheaș,' the apprentice said to the man.

'It is, indeed.'

'Its *life oil* is wasting away...'

'Yes!'

The boy tried to get closer to the animal as he released his own little knapsack off his back, but the wolf snarled at him.

'Not so fast, Alidor!' the man trounced him. 'He'll waste his last breaths fighting you off.'

Then he advised the boy:

'Talk to him, as I taught you. Gently now, go on!'

The young one remembered the wise words of his master he was told while under the Mountain. The beasts were talking with their eyes, not their mouths. As the wolf continued to whimper, trying to lick his incurable wound, the boy locked his eyes into his.

Smooth whispers started to flow out of the boy's lips as the animal froze, unable to look anywhere else. Ancient words, an old song of hurt and healing. A *doină*.

'What do you see?' the man whispered.

Without blinking or taking his eyes from the wolf's eyes, kneeling close to the now quiet animal, the boy whispered back to his teacher.

'I see men everywhere. I see people with wagons and cottages as tall as the trees. I see horses. I see animals being skinned and turned into gold...'

'And what else?'

'I'm running through the forest, Uncheaş, as fast as the wind. I'm running after the man, and he throws arrows at me. He won't come back today. I have him on the run.'

A long howl reverberated in the forest. As the boy spoke to the animal, the Old-Man opened the filthy trap the wolf was caught in. The wolf used his remaining strength to drag itself away from his saviour, limping and squeaking. Blood was dripping from its fur onto the snow. It took everything from the beast to hide away from the travellers, and soon it creeped through the tree trunks, becoming one with the shadows.

The boy looked at it as it was going away. His teacher once told him that was the way of the wolves; when dying, they leave their pack. He wished the wolf had stayed. He could have at least tried taking away its pain with the herbs he had in the knapsack. But the wolf was gone. He turned to the man.

'We have come all this way to free the beast from the trap only to let it die in agony?' he asked.

The man didn't answer. As the darkness took over the forest, he took a knee in the snow. He dug and grubbed in it with his bandaged hands and brought to the surface a dry wooden branch. He took from his sack a piece of rag that he reeled around one of the stick's ends, then poured some oil out of a corked stone cruet. He lay the stick on his foot, above the snow, as he started snapping two pieces of flint against each other.

The sparks were throwing ephemeral lights on his sombre figure, while the sounds from the knocking stones were echoing through the woods. Then the torch caught fire. He stood up grunting with the torch in his hand, then he half-dug up the iron trap with his foot and pointed at it.

'Carry that, boy!'

The boy touched the surface of the still warm and sticky teeth of the iron claw and raised it off the ground with both hands, carrying it like a treasure chest. He looked at the Elder, but before he could ask anything, the man turned his back, mumbling.

'Now follow!' he said.

Pushing through the frozen darkness of the forest, the boy didn't take long to understand the path his guide took. The flickering, sinister light of the torch was revealing the trace of blood the wolf had left behind him. Stains of dark matter were scattered everywhere, some barely scratching the surface while others dug deeper into the snow cover.

As soon as they reached the forest's edge, he felt the blunt blizzard the trees had been protecting them from until then. Particles of glimmer and hoarfrost were whipping his cheeks and eyes, making it even harder to pierce through the snowbanks, with his bag on a shoulder and his hands now brazed to the lively metal of the chains of the trap. The man was too busy fighting to keep the flame alive, chanting old words in his beard. It didn't take long for the storm to dissipate, but once it did, the boy looked around for the wolf's blood marks. The wind swept them away.

Even if it was almost pitch dark, the man quenched the flame in the snow with a dry fizzle. They needed its guidance no longer, as in front of them, perhaps a hundred steps away, there was another light source, a milky pale glimmer, trembling in the distance. The boy could barely see it through his frozen eyelashes. Perhaps a forester's hut's window. A warm shelter, no doubt, he thought. And his frozen heart seemed to revive with hope as he saw his guide take the path towards it in silence.

In the quiet night, the boy heard distress and heartbreaking screams coming from the cabin as soon as they reached its barren courtyard. The Elder passed the fence and the stables, where the horses were neighing frantically. He used his crooked stick and knocked on the wooden door, covered in frost. The cries continued, but the other voices died out as the knocks continued.

'May God bless you, good people, if your hearts will let you help two travellers with some food and warmth for the night!' the Old-Man prayed at the door.

The screams went on as no one opened.

'Good men and women,' the man muttered while continuing to hit the frozen door with his stick. 'We've come from far away, and the freezing darkness caught us on the road!'

The boy heard footsteps rustling on the wooden planks floor and saw the Old-Man taking a step back as the door was unlocked and open. A sallow heat hit the boy's face, and his eyes started to tear up. He raised his head, and in the doorway, he saw a young chap with a lambskin hat covering his head and a sheepskin thick coat covering his back. He seemed strong for his age, and he stood in the doorway as if he were guarding it from strangers.

He quickly looked at the man and the boy, and he turned his head, almost shouting.

'There's an old beggar and his offspring at our door, mother!'

A young woman with her hair wrapped in a dark linen scarf showed up. Her face was washed-out, and her eyes were tearful. Her face has wrinkled too soon, making her look much older than she was. She first looked at the boy carrying the trap, then her eyes turned to the old wanderer, whose eyes twinkled under his thick and rimy eyebrows, with his hemp hood drawn over his white hair. When she saw his forehead mark, her legs melted. Tears started flowing on her dry cheeks, and she fell to her knees, grabbing the traveller's legs in a desperate embrace.

'Mother!' the young man gasped, holding her shoulders as she crumbled.

The woman looked up at the stranger and started pleading:

'The Lord and *Sântandrei* brought you to my door, Old Master!' 'Help me, Wise One! I beg of you!' she wailed. 'Oh, please! Make it so my son lives!'

The young lad helped his mother stand up, and the woman grappled the stranger's arm, rushing him into her abode as the boy stood still in the doorway. Her son grabbed the trap off his hands and threw them in the middle of the courtyard, blasting curses.

'Get in!' he then shoved the boy indoors, closing and locking the hut behind him.

As the boy felt the warmth quickly permeating his skin and bones like a fever, he looked around at the others. He counted six other lads, all younger than the one who opened the door, all of them husky, well fed, and with palms as large as the shovels. Boys who became as strong as the trees they were chopping to bring in the village to earn their bread. Some of them had hats like the one their older brother was wearing, while others were keeping them tight to their chests, squeezing them as their faces barely noticed his presence.

Their eyes were turned towards a bed, close to the burning stove, where the screams were coming from. There was a boy younger than the rest of them, unclothed, tossing around, and crying, losing his voice. The woman guided the Old-Man towards the bed, shoving her sons out of their way.

The apprentice's eyes lay on the boy's wounded leg. His flesh and bones were coming out through his skin, and blood was dripping on the woven blanket and on the floor. He was almost as pale as the snow outside.

'Mother!' he raved. 'Mother, don't let me go to the heavens!'

The Old-Man said to the ones around:

'Boil some water!' then turned towards the apprentice, his eyes finding him through the woman's sons' forest of legs. The boy was ready to let himself fall into a slumber. From the heat and from the scene unfolding in front of him.

'Come over here, come!' he said. He swallowed as his mouth turned dry, but he followed his teacher's order and came to the front as the lads made way for him.

'Master-Mason...' the woman whimpered.

'Here, look and tell me, what do you see?' the man asked him, ignoring the woman's prayer.

The boy looked at her son's leg. Then he looked into his wide eyes, flooded with tears.

'*No beast will turn to gold...*' the boy whispered.

'Woman,' the wanderer said to the woman. 'Bring a saw and a pipkin. Your son shall live, but his moon-howling days are forever behind him.'

Crushed by the Old-Man's words, the woman buried her face in her palms, as her oldest son stormed out of the cabin looking for the tools the stranger asked for. When he came back, the Old-Man took the saw and gave the boy the clay pot.

'Now, boy, set his flame free!' he demanded.

He knew what he had to do. He took the pipkin and made his way towards the stove, from where he grabbed an ember and tossed it in the bail. His hand reached into his knapsack and brought up a knot of dry leaves, which he then crushed in the pot with his fingers, covered with his hand, and blew into it to catch fire. A sweet, milky smoke rose then from the bowl, and when it was ready, he came closer to the young boy's bedside. He brought the pot close to his face and blew into it, the smoke covering his figure like a mist.

The apprentice then chanted softly, repeatedly, as the young lad was falling into a deep slumber:

'*May the bad dreams wash away.*
*Let the good ones come to stay.*'

While this was happening, the Old-Man had already taken the boiled water from the stove and poured it on the saw's blade, then covered it in oil from his own bag. Then poured some more water onto the wound.

'You there,' he said to the oldest son. 'Come to your brother's headboard and keep his shoulders down.'

A last howl to the winter's moon echoed through the valley as the blizzard started blasting, swallowing the wolf cry, and carrying it far over the mountains.

***

*Cioclovina Forest, May 1459 (6967)*

*'Kill them, kill them all!'*

As the jail wagon's wheels were crushing the stones on the path, Codru was trying in vain to gain his thoughts back.

*'You will die in here, worthless scum!'*

He hadn't eaten in days, and his strength and patience were both gone. He was weak; his anger was swiftly replaced with slough and blight. His head was cracking with pain. The Ravens were going to hand him over to the Voivode. It was as clear as day that he was going to die; he knew that much. Holding on to his precious pride was only going to get him there faster.

He knocked with his head against the wagon's reinforced wooden wall, the sound barely making it over the horses' trot and dogs' barks. He knocked again, but the party continued its trail untrammelled. It wasn't until he dragged his body to the back of the wagon that he stuck his face to the small, barred window and bleated:

'Water! Give me water!'

He heard a man shouting, and the wagon stopped.

'See if his tongue has untwined, Toma!' the captain's voice reached his ears. 'We'll halt here!'

As the coachman reined the animals in, he heard a horse coming around, and then he saw through the window, the knight that rendered him defeated. The man got off his buttery-white steed, untied his water flask off the saddle, and walked slowly, approaching the wagon's rear. He saw as his axe, his curbed sword, and his own knapsack were all hanging on the same saddle, as prizes.

Codru pierced him with his eyes, grinding his teeth, but didn't say anything. The man scouted him from under his brows. When he arrived close enough to maybe two steps away from the window, he took off the flask's cork and ordered him:

'Open your mouth!'

They would no longer make the mistake of untying him, nor would they give him the benefit of the doubt, treat him honourably, or let him use his hands. It really was the end of the road for him. But he accepted the shame, as the drought began eating at his tongue and his headache was throbbing.

He stuck his chin between the rusty iron bars of the window and let his head fall back, opening his mouth and closing his eyes. The Raven let the clear water flow off his flask and down the prisoner's throat. After a couple of gargles, Codru started coughing. He was so dried out that his throat forgot how to swallow. The knight stopped pouring for a while and gave him another try once Codru came back to his senses.

'Here!'

And he gave him a few more sips. Codru felt the water reach straight to his stomach. He sighed and breathed over his mouth as he rested his head on the window, his eyes still nailed on the man who had watered him. He noticed his longsword fluttering at his waist, peeping from under his dark mantle—the same sword that disarmed him a few days ago. The knight now had his long silver-streaked blonde hair tied up in a tail, reeling on his broad back. As he covered the flask, he was scouting Codru as well, as if he were waiting to see if he was going to talk. His wait was fruitful.

'My pouch,' Codru muttered. 'I need it.'

The Raven seemed almost dissatisfied with his request.

'Is this what you wish to speak about?'

'*He won't listen...*' Codru told himself as his temples were pulsating. '*Don't lose it!*'

'You don't understand, my head! It's killing me.'

Toma turned his head to his saddle and then back to Codru.

'Your head is the only thing keeping you alive, my friend,' he said. 'What's in there that you want so badly that you can't live without?'

He walked to his horse and grabbed Codru's knapsack, which he then opened as he was coming back slowly, closer to the wagon.

'What kind of *lefegiu* are you?' he asked himself, searching into Codru's bag. 'What's with all these herbs and vials?'

If he could, Codru would have chewed the window's bars with his teeth, jumped out of the wagon, and pulled the knight's arms apart for daring to ferret out his possessions. But he had to be quiet and docile if he wanted to even have any hope that the man would fall for his pleas.

'Is this poison?' the Raven asked, taking out a bundle of parchment and sniffing it.

If gods existed, they were now favouring him. In the palm of his hand, the knight was now holding the one thing that could have made it all better. Codru remembered the first time his tongue touched the same dark matter that was now wrapped carefully and resting on the Raven's leather glove.

The heinous guild of criminals he grew up around were chewing that ungodly mixture to be immune to pain, unshackled from guilt and morality, but forever chained to the poison itself. Their leader forced him to eat it too. It was then that he realized that those earthy, bitter crumbs had the power of making his headaches fade away. He cursed that day, and he made sure that man paid for making him know of it too.

'Tell you what,' the knight said, fidgeting with the little bundle between his fingers. 'I'll let you have this if you tell me your name.'

Codru continued to grind his teeth. He was so close to the cure that he had to accept and play by the man's rules.

'What do you gain from it?' he asked the knight.

The Raven answered:

'Nothing. But may there be someone kind enough to remember one's name on the day they hang. Being forgotten is worse than being dead!' the knight concluded.

Codru took another look at the man answering to the name Toma and spoke through his teeth:

'Codru. That's my name.'

Toma shook his head slowly, recalling the prisoner's name, and then he came closer to the window. Looking over his shoulders, he unwrapped the parchment, revealing the brown, pasty lump. He made a wry face as the musty scent made its way to his nostrils. He brought the poisonous essence close to the wagon.

'Back away!' he told Codru in a low voice. 'I don't want you to get any ideas!'

'*Fair!*' Codru thought. He helped himself with his arms tied up in front to pull away from the end of the wagon, waiting for his prize. The knight took one more look around him as his comrades were getting ready to resume the journey, and then he brought the ointment to the window and let it drop inside. He took another look at the captive and then said:

'Here's your last supper then, Codru!'

The knight stepped away, threw the prisoner's bag over his horse's saddle, and grabbed the animal's reins, pulling him away. As soon as that happened, Codru rolled over to the semi-wrapped brown coal Toma gave him, and resting his back on the wagon's side, he let his head fall on the back with his eyes closed. The cursed poison he had to taint his tongue with for merely a drop of peace and quiet.

'*Take it, you degenerate!*' inner voices whispered violently while his head was spinning. '*EAT IT!*'

He bit his lip one more time before hitting his head against the wagon, then he pinched a nibble from the dry paste with his fingers and shoved it in his mouth, between his lip and his gum. As he chewed it softly, the paste softened and melded with the spit and warmth of his trembling mouth. His heart was beating rapidly now, but he knew that soon the headache and the voices would fade, the veil of relief taking their place.

Looking over the small window, he felt himself drift away as he heard the captain's order to tread on it and felt the wagon moving. His body soon became weightless, and his eyes fell to the back of his head while darkness started wrapping his mind in its safe and welcoming grip.

As he was floating, he began to remember the path the Ravens took on their trip. It was familiar. He could swear the mountains he saw through the barred eye of his prison were the mountains his feet had crossed before, when he was a boy.

'*Brave men, as you are meant to be one day, defeated the Uriași wandering these realms,*' the Elder's voice sounded. '*One of them sank into a lake, and his remains tarnished the sacred waters; one other turned to stone when he was beheaded... Look over there, high on the crest, the Mountain without a summit!*'

He remembered the smell of the earth, pine, and juniper. It was one of the many places the Master brought him to learn the herbs and their riddles. Not too far away, if his memories were not tricking him, were the ruins of the age-old city of *Sarmizegetusa*. He remembered the thick walls of white stone and the round sundials, echoing the night sky.

'*As above, so below*' were the last words he remembered as he woke up from his hallucination.

When he opened his eyes, it was pitch dark. As the wagon ceased its journey, he fell onto his side. His mouth was dry. He grunted as he propped, squinting his eyes for a drop of clarity, and straining his ears for any sound he could hear from the outside, just to get a sense of the time and space he was in.

He heard the soldiers moving their horses and trying to make a fire. The captain seemed to decide who and where to stand guard, as his voice could be heard above the rest, echoing in the valley. As the night set in, he understood that the knights would camp and continue their journey at the cockcrow.

Codru came to the small eye of the window, and he began to distinguish the rocky, broken ground covered in thick grass and moss and the trunks of a few trees lightening up on one side, as the campfire was coming to life nearby. The cool, refreshing breeze of the night was soothing as Codru let his face touch the iron bars with his eyes closed. He felt the mist floating around, clearing his lungs, and seemingly bringing him back to life.

His stomach hurt, but he had no will asking for food or water. If he was going to be dangling by a beam tomorrow, he could do it hungry too. It wasn't until he felt the smell of the game the knights seemed to cook over the fire that his guts started to churn. He heard them laugh around the camp, sucking bones and then throwing them to the dogs accompanying the party. He thought a few times to at least ask for water but gave up as his strengths were barely enough to keep him awake.

He was almost giving up on the thought when he heard boots rustling through the leaves around the wagon. It was Toma again. He had with him a burning dry rot he carried as a torch in one hand, while in the other he had a roasted bird leg. He squinted his eyes, pointing his torch at the wagon, trying to see inside.

'Psst!' he said. 'Take this.'

Then he fit the cooked meat between the window's bars. If he knew it would help him escape, Codru would've broken the man's arm right then and there. He wasn't a dog.

'Turn away if you want to keep your limb tied to your body' he snarled at the knight.

The man left his hand hanging there for a while, looking at him almost daringly.

'Is that so, Codru,' he said. 'I wager ten *dinars* that the pig dung you swallowed earlier filled up your belly.' Then he left the bird's leg fall inside the wagon.

'Toma!' the captain yelled. 'Let him have his way and starve!'

Codru sniffed as the Raven left, returning to his comrades. He squeezed his fist while the leftovers of his precious headache cure turned to mush and then he thrown it in his pocket, cursing. He wiped his hand on his breeches, and then he tumbled until he reached the piece of meat the knight left behind. As he brought it to his face, the grease started to roll slowly over his dirty, bloody, and blackened fingers. The meat was covered in hay straws and dust crumbs, but his hunger was too great to care. His teeth dug into it, and he started munching voraciously, like a famished wolf.

As the meat was rolling down his throat, he suddenly felt a heavy breeze disturb the smooth air. He stopped chewing so he could hear better as he closed his eyes and dropped the bones on the wagon's bed. He didn't hear anything, nor could he see anything, as his eyes were scouring past the heaped opening, dipping into the shadows. But he sensed it. And so did the animals.

The dogs started barking in the night, while the horses snuffled and neighed. He heard the men swarming around the camp.

'What's there, Iorgu? Muşat?' they asked the hounds.

The captain was calling out to his watchmen, but none of them answered.

'Gather around,' he said to the Ravens around him. 'We're being watched!'

'Iorgu!' a man shouted as the dogs scuttled away like hell into the night. After a short silence, the animals began wrestling and were heard barking and beating through the woods. The reckoning didn't last long, and soon after, it ended with a long squeal lost in the darkness.

Codru jumped from his place towards the opposite side of the wagon, hitting with both fists the solid wood.

'Let me out!' he shouted. 'Release me...'

His quarrel was quickly distracted by a lisp in his ear that he caught behind the wagon. Over the knights' battle cries, he heard sinister gurgles and sniffs right outside. The sound of what seemed like fingernails was dancing almost carefully on the wagon's wood, grazing it. Codru held his breath, trying to hear more clearly without moving a muscle.

He followed the source of the murmur with his eyes, sensing it around him as it was circling the caravan he was trapped in. Not after too long, as the Ravens kept their mouths shut waiting for the enemies to reveal themselves, Codru noticed a black shape peeping through the iron window. He couldn't see anything other than a dark figure, framed by the deep blue and green of the forest. But the apparition saw him.

The gurgles turned abruptly into screeches, sounds he had never heard a man make. His blood turned to ice as the creature grabbed the window's edges and started shaking the wagon. Then the shrieks and grunts began echoing everywhere in the woods' clearing, while men were wailing, some summoning their Creator's name to their aid. As the creature outside his prison was pushing its long and skinny arm through the metal, a sluggish matter was flooding on the wood.

Codru pushed the arm away with his foot as the creature tried to reach it and grab it in its claw. Outside, he heard the knights screaming and the stallions prancing and whinnying. The remaining dogs were yelping, trying to run away instead of protecting their owners, but their growls were shortened by unhuman roars catching up to them.

'Heavens, they're too many!' he heard the captain desperately lament. 'May God save us!'

As Codru dragged himself away to the front of the wagon, he heard another sound on top of it, frantically scratching the planks to break in. The second monster. A long wail left his throat, and then he heard a familiar arrow, followed by another one, vivaciously whirring through the air, and then a muffled tumble on the side of his wagon.

His face turned towards the window, where the creature's shouting was sharply broken by a blade hitting the metal as the shadow's head trundled into the grass, followed by its fleshless body, smearing the window's edge with its unholy lard as it was falling.

The torch that revealed in the frame was Toma's. He threw the torch aside, freeing his hand to unlatch the bar locking the jail wagon's door. He unlocked it and opened its doors wide. His face and gambeson were covered in blood, and his massive sword was pointing to the ground. Behind him was his lean comrade, whose crossbow was pointing forward and shooting, giving Toma enough time to call out to Codru.

'Grab a sword!' he said. 'Come to our aid, and freedom is yours!' then he threw the prisoner's weapons and his sack and roared with his sword up as he ventured back to the camp. The other knight took a quick look at him from under his hood, and he quickly followed Toma.

His freedom was his anyway. Whatever these enemies were, it was not his concern. He didn't know whichever wretched hell they spawned from, but he didn't want to have anything to do with them. He didn't owe his captors anything. The curse that was now plaguing the camp was to him pure salvation. He hastily threw his knapsack over his shoulder, took his axe and his *scimitar*, one in each hand, and made his way out of his box.

As soon as his boots touched the ground, one of the shadows swooped upon him, digging its claws into his chest, and casting him against the wagon's side with incredible force. As it jumped to rip his throat with its mouth, almost impulsively, Codru buried his blade into the creature's underjaw, thrifting it all the way to its skull. As the blood was flowing over his fist, he saw the monstrosity's figure up close: its putrid, ashen skin, its eyeless, worm-filled sockets, and its sharp fangs.

As he pulled the blade out, the walking corpse fell to the ground. He turned towards the flames he could see in the camp as the fire started spreading. He saw the sick demons jumping from the trees over the knights, who were fighting for their lives, hacked, and brought to their knees by the ravenous intruders. Claws and bites were tearing into the men's skin, and the inhuman howls covering the camp were bone-chilling, with dread floating in the air.

He turned, and another demon jumped him from his side. Codru tried to keep him away, cutting the air with his hatchet, but the creature dodged it, and the axe landed in the wagon's wall. The monster attacked, while his arm was stuck on the hatchet's handle. Codru turned and slashed the air with his short sword, slicing the attacker's bony chest and leaving behind a black and thick trace. Evading the next attack, he switched to the creature's side, removing his weapon from its clench, and with a masterly kick well placed in the animal's belly, the monster tumbled inside the wagon.

Without any more thinking time, Codru quickly shut the door locked behind it, trapping it inside as the rabid ghoul crushed itself against the solidly reinforced wood, unleashing deafening growls from its cadaverous throat.

'Lend us a hand!' he heard the men shouting not too far from him, seeing him fight. Codru didn't move. The party was decimated anyway, with the limbs and guts of both the soldiers' and the ghouls' scattered all over the ground. He saw Toma, the captain, the hooded knight, and Grigore still standing while a group of maybe a dozen fiends surrounded them from all sides. All he wanted was to grab one of the horses that was still alive and leave this ordeal behind. And yet, his feet seemed to have caught roots.

As he saw two of the enemies laying their claws on the knight who fed him meat and poppy seeds, he made a sudden move. He threw his bag on the ground and ran towards the fight. He dug his sword in the grass as he squeezed the hatchet's handle with both hands. He raised the weapon with both arms above his head, and after making a great dash, he landed the blow in one of the creature's skulls. He turned with a lightning-quick move and bashed the other one's side of the head before the first one's body even had the time to hit the ground.

The hooded knight spared Codru's back with a timely and well-placed arrow as another cursed foe was aiming to dig into him from behind.

As the flames were dying out, he saw the soldier who guarded him at the Citadel being mauled by another shadow. Toma's sword was too late to cleave the creature, as Grigore's fell on his back, with his eyes lost in the night sky and his blood flowing from his neck and soaking into the thick grass.

A desperate shout cracked through the camp. As he turned, Codru saw the last standing fiend with his arm elbow-deep into the captain's stomach. Toma screamed, his sword almost splitting the creature in half with a cut from its bone-sticking shoulder until its opposite hip. With a kick, he cast the corpse aside as the Ravens' leader fell to his knees, resting his sword in the ground, his face twisted in shock and pain, while his hand was trying in vain to keep his guts in his body. Blood spilled off his lips as he coughed, drowning.

Codru stood a few steps away, during the massacre's aftermath, with his hatchet in one hand and his eyes turned to the two surviving knights—Toma and the archer—resting their captain on his back as he was struggling to inhale. The blonde knight turned to him.

'Help!' Toma begged. 'Your ointments... You must heal him.'

Codru didn't answer right away. He was a killer, not a healer. And the dying Raven was long past what any of his herbs and concoctions might have been able to help with.

'He's gone!' he mumbled. 'Look at him!'

He dragged his feet closer to them while Toma was kneeling, keeping the man's hand in his, and the archer was trying to patch the captain's hole with rags, pressing to keep his innards where they belonged.

Standing next to them, Codru looked into the freighted man's eyes. He has faced that fear countless times, and he remembered all those eyes beseeching him, to no avail, to spare their lives. But now it was the first time he could see. He was facing a man who wasn't dying of his hand, nor was he dying for coin. The captain tried to treat him honourably and gave him a way out of captivity.

'He's in great torment! If you have any mercy, you should end his suffering!' his words left his mouth unwittingly. Telling them this thought was the least he could do. Then he turned and stepped away, recovering his sword from where he had stuck it in the earth.

'Red one!' he heard behind him. The voice could barely make it to his ears; it was the captain's. Codru turned his head and saw the Raven's head propped in Toma's lap, one of his arms lying on his chest, and the other pointing at him, as if he were trying to catch him.

'Please!' the captain ruckled, coughing blood on his beard.

Codru hesitated, but after a short lapse, he returned to the dying man until he stood right next to the three Ravens. The man waved at him to come closer, and so the stranger took a knee.

'Red one!' the man said. 'It looks like I'll be the one laughing as the crows tickle my eye sockets...'

The man tried to swallow his spit and gasped, then he said:

'I don't have much time... I beg of you that once I'm gone, to lend my brothers your arm, as you have done it this ill-fated night.'

Codru's thoughts were still grinded by his thoughts of being unjustly imprisoned. If it weren't for this bewitched ambush, he would've been hanged. He had no reason or will to offer his arm. The debt he owed to Toma was paid.

'I will leave this land,' he answered, 'There is nothing I will find here, and there is nothing holding me back.'

But the captain interfered:

'Should you lend us your aid, the hope of the order to triumph would grow tenfold...'

As Codru kept his mouth shut, the man gasped again, while the hooded knight kept his hand over his own. Catching some more air, he said:

'I don't have much gold, but whatever I have, it's yours... And if it's not gold you seek, know that there are worthier things to fight for. I don't know if it was fate or God who made our paths cross. I don't know if you wandered the *beyond-the-forests* land looking for redemption from your past. If that's your desire, know that this is your chance to earn it.'

Codru looked the man in the eyes, then reached out to his right breeches pocket. He brought to light the soilly dirt wrapped in parchment that he hid while he was in the wagon. He grabbed a piece of it on his finger and said to the captain.

'For your pain...'

The man opened his mouth like a child, and Codru rubbed the ointment on his teeth, closing the man's mouth and forcing him to swallow, as he muttered to himself, almost inaudible:

*'May the bad dreams wash away.*
*Let the good ones come to stay.'*

Shivering and delirious, with his eyes largely open, the captain muttered.

'Will you help my brothers? Will you grant a man this dying wish? Do I have your word?'

Codru wrapped the remaining brown wax and let it slide back into his pocket.

'No!' he answered.

And as the captain's eyes shed a tear on the side of his wrinkly cheek, lost in the night and carried away by dreams beyond his mind, Codru slid his sword between the Raven's ribs, piercing his heart and releasing him from the agony.

# CHAPTER III

*Hollow Mountain, August 1437 (6945)*

THE ELDER KNEW IT WAS TIME. AFTER LONG winters in the upper caves of Hollow Mountain, the boy was prepared to be taken into its depths, down to its primeval, smouldering heart. And then, after one year there, he would bring him back to the surface to continue his apprenticeship. Reborn as the Sleeping God, pure as the Moșii, and hardened as steel, primed to carry the sacred torch further. And himself, closer to ending his long watch and shutting his eyes for eternity.

He understood, however, that for now the boy was not ready. And deep down, he may have had doubts that he'd ever be, although the man did everything he could to cast those out. The young proved to be stubborn, as it was expected. His soul was still yearning for the ones who gave him life, even if he could not even name them. His memories were still tied to the village, even if he didn't know what longing was.

The Old-Man could sometimes see the seeds of vengeance brewing in his deep eyes. The wild and bygone fire he inherited was overflowing through the boy's veins, a wrath that could scorch the earth if not measured or tempered. And it has been the Elder's trial since he took him under his wing—to dampen that fire down, to teach him how to restrain it, and to use it for his life's quest.

The way to the heart of the mountain was long, steep, and narrow. In this passage, there was more than enough room for the boy to pass freely, albeit carefully. But the master was moving ahead slowly, his shoulder's cramping and grazing the walls, his breath quivering for air as his chin was almost constantly pushed into his chest. He'd survive this. He wandered this tunnel for ages.

And the air could barely get here. The upper caves were abundant with cracks in the mountain's walls and long human-made holes reaching all the way to the surface. However, as they descended deeper into the earth, they found themselves drawing breath from an empty well. To not waste it, the master kept a rock in his hand instead of a torch, which was glowing anaemically, but it was enough to show them the edge of the slippery stepping stones of the stairs, old and dulled by time.

'Sing to me again, boy,' the man murmured, without turning, as he was carefully jostling. The apprentice was barely able to tie two words together, but it was all his master had taught him since he learned how to speak.

'*Stain not thy heart with deeds of killing.*
*Corrupt not thy flesh through fleshly feast...*'

As the young one continued to hum his hymns, the man perked up his sharp ears, listening to the sacred words. He ceased his struggle with the tunnel for a few moments, and the boy bumped into him.

'Keep your eyes peeled, even if you walk a path you've walked before!' the man snapped. He turned, grabbed him by the shoulder, and set him back up on his feet.

'Carry on!'

The disciple cleared his throat and continued humming timidly:
'*...Capture not thy soul in lustful snares.*
*Utter not deceits, for verity is thy beacon.*
*Seize not hath... Seize what...*'

'...Seize not what hath not been willingly bestowed!' the man grunted. 'You'll learn it! Again!'

Soon, the passage began to widen. The man's shoulder could pass freely without touching its walls. The torch was losing its glow too, but as the earth beneath their feet began to flatten out, hinting at the end of the long torture of treacherous stairs, a dim and warm light was cast from ahead. The boy could see the shape of the man's crooked figure in front of him, and, distracted by the novelty unravelling onward, his chants diminished until soon they completely disappeared.

'Your feet are walking the very ground your forefathers touched before you, all the way until the Awakened One, and then long before him,' the master spoke, dragging his feet on the cold, chiselled rock.

'The wonders and the secrets this Mountain holds, boy!' he said, his sombre voice echoing. 'And soon, you'll be their steward!'

The passageway opened widely in all directions, revealing the vastness of the Heart. The man stepped slowly further away, distancing himself from the boy, as the apprentice's feet froze under the breathtaking colossalness of the chamber.

Radiant boulders of glowing stone in all colours adorned the grand walls that surrounded him, casting light and bringing the chamber to life. These stones also encircled the massive, earthen pillars firmly anchored in the floor, stretching upward until they vanished into the abyss of darkness. He could see round and wide caverns opening in all corners, making way to other chambers. Through this labyrinth, he could hear water gushing and hissing in silky, untarnished waterfalls.

The ancients adorned the chamber with enormous, bearded statues, masterfully carved into the Mountain's rock. So full of life were they that the boy was almost moved to fall to his knees before their austere eyes. Around and above the statues, great wheels of wood and metal spluttered in the shadows. The smallest among them was as large as a mill wheel. These large and heavy circles rolled slowly and frantically, their arms and pulleys squeaking and crackling in a sunken murmur.

When the young one finally woke up from his stun, the Elder was already far away from him, reaching the chamber's core. The man lapsed on his way for a moment, looking at the boy as he was catching up to him, as he understood the bewilderment. It has been a great many winters since he was at the boy's place. The memory of his old master was so grey that he no longer knew if it was indeed a memory or if it was all a dream. But he didn't wait for too long.

'Come,' his voice thundered. 'We're nearly there!'

And as their leather boots clamped on the polished floor, the two of them closed towards the middle of the seemingly endless room. Out of the cavern's rock, as if they had arisen from the earth, there was a large, fine, and wrought slab, carefully chiselled, surrounded by other boulders, crafted in the same way. A monumental table, ringed by numerous seats. In the middle of the massive board, held by a pair of stone hands, stood a great, shining metal plaque.

A great furnace was carved into a pillar merely fifty steps away from the table. A column thicker than the rest of them was diligently built inside the room, right at its centre, as an enormous tree trunk that had the night itself as its crown. Flames were quietly simmering in its veins, and their heat was reaching out to the wanderers, suavely stroking their cheeks.

'Behold,' the Old-Man said gravely, approaching the table. 'The Tome of Light!'

The boy approached the table cautiously, taking care not to touch it. His gaze was captivated by the metal plate, proudly perched upon the dark stone surface. A pale, scattered ray of light was falling from the dark and endless chamber's dome, resting on the golden surface of the tome. Ancient signs were carved in it, crowded like ants. Overlapping whispers of the past seemed to beam from the cold treasure, and each of them was telling a long-forgotten story.

The Elder let the boy wonder.

'Yes,' he said. 'You do hear it! That is good, boy! Listen...!'

As the apprentice stared in awe at the precious book, the man hovered around the large stone table, leaving the now extinguished rock he used as torch to rest on it.

'When the great Fire-Knights arrived on these lands from the midnight and sunrise realms, they made home on this mountain. There were many such places they encountered on these domains, but the Hollow Mountain stood out above all of them...' he said with a long-winded pace.

'They were *Polistai*. Creators, builders, masons. Architects of worlds. Earth was their sister and their mother. The endless Sky above was their brother and father. They drew their flame and might from them both. And they travelled both.'

The man sat down on one of the cold boulders, resting as he closed his eyes, trying to awaken the past.

'Oh, if only we could have witnessed it, boy!' he said. 'The mighty beast tamers, in amber glittering armours, with manes set ablaze, dismounting their fire breathing stallions and surrounded by obedient dire wolves... Bringing with them wisdom and mastery of the elements.'

As the man continued his story, the whispers coming from the golden book grew louder, scattering, and chanting voices were coming from all the corners and crevices of the labyrinth. The boy was scared, startling out of his reverie, but the Elder rested at peace, with his eyes closed, mumbling his words.

'When the Earthborn, the men living here, witnessed the Fire-Gods' arrival, they fought to protect their people and the woodlands they had arisen from. But their stone and bone pikes had no strength against the almighty wayfarers' bronze swords and hatchets. The Earthborns' starving cattle were not a match for the godly, wild beasts the Fire-Knights were mounting.'

As the voices dispersed, lost in the shadow, and seeing that the master wasn't heedful of them, the boy followed his way and rested on one of the chiselled rocks.

'Were the Fire-Knights evil?' he asked.

The man stayed quiet for a moment, then he answered:

'There is no evil, young one, as there is no good either. We are all both, and if there is such a word for it, that is what we are. And that is what the Fire-Knights were.'

'You see,' he continued, 'when the fighting ceased and the ill-blood embers died out, the bronze knights shared their wisdom with the Earthborn, as it was their unrelenting mission and legacy on their path. They taught them how to melt the stone and turn it into a blade or hammer. They gave them the great gifts of the plough and the wheel, guiding them to nurture their crops for food and revealing pottery to keep their food. They taught them the *Earth's sacred tongue*, to make the wild animals bow their heads before them, and the Sky's, to tame the winds, the rivers, and the mountains to their will.'

The Elder rose from his seat and then looked at the treasure laid in front of him on the slab.

'And they had many places across the millennia that they travelled through, and many places they called home. But it was only here, in the depths of the Hollow Mountain, that they ended their everlasting journey and built this ageless temple.'

'An eternal vault to store their wisdom and glory, all of it engraved with secret letters in this book.'

Then he turned, pointing his stick towards the high walls.

'So, they laid the first bricks to the foundation of the world itself, building the great spinning wheels you see all around you,' he said, then his eyes and stick fell on the great, searing stove in the middle.

'And ignited the Mountain's Heart, shoving *rock-wood* in it, *brimstone* and ancient moss they could find in the caverns, to keep the world's wheels working.'

The apprentice dipped his eyes once more at the radiant tome.

'Will you teach me, master?'

The Old-Man looked at him from across the table, his lead-coloured eyes sparkling through the milky ray falling on the book.

'I won't,' he said. 'As my master hasn't. The world has long forgotten Earth's speech. I have raised you for five winters, up in the caves, showing you the ways of people. But to learn the ways of the gods, you shall do so on your own!'

He then started circling the table, returning to the boy.

'The time has come that you shall spend your last year under earth here, in the Hollow Mountain's heart, as so did The Great Sleeping-Bear *Zalmos*, once a slave to the faraway *Samian astrologer...*'

'And when you'll be reborn to the surface and awaken from your slumber, you shall spend the rest of seven winters to nurture, use, and let the gathered wisdom settle down.'

Shivers rolled down the boy's spine, his eyes largely open and flickering under the golden glow of the sacred tablet. He was scared, and the Old-Man knew that. His time in the mountain's belly could have meant almost certain death. He was on the brink himself during his time here. But if he survived, as a child whose blood wasn't thinned with fire, then the boy who carried the gods' fire itself in his veins would survive too.

'Uncheaş,' the boy whimpered, reaching for his hemp robe. 'Don't leave me here!'

The man looked down at his apprentice, whose tears were running down his cheeks.

'You shall spend twelve moons here, my boy, guarding the tome and tending to the heart's fire. And if you prove yourself worthy, the voices of the Moşii will reward you with their teachings and grant you life.'

He then reached out for his knapsack as the youngster's sobs echoed through the chamber, hitting the walls, and disappearing into the labyrinth. The master dug out from the bag a thin roll of pale bark he had, tightly wrapped. He unrolled it and showed it to the boy.

'Here, young Alidor, take this birch-skin. Make of it what you will—burn it and keep the fire alive for a blink of an eye or scribble on it what the whispers may tell you in their *Old-Tongue*, and thus keep the fire alive forever—that choice is yours to make.'

The boy wiped his face and took the scroll the Elder had given him. Before he could open it, the old one grabbed his hand and pulled him to follow. He was sobbing, scared of the long-time of darkness and solitude awaiting him in the depths of the temple. But he followed the Elder obediently towards the furnace.

'*Rebo'ditas, per'skrumb!*' the man said. '*Rebo'ditas!*'

The heat was growing as they reached closer to the forge. The dark stone had cracks marred by crimson, blazing veins from which billowed smoke and steam. The heart was wide open, and the flames were gone. There were only the embers left behind, covered in ash.

As the Old-Man gazed upon his apprentice one last time, a smirk crept across his face. He noticed that the tears had ceased, replaced by a glimmer of golden fire in the boy's eyes.

\*\*\*

*Cioclovina Forest, June 1459 (6967)*

Codru's eyes turned away from the fire that consumed the camp. As the morning sun pierced through the towering tree crowns, he found himself surrounded by the haunting aftermath of the carnage that had unfolded mere hours earlier. And yet, he was numb. The hunger, the rancid potion, the fighting, and the sick apparitions that attacked the company almost disarmed him.

He needed to rest, and yet he couldn't. He knew he had to leave as soon as he had the chance, but the lack of gold or even a horse made that a struggle. He also knew that fighting the two surviving Ravens for one of the three horses left alive after the purge was not the wisest choice. The weakness creeping out through his bones and muscles was as discouraging as the memories of the rabid pestilence he happened to witness in the night.

While in Scodra, he heard about the *magna mortalis* that ravaged the world many years before him. A miasma sent by God that would turn human flesh into deadly black rot. He once saw a woman writhing in agony, reaching with her foaming mouth to bite the priests who were purging her sins away in the river.

He had long lost any shade of faith in gods, but he knew there were illnesses out there that would turn humans into beasts. Some had cures brewed by masked healers; some didn't. But the horrendous face of the creature he first struck was now carved in his mind for a long time. And none of the stories he heard before could make sense of any of it.

As he rested on a fallen tree trunk, trying to breathe in the cool air, bitter from the smoke and ashes, he thought of the name the Old-Man gave him, as he saw fit. The voices were quiet, and his head was clear, but a restless feeling of pending doom was resting in his stomach. The mercy kill he gifted the captain was also following him.

So, closing his eye, he turned to the misty face to which he was always turning to find his peace. While others sought solace in statues and icons during their prayers, he found his in that vanishing, ethereal figure, with its delicate contours framed by a cascade of dark hair.

He opened his eyes and looked at the two men, who were now too caught up in tending to their dead to care if he ran away or stayed, but his feet were not going to carry him anywhere anytime soon. Toma and the hooded knight spent their morning digging a large hole in the forest clearing's ground.

He saw them as they dragged their dead comrades into it in sombre silence. The knights had their faces covered in rags to stay clear of the evil air floating around them as they covered the pile of the creatures' remains, they gathered on the old campfire with sticks and brushwood.

Codru saw the archer taking off his hood and revealing his coarse, dark-grey hair, thinning at the top of his scalp. He was maybe a few years older than his helpmate, but time didn't seem to have shown him mercy. He looked weary; his face was dry, livid, and wrinkled, and his eyes were darkened by heaven-knows-what hardships.

Standing now on the grave's edge, he was holding a small, black leather book in both hands. He had his head bowed down, as did Toma, who held his sword's hilt with both hands, resting its blade on the ground. As Codru carried on watching them, none of them spoke a word for what felt like forever. But the silence of prayer didn't last long. However, by the time the two finished covering the grave, the sun was already climbing up rashly over the summer's sky.

Codru allowed the clear and warm rays to wash his face as he kept his eyes closed, slowly breathing in, and exhaling through his lips. The heat turned sour shortly when the smell of the burning and plagued cadavers began to broil in the middle of the camp. He had to spit to get the taste of filth out of his throat. As the creature's bodies were sputtering in the fire, he unexpectedly heard a now familiar growl coming from the jail wagon. And then he remembered the beast he had locked in it during his first brawl with the night creatures. It survived.

He suddenly stood up, reaching out for the axe he now had hanging at his waist. Toma and the other Raven were rushing the fire, throwing looks towards him in silence as they noticed he rose from his place on the tree trunk. He turned away from them, quietly moving towards the wagon, trying not to disturb the monster, if that's what he was hearing. He had both hands' fingers wrapped around his hatchet when he finally reached behind the wagon. He eyed the tight, barred window, as there was indeed movement to those grunts. The reinforced door still had the latch on, just as he left it during the night when he trapped the beast inside.

After a few steps towards it, a crack burst under his boot. A dry branch sticking out of the leaves. It only made a muffled, subtle noise, but that was more than enough to startle the fiend. As soon as the branch popped, the monster's teeth smashed violently against the window, the roars scaring the birds away in the nearby trees as they took flight Codru instinctively raised his hatchet to his chest, taking a step back to prevent any possible attack. But the solid door of the wagon didn't even flinch. And he understood—the beast was never going to leave that cage on its own.

A hand touched his shoulder, and Codru turned around with a hitch, ready to wet his axe, only to quickly come to his senses once he realized it was Toma, looking at him from under his blonder brows.

'Easy now!' he said defensively, raising his palms in front of him. He slowly left them down, almost at the same time Codru dropped his weapon back to its strap. Toma took down the rag covering his mouth and nose and stroked his short, white-gold beard. Codru looked at him as the Raven tried to see past his shoulder and behind him.

'Daniil!' the knight shouted suddenly. 'Come over here!'
The archer approached the two men standing behind the wagon quietly. Codru looked at him, joining Toma's side, his sombre, haggard eyes following the direction of his comrade's. Both seemed to have forgotten about their once-prisoner's existence, absorbed by the trapped ghoul rustling in his cage.

'Codru!' Toma told him without taking his eyes from the

prisoner. 'You captured one, didn't you? All this death wasn't for nothing, after all!'

Daniil passed Codru over, getting closer to the wagon and peeking inside, while the beast was grabbing the window's bars with its sallow, veiny claws and sticking his hole-riddled tongue out between them. He looked at the imprisoned beast, lost in his thoughts, with something resembling compassion. He turned his head towards Toma and nodded.

'Follow us further, out of the woods!' Toma said, fixing his eyes on Codru. 'Whether it's to your liking or not, your fate is now tied to ours.'

Codru didn't answer right away, as he didn't know where the Raven was going with it.

'We'll leave before the sun reaches the mid-sky. We'll try to rest, care for our wounds, feed ourselves and the horses. Then we'll be on our way. We must get out of the forest before the sun sets again.'

He pointed his forehead towards the wagon as the animal continued to throw itself against the walls.

'This creature's den we stumble upon isn't the only one. And it's only at night that they come to life. If I were you, Codru, I'd rather not be on my own in the forest tonight. There's a longer way back until you reach out of the woods than if you join us.'

Codru was silent. He couldn't argue. He wouldn't survive another encounter with the beasts on his own. He didn't earn back his freedom only to be torn apart by monsters.

'Where are you heading?' he asked the knight. Toma's eyes twinkled, aware of the man's doubts. He said:

'Two days on horseback to the sunrise from here, there's a place—an old, sacred temple, built way before our ancestors' time. We'll take our new prisoner there.'

'Why not end its breath?' Codru asked.

'Because it's the first time we captured one. Daniil here always had a suspicion he shared with the captain. He believes they're people the devil spirited away, preying on their souls. He thinks he can save them. And with your aid, we'll now be able to follow this thread through.'

'I know that men died last night, but the Brotherhood will endure. We owe it to our fellow Ravens to continue its sacred quest,' he said, getting closer to the lock and making sure it was solid. Then he turned to Daniil: 'We should cover the wagon! We'll have to keep this quiet.'

The archer climbed up to the cart's bench and loosened a heavy leather blanket that had been tied up in iron grips until then at the end of the wagon's roof. The large canvas unrolled over the wagon, with dust and leaves scattering about, and then Toma caught its edges in wooden frames surrounding the wagon's belly. Once the cover was fastened, Codru heard the beast turn dead silent. There was no doubt that darkness was its wretched home.

The knights gathered the three surviving horses, who had been tied up to the trees around the camp until then, not too far from the carriage. The steeds were still unsettled, pulling away their heads, and one of them had a large bite mark close to its neck. The blood had dried out and turned dark on its grey skin. Unless the monster was spreading his vile sickness with his mouth, the horse would survive, Codru thought.

'There, Golden-Sun... There, shining one!' Toma soothed the mustard-coloured stallion, smoothing down its mane and feeding it an apple. Then he turned to Codru and threw him one too. He caught the red fruit and nodded to the man, as his belly was surely demanding it. He walked to the fallen tree trunk he rested on just before he heard the prisoner's rales and took a ravenous bite of the fruit.

The crossbow bearer left the two behind as he was smouldering the funeral fire that seemed to have already swallowed all traces of limbs and guts that tainted the grass. Toma followed Codru, chewing on his own apple. He didn't sit until Codru looked at him as he was standing, blocking the sun. Codru agreed.

'He spoke the truth,' the knight said, breaking the silence without turning to him.

Codru chewed his apple quietly and swallowed.

'The Captain, I reckon!' the knight continued, making use of Codru's pause. 'You should join us on our path and see this holy mission brought to its completion, in God's name...'

'I care not for it or for your peacock god,' Codru cut him off, discouraging the man to continue. 'Give me a horse, and I'll be on my way!'

Toma turned to him, not taking the man's words to heart. He continued to listen.

'God was nowhere in sight when my home was plundered, and my family killed. Nor when I was enduring pain just for the sake of it...' he continued. 'I am my own god!'

Toma nodded.

'Then do it in your own name!'

Codru looked at Toma's face. There was some hidden truth to his words, and deep down he knew it, even if he wouldn't allow himself to believe it. He chose to remain quiet and took another bite of his apple as revenge. The knight chose to continue:

'I can see the dark cloud above you, wanderer. The burden of shame and guilt hangs on your shoulders. And the reason I see it is because I too have known it,' he said, and then he turned his eyes to Daniil, who was away from them, standing tall and bowing his head close to the mass grave.

'And so did he. And many other men who died last night. Some of them were bandits or outlaws in another life. I was a treasure hunter. Daniil there outcast himself from his village, chose to be a monk and took his vow of silence. You see, Codru, we were all lost when the great Raven, Hunyadi, swore us in. He gathered lost men, like you and me, men who had nothing to lose, and promised them absolution and a place in the heavens.'

While Codru was listening, Toma turned his head back to the covered cart.

'It is said that more than ten winters ago, a cursed sickness began spreading from the south. An odd one, spat out by the devil. A sickness of the soul, not of the body. It appears that one day, suddenly, the dead men and women would awaken from their graves under the moonlight and drag into them the living, who would then carry the curse further.'

He lapsed for a few moments, aware that Codru was listening, then carried on:

'We call them *Strigoi*, due to their god damned howls. And so, our late Voivode Hunyadi founded this Brotherhood under his house's crest to safeguard the living from the undead and to discover the sickness's roots. The *moarte-neagră* took him before he could see the fruits of his labour; may he rest in peace!'

Codru shook his head.

'Dead don't kill people; the living do!' he muttered in frustration, throwing his fruit's core away in the grass.

'My blade put many in the ground, and none came back. I have been taught foolish, hogwash stories of otherworldly beings. Superstitions, just like this one. Your Strigoi seemed dead enough to me after their heads rolled on the ground.'

'And we burned them to stay that way,' Toma added.

Codru suddenly left the wooden log.

'Your gang of pious murderers died, and the man who rounded you all together is long gone,' he said. 'Why not give up and live the rest of your days away from this?'

'What are you scared of, Codru?', the Raven asked.

'Nothing scares me!' he snarled.

'Well, I am scared,' Toma continued. 'I'm most afraid of not having a mission or not leaving a trace that I once walked this earth and that I left it better than when I came into it; proof that I fought, and that even if I didn't emerge victorious, at least I left my claw marks on its surface. You may not be a man of faith, stranger, but we all want and need meaning.'

Toma shook his head, hinting at the carriage behind them.

'Otherwise, we're not much different than this poor, aimless soul.'

Codru's eyes were cutting through the man's stare like blades, as words such as these had been the vain promise the Old-Man always made to him, just to be turned away when he returned to him. A promise of purpose and legacy. He turned his back on the knight, clenching his fists. What did the knight know of his life and the things he had to do to survive? 'You know nothing of me, Raven!'

'I don't need to!' the knight said. 'Last night I saw a man who fought besides my brothers and showed mercy to a dying man. And for me, it's all I need to know.'

Then he stood up and said his last words to the stranger.

'Worry not, Codru. If you need a horse, I'll get you one. The wiser one which will surely help you find your way out of the forest. But should you decide to accompany us, a reward of gold awaits you at the journey's end. And perhaps a way out of your suffering.'

The knight left Codru there, sunken in his thoughts. The Raven joined the other knight as he harnessed two of the horses to the wagon: the pale yellow one and the grey, wounded one. The monk ended his watch on the now-dead fire with his head covered. He walked towards Codru and brought with him the last steed, the black one, as Tome had promised. When he got close enough, he raised his hand, showing Codru to take the stallion's harness.

As both Toma and Daniil climbed up on the wagon's bench, drawing the horses' reins, Codru grabbed the animal's saddle's horn and fit his boot in the stirrup, mounting the dark animal. Toma turned his head towards him one last time, then he barked:

'Giddy up!' and the wagon creaked, resuming its path.

Left behind, Codru watched the knights get further away, and his mind pondered the undead monstrosity, devoured by the devil, and ensnared in darkness. He didn't want to be one.

The claw tied up around his heart loosened its grip for just a moment, and that was when his boot's heel poked the horse's side, letting the animal join its brothers on the path.

# CHAPTER IV

*Härmeschtat, June 1459 (6967)*

'THERE IT IS,' SAID TOMA, 'THE RED FORTRESS! Halfway on their path to the old temple there was a great city of traders. The blonde-haired Raven told Codru that if he wanted his pay for helping them, they had to pass through it and pay a visit to his brother.

As Codru and the two Ravens were approaching the city, the massive brick walls were arising in front of them. A chain of great, white mountains towered in the distance, protecting its southern side, while sneaky, crimson rooftops peeked from behind the walls and bastions. The road to the fortress gate bustled with horse-drawn merchant wagons, some departing and others arriving.

The travellers did all they could to hide the massacre traces off their bodies. They washed away the dry blood off their clothes hours ago, when they passed by a well where they slacked their thirst. Codru took the Raven's word and kept the horse close to the covered cart, at the road's dusty edge.

He covered his face and his weapons with the cloak he was stripped away of when he got caught. He kept his head down, covered under the hood, but even so, inquiring eyes were measuring his figure as they carried away in their caravans. They couldn't see his face, but his long, rusty mane flowing on his shoulders and the curved Ottoman blade hanging on his side—they were all omens for the people. Word would travel; that was certain.

But for now, he didn't think much of it. He agreed, forced by unfortunate occasions, to escort the knights to the temple. His empty pouch longed for the coin. Codru also thought that the Brotherhood, or at least what remained of it, could be of use. They could roam the realm under Voivode's protection, and they could cross nearby borders without a written word or having to deal with guards. And when the time came for him to leave Transylvania, that would come in handy. The gates of Härmeschtat, as the travellers were calling the red city unravelling before him now, would prove to be one of these trials.

As the three arrived at the gate, a bell rang from the top of the gate tower. Two bearded men with rugged looks, dressed in brown gambesons with chainmail covering their heads and halberds at the ready, hailed as the newcomers approached. One of them raised his arm, waving at Daniil to restrain the horses and halt the wagon.

'Be welcome to Härmeschtat,' he said to the knights while he approached the cart. Codru couldn't speak the Magyar tongue, but he understood bits of it. It only took the wanderer a quick look from his hood at the guard as he was getting closer to know his kind. He was one of those.

'State your business, strangers!' the guard said sharply, waving his importance while eyeing the cart with overzealous scrutiny. He spat in the dust to underline it. The man looked and walked like a troublemaker.

'Only to idiots not to give power!' Codru thought to himself.

Toma sensed it too, indeed, but he kept his wits about him, preferring to choose his words carefully to not catch any undesired attention.

'We are knights of the Raven Brotherhood, bearing the noble name of the late Hunyadi and the protection of Voivode Rozgonyi!' he stated.

'I'm not blind; I can see your seals clear as day!' the guard cut him off. 'Your kind settled down at the border, at the old Mehadia Citadel; is what you are doing here that I'm more curious about!'

Before the Raven could answer, the guard pointed his chin at the covered wagon and asked:

'What do you carry in here?'

'A sick prisoner, you see, covered so it won't spread his miasma!'

Toma answered. 'I welcome you to search it, but it is safer for you good people to stay away from such disease.'

'Is that so?' the guard grunted. 'Then you'll have to turn around, won't you? No sick or plagued man is allowed to trespass, mayor's orders.'

The guard scratched his beard, squinting his eyes as if he were trying to peek through the leather blanket.

'I'm sure the young physician Saltzmann would appreciate a trial subject for his theriac. Not to rush you, but the poor soul is running out of days in there,' the knight said persuasively. 'Surely, there must be some way to get to some kind of good arrangement for all of us.'

The guard smirked, stepping a way back and looking at his guild fellow over his shoulder, then returning to Toma.

'An arrangement, you say...' the man grinned, revealing his yellowed teeth, clearly tempted.

Toma reached out under his dark mantle slowly, which caught the guard's attention, who barked for a moment with his hands firm on the halberd. The knight showed him quietly that he was simply reaching for his waist, where his pouch was hanging. Reassured, the guard allowed it and got closer to him with his weapon still pointed. The Raven plucked his pouch from his belt, shook the coins in it to check for plenty, then leaned in, hushing his words:

'Perhaps a humble contribution to bolster the guards' coffers, as a humble gesture of goodwill, might smooth our passage. After all, we all know of soldiers' meagre wages, and these are trying times we live in.'

The guard frowned and raised his eyebrows, sniffing in the now-open pouch. He glanced around and then clawed the pouch from the knight's hand. He slid his fingers in it, rustling the gold, then nodded, sucking his teeth, and clearing his throat.

'Very well, honoured knights, let's not make this a bigger problem than it is.'

He then tucked the pouch under his gambeson and turned his head to the other guard, who understood the task and shouted at his comrades in the tower to open the gates.

'Enjoy the city's hospitality!' the guard giggled.

As the wagon's wheel started turning, the iron gates of the city widened slowly, creaking and clanging. Daniil armed the steeds with a loose rein as Toma forced a smile and nodded at the other guard as they were passing through the gates. Codru fell right behind the wagon, keeping his head down, sensing the storm was yet to pass. And he was right.

When his cloak revealed his sword, the first guard's voice rose behind them.

'Ay, stay right where you are!' he said to him, while the guard's comrade raised his arm and halted the carriage.

'Curses!' Codru grinded his teeth, his eyes meeting Toma's, who shook his head slowly to not do anything reckless.

'Since when do the Ravens' Order's members carry Ottoman blades?' the man shouted at him, trying to see his face hidden under the hood.

Codru refrained from saying anything. He thought the charade was over. He would certainly be taken for a spy; the fight would break out, and even if he took some of the guards' heads, the journey would soon be over.

'A trophy, no doubt, from the last crusade!' Toma barged in, almost doubting it would work. But the guardian's greed blinded his mind, letting ignorance take place.

'A handsome one, at that!' the guard admitted. 'Tell you what, fair knights, throw in the precious sword, and we'll remain friends! What about that?'

Codru frowned, but he understood that the obvious thought didn't even cross the guard's mind. He just wanted the blade, and he surely wouldn't let go easily. He didn't wait too long to make it his own, either. While Codru kept calm, the man suddenly reached out to his scabbard, ready to pluck the sword.

'Don't!' Codru hissed, unable to restrain himself. 'Touch it, and you are dead!'

The guard froze, taken aback by the unexpected surge of hostility from the newcomers. His face turned red, and his nostrils pumped air like a bull in heat, while his lips revealed once again his nasty teeth, ready to give the order to seize the intruders.

But then, Codru said:

'It's cursed! The blade, that is. Charmed by priests!'

The fury on the guard's face gave way to outrage. Codru continued:

'The last man who touched it lost his arm! It withered and turned to dust.'

The man grimaced as he took a couple of steps back.

'Charmed?' he mumbled. 'Lost his arm?'

'Indeed!' Toma jumped in. 'I've seen it with my own eyes! Brother Daniil here cast the spells himself!'

The monk knight turned to the guard and nodded, rolling his thumb at his neck, and unearthing from under his gambeson a small, silver crucifix, which he then tucked back in shortly after.

The guards looked at each other with their eyes wide open, and then the greedy one almost shouted, swallowing the nonsense:

'Lord in heaven!'

Then he continued, cursing:

'Well, go on, then! Keep your cursed sword and your filthy wagon away from me! Hurry your horses before I change my mind!'

Daniil gently urged the horses forward with a tap of the reins, setting the cart into motion once again. They left the iron gates behind, their creaking sounds fading as the guards continued their bickering.

'I'm surprised you didn't lose your wits, Codru!' Toma sniffed. 'And that curse story was not bad either, for a faithless man.'

Codru rode silently for a moment before responding:

'I merely preyed on your people's weakness for old wife's tales, nothing more.'

'So, there's no cursed blade after all?' Toma chuckled.

'There is one truth to it!' Codru said, raising his head and meeting the knight's gaze. 'A man did lose his hand!'

***

The red brick walls of the city mirrored the wooden roofs of the tall, sand-coloured houses strewn on the maze of alleys. The roofs were adorned with unusual eye-shaped dormers that seemed to unrelentingly watch over the townsmen. All sorts of artisans and merchants, brought here from different parts of the world and speaking in all languages, were hustling, and rushing the people into their shops, promising them exquisite wares.

The noise, the lively people, the streets—they all reminded Codru of his days in Venice. As Daniil continued to drive the hidden cart through the heart of the market and Toma rested silently on the wagon's bench, the stranger scouted the vibrant buildings and the alleys from under his hood. More layers of walls and numerous towers seemed to have been raised up to the town's core on the hill, which he could glimpse from afar by the great, cathedral roof pointing sharply toward the amber clouds of dawn.

'The newest gem in the Red Fortress, praising Saint Mary,' said Toma. 'As tall as its twin that rests in Byzturch, up north. Crowned with its four small towers, the roof serves as a gentle reminder that here reigns the law of the sword. Townsmen don't need the Voivode's clemency to execute their outlaws.'

'Thank to God we didn't just become of that sort, don't you agree?' the knight raised his eyebrows.

'Where are we heading?' Codru asked sombrely, not playing into the knight's playfulness.

'As I promised you, here is where you'll get paid for joining the quest,' the knight reassured him. 'My brother is the town's, if not, I dare say, the realm's greatest blacksmith. He's also the one who keeps safe the treasures I hunted in my youth.'

Codru just came to realize that the knight would offer his own gold only to have his arm by their side. That could have either meant they were desperate or that he was just naive. Poor, reckless reasoning. Alas, he thought, coin was coin. And if Toma was willing to give it away just to solve a mystery, that was his choice alone.

The bells rang again from the towers, letting the people know the horologe had struck seven. The area where Toma's blacksmith brother had his workshop was quieter than the rest of the town. The wagon's wheels and the horseshoes clanked on the stone-paved alley as the sun was setting and the fires were set alight on the bastions, flickering through the shops and houses' windows as well.

Hammers hitting the anvil and a smoke scent were the first signs Codru noticed when they arrived at their destination. A three-story building, with its wall pushed blatantly right into the alley's edge and covered with the same watching roof eyes as almost all other buildings, presented itself to the visitors.

Daniil stopped the wagon, and while both knights went down, Codru dismounted his horse, pulling its reins after him. He saw Toma craning forward and circling the house, getting around the blacksmith's workshop. He whittled a few times until the hammering stopped.

The knight walked in under the elevated wooden roof that covered the yard, avoiding hitting his head on the glass lamp flickering on the beam and staring at the closed workshop's door in front of him. Both Codru and Daniil were waiting in the alley as a shadow rattled through the window. Metal clanking could be heard as the host was trying to unlock the door, and then, once opened, the shadow holding what looked like the hammer showed up in the doorway, framed by warm, flickering lights cast on the interior walls.

'Who goes there?' the voice yelled hoarsely in Magyar.

The Raven cleared his throat, then said out loud:

*'When the scarf is torn at the edges,*
*There is hope for your brother's head.'*

The shadow stepped forward into the lamp's light, showing his figure, and said:

*'...When the scarf is torn in the middle,*
*Then you know that your brother is dead!'*

'*Greuthung*, brother!' the man cried out. 'Is that, in truth, your ugly mug?'

'That's my ugly mug, indeed!' the knight answered laughing, and the two men grabbed each other in a tight, wayward embrace, shaking each other off the ground.

'And you brought two more rascals like yourself with you, bless your heart!' the man chuckled and then looked back at his taller brother's face, grabbing his shoulders, and roughing him up.

'The years in Hunyadi's service, at that rat-hole of a fortress at the realm's edges, really stole your youth away, haven't they?'

The knight looked back at his brother and didn't say anything. The blacksmith whistled towards the doorway.

'Ay, István, get your scrawny bum over here!'

Another shadow came into the doorway. A young man wearing a leather apron stepped forward.

'What do you need me for, master?' he asked the blacksmith.

'See those horses? Be kind and pull them in the back to the stable with ours. And feed them the good oats, you hear me!'

Then he turned to his brother, while István crossed the yard in one breath, landing his boots in the alley, grabbing the reins from Codru's hand like a whirlwind, and pulling the animals from the alley, as he was told. Daniil looked after him until he disappeared in the dark, worry showing up on his withered face.

'Come, my friends, come!' the blacksmith said, waving at Codru and the monk. 'I've got some smoked boar and some *palincă*, so glorious you'll beat up your mothers!'

Daniil shook his head at Codru, inviting him to take the lead, which he did. He stepped into the yard, passing by the lamp, while outside it turned darker and quieter. He followed the two brothers, with the shorter of them having his thick arm around the knight's shoulder with his sleeve wrapped up, carrying him through the workshop's doorway. Once he crossed it, the monk and, right after him, István followed too, closing, and locking the door behind them.

The workshop was like an old stable that still stank of manure but replaced the living cattle with iron and steel. A massive workbench, crowded with tools, was surrounding the walls, decorated with masterfully crafted blades, axes, and shields.

A great brick forge, now chocked of its fire, was walled up in the corner. In the winters, it must have also served as heating for the blacksmith's living area upstairs. On their left side, a wooden stairway led up to a door. Barrels and buckets of water were cluttering half of the ash and hay-drenched floor. And in the forge's right corner, there was a wooden trap door in it, locked and strengthened with steel bars.

'I urge you to leave your weapons here, in the workshop, will you? There's no room for swords amid a reunion now!' the host said.

While the knights agreed immediately, the blacksmith saw Codru hesitating.

'Your steel, too, needs a good polishing!' Then he peeked at the stranger's waist as he eventually decided to follow the rules and pulled his cloak aside.

The man saw the axe. 'That's not a common thing, carrying a wood-cutting hatchet as a fighting axe!'

Codru grinded his teeth, but he chose to ignore the remark, throwing his axe and sword on the workbench with the others. Once he disarmed his guests, the blacksmith guided them through the crammed passageway to the stairway and then waved for them to follow him up until the door that stood open above them.

The apprentice remained downstairs, seeing to his chores, while the rest of the men climbed up to the door and entered the blacksmith's home.

The room, softly illuminated by a handful of wall-mounted lamps, had a simple, albeit spacious, feel to it, despite the sense of confinement given by its low, wooden ceiling. Strings of garlic hung from the ceiling beams, and the nightlight filtered through the glass windows facing the alley. A thin rug nearly covered the entire wooden plank floor, serving to muffle the resonating clatter of the men's boots. At its centre, a sturdy table with a candle in the middle was surrounded by three chairs.

Upon entering, Codru noticed that the left side of the room was lined with shelves, displaying some of the blacksmith's tools and numerous bottles of liquor. The largest shelf, doubling as a table, held bread covered with a white cloth and dry sausages, all resting on a thick cutting board. On the right wall, a set of stairs led up to another door. With no bed in sight, Codru understood that the upstairs area might serve as the blacksmith's sleeping quarters, before reaching the attic.

'This is my sworn brother, Sándor!' Toma said, turning to Codru and the monk.

The blacksmith was what the knight was not. Shorter by almost a head, he had dark, curly hair between his ears, rolling in brushy sideburns on his temples, which came together in a thick, bushy black beard. He shared his brother's robustness; however, the meat and the good life in the city gifted him with a healthy paunch, stretching his stained work shirt and the edge of his leather blacksmith breeches.

He nodded as he looked at his guests' faces with his dark, rich eyes and scouted narrowly when they met the wanderer's long crimson hair and his forehead sign.

'Our new outlander friend here goes by Codru.'

'Any friend of my Toma is my friend!' the blacksmith didn't hesitate to shake his hand.

'And you remember brother Daniil, of course!' Toma concluded.

'Ever silent as God during Sundays! How could I forget?' Sándor tilted his head with respect.

'Well then, welcome to my home, travellers!' he continued, rubbing his palms. 'Take the chairs, friends; I shall bring the promised offerings at once!'

Codru, Toma, and Daniil followed Sándor's words and grabbed the chairs around the table, while shortly after, the blacksmith came holding the cutting board with meats, onions, and bread on it in one hand and two pairs of short glasses in the other. He laid them all on the table while Toma made room, pushing the candle to his side. Sándor left for a moment, and when he returned, he had one of his bottles on his chest, holding it like a newborn.

'Behold one of my prized babes,' he chuckled. 'All the way from the Körös' Meadows!'

He unsealed the cork, and then he poured its sap into the glasses, with the unclouded, golden potion twinkling in the candlelight. He crammed the cork back in and then rested the bottle in the middle of the table. He took one glass and raised it above him, inviting his guests to follow.

'To your health!' he said, and he downed the liquor, as did the knights. Codru took another glance at the potion, and then he threw it down his throat. The nectar roasted his chest as it ran down to his stomach, while an instant sweat burst on his temples and an unexpected cough followed.

'That's Queen's Water for you, friend!' Sándor laughed. 'It cures like Heaven's heart and burns like Hell's arsehole!'

The blacksmith left them for a moment and came back with another chair, which he then sat on, helping the men share the food.

It has been a long time since Codru had such a feast, and he kept his silence while filling his mouth and listening to Toma's youth adventures as told by his brother. Glass after glass, while the candle was slowly melting away, the men almost emptied the bottle.

'Do you remember Hanna, my little brother?' the blacksmith smirked.

'Sweet Hanna...! Who could forget her?' the knight grinned, prompting his back in the chair, embracing nostalgia.

'Or her bountiful bosom!' his brother howled. 'Her Boyar of a father almost got me in chains because of her, Codru! You hear? She's married now and has four little baron sons of her own.'

Then he turned to the knight.

'A lunatic, this one right here broke many virgins' hearts the day he swore his oath. He broke my heart too; you see, I had to leave the *Dacian* gold days behind, and settle, earning by crafting swords and maces.'

'The treasure hunting days are long behind us,' Toma elbowed him. 'But you can't cry to me; look at you and the restful life you built here!'

The blacksmith sighed and nodded, looking far into the candle.

'You're right, my heart is at peace!' he said, vaguely disappointed. 'So, I'm taking it you didn't bring any precious goods in that hidden wagon that rests in my stables now, did you?'

Toma looked around at Codru and Daniil, leaning on the table, then returned to Sándor, saying:

'I'm afraid, dear brother, what I brought with me this time is precious but far from good.'

As if a dark cloud suddenly rested above the table, the

blacksmith's face, red and vivid moments ago, seemed to slowly pale with worry.

'I see!' Sándor said. 'Tell me, then! What can I do for you, Toma?'

The knight took another sip of his drink and then cleared his throat.

'You are surely aware of the mission of our order.'

'Finding the living dead curse's roots and guarding our lands from them. By now, even the new, young King himself has heard about it, I'm sure.'

'Precisely,' the knight said. 'We were on our way to Hunyadvár when a horde of them, unlike any we had encountered before, assailed us in the dense forests of Cioclovina.'

He paused, during which time his brother thought it was fit to open his shirt's bead and spit symbolically down his chest to cast the omens and bad spirits away.

'What happened?'

Toma looked at Codru and Daniil and answered:

'We are the only survivors out of a dozen men of the Brotherhood!'

'God's mercy!' Sándor rumbled, refilling his glass, and shoving it down his throat. 'But there is no such thing! God turned his face away from our domain,' the blacksmith pondered. 'And it's all that devil of Prince-beyond-the-mountain's fault.'

'How do you mean?' Toma asked, distracted from his story. Sándor didn't hesitate to explain.

'I heard that three moons ago, he cruelly murdered all the Boyars' families that he found guilty of his own family's torture and death. On the very Easter Sunday, no less. He enslaved the able men to build his Poenari Watchtower without food or water. But that alone didn't fill his lust for blood.'

He took another drink, wiped his temples of sweat, and continued:

'He even turned on his own, the bastard, his old northern allies! He had almost four dozen merchants from Kruhnen impaled a month later for breaking the Wallachian laws. He burned to the ground the lands and villages around the city too.'

'They say that since he took the throne, Wallachia has turned into a filthy, doomed wasteland.'

'Where did you hear it?' Toma asked, his curiosity growing further.

'The merchants from all over, of course, who are passing through our city!' Sándor answered.

'You should hear their dark-hearted tales of dead walkers, the kind you're hunting. To the south, there are cattle dying of unholy witchcraft sickness near Dlăgopole, as the Wallachians call it, and the wheat fields are turning to dust and mold. Further beyond the mountains, to the sunrise, close to the Black Sea, there are stories of faceless *Akinji*, covered in foul adder skin, plundering the villages of Braylan and kidnapping virgins. We are witnessing the end of days, the one from the book; you just mark my words!'

'Faceless plunderers, you said?' Toma seemed to have suddenly awakened.

The blacksmith nodded subtly, coming to realize he may have spoken too much as the knight went wool-gathering and his face turned pale. It was enough for Codru to notice there was something amiss. However, Toma quickly collected his thoughts, expressing his concerns about the matter at hand.

'The Strigoi turned bolder, brother; I can almost sense it,' he sniffed. 'They went too far north from the mountains, as if they gained more strength. They ambushed us cleverly, not as the mindless ghouls we've known them for years.'

'What does this mean?'

Toma sighed.

'It means we're running out of time and that this curse is spreading quickly. The only way to end it is to cut off the snake's head! And that means we need to find it! Tell me more about the dead cattle; it could mean something to the quest.'

Sándor tried to remember if he indeed knew more about it. He did.

'I may have something, but I heard it from a Genoese peddler that passed by, and we could barely understand each other. He only said that the town's *pârcălab*, a Black Boyar by his title, promised gold to whoever dared to bring him the guilty witch's head. The townsmen think the Boyar lost his mind, and there's no witch—only God's punishment!'

'Don't tell me you're thinking about crossing the mountains to Wallachia!' he suddenly reacted.

'I will,' the knight said, 'if that's where the path leads! The Wallachian Prince knows our Brotherhood's name and Voivode's safeguard we bear, so we can roam the region. It's his land; he has to offer his help if he doesn't want to rule over a cemetery.'

'I wouldn't count on it. It was the great Raven, your very leader, who gave the order to have his father and brother executed, remember? If you're looking for hope to reason with him, you'll find no such thing. The man flays mothers and infants for pleasure; may he be forever damned!'

'We've taken an oath, and we have a duty to fulfil it!'

The blacksmith sighed, pouring another glass of the honey-coloured potion, and shook his head.

'If I cannot change your mind, at least do not travel bearing your order's sign. Do it as a peddler! Go to Kruhnen and find Georg Lang, the city's *Județ*. He owes me a favour, so ask him for a merchant safe passage letter. The Prince welcomes those following his law.'

'If God wills it, we won't have to get there.'

'The caravan! What do you have in your caravan, Toma? You were going to tell me.'

The knight landed his hand on his brother's shoulder and said:

'If fate wills it, the answer to our prayers! We captured one, Sándor!'

The blacksmith's face turned yellow, and he overturned his chair, sheering as he rose from his seat. His voice thundered.

'Are you mad? You brought one of those into my home? What for?' the man said, the liquor visibly taking hold of his tongue.

'We'll be gone before the sun rises. The wagon is safe as long as it's under the pitch-dark cover. Your home is but a halt on our journey, Sándor. I came to you because I need gold—lots of it. The time has come for me to tap into our vault.'

Toma's brother seemed disheartened by his words. Codru saw him fall silent, his eyes far away, while he struggled to raise the chair, grunting. The knight tried to help.

'Let go of me; I can handle the damned chair!' he muttered, straightening the seat, and turning his back, moving towards the shelf.

There was a knock at the door, and shortly after, István showed up and broke the tension.

'Take the night, lad!' the woozy blacksmith told him.

'Very well, master!' the young man nodded, then vanished.

While the young man was closing the door, the knights were changing looks in silence as Sándor quarried through his bundle of trinkets lying all over the shelves. He came back to the table holding a small, bulky, clay-made object and a long hay straw in one hand and a keychain in the other.

Codru recognized the pipe. They used to smoke that in Edirne. His nose caught the sweet scent of the mullein herb that was chugged into it. The blacksmith leaned over the table, lit up the straw from the candle stub lying in front of them, then shoved the clay whistle in his mouth, sucking and puffing as the herbs caught the hay's flame and the smoke rose to the ceiling.

As the smoke flooding in his lungs seemed to have soothed him enough, Sándor returned to his seat, lay on his back, continuing to puff from the pipe, and turned to Codru, now piercing him less friendly with his black eyes.

'The gold is for you, friend, isn't it?'

The wanderer didn't turn away.

'It so appears!' he answered.

The man blew the smoke up in the air, smacking his lips, then continued:

'I should've known you're no knight; the coiled snake sign you bear over your eyebrows... I've never met one of you before, but I heard of your kind as a child. Wandering the mountain villages as old beggars, blessing people with rain and good harvest in exchange for bread or milk.'

The blacksmith took another pause, waiting for a reaction from the crimson-haired man, but that didn't happen.

'But I don't see you blessing anything. You sold your soul to Satan, no doubt. You have only blessed the unfortunate with your blade, haven't you? You strayed far from your path. And you did it for the gold, not for the bread.'

'Who the hells are you, and what land are you coming from?'

'Enough, Sándor!' Toma grabbed his brother's shoulder.

'Enough is when I say is enough! Next time, better tell me whom I let in my home!' Sándor barked.

'It's only thanks to this man that we are now at your table,' Toma said. 'He's also the one who reignited hope in our mission, trapping the Strigoi!'

'Don't soil your underpants!' Sándor said to the Raven while turning away from Codru. He poured the last drop from the bottle into his glass and drank it. He then stood up and grumbled with an annoyed tone:

'Well then, let's give the devil his bounty, shall we? I don't want him under my roof more than needed.'

The stairs seemed steeper on the way down to the workshop, and Sándor was surely overusing the wooden, creaking rail. The weapons they had placed on the workbench were now concealed beneath a heavy cloth. István only left a couple of lamps burning on the walls before he left, but it was enough light to show them the way. Sándor released one of them from its bracket and guided his guests through the clutter as quietly and carefully as he could.

'Don't we dare wake up the Strigoi from its nap!' he mumbled.

Codru walked behind Toma, who was following his brother, but even so, he could tell they were heading towards the trapdoor he noticed earlier in the corner. When Sándor reached its edges, he took a knee next to it, gasping, and gave the lamp to his brother to hold it while he struggled to fit the tinkling keys in the lock that was holding the iron chain guarding the hole in the floor. After he unrolled the chain off the rings, he raised the trap door up, revealing the dark emptiness of the vault. Two wooden bars were visible on one side of the entrance's frames, giving a glimpse of the top of a ladder.

Sándor looked up at Toma. The blacksmith's forehead and temples were glowing.

'One of you should remain behind, just to be cautious!'

Toma turned back to Daniil, who understood his task without any other words. The blacksmith grabbed the wooden ladder's end and sank slowly into the darkness, under Toma's watch. A few firecrackers and curses later, a weak light started to flicker from below, a sign that Sándor had lit a lamp in the basement.

Toma used that as a signal and left his own on the table, following soon after into the cellar. When Codru's boot touched the stone floor of the basement, he realized the space was larger and taller than even the blacksmith's room upstairs. When he turned, he could hear the blacksmith swearing as he was trying to light up the last of the lamps, rubbing a flint and a piece of metal together. When he finally succeeded, he placed the lamp in the last empty bracket and turned to Toma, whipping his ooze out of his face.

Codru couldn't help but wonder how long it must have taken to build the vault. There were three walls, with only the one to his left that was covered with stone bricks and now holding the light sources and bearing a few shelves covered with small chests and wooden or iron boxes. The front and right walls looked more like the cell he was kept in at Mehadia. But, unlike that one, these two cells were keeping others from getting in, not out.

Walking towards the two brothers, he could see through the iron bars numerous large chests, one on top of the other. There were masterfully crafted armours placed on their racks, shining coldly in the low light. In the front cell, he saw animal pelts, precious rugs, and carpets, and even tools and weapons of unknown origin, even for him. One of them looked like an overgrown sickle.

'I call it *falcă*; we found many of them iron blades in the deep bed of the Olt River,' Sándor said. 'But that's not why we're here!' he grumbled, turning to the cell on the left.

While the blacksmith took his time unlocking the metal door, Codru saw Toma's head turned towards the other cell, almost as if he didn't care much for the reason they were here anymore. He only woke up from his reverie when he heard the door chains hit the stone floor. Sándor stepped in while his guests waited. He kneeled next to a chest and raised its lid after his keys unbolted it. The knight peeked through the bars as he approached the cell.

'Hand me those two pouches!' he asked impatiently.

Sándor sniffed, eyeing the chest's treasure.

'That's worth almost 500 gold ducats; you surely must have had too much to drink!'

As the knight kept quiet, his face expression not twitching, his brother understood that there was no way to change Toma's mind, so he grabbed the two pouches and threw them one by one to him.

'I pray to God he's worth it,' Sándor whined, side eyeing Codru.

'Here!' Toma said, throwing one pouch at Codru, who caught it and shook it. 'One now, one after we fulfil the task, agreed?'

The coin he just got was already more than he had ever been paid for one kill. He leaned his forehead quietly and fit the pouch under his cloak.

'Very well!' the knight concluded, following his new ally's way, and hiding the other small leather back under his own mantle. He then spoke to the blacksmith:

'There's one more favour I require, brother!' then his face turned to the other cell, where the weapons and pelts were. Sándor stood up, his face losing its colour once again.

'You must have completely lost your senses, Greuthung!'

Toma approached him and laid one hand on his shoulder. He

said, with a lower voice, looking him straight in the eye:

'I need to put this to rest, once and for all! I may never have another chance!'

Sándor sighed, bowing his head. He turned and locked the cell door behind him. He crossed the cellar towards the other one, quietly and surely, as if the liquor's vapours had suddenly left his brain. He unlocked the cell in silence, and after he opened the door, he moved out of the knight's way, handing him the keys and waiting outside.

Toma stood there like a statue for one moment, but once he entered the cell, he pulled a bear hide to the side, revealing another massive wooden chest. His keys unlocked it, and as if someone or something urged him to follow, Codru got closer to the cell, surprised that Sándor didn't even care to say anything anymore.

He peeked over the knight's shoulder, and as the flickering lamps dared to cast their lights inside the chest, he saw two objects like nothing he had seen before that seemed to have caught fire themselves, glowing ominously: a helmet and a mace.

\*\*\*

'My brother barks, but he won't bite!' Toma pulled him aside that night after they returned to the surface. 'We'll rest here, shall you agree, and we'll resume in a couple of days? I have another request for Sándor. Meanwhile, be welcome to roam the city.'

He didn't have the desire to do so. What he needed was rest. For the last two nights, he laid his bones in Sándor's attic while István, sent by his teacher, knocked two or three times on the door, bearing with him food and drinks.

He slept on a thick, woollen quilt on the attic's floor. When he woke up the morning they were supposed to leave, he felt rejuvenated, he couldn't lie. Rays of lucent light, through which diluted dust was floating, reached out to him through the two roof eyes that also served as windows. He sat there quietly with his eyes closed, rubbing them to regain clarity.

He turned to his knapsack, thrown on the wooden floor next to the quilt. Usually, he'd get a taste of one of his foul potions in the morning to regain his vigour quicker. He grabbed the bag and rummaged through it. He unveiled a small vial with an oily, green, curdled, dark essence that left traces on the vial's solid glass. He threw it back in the bag and stood up. He hadn't indulged in it for the past few days.

He walked toward one of the small windows. In the alley, he could see that Daniil was already harnessing the horses to the cart. The blacksmith's apprentice was nearby too, petting them and treating them with buckets of water. Codru could see the sunup already, way past morning.

As he was getting his boots on, a jumble of thoughts started creeping into his mind. He didn't want to give in and start trusting all the crap he heard. There were no such things as spirits, the undead, or witchcraft. But he knew there were terrible, unknown maladies out there, such as the one their prisoner had. And he knew the vile nature of man. He's seen it and felt it on his skin. The stories of pillagers or ruthless princes were just proofs of it. If life required him to, he would resolve them both with his sword.

He tied up his mantle around his neck and took his knapsack, going down the stairs and reaching the room where they had their feast, now flooded by the morning sun. The door was open, and he could hear the voices of Toma and Sándor arguing. When he appeared in the doorway at the top of the stairs, they both ceased their bickering and turned their heads up to him.

'Are you feeling prepared, Codru?' the knight asked. 'You certainly look rested. It's way past early morning, but I thought you might need the shut eye, so we delayed our departure until noon.'

Codru hummed.

'Very thoughtful. It helped a great deal not being in a cage or chains the whole time.'

Then he asked:

'Where are my weapons?'

'Easy, wicked one!' Sándor said, clearly still holding grudges. 'You shall have them. Let me see you to your wagon.'

After following the two brothers down the stairs to the workshop, he noticed that Daniil had already taken his crossbow while Toma was just studying his long sword.

'Balmut is, to this day, one of the works I'm most proud of!' the blacksmith measured his brother's reactions with his arms crossed.

'Right you are!' said the knight, putting the weapon away.

On the table were only his scimitar and his axe, their hilt and haft looming from under the cloth. Toma moved along, exiting the barn, while the blacksmith remained behind. He approached the wanderer and reached out to the workbench where the weapons were waiting before Codru did.

'I took the liberty to feed and care for your precious tools, you devil,' he mumbled without looking at him but rustling the rag cover. 'Here they are!'

Codru laid eyes on his belongings. Even in the dim light of the workshop, he could notice a clear polish on the blade of his curved, freshly sharpened spade, as the blacksmith surely took care of that. He raised it, balancing it on his palm. He winged it slowly and precisely around him, the blade roaring like wind and shielding him in a protective, invisible shell. His eyes looked back at him, reflecting from the scimitar's edge as clear as a silver mirror.

'Good work!' he said, almost pleased and impressed by the man's craftsmanship.

'They don't call me Earth's Hammersmith just 'cause I have a big hammer. Here's your axe too!' Sándor raised the tool off the table and gave it to Codru with both hands, as if he pledged an offering to the gods.

Codru looked down at it, and his first impulse was to strangle the man. The hatchet's faces were sleek, and its edge was sharper than it ever was. That wasn't what made his blood boil. What did that, however, was the sign the blacksmith had carved in its steel. On one side of the hatchet's neck, an inscription of a coiled snake reaching out for its tail was now guarding the weapon's head. Down on the wooden, varnished haft, an array of runic signs was spreading from head to toe.

Seeing the man struggling to understand what had happened to his weapon, the blacksmith broke the silence, almost satisfied with his deed.

'Now it will always be a fighting axe and not a wood-chopping hatchet!'

Codru held himself back from grabbing the axe and using it on his own restorer. He grasped it in his hands and grunted.

'I did not ask for this!'

'It matters not to me!' said Sándor. 'I merely just sharpened it to serve you well in battle, and I gave it your forehead seal, so it will be true to who you really are.'

'Now they'll know its bearer is not a knight!' he concluded.

Codru pierced the blacksmith with his eyes while dropping the axe in its clutch under the cloak. Sándor looked at him defiantly, with a hint of a smile in the corner of his moustache. He got closer and said:

'I know you'd be glad to send me to my maker right now, but then you won't get paid. Know that I am not afraid of you, nor do I need you to like me.'

He then continued speaking while heading towards the doorway to the yard:

'My father used to say that if you want to keep the starving wolves away from your herd, you need a hound as starving as them. I need you, hound, to have my brother's back, and for that, I blessed your weapon with all the protection my guild elders taught me. Those runes may one day save yours and my brother's lives!'

Then he left the workshop.

When Codru followed them outside, the brothers were saying their goodbyes, and Daniil was already on the cart's bench. The wagon remained covered, the beast silent, and István was finishing strapping on its roof a long wooden pole with an iron, circling claw at one of its ends. Some sort of longer staff of Sándor's devise that he crafted on Toma's request. It was like what dogcatchers were using to trap rabid animals and keep them at a distance. Codru understood what this one would be used for.

'Your horse, *Uram*!' he heard the apprentice approaching him while pulling the reins of the dark horse the monk gave him.

'Great beast!' the boy tried to converse, clearly intimidated by his appearance. He nodded, taking the reins, and looking into the deep black eyes of the stallion. He agreed that it was not a bad-looking animal.

'Does he have a name?' the young man dared, despite the stranger's sourness.

'Names keep you tied where you don't belong!' he answered to the boy. 'They matter not!'

'All horses must have names, *Uram*! His is Shadowfire—when I went to the stables early in the morning holding the lamp, the fire burned in his eyes. He was so black that he looked like a shadow on the walls. I called him Shadowfire when I gave him water, and I swear, he was very pleased with it!'

Toma overheard and laughed.

'Name all the horses in the city when they're thirsty and then give them water; you'll see how happy they are with their names!' Sándor poked him. 'Enough with the chatter; there's work to do!'

István scratched his head, confounded, and left the yard, going back to his chores. Stupid, innocent soul, Codru thought, untarnished yet by life's meat grinder. When he looked back into his horse's eyes, his mind clashed to the back of his skull. He landed on green field, surrounded by mountains that flashed through his mind. He blinked and a thunder of hoofbeats ploughing the field stabbed his ears. A battle. Swords bouncing off each other. Men roaring. He galloped through them like a scythe. He saw his dark, majestic reflection in the churning puddles scattered across the land. His mane and his hooves.

He came back to his senses, staggering, taking a step back and regaining his senses, while his ears were still singing. While still in shock, Codru turned around quickly to see if anyone saw it, but none did. He exhaled with relief. It has been a long time since he had one of these visions. His heart pumped as struck by lightning felt alive. The horse spoke to him.

'Greeting to you too, Shadowfire...' he whispered pensively.

Then he tied his knapsack to the saddle, pulled its horn, and hoisted himself on the animal's back. In front of him, he saw Toma giving his brother a last embrace and finally joining the monk on the wagon's bench. He turned towards Codru to see if he was ready, then shook his head at Daniil.

The monk gently whipped the horses with his reins, and the wheels started spinning in the alley, leaving the city, Sándor, and his workshop behind.

# CHAPTER V

*Old-Şinca Cave, June 1459 (6967)*

'WHAT IS IT THAT YOU'RE DOING?' TOMA startled him from his musings.

Codru raised his head, half surprised he didn't hear the knight's footsteps getting closer through the grass. He was in a hurry to hide away the odd roll of bark he had been staring at for the past few long moments. Toma saw him pulling the bag the wanderer kept lying on the ground between his boots.

'That's not a parchment...' he said without breaking eye contact with the object. He took a long drink from his freshly filled-up leather flask, then tried to hand it to his comrade.

'No,' Codru mumbled, declining the flask with his hand. 'It isn't.'

'I know what you're trying to do!' Toma continued, taking a seat next to Codru on the tree trunk he had been resting on until then, while the monk was still climbing from the valley where he and the knight refilled their flasks from down the spring.

'You are trying to decipher my brother's inscriptions that he engraved on your weapons, aren't you?'

Taking advantage of Codru's silence and watching him finally tuck the peculiar roll of parchment inside his knapsack, he continued:

'Whatever script it is that you so carefully try and fail to keep a secret in there, it won't help you translate Sándor's runes. But I can; shall you still be curious to find out.'

Codru ignored him. It wasn't that he wanted to know what the blacksmith carved on his steel as much as why he did it. But that could wait. Right now, he was more curious when the knights would decide to resume the journey.

He looked at the sky, and it was past mid-day. It was their second day on the road, and they were now travelling through a thin forest. As dusk was approaching, he didn't want to be caught in another trap of forest creatures on the road.

'How far is that temple?' he asked the knight, completely disregarding his previous interests.

The knight raised his eyebrows, expressing 'as you wish' and stood up from the trunk.

'It isn't far at all,' he said, turning away from Codru and walking towards Golden-Sun, who was shaving the grass with his muzzle. Toma strapped his flask to the horse's saddle. The eerie glare of the artifacts he took from Sándor's vault loomed from under the covers. He said, gazing towards the valley as the monk was approaching too:

'We only made this halt to gather our strengths in preparation for the night. We'll need those when we bring the Strigoi out. But we are closer than you'd think!'

When Daniil showed up, he looked more tired than usual. It could have been the labour of the hill he had to climb from the stream, or it could have been something else. But as the monk was slowly circling the carriage, Codru could sense the same worry weighing down on the hooded knight's face that he noticed a few days ago, before they entered Sándor's workshop. He revisited time and again the dog-catching staff the blacksmith made for them. He rechecked it for resistance and durability. If it was properly tied up or loose.

'What happened to him?' Codru asked Toma while mounting Shadowfire.

Toma looked toward the priest.

'You are not the only one running away from their past.'

He then ended on a side note, leaving the area, and beginning to walk towards the cart:

'Unlike yours or mine, however, his past would catch up with him before the night is through.'

The way through the willowy beech and ash-tree forest was rather quiet. Ancient boulders of rock, covered in sheets of moss and spiderwebs, taller than them or the horses, rose from the earth on both sides of their track, guiding them. The stillness was only broken by the horseshoes rustling through the leaves, the wagon's wheels creaking, and the wild, huddled up chirps of blackbirds and starlings quivering through the high crowns.

The sun was almost set as the three journeymen approached a man-made road, peeled of its grass and showing the bare ground underneath, battered by time, hooves, and carts. A settlement must have been nearby, Codru believed.

'There is a small Christian village in the valley; there are not more than two hundred souls in it,' the knight said, almost as if he answered Codru's thoughts.

'We've been roaming the Făgăraş's old lands for quite some time now, as old as the *Râmlani* themselves. There are still ruins of their old forts standing nearby.'

'Făgăraş? I heard of this place before,' Codru said half-heartedly.

'The Besenyő, or the Pechenegs, the barbarian raiders who settled here, called it as such hundreds of years ago due to the ash-trees that swarm on its grounds. They are long gone now, but the Christians here endured. And this land protected them.'

'What do you mean?' Codru asked, continuing to ride his steed close to the wagon on Toma's side. The knight replied:

'You see, they found old temples gouged in the rock of the mountain or deep in the ground. These sturdy and hidden oases, unbowed by time, provided shelter and shielded them from the invaders. Now they are still using them as churches. Their grounds are sacred. Men thought God answered their prayers and that he built them out of ether for them to hide, but the temples were here long before them, or the invaders' ancestors were even born.'

Codru's memory spiked. Long lost visions of a cavern deep beneath the earth began taking hold of his mind. There were flashes of an ancient temple and an underground labyrinth. There was the Elder's sombre and grave voice reeling his histories of the mason Fire-Knights.

He just began to realize that their destination could have been one of the mysterious ancient places they left behind before they were swallowed by the sands of time.

\*\*\*

'They call it the Temple of Fates!' the knight said, looking ahead towards the entrance of a grotto opening its jaws in the hill. Codru could finally see the place he heard the knight blabbering about for so long. The caverns of unknown origins that people older than the Dacians have carved into the soil and rock.

Daniil's boots touched the ground, and the horses seemed unsettled. He ran his hand over their manes to calm them down, while Codru dismounted his steed, haltering it to the nearby tree. The darkness of a clear night was approaching, but there was an unusual mist and heaviness in the air. It came as no surprise that the valley's villagers firmly believed the ancient cave harboured enchantments beyond their wildest imaginations. They turned it into a church and shrine for pilgrimage. They claimed, Toma told him, that they would come here sick, and leave cured and that their wishes made here would turn true.

He saw, from a fair distance, the priest-knight's jaw pulsating on his emaciated face. The monk has taken out his crucifix and kissed it with his eyes closed, as he was undoubtedly praying. But Codru only wanted to get over whatever the knights had come here to do. He was counting on their victory too. The sooner their quest was over, the sooner he could part ways with them and leave this place behind. He even hoped the fates of the temple would be on his side, if that was what it took.

'Help me here!' the blonde Raven asked, with one hand touching the leather blanket covering the jail wagon.

Codru closed in on him and clutched his fingers together. The knight grabbed his shoulder, rested his boot in the cup of Codru's palms, and pushed himself up, reaching out over the wagon's roof. Toma untied the long wood and iron staff his brother crafted for them and then grabbed it, lifting it up. He also took the thick rope the staff had been tied with. Once both were secured in Toma's hands, he let himself back down, jumping to the ground, while Codru whisked the dust off his gloves.

Daniil was waiting, almost petrified, behind the cart, looking at its covered door, as he could already see the sick prisoner through it.

'Brother Daniil knows the inside of this temple,' the knight said to Codru. 'There should be a few old, rusted shackles pinned in the underground walls of the shrine.'

Then he threw him the large roll of rope. Codru caught it with both hands as it was unfolding. He frowned, then he spoke:

'You want me to be the one tying the prisoner up.'

'Let's say the second pouch of gold comes as a hazard reward,' the Raven grinned.

After that, he circled around the wagon carrying the dog-catching staff with both hands, reaching behind, where Daniil seemed to have ended his prayers. He looked at the two men approaching with cheerless, sunken eyes. He let his hood hang on his back, revealing his grey-dark, greasy hair and his thin skin stretched over his temples.

'Daniil shall crack the door open, and I'll swiftly try to catch his neck with this,' said Toma. 'Once I have it trapped in the iron claw, you'll use the rope to tie its arms behind.'

Codru turned his head toward the wagon as the monk dug his fingers into the leather cover. It only took a few moments of light hitting the iron bars of the tight window and a violent roar unleashed from the carriage. The face of the prisoner knocked on the door with such force that his thick spit burst through the wind. The horses started frowning more agitatedly than before, with their horseshoes scratching the dirt.

The three men looked silently at the desperate, mindless being. Codru pondered pensively, observing its figure again. The man, if it could have been called that, had no right to exist. During the whole time the travellers spent between the forest ambush, the journey to Härmeschtat, and finally this ancient shrine, no one fed it or gave it water. But if that didn't end his cursed existence, the worm-swarming, flesh-eating disease he must have been carrying should have taken him long ago. Maybe, Codru thought, that was the disease: restless death.

Daniil pressed his right shoulder and left palm into the reinforced-wooden door of the wagon while his right hand reached for the iron fastener that kept it locked. He looked at his guild comrade as he tried the mechanism of the pole. He pulled a lever built in the pole, and the thick iron ring at its end opened wide, like a claw.

Toma pushed it back, and the claw closed. Sándor's beast-catcher worked like a charm. As the knight opened the claw once more, ready to use it, he dug his boots into the ground, bracing himself. He nodded at Daniil and then at Codru, who unravelled the rope and prepared a solid knot, ready to trap his arms on Toma's wish.

One last rapid breath, and the priest pulled the lock, cracking the door open. The wagon shook like a tempest when the creature's arm creeped through, vainly grappling the air for freedom. Daniil leaned more into the door as his feet sank into the grass under it.

Codru saw the small chance and took it. He didn't wait for Toma's signal, and as soon as he laid eyes on the beast's arm, he passed the knights and threw the noose around the putrid and slimy arm of the Strigoi. He quickly pulled, and the noose tightened rapidly around its elbow. While the beast bawled at its captors, his rotten teeth pushing through the cracked door, Codru doubled the noose and signalled Daniil that it was ready.

'Now!' Toma shouted over the creature's grunts, and Daniil let the door open just enough more for the prisoner to reveal its sallow skull. Toma opened the claw and tried to find its neck, but the Strigoi barked, biting the iron, and braying its cracked teeth in it. Toma panted, trying his luck one more time, as the priest released the door once more. With a knack, Toma pushed back the staff lever, and the claw wrapped around the monster's neck.

Toma was a vigorous man, but the creature was stronger, easily overpowering him.

'Daniil, let the door open!' he said. 'Curses! I need you here!'

It only took half a moment for the monk to abandon the wagon's door, and it knocked on its side, just in time for the man to lay his hands on the pole next to Toma's. Both men were fighting for their lives to keep the creature at the pole's length, away from it and its dark, skeletal claws, as it got out of the carriage.

While the knights continued to struggle to hold the prisoner in place, Codru leaped behind it and threw another loop from mid-rope around the Strigoi's free hand. When he pulled, both creature's arms tightened together behind its back, in such a violent and harmful way that the mercenary could hear its bones crack and his shoulders jump from their sockets. The prisoner wailed.

'It's time!' Toma yelled.

Daniil and Toma began pushing and guiding the Strigoi in the direction of the temple's entrance, restraining it so it wouldn't deviate from its path. Codru rolled the remaining rope around his knuckles and wrists, and it was biting away at his skin as the prisoner was jolting and twitching. The horses didn't calm down, not even when the men succeeded in taking distance from the cart, their neighing reverberating through the trees as the mellow darkness rested on their crowns.

Codru grinded his teeth, drops of sweat rolling on his temples and his eyes moving from the Strigoi to the heaped mouth of the rocky hill, which seemed to open to swallow them in its belly. If it was the shrine Toma told him it was supposed to be, it didn't look as such. He had his share of caverns, and this was merely one of them. The fate that the temple bore in its name was merely foreboding the fate of the creature and nothing else.

None of Codru's travelling companions had any way of bringing light for guidance. More so, the only one who happened to have already been here before was Daniil, but he was not speaking. Even without their captain, for a pair of men who took pride in their knighthood, Codru believed they could have been more prepared for this, but they were not. And as such, it fell onto him and his darkness-hardened eyes to guide the knights further down.

'Follow me!' he eventually said, grunting and straining. Relentlessly holding the beast-catcher in place together with the priest, Toma heard the mercenary's words. His intrigued expression disappeared as quickly as it loomed on his face, shaking his head like a child who was promised to be taken care of and agreed to follow Codru's words.

The cursed voice of the Strigoi dispersed in the shrine as they succeeded in crossing its sombre entrance. By the sound alone, Codru could tell the cavern was neither too deep nor too wide. But it was as dark as expected.

Getting ahead of his fellows and closer to the tied-up prisoner, he could sense the rotten flesh's smell rushing into his nostrils. Peaking over its bony shoulder, he could glimpse at the moderately steep path that has been carved into the hill, with other great holes dug on each other side of the passage. At the end of it, a haze of blue light seemed to come from above, scattering through the cave's sanctuary. It was the moonlight that somehow broke through the hill's top.

The men, led by Codru and the monster ahead of them, belching his infected slobber over his chin, descended through the temple, which resembled a mole tunnel more than the church it was used for. Some of the bleak side entrances had old, almost hollowed-out rust-iron broken bars. The Strigoi wasn't the first prisoner ever brought here. Codru wondered if this had happened before.

'The shackles!' Toma bellowed, unable to continue his plea as his hands loosened the grip for a moment, giving the Strigoi enough room to pull away but not too far to lose it.

While the rope scraped through his skin, Codru scrutinized the eerie chamber. The moonlight falling through a tall eye in the tower-like ceiling made his search easier.

There were no shackles on the chiselled walls of the grotto. However, between its centre and the wall in front of them, an iron, solid stake rose from the stone. Its unusual shape and inscriptions made it difficult to guess what this pillar had been used for before. But the only holes he could find in the cave were the ones the iron stake had on its edges, like a lace of metal surrounding it.

He pulled the rope after him, while the prisoner's neck twisted in the tight iron collar, peeling its skin off. As the Strigoi was now facing his captors, Codru passed the rope through one of the rings and pulled it off the other side with strength, dragging the Strigoi's arms closer to it. While the sick one continued to cry out, Codru continued to stitch the rope through the rest of the holes. Once that was ready, he used the remaining rope to roll it around its chest, avoiding the Strigoi's mouth as he did.

The knights finally released its neck from the collar, and for a few long moments, the three men simply stood there, panting, wiping off their sweat, and mending their sore hands, until Daniil took a few steps back and left the sinister chamber.

'He'll be back soon,' the Raven said, noticing Codru's inquiring frown. The knight prompted the beast-catcher to lie on the floor and let it rest on the tuberose wall. The prisoner's howls were relentless; his hoarse throat snarls hit the men's eardrums like nails on a coffin. The blue-hued moonlight spread on its meagre cheekbones and chest, exacerbating its ghostly, unreal appearance.

Codru has given a thought or two on how the knights planned to use the Strigoi to find the disease's source but didn't give them good odds that they would succeed. They kept this creature alive longer than they should have. It appeared that mercy wasn't in the books for the so-called virtuous knights when there was a higher purpose at stake.

Daniil came back with his saddlebag, his crossbow, and a wooden bifurcated pike he had until then strapped to the side of his horse.

The knight kneeled ceremoniously between Codru and Toma, near the iron pillar, right in front of the Strigoi. After he rested the pike and the crossbow on his sides, he made the sign of the cross with his eyes turned to the hollow ceiling through which the light fell on his pale face. Then he opened the bag and revealed a couple of long wax candles. He used his flint stones to light one up, and then he melted the bottom of the other one with it, sticking it on the floor between him and the monster.

Once he lit it up using the first one's flame, he continued to encircle himself in a spread of several candles he kept taking out of his knapsack. A sweet, feverish scent flooded the cave when the monk took out a small metallic scoop and held it over one of the candles until white filaments of smoke formed above it.

He stood up and moved his lips in silence as a prayer. He crossed the prisoner with incense from a safe distance, making it even more agitated. He then looked in turn at each of his witnesses. He quietly laid the incense burner on the stone floor while still fumigating and picked up the two items he brought with him. He handed the crossbow to Toma and nodded.

When the priest turned to Daniil, he raised the bifurcated pike in front of him and spoke for the first time:

'Take this!' his guttural, mellow voice sounded. 'You'll know what you'll have to do if that moment arises.'

Then he turned his head towards the entrance. Codru could see the muscles in his jaw waving frantically. The priest turned back to him and looked straight at him.

'For all our sakes, hold hope that it never comes!'

Looking confused at the simple wooden stick he had been given without any other counsel, he gazed at Toma for answers. But the Raven didn't meet his eyes. He stood still, with his face towards the sickened and his hands tight on Daniil's weapon.

The older knight ceased his slow movements inside the circle of candles and suddenly untied his cloak and threw it on the floor, outside the circle. He then began removing his gambeson, his tunic with crow motifs knitted on it, and casting them one by one over the hood he had already chucked out. His clothes piled up until he stood half-naked, wearing only his breeches and his boots.

Codru's eyes fell on the monk's bony back, through which his crooked spine looked as if it was going to pierce his pale skin. The wanderer saw now that he wasn't the only one bearing ink markings. Daniil's back and shoulders were almost entirely covered in Cyrillic letters, which Codru never had the fortuity to learn so-far.

Clouds slowly shadowed the moon, which had been serene until then, with the light coming from above dimming more and more.

When Daniil grabbed his silver crucifix dangling around his neck, the candles began to flicker as streams of chilling air hissed through the cavern.

Daniil's voice thundered, trying to cover the Strigoi's scream. The moon disappeared completely. The priest broke the crucifix from his chain and raised his arm, keeping the silver as some sort of shield in front of the creature.

He started chanting words in a broken tongue. An old incantation that made the Strigoi drop to its knees as if a mighty god struck it down.

'Ot"gon'em vo'z' v' ot'nos nas, k'to bi 'vo' t'y b'y,' Daniil continued his rite. 'n'ch'shni du'khi, vse satan'sk'i s'ly, vse p'r'd'n'i na'val'n'tsy...'

And then, even in his lack of knowledge of what the monk said, Codru finally understood. They were never going to heal the sick. They were going to try to cast the devil away and save its soul instead. He began believing the mission was never to find the sickness's source and destroy its roots with herbs or potions, but to summon in the Almighty's power and hope their belief in providence would be enough. He has been hired to witness these idolatrous, self-righteous fouls failing. He has never earned gold in an easier way.

His thoughts broke when the wind started suddenly to sweep through the entrance, almost blowing all the candles away. Both him and Toma turned their heads towards it, as something seemed wrong. Daniil began casting his exorcism even louder, doing everything he could to cover the wind and the monster, which was now raising from the floor, despite the monk's resilient attempts to submit it. Whatever he was trying to do was not working. Toma relit the blown candles while at the same time shielding them from the wind under the cover of his mantle.

The wind kept howling. Daniil's eyes turned quickly to Codru for a moment. And in that glimpse, the mercenary saw pure terror. His sharp ear caught the wind's roar, and then the hair raised on the back of his neck; it was not wind. It has never been the wind.

'They're coming!' the monk wailed, gasping, and breaking the incantation.

It was then that the Strigoi released a long, demonic shriek that came along with a blast of wind that burst from his whole body, lifting the three men off the floor with incredible force, throwing them across the sanctuary, and scattering the sacred circle of candles in all corners.

Complete silence and darkness. And then, a dying moonlight poured through the ceiling once more.

'Stand up!' Daniil cried out, already on his feet. 'Both of you, now!'

A rattle broke the darkness from where the Strigoi was tied. The throat-cracking sound became louder. Then it slowly turned into a sound, and hearing it threw Codru shivers down his spine. It was laughter.

'*Da-ni-iiiiiil...*' the voice permeated the shadows. '*Da-niiii-IIIL!* *Daniil, I'm talking to you!*'

The monk's legs turned to mush, overwhelmed with despair.

'*Let me see you, Pike! Where are you, Pike?*'

The morbid quietness weighted heavily in the mouldy air of the temple. Codru had the feeling that whatever it was he was now partaking in, was greater than him or his whole party. He recollected off the cold stone ground and watched Daniil figure do the same, half-heartedly. He heard him grunting as his hands searched the floor. He recovered his flint shards, and after clashing them between each other a few times, he eventually lit up the first candle.

He raised himself off the floor, holding it in front of him, breaking the obscure shadow and revealing his scrawny chest. Toma joined him, lighting up another candle from Daniil's own flame. Their tall shadows were trembling on the cave's sinister walls.

Codru grabbed the bifurcated stick he had been given and followed the knights as they walked reluctantly towards the Strigoi. He heard the creature chuckling in his throat, a sound that resembled water dripping in sizzling oil.

The candles revealed its form shortly. The creature was on his knees, with the head bowed down, and a sluggish drivel was dangling on his chin. The Strigoi raised its head suddenly, with its empty eye sockets scouting towards the approaching men.

'There. You. Aaaare!' it harrumphed.

Its jaw was moving unnaturally as it was struggling to speak, the rotten muscle snapping with each movement, almost as if another move would have its jaw separate from the head.

'Thieeeeef!' it said.

'What are you looking at, sons of whores?' he growled out of nowhere, shaking its head at Toma and then Codru, who were now standing by the monk's side.

Seeing that Daniil was shaking his arm as he held the light, lost in his own dark thoughts, Toma barked, seizing the attention the monster gave him.

'Who are you, viper?' he asked.

'I'm your nightmare!' the monster answered. 'Pleased to meet you!' Then it continued in a horrid, suave voice: 'Little Toma, the Greuthung! Do you know what happens with the unborn children, Little Toma? They come to us, and we make them into a stew!'

Codru saw the knight clenching his jaw, his hand reaching to his sword's hilt.

'They're both down there, you know! Your unborn child and his whore of a mother! Legions shall have their ways with her soul as those bandits had their ways with her body!'

'Shut your cursed mouth, you Satan,' the knight roared, his sword hissing as he pulled it from its scabbard, ready to swoop upon the Demon.

'No, brother!' Daniil woke up from his trance. He raised his arm to Toma's chest.

'He finds your weaknesses and twists them for his unholy game. He takes pleasure in preying on mortal's fears and dark thoughts.'

'I know of this devil,' he said. 'It goes by Maledictus in the Old-Tongue of the Râmlan. On these lands, they call it *Michiduță*.'

The devil giggled.

'Why have you come?' the priest asked. 'What have you done with this poor man's body you made your home in?'

'Oh, I merely borrowed it, Pike!' he ruckled in a pretend shyness. 'It was dead when I arrived!'

'They say that is beneath you, scourge of the earth! When did your wretched all-father begin raising the dead? Is the living no longer enough? Or aren't they listening to your treacherous bargains anymore?'

The Demon sucked on his putrid teeth.

'Bargains ought to be treacherous, Pike!' then he laughed. 'And this,' he said, looking down at his body, 'isn't our doing!'

'Whose then?'

The Strigoi grinned, showing, and licking his cracked, ashen fangs.

'It has never been more painless to corrupt your kind! Our kingdom flourishes. We have your kings' souls in our pockets!' his voice echoed. 'We don't even need to go home anymore. These lands feel more and more like it!'

He laughed again. A long howl broke the silence outside.

'Do you hear that, dear Pike?'

Daniil turned his head to the cave's entrance.

'They're here for you! You've been hidden for so long that we began giving up on searching! But then you spoke.'

'What is this creature talking about, monk?' Codru interfered, seeing Daniil lose his head once more.

'Oh, the men-slayer talks!' said the Strigoi, measuring Codru with his eyeless sockets. 'We have a warm place of honour in our realm. All those souls you've blessed us with. All that guilt!'

He closed his withered eyelids and licked his rotten lips.

'Oh, so savoury!'

'Daniil!' Toma shook the priest's shoulders. 'Tell us what's coming!'

'The *Paralei*. The soul-reaping spawns of the underworld.'

He then hitched the bifurcated wooden stick from Codru's hands and, with a ferocious twist of his upper body, plunged it into the Demon's skeletal chest. A loud scream untwined out of the Devil's throat, and a sudden white flame overtook its body out of nowhere, smothering it to ashes.

'It couldn't be saved!' he mumbled.

The more he was witnessed, the harder it was for the wanderer to make any sense of it all. While the cadaver was burning at stake, Toma handed over the crossbow to Daniil and readied Balmut, startling the man from his confusion.

'Come with me!' he told Codru, and he headed towards the exit. Behind them, the priest gathered his belongings like a storm—his attire, his incense burner, his saddlebags.

Once at the surface, they scoured the thin forest, looking for the howling's origins. The clear night sky made it easy for them to see at a fair distance, and for Codru, it was almost as clear as day. He saw the horses trying to pull away from the wagon while Shadowfire was neighing and prancing tied to the tree.

'We could take the horses and outrun whatever is coming!' said Toma, panting.

'There's no use!' said the monk. 'They'll follow us relentlessly until they catch up to us. We'll have to make our stand!'

'Have you faced them before?' asked Codru, cutting through the air with his axe.

The priest turned to him.

'Only once, many years ago...' he said, bowing his head for a short moment, then turning his eyes to the bushes.

In the woods, several pairs of eyes lit up and shone like embers in the moonlight. Muffled growls, born in fiery ribcages, followed. The priest did not wait. As soon as the first cursed gaze sprouted in the shadows, he stuck the pike in the ground next to him, fit an arrow on his crossbow, and let it whirl towards the unknown, lurking predators.

A long groan let the men know the arrow had met its target. But then hell on earth was unleashed. The howling echoed off the woods, and the Paralei burst out of their hiding, surging, and racing towards the travellers. Ravenous and rabid, larger than the largest hound, with brewing, dark manes covering their necks and backs, all the way to their long tails whipping like lashes. Traces of smoke were raised behind them. The grass and leaves sparked, turning into ephemeral flames, while the ground trembled under their claws. Their barks were omens of the devil's wrath.

Codru bit his lower lip, bracing himself with both his hands twisting on the axe's throat. He didn't believe his once-captors that the stories they kept talking about were true. But who could deny the pack of beasts running towards them now? If that was all real, now he hoped the runes Sándor cast into his weapon would be too.

As the pack approached them, Daniil released another arrow, aiming for the same Paraleu he hit before. Once he missed, he disembarrassed his weapon and grabbed his wooden pike.

The first beast made a large leap towards Toma, aiming at his throat. The knight dodged it, and his long sword raged through the air, missing the agile hound. Codru didn't wait. He ran towards the closest of the animals and struck it with the axe, cleaving its muscular shoulder right under the mane.

The wounded creature twitched, grappling, and digging the ground under its talons, and his muzzle opened wide, revealing its large and warped fangs. Codru stumbled on his back. The Paraleu flew above him right away, splattering tar out of its shoulder wound. With a quick movement, Codru drew his scimitar just one blink of an eye before the monster prepared to bite. He plunged the spade right through its red, radiant heart, pulsating in the beast's chest. The white, blinding flames took over the hissing hound, who fell, squirming and wailing in the grass.

'The hearts!' he yelled, dragging himself away. 'Aim at their hearts.'

His discovery was fruitful, as one moment later, Daniil's pike set one more Paraleu ablaze.

The remaining Paralei—maybe a handful of them—attacked even more ferociously. Two of them cornered Toma close to the temple's entrance, almost driving him inside and entrapping him. Codru stood up and ran towards the Raven, while another beast was already in his own footsteps. Just before he reached the fight, Toma's long sword dove into one of the creature's mouths, cracking through the back of its skull, doing nothing more than have the man disarmed and jolted to the ground.

Codru's axe hit the same hound in the back of its neck. He hit again. And again. Splattering the muddy blood on his face and screaming until its thick throat was completely open, letting its head fall with a rumble into the dirt.

He screamed. The fangs of the second hound cornering Toma before grazed his shoulder, missing its target. The wanderer fell to his side, leaving a worthy chunk of his tunic as well as his skin behind. Toma returned to his feet and drew his sword from the Paraleu's skull, pushing it away with his boot and used it on Codru's attacker, digging it between the hound's ribs and bursting its heart into violent fire.

There were only three of them lion-wolves left, and one was taunting the monk, frantically barking and snarling, revealing its tongue through its teeth while keeping distance from the man's bifurcated stick.

The other two came like the wind towards Toma and Codru, who by then were already on their feet, away from the blazing hound, which was yelping his last moans while turning to charcoal.

Codru rolled on his heels to gain momentum, and with a lighting fast turn, he released his axe into one of the attacker's foreheads. The strike was so mighty that the monster stumbled in its run, his muzzle crashing into the ground and having him thrown up-side-down right to the mercenary's feet, who blessed his large and exposed belly, ripe for killing, with his scimitar's edge, slowly dug into his amber, flickering stone.

The lights of the fire were a godsend for Toma, who thrust himself at the other attacking hound with both his hands on his sword's hilt, swinging it through the wind until its edge crossed a wide cut across the monster's face. The hound bellowed, and its attack was in vain as the knight turned quickly to his side, and with another strike, he sliced the creature on the side, from the front legs to the back ones, dragging a long, fresh scar on its black skin.

Codru recovered his axe, and with another twist, he released the hatchet violently, panting once more from a distance, aiming at the Paraleu, which was cornering and biting away at Daniil. His axe stuck on the beast's back, and this was enough for the monk to come from the other side with his staff, sticking into the demonic dog's heart from the opposite side where it had been hit by the axe. The white fire almost coincided with the one Toma left behind him once he slayed the butchered Paraleu.

The fighters turned their heads around them, scouting for more attackers and listening to any howling they might've been able to. But amidst the eerie silence, only the crackling of the coal, remnants of the fallen hellhounds, resonated through the air. It was done.

***

The morning loomed over the mountains, their white crests glowing in the misty rays of the yet unseen sun. Flashes of the events that occurred just hours ago still weighed on Codru's mind. His shoulder wound was stinging, but he would live. Standing next to his horse, he squinted, stretching his neck, and struggling to mend it with a mixture of herbs he found in his old bag. Toma approached him.

'I can give you a hand,' he said.

Codru only sniffed and continued to gasp, shaking his head. But the knight didn't leave.

'Is there something you need?' Codru asked, almost sceptical. 'You proved me wrong; is that what you want to hear? That Demons exist?'

Toma shrugged.

'A man's beliefs are his own,' he said. 'The things you've seen last night, many haven't. The knights of the Order haven't either. I am, however, more hopeful now.'

'And why is that?'

'Now that you know what lurks in the dark, you can't unknow it. And I could dare count on your allegiance. The Order could, perhaps!'

Codru covered his ointment-treated wound with a string of cloth and tied it using his arm and mouth. He let his cloak fall over his shoulder.

'That won't happen!' he spoke, throwing the parchment packet he had the herbs in back in his knapsack. 'We agreed on joining you until this temple. I did. Those were the terms. I'll have my other pouch of gold and then I'll be on my way.'

The knight frowned, irritated. His patience was breaking as the fight and the hindered mission began eating away at him.

'Where to?' he mumbled in his beard. 'There's nothing waiting for you at the end of the road.'

The Raven's words were said in a calm way, but they were meant to hurt, and Codru felt them. And so, he bit back:

'What is there waiting for you, then? Your dead woman or your unborn child?'

Toma's dark eyes lightened with sudden rage. He grabbed Codru by his chest and hissed gravely through his clenched teeth:

'Don't you dare speak about it.'

The monk, now wearing his hood, approached the two men, raising his hands to pull them apart from one another.

'Fellows!' he said. 'We survived a Demon's possessed Strigoi and a pack of Paralei. Let's not begin murdering each other.'

Toma let go of Codru, who didn't react to the knight's threat but had his hand on his axe's head the whole time.

'So be it then!' the Raven snapped, with his nostrils pumping and his eyebrows shadowing his eyes.

'Here, gold-famished son of a whore! Take it! Go back to your wretched work.'

He plucked the second pouch from his belt and threw it to the ground at Codru's feet. Then he turned around and made his way towards the cart, leaving the other two men looking at him as he walked away.

Codru knew deep down he shouldn't have said those words. But if he had to be hated to be let go of, he thought it was worth it. He smoothed out his tunic and grabbed the pouch of the ground, hanging it at his own waist.

'Brother Toma is not wrong!' Daniil turned to him, daring to speak on the knight's behalf. 'The Order still needs your axe.'

'We have done what we had to do, have we not?'

Daniil looked at him, sighing, and said:

'The mission was always greater than this. We only found crumbs of answers. We know the dead are cursed, and they wake up, but we don't know why or who's calling out to them.'

He looked at Codru, then continued in a grave voice:

'The Holy Book talks about Judgement Day and about the dead walking the earth as a sign of that day approaching.'

'What about that Demon you spoke to?' Codru asked, as it was one of the few things he found difficult to wrap his mind around. 'It surely could have been the one who raised the dead.'

'Far from it,' the priest said, shaking his head and looking away. 'That was only my past following me.'

He continued, seizing the moment:

'Decades ago, I struck an unfortunate bargain with someone I believed to be an angel. I was promised wealth and strength. Even foresight. All of those to be mine for ten winters. I was young and naive, so I took it. But as I grew older, I realized the terrible mistake I'd made. Ten years of wealth isn't worth eternity burning in hell. So, when the time came, I refused to pay.'

'One night, there was this creature outside my hut. I could see it through the window, out there, digging my grave. I've waited inside, crying, and praying all night while it was scratching at my door. Then I heard the roosters, and the scratching stopped. When I got out of the hut, I saw the Paraleu leaving my yard. I grabbed the first thing I could get my hands on from the shed—the pike—and stabbed the hound in the back, and it burst into flames.

And then I ran to the closest hallowed ground I could find, a monastery up in the mountains. I had Saint Basil's prayers carved on my back for protection, and I decided from that day on to hold my tongue forever so they wouldn't hear me, hiding in the sacred home, away from the devil.'

'Why didn't you remain there?' Codru asked.

'I got tired of living in fear and shame. I made a crossbow out of a wooden crucifix from the monastery. I offered it, alongside my arm and my foresight, to the Moldavian prince, where my home is, a long way up north. When the prince was usurped and killed, I turned to Hunyadi, the founder of the Raven's Order, who swore me in.'

Codru was bothered by the naked honesty of the withered knight.

'Why are you telling me all this?' he asked.

'Because if you abandon this quest, you'll end up like me. Last night, I spoke for the first time in many years. I forgot what my voice sounded like, or even that I had one. I thought that fighting the

Strigoi while keeping safe and silent would be enough to wash away that deep-rooted fear that grew vines around my heart, but it wasn't. I was fighting an evil, but not my evil.'

Codru looked at Toma, who was unharnessing the horses from the jail wagon.

'The hounds we fought last night were just the scouting party. More will soon follow. It is my soul they want, so I'm heading back north to have them follow me there, meaning we'll part ways here,' Daniil said. 'As for Toma, he would dare to go on further on his own, unless you would stand by his side. Crows fly swifter if they do so in a pair.'

Daniil began stepping away from him.

'There are things I wish I had time to tell you. Things I've seen since the first day we met at Mehadia. Terrible things may one day befall you. But there's no time for it now. If I can leave you with any words of wisdom, remember that running away from your past won't serve you well; standing your ground and repenting might.'

'And forget the things that the Demon said last night; you don't belong to them. Maledictus was right when he said that all bargains are treacherous, but he was wrong to think they were only in his favour. You see, you can strike a bargain with the devil and then refuse to honour it. I am living proof. Because your soul cannot be taken; it can only be offered.'

# CHAPTER VI

*Cozia's Groves, June 1431 (6939)*

'DID YOU HEAR THAT, OR NOT?' MIHNEA ASKED. But Horea did not. However, he knew that they were not supposed to be there. This was hallowed ground. And it was a hallowed day. Many years ago, by the fireside, his elders warned him that foolish men who ventured into these groves during the night would become lost, never to be seen again. Others, it was said, would simply lose their minds. Sometimes, lone wolves were seen lurking at the forest's edge, as if keeping vigil.

But Mihnea and the rest of his band of poachers thought it would be best to trap the nocturnal wild cats under the moonlight. He and his comrades had woollen, earth-coloured cloaks, and bows. They walked half a day from the forest edges until here. They spend the evening scattering dead rats around the nearby glades, and they set snares and traps close to the baits.

Horea was not made for the poacher's life. His father had been close to the town's pârcălab, and he had hopes that his son would step into his shoes. He spent silver on Wallachian and foreign masters to teach him reading and writing. If God allowed it, who knows? He might one day be seeing to the town's affairs. But young Horea's heart, however smart, yearned for gold too, as many men's hearts often do. He consorted with these rogue hunters led by one

Mihnea a few moons ago. They would track foxes, deer, lynxes, and sometimes wolves. The rarest the pelt, the better.

They'd begin preying in the early springs, right after snow melted, and end their year late in the summers, when the first birds would begin migrating, taking their riddled cart all the way to Târgoviște or even to the closer fairs to turn the furs into precious coins.

The young poacher swore to himself that this was going to be his last hunt. Mihnea wasn't the most honourable or merciful man. His disregard for the woodlands, its animals, or even the sacred night the villagers living around these forests were celebrating was going to bite him in the arse one day. And with him would suffer the rest of his gang as well.

The man raised his head from the bushes once again. His hands were ready on the bow, and his eyes were nailed to the closest beech-tree-trunk they had hidden a trap under. There were the other three of his men, hidden as well, in all corners of the clearing. But he only kept Horea, the weak one, close to him.

'There's something out there; I can feel it!' he told the young poacher. 'Did you split that rat open as I've told you? Are you sure?'

'I did as I was told!' Horea whispered his answer.

Breaths of warm air whistled through trees as fireflies swarmed calmly through the night's stillness. A long hoot rustled through the night, echoing not too far away.

'You heard it this time?' Mihnea turned to Horea. 'I told you I heard something.'

The young hunter heard it. It was the haunting hoot of a little owl, no doubt. He shivered. They said it was a death's omen.

'We need to leave!' he mumbled. 'We ought to not be here. Not during the solstice.'

But Mihnea shushed him. The bushes crackled, and some noise came from nearby the trap. The seasoned poacher grinned with satisfaction in anticipation of a precious lynx pelt. Quietly, he placed an arrow on the side of the bow without stretching its string. All he did was get ready to put a bolt in the future trapped beast. He looked at Horea toughly, urging him with his eyes to bring up his bow too.

The little owl closed its beak, and now there were only the steps of the hidden, unseen beast dragging through the leaves. Its shadow revealed itself. The barely visible shape of its head and its torso. Fearfully approaching the split-open dead rat lying in the trap's iron teeth. Sniffing it cautiously.

Both Mihnea and Horea raised their bows while their arrows peeped through the bush, their heads sparkling under the gloomy light of the night sky.

A branch the animal stepped on suddenly snapped, hitting the trap. The trap's jaws closed with a violent clench, and the older poacher's arrow flew impatiently off its bow, slashing the air and missing the target. The animal jumped on its feet, alerted, and dodging to its side, as the trap only swallowed the branch. A few more arrows gushed from the neighbourly hideouts, all whirling close to the creature and failing to hit it.

'Do it, you scalawag!' Horea heard the leader taunting him, drops of the man's spit hitting his cheek. He quickly aimed at the animal, drew his bowstring, and released the bolt. Just as it left his hand, the moonlight revealed the creature: a pure, silver-white deer, glowing in the darkness and staring right at him. His arrow whistled through the air, cutting across the beautiful animal's face before embedding its blade into the tree trunk. He missed.

Before he could even move, star-struck by the godly apparition, the deer stood its ground, piercing the darkness with its eyes, looking deeply into Horea's from a distance. It dug its hooves into the leaves and bent its knees, then scuttled away through the bushes it came from, running.

'Chase the deer, you rascals!' Mihnea blustered. 'Don't let it escape; it's worth more than your own lives!'

He jumped from the bush, dragging Horea by his coat to follow. Three other archers whipped out of their hiding as well, grunting and running, either bringing up their bows forward or holding their knives. They no longer cared about the noise and commotion they made; they were now charmed by the sight of the luminous deer galloping through the groves, putting distance between itself and the predators.

They ran through the night, puffing and blowing, stirring the ground under their boots. Horea heard the poachers cursing and casting arrows at will, pushing away the leaves, branches, and spiderwebs smothering their faces.

'Shoot, bastards! God damn you, shoot!'

Their yelling awakened the woods, with crows and little owls fluttering their wings through the trees. Ahead of them, the scared white deer jumped over fallen trunks, zig-zagging its way forward, cheating and making its hunters stumble and lose their ways. Horea ran too but fell behind, as his head kept turning back occasionally, vainly trying to remember his way back. His heart pumped in his ears, ready to break his chest.

The eyes of the moonlit deer haunted him. It made him start to hear things. His memories of men losing their minds flooded his brain, and that's when he understood the gang of poachers were on their path to becoming one of those men he heard stories about—men that would never be seen again. He suddenly halted his run, attempting to fill his twisted, pressed lungs with air. He dropped his bow purposefully amidst the weeds and placed his hands on his knees, gasping for breath. In the distance, he could hear his companions growing farther away, raising a ruckus in the night.

'Wait, wait for me!' he wished to shout, but his voice had yet to recover. 'Don't run after it; we have to return!' he wheezed.

But none heard his pleas. He turned his head, and he could try to leave them behind. His mind told him to. But his heart was a moron. He had to do everything he could to make them abandon their hunt before it was too late. Before they crossed the edge of no return. He raised his bow, threw it on his back, and began his run through the dew-soaked graves of leaves. Bolting in one breath, he followed the noises the men could still be heard making. He was younger than most of them, and his legs were long. He soon caught up to the hunters, and he began to see glimpses of the pale deer, wreathed in the obscure green of the woodland, long way ahead of them.

In the deep silence of the night, broken only by the men's grunts and rustles, a chilling bloom of wind came out of nowhere, thrifting the weeds and the tree crowns. And it was gone as quickly as it came. The men suddenly ceased their run. They looked around, searching the area.

'What in the name of...?' Mihnea murmured, scouting the tenebrosity. Another wind's roar, a stronger one, suddenly followed from the other direction, laying the men to the ground as it passed, like a sickle, and having the hunters cover their heads and hole up in the long grass. The full moon broke the night and the branches like an awakened eye in the sky. The strange deer was gone.

Horea heard the poachers' leader cursing in his beard, crying for his lost bounty. But the other men, himself included, barely moved, their faces scouting the pitchiness of the high arbours. The legends seemed to have suddenly arisen from their own memories too, and their swift, muffled laments were beginning to take shape. But wind cut through them with an instant, breaking from two or three different places at once.

One of the men bewailed and was cast off to the ground. Horea had not been as sure that something was now onto them as he was at that moment.

'We must leave!' he pleaded. 'Let's leave!'

He then saw one of the men, a different one than the one who fell to the ground, being lifted in the air. He screamed in terror and confusion while his eyes sparkled in the moon's rays and as the wind raised him up from the ground and threw him with unseen force towards one of the trees. He fell into the bushes and moaned in agony, unable to catch his breath. Before the hunters could even begin to understand what had happened, a new wave of wind pierced through the company, plunging into another man.

Horea saw it and given the way Mihnea himself turned to stone in horror, he gathered that both the leader and the other men standing saw it too. The wind that mowed the last hunter to the ground took a sinister, unbelievable shape, bending the air around it. As if it were not wind at all, but a phantasm wearing the robe of nothingness itself.

And this spectre did not come alone.

The men, already shattered by the winds, screamed almost at the same time as untouchable presences began dragging them through the branches and bushes by the head and ears. The poor, hopeless men cut their palms through the weeds and thorns as they grappled into the dirt, vainly trying to save themselves. Both standing men stumbled backward, shouting in alarm as they watched their comrades being pulled away by the relentless wind, into the darkness. They knew they would soon share the same fate. And they were not wrong.

While the distant voices of the lost men still echoed, beseeching, and crying out to God, several other gusts of wind swirled around the remaining hunters. Mihnea continued to shoot his arrows relentlessly in the darkness, abandoning the men to fend for themselves as he sought to find his own way out. Another man flew across the circle, his scream hitting Horea's ear as the poacher passed by him through the air. He followed the others into the night.

'Come at me, you bastards!' Mihnea belched at the spectres, beating his chest as he wasted his last arrows and pulled his daggers out. 'Come out, show yourselves!'

The last man standing beside him and Horea dared to run, but before he could even make a few steps, ivy strings tangled his boots, letting him drop like a sack of potatoes into the vines. The wind rested above him.

'No!' he cried hopelessly. 'No!'

His eyes finally met the presence's real face, taking shape out of the air, revealing long, silvery hair floating in the air as in the water and a pale, luminous figure, marked only by deep, darkened eyes. This predator stretched its thin arms from under its translucid cloak, leaning and reaching out to the fallen man's face. The whisper it made got to Horea. Threats were made in the ancient, unspoken tongue of the storm.

He saw the man's face being twisted unnaturally under his eyes as the presence's long fingers dug in the hunter's mouth and eye-sockets. It bent his face as if it were a chunk of clay. The man's plea shut, his deformed mouth remaining wide open, like a fish thrown on the sand. His eyes were lost, stuck in the endless night sky.

The predator rose in the air and moved slowly towards Mihnea, while its legs began to take shape as well, resting softly on the grass. The earth cast sparks under its feet. The closer it got to the only two remaining hunters, the more the woodland apparition embraced its earthly appearance. Behind it and to its sides, the other winds also revealed themselves, beginning to take form and shedding their invisible covers.

Mihnea continued to hold his daggers in front of him, trembling in his hands, but his voice long vanished. Horea could only hear him whimper like a cornered, beaten dog. The being turned slowly into a bare maiden of unmatched, never-seen-before beauty, with her long hair floating and covering around her pure, radiant skin like a white rose bud, ready to bloom. Her eyes were like two flaming jade stones, lightening under her eyebrows. A pair of small horns loomed on her crown through her rich waves of white-golden hair. Her unblemished right cheek bore the slender, crimson mark of a fresh wound that was left behind by a cursed arrow.

The being's sisters joined her, their breath-taking visages and their flaming eyes making the two men's feet grow roots in the ground, unable to move or even blink.

As the woodland woman floated right in front of the hunters' leader, her red lips opened, her voice being the forest's singing itself. Horea didn't know it, but he did feel it. They were threats, cast out in the sombre language of the ether. Curses the woodland maidens laid upon them who traversed their realm on their day, the only day of the year it was forbidden to. Charms were bestowed upon the poor souls that dared to draw their bows at her.

Horea's heart wept, burdened by unspoken remorse, begging with his eyes for mercy as he knew he'd soon find his bitter end, as his companions had. But the spirit didn't even look at him. Her eyes were on Mihnea.

A long whistle broke through the bushes as the maiden's voice resounded above those of her sister's. She raised her arm, digging into the wind and out of thin air, her fingers wrapped around the hilt of a sword born under the men's eyes. Lilac and emerald flames burst out of its edges, and the light flickered into the dark with a sound, flooding over the men's faces and catching their eyes, while the other maidens continued to wail their punishment-bringing chants.

Mihnea dropped his daggers, and his arms fell by his sides as he kneeled, looking up to the woman. Silent tears crawled down his cheeks.

'Please!' he begged.

But the phantasm showed no mercy. First, her blade cut viciously through the darkness, and its glowing peak slashed the man's face, throwing him to his side in agony while thrashing in the ferns. But that wasn't his punishment. Horea's eyes watched in terror as the man's wound began sprouting. Long and twisted grapevines sprang out of the warm scar, pushing out and growing quickly between the man's fingers as he was holding his face. Mihnea dragged himself through the grass, trying to snap the vines and roots of his face, breaking their growth. But the more vines he broke, the faster they grew.

Under the watchful, silent gaze of the ladies, tendrils and bindweed soon besieged the hunter's head, slowly clawing and covering his nose, silencing his shouting. Breaking through his eye. Until his whole face became one with the weeds, as he was being snatched by the embrace of the thick forest soil.

A tear dripped from Horea's eye onto his cheekbone as his petrified body was the last offering the witches were going to make to the ancient groves. The wounded apparition's eyes fell on him, and unclenching her fingers off the sword, she made the blade vanish into the same fog it had been pulled from. Her sisters surrounded him too, their chanting resuming as the wind began howling through the trees. And when both the chants and the wind suddenly broke, the cortege thrust itself at him like a thundering cloud that swallowed him entirely and disappeared, leaving behind no trace of the ambush that happened there.

In the serene, moonlit clearing of the groves, a little owl began hooting.

\*\*\*

*Kruhnen, June 1459 (6967)*

'You better hear me out, idiots! The Wallachian son-of-a-wench prince will one day soon hunt down our dear citadel too if we don't do anything! Let people have their justice!'

The drunk man staggered in his chair.

'He's already calling himself lord of both Amlaș and Făgăraș, for God's sake!'

'Hold your tongue, old scrapper!' said one of his younger drinking buddies. 'People are watching; they could hear you!'

'It's no skin off my nose! He's not my prince!'

'It may as well be!' said another one, sitting at the table across from the drunkard. 'Haven't you heard the Ottoman's man-whore is now in cahoots with the Hungarian crow-fledgeling? Guarded envoys carrying letters have been seen crossing the Ardeal, all the way from Târgoviște to the young Matthias's court, once every moon.'

'So what!' the old man tossed off his short glass of queen's water. 'You all know the young'un has no power. It's his uncle who rules.'

'Precisely!' the man sitting across nodded with satisfaction. 'The same man who Vlad helped and calmed down the quarrel he had with our Székely folk. They say the Wallachian even calls him his elder brother.'

'Devils curse them both then!' the drunk man spat on the wooden floor of the tavern. 'Now I need to drink more!'

The other two younger men looked at each other.

'Maybe that's enough for today!' the youngest said, trying to grab the troublemaker's sleeve as he stood up from his chair. A few of the men drinking and chattering at their neighbouring, thick wooden tables raised their heads at the movements and the noise.

'It's not like I drink from your mom's cup now, do I?' the old one mumbled, his tongue twisting in his gap-toothed mouth. 'It's enough when I say it is!'

Stumbling and clamping his boots on the bordage, the old sparrer somehow reached his destination, his hands grabbing the counter's wooden edge to barely stand straight. Behind it, the young barmaid, who was the landlady herself, put on her brave face. She was used to drunkards, drifters, and men of all sorts.

'I'll have you out of my tavern, old-boy, if you don't temper your fire!' she said, giving an eye to the only man sitting at the counter, sipping quietly from his mug, hiding his face beneath his hood. 'You're troubling my patrons!'

'Oh, shut your womanish hatch, will ya? I'm not your husband. Be a good maiden and fill up my pitcher with some more of that brandy!'

Then he staked his clay jug on the plank and threw a silver coin next to it, making a sound as the metal sprang a few times. The woman puffed with resentment, slammed her hand on the wood, and snatched the coin between her fingers and grabbed the jug by its handle.

'Pardon this old ploughman's rudeness, traveller, will you?' she excused herself to the man sitting by himself. 'The soldiers don't know how to treat a woman; they're used to shag each other down at the tower...'

'Ay!' the man said, causelessly prying the stranger. 'Why sit here by yourself, huh? Come join us; we drink to the Wallachian voivode's perdition!'

The traveller didn't answer, continuing his quietude while the woman was relieving one of her small barrels into the old man's jug. The jug wouldn't fill up fast enough.

'What are you, dumb? Can't talk? I'm talking to you!' the man bickered, stepping towards the stranger, helping himself to the counter so he wouldn't fall.

'Hey!' he barked in frustration, and he laid one hand on the quiet man's shoulder. He shouldn't have done that.

With a quick move, the man's chair fell to the floor when he stood up. The old man's arm twisted from his shoulder in the lightning clench of the traveller's hand, and his head clashed with the counter's wooden plank under the stranger's glove.

The sudden scream and the noise of the account had the rest of the men in the tavern turn towards the scene with curiosity and outrage. However, none thought it was worth it to interfere. Except for one of the old man's mates, surely the one telling stories of envoys and secret brotherhood.

Codru's face grimaced with his jaws closed. His dark grey hood fell of his head during the reckoning, letting his rusty mane flood his shoulders and his face subject to the men's scouting eyes. It was enough for some of those sitting at the tables to stand up quietly and move backwards with their hats in their hands, towards the tavern's door.

He looked down on the squirming old man, trapped in his grasp, and at the barmaid, who was now quiet as a mouse, covering her dressed head under the counter's cover.

He felt somewhat sorry for her and angry for the piece of crap drunkard who disturbed him. She hasn't been anything but welcoming to him during his stay under this roof since his arrival in town. And this old rambler had to ruin it.

'Let the man go!' the drunk's companion yelled from across the room.

Codru turned to face him, noticing the man's hand resting on his sword's hilt.

*'This isn't good,'* he thought, realizing they must have been guards or, worse, men of the law. He had committed no wrong, yet it made no difference. His hair, his marked forehead, and his attire all served as unwitting invitations to harassment and disdain. However, he thought, based on what he overheard from the men's conversation and on the fact that he hadn't yet thrust himself at him with his spade in the air, that the young guard wasn't as stupid as his senior. He could surely see reason.

Codru released his hands from the old man's arm and face, and the drunk one fell to the floor. Crying, cursing, and rubbing his shoulder, the old man walked in his fours towards his men's table.

Codru showed his palms, raising them to his chest.

'Nothing has happened!' he said gently. 'Nor it has to!'

'Devils curse you, freak!' the old man poured oil on the flame. 'You almost broke my bloody arm!'

Seeing that his comrades were still pondering, he yelled at them:

'What are you waiting for? To the dungeons with him! He needs to be pulled to pieces!'

The youngest of the guards urged the drunk man to stand up, pulling at his shoulders.

'We'd better go!' he said to the other, whose hand was still on his sword and his eyes still on Codru's surrender.

'Brother, forget about it; it was noth' but a tavern brawl.'

Codru sensed the man's unease. His eyes squinted in silence from the other side of the tavern, almost as if he tried to understand what sort of man he was or even if he could take him, should it have come to this. Regardless, his decision was made.

'We can't turn an eye on this!' he spoke, and his words were as told to his young fellow as they were told to Codru. 'You'll have to follow us to the tower. The chief would know what's to be done!'

Codru bit his lips and let his hands down. It was pointless. They wouldn't let him go in peace. He thought it was better to at least finish his drink. He sat back on his chair, turning his back towards the guards.

'I'm not going anywhere!' he let them know while taking a sip from his glass.

The guard pulled his sword. The sound reached Codru's ear, and he sighed as he left his empty glass resting on the counter. He did not turn, not yet. But his axe, hidden under his robe, was itching. Then he heard the grave, familiar voice of his travelling fellow.

'There won't be any need for that!' it said. When Codru turned, Toma was standing in the doorframe, holding a large sack in his hand, the outside light revealing only the shape of his mountain of a body and his dark cloak. The guard looked at him and seemed to have recognized the man's crest knitted on his gambeson.

'A damned raven!' the drunkard grumbled. 'That's what's needed right now!'

Toma stepped indoors as the men looked at him with contempt. The bar maiden peeped as well, her eyes looming curiously from behind the wooden board.

'You have no business here, knight!' the guard said. 'This is the town's matter!'

Toma checked on Codru from across the tavern, then he turned to his new friends.

'I have Voivode Rozgonyi's protection, as you know,' he said. 'If you don't agree, take it up with his lordship Lang first, and if he wants this man behind bars, I'll not stay in the way. You're men of the law, so do it then by law!'

'Devils!' the old man spat, prompting his shoulder into the tavern's wall.

The young constable grunted, but he knew the knight was right. He sheathed his sword and told the youngest of them three.

'Let's go deal with it! Man's speaking the truth!'

On their way out, with the youngest man holding the old one's arm over his shoulder to not fall in the mud, he turned to Toma and said:

'Don't overstay your welcome!'

'Worry not!' Toma replied. 'We were just about to leave the citadel!'

Then they disappeared into the alley, leaving the tavern behind. The curses of the old drunk man soon were swallowed by the sound of carts, horses, and townsmen passing by.

Feeling safe enough, the barmaid dared to raise from behind the counter, keeping a safe distance from both Codru and Toma, who walked his boots on the plank floor until he joined the wanderer. He didn't take a seat. Instead, he raised the sack he had been dragging with him all along and threw it into Codru's lap as his elbow rested next to his now empty glass.

'What's this?' the stranger asked, confused, rustling through the large hemp bag, poking his hand around. It was a thick, dark piece of cloth, both thicker and darker than the one he was now wearing.

'You got me a cloak? I have one already; what am I supposed to do with this one?'

'You'll be wearing it and discard that old Venetian rag you've been taking so much pride in and so much trouble with.'

Codru puffed in disagreement, letting the cloak in its sack, and dropping it on the floor next to his chair.

'You can take it where you got it from; I don't need it!'

Toma bit his lower lip, a grimace deepening the wrinkles around his eyes, and he sat next to the red-haired fellow. He threw an eye at the barmaid and shook his head. The woman hesitated at first, but then she grabbed a glass and posted it in front of him. She poured from the jug the old drunken man paid for. The Raven thanked her and downed the palincă in one go, letting his glass on the counter.

'More!'

The woman poured again. Toma dropped a golden coin on the wood and said:

'For the mess my man here made, and for your discretion.'

The woman looked at the coin, then at the knight. Her eyes fell for a moment on Codru, who looked away when he met hers. Then she left the jug on the counter and grabbed the coin.

'Thank you, Master Raven! God bless you!'

And she disappeared through the door behind, closing it and leaving the two men alone.

'It's wiser you will wear it, so I don't have to keep getting you out of the gutter!' Toma spoke in a low voice, but his frustration could crack through it.

'Forget about the fact that you're walking around wearing a mantle torn apart by Paralei. There's not much we can do about your face either, but this will at least let you lose yourself easier in the crowd.'

'Besides, it's a merchant's robe. If we're to pass like ones, we must look like ones.'

Codru raised his head and took a long look at his comrade.

'You mended it, then!'

Toma took a sip from his glass and nodded.

'I did!' he said. 'We're now owners of a cart loaded with fleece and cloth, ready to traverse the toll gates. And that's one of them!'

Codru looked at the sack. He'll wear it, damn it, he thought to himself. It's the least he could do. While he had been lying low in the upper rooms of this tavern for the past couple of weeks, the knight relentlessly walked Kruhnen to gather the necessary materials for their cover.

Codru could've abandoned him at any given time, still. Toma was aware of it, and the stranger didn't hesitate to throw that in his face occasionally. But, somehow, he chose not to leave.

The words of the hunted and haunted monk lingered, even if he continued to deny it to himself. Much of what the cursed priest told him reached out to himself. He and Daniil had many things they shared, and the troubled past was just one of them. He did not want to spend his years on the run. Maybe this wasn't his salvation, nor did he ever look for it. But his mind was darkened enough as it was, with or without the nightmares.

Another thing he could not deny himself was his curiosity, which by now had begun to sprout in his brain. It was now a reality that there were unnatural beings and events at play, and he could no longer turn his eyes.

When he told the knight he'd join him over the mountains, although he had already been paid for the done deed, he expected more gratitude from Toma. But the already disappointed Raven had enough of his crossness, and frankly, he most likely assumed he'd have to get to the bottom of his mission on his own. 'Go suck a horse!' was his then-reply.

Regardless, as they set out to travel to Dlăgopole, the town where the so-called Black Boyar had his manor, as Sándor told them, they had to first visit Kruhnen to get their affairs in order. Codru did hold hope that the 'unholy witchcraft sickness' people were talking about, brewing in the South, was related to the dead folk abandoning their graves. That would at least put his curiosity to bed.

'Go grab your belongings from the rooms, and I'll meet you by the stables,' Toma woke him up from his mind drifting as he put his glass upside-down on the counter. 'The județ Georg won't wait for your sorry arse.'

Then he left him and his sack alone in the tavern, vanishing off the door.

Later, when they met behind the tavern, where Golden-Sun and Shadowfire were still rummaging with their snouts through the scattered hay in their animal pen, Codru was now wearing the dark, woollen mantle the knight let him with. He had his old sack with him in one hand and his axe in the other. He left the old, ripped robe with the bar maiden, who said she'd keep it with the rest of the junk she was piling up somewhere in her tavern's attic.

'I'll just keep it in the hope-chest with everything my guests left behind over the years,' she said when they bid their farewells.

Toma was just untying his horse when Codru arrived. When he saw him wearing the cloak, he grinned, ready to perhaps throw a joke, but he kept it for himself.

'Maybe restrain that pile of hair you have there too, and you'll look just like an *Oltenian* merchant,' he contented himself to say. 'That's an *ipingea* that you're wearing. The only one I could find with a hood around here, to suit you.'

'It will do,' Codru answered.

Toma nodded and pulled the pale-yellow horse after him.

'The wares cart is right around the corner,' the knight said, then reined the animal along.

Shadowfire swung his muzzle when Codru approached, seeking a comforting touch. The man looked away, avoiding speaking with the stallion once more. He was running low on his potions, and a headache-giving trip into the animal's cluttered mind was the last thing he needed now. Nevertheless, he gave the dark horse an affectionate pat, running his calloused fingers through its coarse mane. Once he rested his belongings on the horse's back, he untied it and pulled it after him.

Right next to the tavern, Toma had already harnessed his horse to the new cart, filled with sacks, bundles of cloth, twine, and rolls of rugs. This must have cost a small fortune, Codru thought. The gold the knight had earned in his youth was truly proving to be useful now. It was a much nicer cart, too, than the jail wagon they abandoned in the woods when Daniil took the third horse and took the road north.

'This is it!' he told the stranger after he removed his things off Shadowfire's back and placed them into the cart, next to his own bags.

Codru let him, although he didn't lose them from his eyes. Once Toma harnessed the dark steed to the cart too, the knight tied up his grey-blonde hair in a tail and hid it under his own hood, closing his knightly mantle to cover his crest. He suggested to Codru that he do the same, which he did half-heartedly. They both put on their gloves and jounced on the cart's bench. The knight urged the horses forward with a soft cluck of his tongue, beginning their roaming on Kruhnen's battered streets.

'The Praetorium, the Town Council, isn't far,' said the Raven as the wagon's wheels spun on the road. Codru noticed many similarities between this town and the Red Citadel, although the all-watching eyes were missing from the houses and shops' roofs. Right ahead, he could see the tall spire of a church arising from the city's heart, covered in heavy scaffolding. Even if it was still under construction, he could tell that by the time the masons finished their build, it would have been a great one.

The walls and towers of the city itself were some of the greatest too. Before reaching the city, Toma took his time and described to him the foundation of the city's thick and tall walls, its bastions, and its countless towers that the old Hungarian King watched over himself before he died. The city turned, the knight has said, into a durable, impenetrable keep; the last gate of defence of the Christian world in the face of the Empire, shall the Ottomans ever thought to march their armies over the mountains.

The Raven told him each bastion was taken care of by its own guild and that all its towers and *zwingers* of them had ingenuous defensive holes for oil or tar and even for the bombards. 'Heavy and frightening machinations made of bronze, eaters of the devil's powder, capable of massive destruction,' the knight added.

'Once we get our hands on that letter the Wallachian ruler holds so dear for the merchants to have, we travel straight to Bran's tollgate.'

Toma was mostly just thinking out loud and planning their journey ahead for himself. He knew his companion didn't give a rat's arse about it. But Codru decided to speak, his head turning up, watching the tall roofs and the townsmen as he did.

'That Vlad, huh? Quite the character, isn't he?' he wondered.

The knight turned to him.

'What makes you say that?'

'I remember your brother speaking of him not too fondly,' the wanderer replied. 'And those drunken fouls at the tavern kept blathering about him too. They said he'd one day rule over this city.'

Toma grunted.

'I'm sure that would please him,' he said. 'This place holds a special place in his cursed heart. Not too long ago, he was tasked by my Lord to protect it during his exile. This place is also the crossroads of many trade paths, ripe for levies and riches. Letting merchants come from and to his lands means more to him than bringing in the gold; he wants craftsmen and builders to come and stay on his lands. He surrounds himself with skilled, incorruptible, and people devoid of any allegiance, from all over the world. His *Viteji* are loyal and entitled farmers, as he doesn't trust the noble Boyars. The *Sluji*, his own private guard, consists of Russ, Serbs, Anatolians, and Gypsy slaves. *Egyptians*. Even women, some say.'

'Sword maidens?' Codru interrupted.

'You heard me!'

Then, as he slowed down the cart, squinting at the gathering that was forming ahead in the town's square, he ended his chatter:

'The Pope himself talks highly of him behind closed doors. If Kruhnen is Christianity's gate, Vlad is surely a good candidate as its guardian. He's smart and cunning. But too young, if you ask me, too hot-blooded and cruel to be a ruler.'

Codru said:

'Well, the blacksmith said that if you want to keep the starving wolves away from your herd, you need a hound as starving as them.'

'Then I suppose that you and the prince would make great accomplices.'

The Raven's final words were abruptly cut off by the sudden commotion that swirled around them and their horses, like a turbulent river. Both men raised their heads to peek above people's heads and see what had happened that townsmen gathered in multitudes, shouting, and throwing curses.

Codru thought they'd get noticed quickly, but people cared not for them much. Their faces were twisted with anger. Some of the folks were swinging sticks and pitchforks. Others came ready with rocks hidden in their fists. Whatever was going on, they were out for blood.

The Raven jumped off the cart and joined a group of men, trying his best to blend in.

'What's the hold up, friends? What's happening in the square?'

He was generally ignored; people being too caught up in their rebellion to take care of this man's questions. Codru thought he could give him a hand, against the knight's protests, who thought it would have been wiser for him to stay put.

But the stranger was right. As they left the merchant's cart in the middle of the street, both men succeeded in cornering a black sheep of a man, left behind by the crowd but who felt like joining the herd.

'Why can't we pass?' the knight asked the man, who was trembling like an aspen leaf.

'Who are you? You're not from around here? You don't know?'

'Answer the man's question!' Codru leaned over him, prompting his arm into the wall as the man tried to evade the strangers' trap.

'Alright, alright, hold your horses!' the man raised his hands in defeat. Then he chirped:

'It's the guild master Siegel's daughter; they hitched her to the Pillar of Infamy in the square.'

Codru turned to Toma, vaguely confused. The Raven nodded that he understood, biting his lips.

'Why?' he strong-armed the cowardly townsman with his voice. 'Speak!'

'It's mid-...midsummer, longest d-day of the year,' the man stuttered. 'They thought to put on a farce on her... with the Day of the Sânziene and all!'

'It was meant to be harmless!'

Toma seized the man firmly by the shoulder and delivered a swift kick to his rear, helping himself with his boot to set the man in the right direction.

'Get out of my sight!'

Returning to their cart, Toma scratched his nose and tamed his beard, thinking.

'This could be a bit of a hurdle!' he said.

'Who's this guild master?' Codru asked, still peeking over the men's heads. 'And what did his daughter do?'

'She bedded the wrong person!' the knight answered almost immediately. 'The Wallachian prince himself, during his stay here at the citadel.'

Seeing his comrade's confusion all over his face, he continued.

'Remember my brother's tales of Vlad scorching the outskirts of Kruhnen? The mass execution of corrupt peddlers? Well, it seems like the people found his weakness, and this could be their retaliation.'

'We'd better hurry; we'll have to push through the crowd anyway!' he then said, climbing back in the cart while Codru followed.

The horses shook their heads as they dragged the merchant's wagon like a plough through the herd of peasants and rabble. The council they needed to get to was on the opposite side of the square. As they hardly made it close to the market's centre, Codru tried, almost without knowing, searching for the punishment pillar the scrawny man was talking about. It didn't take him long to spot it. He didn't know much of this day the folk were celebrating, but it certainly could not possibly have been that way.

In the middle of the square, there was a tall, wooden pillory. The kind of which he's seen before in Venice. Chained to it stood a young, blonde woman, stripped of her clothes. She was with child. Her hair, once long, looked as if it had been shorn with a knife, her uneven locks stranded in the wind. Her assailants adorned her hair with a yellow flower crown as a mockery. Men and women alike had been throwing rotten fruit and stones at her, smearing, grazing, and bruising her body. They laughed and taunted her as she kept crying, yelling, and pleading to end the punishment.

'Where's that dream sweetheart of yours now, *Sânziano?*' some woman mocked her as the helpless girl begged out for her father. A man closed in on her with a wooden bucket filled with filth and dumped it on her, covering her body in wretched hogwash.

As the cart moved along, her reddened eyes stood out amidst the bustling crowd. She had noticed the foreigners, men who didn't partake in this nightmare. Her tears ceased, and hope flickered in her eyes, reaching out straight to Codru's. She uttered no words, yet her silent plea resonated loudly in his heart: *'Please, help me! Please, help my child!'*

He felt a curl in his chest. A mother's cry. The kick he felt in his gut sent him back in time. He was on the floor, crying. He heard a woman screaming and looking at him from across a tight, darkened, burning room. She was vainly reaching out her arms to him as strange men were tearing up her dress.

'Don't dare do anything; we need to keep our heads down!' Toma shook him up. 'Stay out of it; you're not her saviour!'

Codru's eyes cut him off as he pushed himself out of the cart.

'God damn you!' the knight followed him, cursing and shouting his name. He abandoned the cart in the square and went after the man as Codru was pushing people to left and right, ploughing through the crowd, grunting, and swearing. His eyes and the woman's didn't break their tie, and his heart was boiling, his axe ready to be released from its clench. He felt a hand on his shoulder, pulling him violently.

'Codru, enough!'

He ignored it, his rage poisoning his mind as his ears flooded with laughter and crying at the same time—the crowd and the invaders of his once home, his mother and the woman tied to the pillar.

'Codru!'

He turned like a whirlwind, snarling at the Raven.

'Let go of me; I'm doing your knightly duty!'

'Enough!' Toma cut him off, pointing at the scene unfolding not too far away from them. 'Look!'

A group of people suddenly emerged within the crowd. A few dignitaries, most likely surrounded by guards, broke the noise, pushing the people away from the woman. An older man, her father, covered her in a blanket as a smith worked on removing her chains. The leader of the magistrates unrolled a parchment and started reading it loudly, trying to cover the crowd.

Codru kept watching the young woman being taken away under the guild master's wing. She turned her head once more to him before she lost herself in the crowd, as the guards weaved for her a path through it.

'It's over!' he heard Toma's voice. 'We need to go.'

\*\*\*

The man gasped as he climbed down off the wooden ladder. He could barely hold the large, dusty register covered in husky leather. Its thick, yellowed pages, with rodent marks on their edges, made the book look older than it was. He grunted as he approached his low podium, where his engraved cherry-wood desk was.

When he laid the book on the stand, dust and rat piss whiff rose from it. The powder flickered in the warm rays of sunset gleaming through the stained glass of the windows placed on the higher parts of the walls. The noise made some of the young scribes sitting behind turn from their own panels, where they were squinting assiduously into their bulks of parchment and scrolls under the heavy light of their candles.

'I find it very, very hard to believe master Sándor's kin, the Greuthung I heard so much about, turned to peddling...' the man grunted, measuring the two men over the spectacles he brought to his hooked nose.

The Județ poked where his hooked nose didn't belong, Codru thought. As far as he understood, the man owed Toma's brother a favour, so his questions should have had no place in this encounter. But he did expect it.

When they entered the Praetorium, they were welcomed by a large painting depicting a full-body portrayal of this man wearing a lustrous armour placed above the door. Codru recognized the same pestilent opulence he'd seen in many of the Venetian and Genoese noble's homes years ago.

Upon meeting Magister Georg, Codru noticed his many rings, his golden-stitched bonnet, his velvet robe and breeches, and his high-heeled shoes. In return, the județ took note of the wanderer's face, but he was pleased to keep his remarks to himself at the time. Until now.

Seeing that Toma didn't answer his inquiry, the man turned to Codru.

'What about you, sire?' he said, soaking his writing feather in the inkwell resting at the corner of his table, with the large book open under his grey beard.

'Where have you travelled from? You don't seem to be from around these parts.'

The knight interfered before Codru could ruin the encounter.

'He doesn't speak the tongue, Master Lang! But I vouch for him.'

'Vouch? That means nothing to me!' the *burgher* replied. 'But I suppose I don't want to hear it! No questions are needed.'

His feather grazed the book's parchment while the man's lips formed words without saying them, his scruffy eyebrows crushing into each other.

'Pelt merchants... Buda... to Târgoviște!'

'Sire!' one of the young scribes suddenly approached the magistrate with a large scroll in his hand.

The boy could not have been older than sixteen or seventeen winters, and he was certainly younger than the rest of his fellows in the back. He was dark-haired and supple. His earth toned clothes, although shabby and patched around his elbows, were clean and well maintained.

'I have finished it!' he began saying out loud, trying to hand over his piece of work. But as quickly as his words poured out of his mouth, the older man turned and slapped him, making the young man stumble and fall back a couple of steps, covering his face.

'You wicked pauper!' Georg broke out. 'You crawl behind my back like a bloody mouse and then scream in my ear! You almost made me spill the ink; you bugger!'

"Beg your pardon, sire!' the boy complained, his eyes turning quickly and shamefully to the strangers, then back to the județ. His tone, however, didn't change.

Master Lang stood up from his chair, puffing, and grabbed the parchment from the boy's hand like a hawk, reading it jitterily. He then barked at the scribe:

'Out of my sight, hireling! Back to your station! Now, I said!'

And as the young'un turned, the master blessed him with another whack over the back of his neck.

Codru looked Georg dead in the eye as the nobleman took his seat, muttering curses and whipping ink with the cloth of his ringed fingers.

'Anything you want to say, merchant?'

The traveller swallowed his words, but his eyes told enough.

'Don't you dare pity him!' the județ blabbered as he dragged a piece of vellum off a drawer he had on the desk.

'I took him off the streets,' he continued. 'An orphan, deaf in one ear, this one! But devil damn him, he knows the letters and the illuminations like no other...'

'Why does he deserve the beating, then?' Toma asked him somewhat calmly, so Codru wouldn't barge in.

Master Lang grinned beneath his moustache as he began writing the letter. After a short pause, he spoke without raising his head.

'You like your horse, don't you, Master Toma, the Greuthung? You're surely proud of it, too. It's a fine horse, a working, beautiful steed, no doubt. But you still whip its back and kick its belly as you ride it.'

Despite all the knight's efforts, Codru could not turn his eye. It had never been the sense of justice that burdened his shoulders. He, of all people, felt he had no right to even feel that. The harm he has caused for years could not have been erased by good deeds. So, he didn't attempt to. Following the Raven without pay in his quest or his desire to free the woman in the square were acts driven by instinct, not reason.

So, when he heard the magister beating his liege without any grounds, all he could think of ware the scars he still bared on his back from his years in the sultan's service.

He did wait patiently until the județ melted the wax on the letter and pressed it with one of his golden rings, sealing it and then handing it to Toma. But once that happened, his words almost left his mouth without his permission.

'If you treat humans like beasts, they become beasts,' he said, his eyes lightened by the candle on the master's table. 'And a beast can take a beating. Maybe years of it. Until one day, when you try to feed them and they rip out your throat, however dutiful and loyal they had been until then.'

He threw a look at the young scribe, who turned in his chair with his mouth and eyes wide open. Georg's face grimaced in anger as he stood up from his chair and looked down on Toma from his podium.

'Lying vipers,' he snarled. 'I could have your flayed in the square, tied to the Pillar like that whore! Your brother's armour is not worth this treason!'

The knight muttered a curse, shaking his head and stepping backwards.

'We'll leave now!' he said, signalling Codru to follow his lead and pointing his forehead at the door.

'I swear on my father's grave, if I ever find out you set foot in the citadel, I'll have you dismembered, you maggots! You hear me?'

His shouting only became inaudible when the two men closed the solid wooden door of the chamber behind them.

As they almost flew over the stone stairs at the Praetorium's entrance, they headed straight for the merchant's cart. For as long as the walk took, Toma's head kept turning, looking out, checking if the județ called out for his guards. None were in sight, but as they reached the cart, Codru and the knight stood there, panting, ready to jump on the bench.

Out in the distance, running in their footsteps, they saw only one man running, approaching them directly. The closer he got, the better Codru understood who he was.

The young scribe ran all in one breath, waving his arms in the air as a small leather bundle was hanging on his shoulder.

'Wait, my sires, wait!' he shouted.

'Stay there,' Toma ordered when he believed the scribe got close enough. He was harmless, but he wouldn't take any chances. 'Why run after us?'

The scribe pressed his hand on his knees, gasping for air. He only raised his head a couple of times, swinging his eyes from the knight to Codru, then back.

'We don't have all day!' Codru rushed him.

'Let me come with you, good people! Merchants, is that true? You need a hand with the horses, perhaps! Or carrying the wares?'

Toma sighed.

'No! Go back to your letters, lad!' he said, hoisting himself up in the driver's seat.

'Don't,' the scribe said, almost desperate, getting closer to the cart. 'Don't, I beg of you, masters! I can't go back! I said things to Master Georg. Bad things, mostly about his mother! He'll punish me! Please!'

Codru felt a tad responsible for the young man. But men make their choices, and then they need to live with them. He silently joined the Raven on the bench.

'Wait, wait!' the scribe lamented, his ink-stained fingers grappling at the cart as Toma took the reins.

'I can wash your clothes or cook when you make a halt in your journey. Please!'

'This journey isn't for you, boy,' the Raven said decisively. 'Turn back! May heaven preserve you!'

Defeated, the young man finally let go of the cart. Right before Toma was ready to set the horses on the move, Codru asked the lad:

'What do they call you?'

'I'm Timotei, sire! Timotei of John the Carpenter!'

'I'm Codru,' the wanderer replied. 'Come here!'

As the boy circled around the horses, moving from Toma's side to Codru's, the man reached out under his ipingea and untied one of his pouches. He dug his fingers in it and grabbed a good bunch of gold coins. His arm reached out to the scribe, who hesitantly opened his palm, letting the fistful of ducats fall into his hand.

'You won't need to return to your master now! Go do what you will with the gold. It's more than enough to buy you a roof. Or a workshop.'

'Sire!' the boy exclaimed, choked up. 'I won't forget your kindness, master Codru!'

As the scribe looked at the little treasure he had received, shining in his hand under the sunset sky, Toma clicked his tongue, and the horses pulled the wagon away.

# CHAPTER VII

*Bucegi Mountains, August 1437 (6945)*

'REMEMBER THE 7TH LAW, *PER'SKRUMB*:' THE Old-Man said. 'Lead thy deeds by wisdom, not by fury.'

The journey made the boy tired and on edge. Thoughts of his parents still haunted his scattered mind while under the Mountain. And the year felt like an eternity, spent in silence and darkness. In hunger and thirst. He was like a feral animal kept in captivity. And he was scared. Fury was all that kept him alive.

He remembered the Master leaving him there, all by himself, to tend to a forge he was never taught how to do. He stayed there, next to its warm mouth, and cried until he fell asleep from exhaustion. He cried for being abandoned once more. He began remembering his mother and his father. Not their faces, but their warmth. A rage he didn't know was there overwhelmed him. But he was so weak that his heart couldn't bear it, so it went away after a while.

When he was waking up, he didn't know if he blinked, slept for days, or fainted from starvation. For days, the embers continued to keep him warm, but after a while, they started to turn to dead charcoal and ash. He was so close to throwing in the piece of birch-bark the Old-Man had left with him, just for a few more moments of sparkle. But, by mere luck, he didn't.

When he stopped crying, his eyes were drained of tears, and his chest was drained of pain. So, his ears began hearing again. And listening. At first, it was the ashes fizzling their last song. Then it was the hiss of the wind, haunting the gigantic dome of the Hollow Mountain, the air creeping in through the cracks and holes. And, eventually, he listened to the quietness, for in the quietness, the secrets seemed to come to life.

He heard again the murmur of the underground springs swarming the caverns, their waters gurgling on dark rocks, and the drops trickling down off the cave spires. He abandoned the forge, looking for the water source. Afraid he wouldn't find his way back through the maze, he fought to stand and collect pebbles from the luminescent stone he remembered his teacher using to light up the passage. They were plenty, but his weak body and thin arms could barely get them. When he gathered a bunch, he began leaving them behind, like a trail through the labyrinth.

Until he reached one of these veins of water crawling through the stones. He fell to his knees and plunged his face into it, killing his thirst and weariness. A still, dark lake lied further along the path, its waters untouched by the sun or humanity, its surface reflecting only the crystals that adorned the tall and tuberose ceiling above. But even in that stillness and fog, his eyes caught things moving, lurking in their depths.

Thirst made him hear the whispers haunting the cave, the voices of the ancestors, as he remembered his teacher telling. But hunger, now long past the feeling of his stomach being ripped open, made him see them too. With his eyes and face wet and pale, he moved away from the lake, dragging his feet, until he found a cluster of ashen mushrooms sticking out timidly from under a rock. He grabbed them and stuffed his mouth. Heavens had been merciful enough, making so that they were not poisonous. He began searching for more.

Days past. Weeks past. He would eat those mushrooms and lichens growing on the walls, and when he couldn't find any, he'd eat worms and other insects. He'd soothe his drought and loath with the cold water of the streams. He'd bathe under their thin falls.

When the cold began to bite away at him, as the Forge's once vibrant and blazing cracks looked deader by the day, he began hearing the voices more and more clearly. The hiss turned to words, spoken out of the mouths of many people at once. A language he couldn't understand with his mind, but his heart could. And the winter told him it was time to find fuel.

He would continue his journeys through the cave, wandering and exploring its many rooms and hideouts. Its secret passages, scavenging for shrooms, waterweeds, and bugs. Sipping from scoops of stone carved on his path. One day, he stumbled upon a piece of ancient wood, washed down from the world above. Putrid, soaking, and petrified. Covered in moss. He dragged it into the chamber and threw it in the Forge, but it wouldn't catch fire. So, he kept it out for days on dry grounds. Waiting for it to cure. He took some time and crushed it with stone shards into splinters, crying and shivering as snot long dried out on his muzzle.

He stemmed a little pile of them in the Forge's mouth, blowing in the last remains of warmth with his trembling puffs and covering them with his frozen hands. And sparks arose from it. And then smoke. And the more stone-wood he'd add, the more the blaze was regaining its life. He rejoiced, and so did the voices. The great wheels began creaking once more. The red veins of ember began spreading, pulsating again on the furnace's pillar. But with them, his rage spread too.

He'd go on his rounds, day after day. Learning to count the days by the light falling on the golden book. Spending the light falling through the roof searching and gathering provisions for him and for the fire. Scribbling doodles he could see in the Book, but of his own making, using shards of stone and ash, in the roll of bark his teacher left him with. Trapping in it all the secrets the winds of the Mountain shared with him for keeping the flame alive. And plotting, in his little child mind, his vengeance. He took an oath to himself, saying that someday he'd find the people who made him an orphan and punish them.

Until one day, when he woke up from his nest he made at the furnace's foot, and besides him stood the Old-Man, prompted in his stick, with a grin in his beard. He told him the trial was over. And that it was time for him to come to light.

'As so the Great Sleeping-Bear once returned, and the people who thought him to be dead rejoiced and followed him and listened to his wisdom from then on!' he said.

He was then fed milk and bread in the Master's den at the Mountain's top. He was washed of filth in the valley, clothed anew in linen rags, while his numb, cracked soles were tended to and covered in wool and leather.

The boy showed the Old-Man the scroll he had been scribbling and carving under the Mountain, but his master refused to look at it.

'That shall be your guide through the stewardship when I'm gone,' he told him. 'I need not read it, nor would I or anyone else understand it. It's your covenant with the Fire-Knights.'

He told the boy that the Forge had only been the first trial he ought to pass. There were two more waiting for him, and that, come spring, as soon as the first snowdrop flowers would blossom, they'd set the path for the following one.

The Old-Man and his apprentice spent the last days of winter in the den, around the fire, repeating the Laws of their caste, feeding on the last of the master's dried fruits and rye, and navigating through the teachings the Hollow Mountain laid on the boy.

'You have been blessed with solitude. Thirst may sharpen your hearing, hunger may clarify your sight, but only in solitude can one truly understand,' the beggar kept uttering. 'You were taught about choices and consequences. You chose to save the bark and write in it instead of burning it.'

However, every time the young one asked about his parents or showed signs of anger at the injustice he had suffered, the man turned sour and asked him to recite the laws instead. He kept telling him:

'You fought your fears and your past while down there. Don't bring them with you to the surface. It's only when you leave them behind that you truly defeat them.' When they left the den, the boy was worried. He asked the teacher:

'What about the fire? Won't it die with no one to tend to it?'

'Worry not for that right now, boy,' the Old-Man answered. 'It's the Heart of the Mountain. Just like with any heart, we must care for it and protect it. But hearts can also beat without being told to.'

When they finally began their trip, the Old-Man had him carrying an old hatchet, making his journey even longer and more relentless than it would have been. The nights were cold, and they couldn't always find a dry place to lay their heads, so they had to carry on. When they couldn't find shelter in a mountain nook, they had to sleep under the sky on the dirty hemp rags they carried on their backs. Food was scarce as well. Only occasionally were they blessed by kind-hearted people who offered them some food as alms or shelter in a cowshed or barn, where they would sleep in the hay alongside the animals.

The next day they would both say *bogdaproste* and would only leave after the Old-Man went out in the field nearby the welcoming hosts' yard and said a prayer in the Old-Tongue, scouting the sky and waving his stick as if he tried to cover the whole Earth under his wing. He would say '*Buris'rouka, visas'kapura*' and then tell the boy what the incantation was for, as he one day would inherit its burden and speak it for those who deserved it.

The apprentice would spend most nights close to the campfire, if they bedded on the road, reading and deciphering his own carving in the birch-tree scroll, deepening them with a nail or with charcoal, so they would last. He was falling asleep reciting the whispers from the Hollow Mountain. Repeating his oath without the Master's knowledge or permission.

One day, finally, as they reached the highest point of the steep ascent on the hill, their journey came to an end.

'There it is,' the Old-Man said, dragging his feet on the field, with the cold spring wind howling on the crest. 'The Last King's head, carved in the stone by the Gods themselves.'

The young one trembled, and his teeth were shaking. His rags, although patched unevenly with fur, could barely keep the wind away from his body. From their trail, he could see the seemingly never-ending chains of mountains still covered in snow and misty clouds. He could see the wide valleys, covered in blankets of thick mountain vegetation, and cracked by sandy veins. He could see the sunrise breaking through it with long, sharp spears of light, casting its shy warmth on the peaks, on the damp and woke grass covering them, and on his face, while his breath was glowing in front of him.

He also saw the great rock the teacher pointed at. The great stone head, much too like the ones of the stern guardians he saw in the chamber, holding the Mountain's roof and mill wheels on their shoulders, and gigantic stone swords prompted in the floor. Not too far from it, great mushroom-shaped stone pillars, washed by winters and storms, seemed to also have been raised from the hill. It was there that the man guided their steps.

'The ancient altar where the Last King offered his own son to the Gods, rests right at their feet.'

Walking by the great stone pillars, the boy felt crushed under the heaviness of the endless blue sky. A huge stone, like the one that had the Tome of Light on it, grew between the monuments, like a tooth rising from one's gums. He did not know it, but the stone was a sacrificial altar, lying there under the clouds. The man stood by it, measuring him from under his scruffy eyebrows, his blurred grey eyes falling on the boy who was approaching, tired yet curious.

They both left their knapsacks on the ground in silence, breathing in the pure air surrounding them with their eyes closed. Resting, as they both would need it. The apprentice saw the man moving his lips as he was muttering prayers in that same strange language of the elders. He raised his hand, touching the mark carved on his wrinkly face, tracing its circle and the lines radiating from it with his nails.

'Climb on the boulder, Alidor!' he said, breaking his silence, his grave looking eyes looking restlessly down on his apprentice. 'In the Mountain's belly, your mind has hatched, much like an egg. The time has come that we crack that egg and release the offspring into the world.'

The boy endured great torment for a long, very long year in the abyss. Not a torment of the body, but of the mind. He'd think that he would not be afraid of anything that he would have to face. And yet, the short, barely understandable words of the Master, awaken the fear in him once more.

'Remember that from today on, pain will become your sister,' the Master spoke, as the boy dropped his own sack next to the stone, accepting his fate and humbly climbing on the bed. 'You will let your sister in, and she'll join you for the rest of your days.'

As the boy rested on his back, under the Elder's watch, the man muttered once more in his beard.

'It brings me no joy to do what I'm about to do, child. But if you are to become one with nature, it is important that you pass this trial too. As I have. As my Master has, and many more before him.'

His words intertwined with the wind as he left his sack at the end of the stone-bed, close to the boy's feet. He first took out a small stone jar and began crushing dry leaves with a short and thick wooden pistil. After that, the Old-Man took his time knocking his flint shards together with his calloused and trembling hands. Carefully nourishing the sparks in the jar. Blowing in it softly and carefully to not spread the leaves' crumbs. Threads of milky smoke rose from it.

When he approached the apprentice's side, he rested the jar under his chin with both hands and nodded. The young one raised his head and let the smoke cover his face.

'Breathe,' the man urged him. 'Here, we're smoke wanderers.

There,' and his face turned to the sky while the boy started coughing, 'there, we are cloud wanderers!'

The boy's let his head rest on the stone-bed, with his eyes getting lost in the white, passing clouds that were covering the heavens.

The cold, the wind, the anger—they all seemed to sink into the back of his mind. He felt tingly and numb at first, and then he felt nothing at all, as if his body began floating above the altar, the air carrying him through the smooth blanket of mist covering the hills and the valleys.

The man began washing his face, removing his greasy, crimson hair from his forehead. The cloth was soaked in oils and concoctions of the Master's making, of leaves and roots he steadily picked up on their journey. Then he reached out to a small, wooden box hidden in his bag. When he opened the trinket, it revealed a handful of small shards of stone or metal and thin, white bird bones, covered in dark carvings at their thickest sides.

He continued to spout his whispers in ancient tongue as he took one of those metal splinters and smeared its sharp head with more of the same oils. His eyes then met the boy's. He told him he would have to lay still. He told him he would want to scream and struggle, but to ignore those thoughts as hard as he could and endure quietly and bravely, reminding him of his sister's embrace.

'Your thoughts caught root in the depths of the smouldering Earth; now it's time to free them and anchor them to the brink of the eternal Sky,' he finally said. And then the blade pressed on the pale skin of the apprentice's forehead, right in the middle.

The cut sent the boy's limbs into spasms. Walled off by the herbs' smoke, his mind was not completely there; however, his body was, and it felt every bit of it. He heard the man's voice, like in a dream, somewhere far away, telling him to cease moving. While blood trickled slowly on his face, it ran further on his cheek, as if he were crying, reaching out to his neck. Perhaps he was indeed crying. But he did all he could to make his heavy, twitchy limbs listen as the teacher ran a thin and deep cut into his skin, reaching all the way to the bone.

Once the man peeled his fresh wound open, revealing the boy's skull and using his oily cloth to suck the blood flowing, another strange blade had its turn. Round, like a very small saw bent into a circle. Its head began at first grazing the very boy's skull, scratching a circle on the bone. Then deeper and deeper, as the Elder dug and twisted it, until bits of the bone began to crack. The apprentice cried and wailed, but it wasn't the pain that made his voice release into the valley, but the thought of his head being unclogged like a wine barrel. He understood that it can hurt more to think of the pain than the pain itself.

'Do not move, boy!' the far-away voice of his teacher kept ringing in his ears as the rain clouds gathered above, seemingly out of nowhere. The master took note of it but did not slow down his ritual.

'It's done!' he finally said. And thunder struck the fields at the same time the apprentice let a roar leave his lungs. The rain began pouring, soaking him and the Old-Man.

The master quickly covered the young one's newly awakened eye with the peeled patch of skin and did all in his power to stitch it together with linen thread and bird needle bones. As the herbs' fever was fading, the boy yelled, as every time the bone needle pierced his wound, it felt like a dagger eviscerating his face.

He wasn't shouting or crying from the pain of his body, but from the agony of his memories that stormed his mind like a tempest. They all surged at once, reminding him of his loss as if it had just happened. As if they were playing out in front of his eyes. For the first time, he was truly seeing. He felt as if he were being pulled into the heavens, dragged through endless clouds of eternal light, journeying through the vastness without moving.

The Old-Man tried covering the boy's head under his cloak, keeping it away from the water. The storm was hastening, with clouds and winds appearing to gather right above the altar, whipping the Earth with merciless lightning that looked like great spider legs made of light, digging into the mountain's peaks. And the man felt, deep within himself, that it was no ordinary storm. He waved his crooked stick at it with his free hand, trying to cast the clouds and the winds away, but the thunder cracked even more grim than before.

And he understood that the Fire-Knights' blood flowing through the boy's veins was only now coming to flow freely. He has been afraid of that since the first day he found him in the ruins of his home. He has seen it in the boy's rage. He tried to smother it. Worried he was not going to be able to finish the ritual, the man quickly left the boy's side and dragged the hemp bag the young one had dropped next to the stone. He knew what he had to do. He took out the hatchet he freed many winters ago from the child's father's stiff hand. He walked through the mud, away from the altar, dragging his heavy feet and grunting, casting his incantations as he never had before. Howling them into the wind, with rain appearing to drown out his words.

When he believed it was far enough from the boy, he raised the hatchet above his head, water pouring from the sky on his leathery face. And with a shout, he drove the hatchet's head into the ground with all his might. Suddenly, lightning split the sky and struck that very spot, moments after the Old-Man could throw himself to the ground, covering his head. The skies howled, the echo of the strike reverberating through the horizon. And that was the last thunder.

He pulled the hatchet from the ground cautiously, as smoke was rising from its dark veins riddled handle. He then returned to the boy and placed the axe at his feet.

For as long as the trial took, the man didn't cease his chants, restlessly keeping the boy's head dry with the cloth until the bleeding stopped. He kept waving smoke towards the boy from the jar resting on the stone-bed. He pushed dry leaves into his mouth, urging him to chew and swallow, keeping it closed with his palm. When he finished piecing it back together, he knew they were only halfway through the trial. But he waited for the skin to dry out. The sky became quieter and quieter until the torrential rain turned to drizzle, while the clouds remained on top of the altar, as if they were watching over the boy's body.

Exhausted, the boy eventually succumbed to a deep slumber as his body finally giving in.

He opened his eyes. His heart was trembling, and even before he could say anything, he turned to his side and vomited. He felt a hand on his shoulder—the Old-Man's hand.

'Easy, boy,' he said softly. 'Easy now, let it out.'

He helped the boy off the stone-bed, handing him a clean cloth to wipe his face. The apprentice held his heavy head. He tried touching his forehead almost without thinking and realized it was wrapped in more of the same rags. He looked around him and noticed he had been asleep long enough that the sky had cleared, and he could see the sunset, but the sun had long disappeared behind the mountains.

He turned to his master, asking him with his blue-grey eyes if it was over and if he had passed the trial. And the master answered him in return, in the same way, his grave, faraway voice resounding inside the boy's head.

'Yes, *per'skrumb*,' he told him without moving his lips. 'You have indeed passed it!'

With one arm around the boy's shoulder, he grabbed the hatchet he left on the stone and handed it to him.

'This was your father's; he died trying to protect you and your mother from the intruders,' the man said.

'It's now abounded in the Gods' very own breath. One day, if that's your fate, you may have to protect someone with it, too, and bring sacred hail upon them.'

\*\*\*

*Dlăgopole, August 1459 (6967)*

'Not all stories are forged, after all,' Codru told himself.

Some believed in Purgatory, a place where souls would go after death to pay for their sins. He was looking at it.

The chance had it so that his and Toma's arrival coincided with a cloudy, rainy day. But the land seemed to have not met the sun's blessing for a long time, if ever. As Shadowfire's and Golden-Sun's hooves were digging into the mud, slowly carrying their cart through the sombre, dreadful town, the scent of sickness and dung made his throat clench and his spit turn sour.

People they passed by would have normally looked at the newcomers, even if they were mere merchants. They should've seen old women scouting from their courtyards, children running after their horses, or, as Toma expected, Egyptian beggars and slaves asking for coin. But they have encountered none of that.

On the way here, the knight told him that the Prince had all of Wallachia purged of vagabonds. He once held a feast where he gathered all of them, or at least all he could find. He then had his men lock the doors of the dining hall and set it on fire.

'They are still around, of course,' Toma said. 'But the Voivode scared them enough to not want to make themselves known anymore.'

However, the Voivode wasn't here, and he wasn't omniscient either. He couldn't have eyes in every corner of this wretched realm. Codru believed it was more than that.

Before they entered the town, he could see men dragging their dead cattle, pilling up their cadavers, and burning them, just as the knights did with the Strigoi. Some men would also dig up big holes out in the fields, afraid that fire was not enough. They would throw the cows' corpses in those deep ditches so they would not come up, some lamenting and swearing the Necurat had taken hold of them and make them move and walk the earth at night.

The curse that was believed to have taken hold of this place seemed closer to the reason why people could not care less about the travellers' presence.

They have been, however, able to drag the words out of the mouth of one old, blind woman, asking her about the whereabouts of the Black Boyar's mansion.

'You are not from here; I can hear it!' she said.

Toma didn't answer.

'Why go there, my love,' she asked them after. 'Do you not have mercy on your youth? Get out of this town while you still can.'

'How do you mean?'

The old woman said:

'I am blessed enough to be blind, and I can't be witness to the wrath that befell this once good place. So, being here does not hurt me anymore. What's your reason? Look around you!'

'No one is safe here,' she continued. 'The ungodly illness doesn't care if you are a king or a slave, a child or a mere traveller.'

Codru looked at the old woman as her voice began fading. She wanted to leave them behind. It seemed strange to him that she roamed the desolate hamlet on her own.

'How come you aren't getting lost?' he thought to ask.

The knight looked at him, raising an eyebrow. The old woman turned her face toward him.

'There's another one who's not from around these parts,' she said. 'You're from far away, aren't you?'

After letting the silence linger, she continued:

'People think that if you are blind, you can't see. But you don't need eyes to have sight, do you?'

Codru frowned as the old woman let the silence linger on the last words.

'Besides,' she concluded, 'I'm not too eager to go home. Death is waiting for me there, so I keep playing hide and seek with her every Wednesday. I hope that one day she will give up searching.'

'If you will, kind woman,' Toma interrupted as the night was coming. 'Tell us where we can find the Boyar's home. He spread the word, all the way over the mountains, that he put out a reward for cutting the roots of the evil this town was plagued with.'

'The evil?' she asked rhetorically. 'Are you perhaps talking about *Muma*? The witch no one has seen, but His Worship blames for the sickness?'

'Precisely!'

'You cannot miss his mansion if that is what you are looking for. I am blind; I couldn't tell you which way to go. But if God wills it, you will not reach it. Many lads came looking for rewards and failed. *Vodă* himself sent his Viteji to help, but they left as clueless as they arrived. Just keep going where you need to go, dear travellers, and leave us to our curse. The only evil plague resides in that mansion. And it will not go anywhere.'

The two men looked at one another for a while, as if they tried to see if the other one knew what the old woman was on about. Then, when they turned to the woman, hoping to get more answers, she was gone, as if the muddy ground beneath her had swallowed her.

'No wonder Death can't find her if she plays the game that well,' Toma mumbled.

She was, however, right. The mansion presented itself not too long after, as all the roads led there. Their wagon's wheels grinded through the sleazy road, sprinkled with poorly cut stones.

Codru was told by the Raven that the rumours he had heard from the blind woman were not far from the truth. No one really knew where the Boyar came from, and people were afraid to ask. It seemed that shortly after the Voivode himself took his rightful throne, the Boyar appeared in the town known as Dlăgopole. The Voivode handed over the town's keys and the highest seat in the *Sfat* for the Boyar to settle in. He decreed, under the threat of the spike, that the townspeople must heed the Boyar's words, as the newcomer would be voicing the Voivode's very mind.

The nobleman's house jutted out like a broken bone through skin, its pale walls and frames appearing to glow against the muted backdrop of the square, distant ashen clouds, and the drab attire of its caretakers. As the merchants' cart approached the gates, a guard promptly presented himself. His intimidating attire, composed of rust-coloured chainmail and a blackened tunic, mirrored the grime on his face.

'His Worship won't see any peddlers,' he spoke. 'Scram!'

Codru didn't even attempt to speak, letting the knight negotiate his way in, as he was usually so skilled at it. Toma left his comrade in the wagon and walked towards the Wallachian guard.

'We have travelled from afar; the rumours of this town's curse reached our ears,' he said. 'I believe we can help His Worship, for a price!'

'More money-hungry scum! Bloody leeches,' the man at the gate cursed. 'What wares could you have that will help our sick and our dead? More potions?'

Before he could send the travellers off, another man joined him, running all in one breath.

'The master wants to meet them; let them in at once!' he said, panting.

The first man turned.

'He wasn't told of their arrival!'

The other one didn't waste time humouring this man's indecision, so he removed the bolt from the musty wooden door himself and invited the men in, sending boys after their wagon and horses.

It seemed strange to Codru to have been invited into the mansion without even being searched. They could have been anyone. They had weapons.

As his and the knight's boots were clamping on the stone pathway from the gate until the abode, the wanderer's eyes scouted the fences and the crenelated walls and roofs of the building. There were caretakers and guards almost in every corner of the establishment, lighting up the torches and the braziers, but instead of giving the guests the curious eye, they appeared to avoid looking at them, with their heads down and their faces away from sight. Even the man who was now guiding them to the entrance. He pushed the large wooden doors to the sides, and together, they crossed the mansion's threshold.

The building was said to be the place where the town's council would hold their meetings. However, the Boyar seemed to have turned it into his own home. Everything, from his subjects to the interior walls and columns of the house, had his crimson toned mark on them, just like the guards' armour. After a short hallway, their guide, who until then had kept quiet, turned, and told them this next door was where he had to leave them.

'The Master is waiting for you on the other side.' And he walked away as suddenly as he appeared.

Toma opened the doors, and the two merchants in disguise were rapidly overwhelmed by a heavy wax scent and misty smoke lingering in the air. Even with all the candles adorned on the walls and leaking from the ceiling chandeliers, the light was still weak, failing to pierce the misty gloom of the chamber. The windows were covered with thick curtains, drawn shut despite the encroaching darkness outside.

'Come, my lords! Come!' Codru heard a hoarse yet tranquil man's voice. It sounded old, and it echoed when spoken in the bleak, large room.

The man they had been looking for was sitting on the only chair, right in front of the new guests. The closer they got, the stranger the man appeared. He was surrounded by loyal acolytes who, like the men Codru had seen outside, had their eyes sunken and their faces aimed at the stone floor, covered in scarlet rugs and pelts. The warm flare of the upper candles and rushlights fell on the Boyar's clean-cut cheekbones, aquiline nose, and wide forehead, hiding his eyes in shadows. Long, thin, leaden hair fell on the dark fur of his large mantle, which unravelled on the floor like a tar blanket.

However, even under the weak light of the chamber, the more Codru closed in, the more he understood the Black Boyar's name's provenance. It wasn't the clothes or his dreadful appearance; rather, it was his skin. Darker than the one of the outside guards' or every Wallachian he has encountered up until here for that matter. He remembered Toma's words that the Voivode had always preferred the foreign company to the native one. The Black Boyar could have easily been an Egyptian—there was no way to tell. He noted how obedient his Wallachian vassals were, which was odd, as he knew how proud and wary of strangers the folk around these parts were too.

'Welcome!' the Boyar said when the two men were close enough that they could talk without raising their voices. The knight nodded, while Codru was content to only measure the man from a safe distance. He felt the nobleman's eyes watching him from under his shadowy eyebrows.

'Two humble merchants, we are, but we are skilled and seasoned in the way of these lands,' Toma began. But the Boyar raised his hand, signalling him to save it.

'I shall spare you the lying,' he said. 'I know very well you are not peddlers.'

His words didn't sound like a threat to the fact that they had been discovered. However, it felt like one.

'If you were indeed a pair of traders, I wouldn't have had any reason to talk to you.'

Codru dared to join the discussion.

'What gave it away,' he asked, mostly rhetorically.

The man grunted, hesitating to speak his mind, but he honoured the wanderer with an answer.

'In this town, I'm his Sire's eyes and mouth. Of course I knew. I have seen you and watched over you since your arrival.'

'The town doesn't look too watched over!'

Toma turned to him, biting his lower lip, expecting maybe an unfortunate turn of events. But the nobleman simply smiled, his grin spreading like a sickle on his sullen figure.

'You are daring, merchant. This is great news. It will serve you well on the mission I have for you.'

After a short pause, he asked Codru:

'Where do you come from? I had not met many Viteji bearing the mark of the ancients. That is a sacred symbol of your caste, is it not?'

Codru's eyebrows entwined. He could have asked the Boyar similar questions. He didn't meet many who even knew what his tattoo was, let alone what it meant.

'I was born around these parts; that is all that matters right now.'

'The Ancients have not been too kind to you, have they?' the Black Boyar smirked. 'Too unyielding, those bastards, some would say. Too... Incorruptible.' Then he rose slowly from his chair, stepping down the thin stairs in front of his throne. 'But you know,' he continued approaching the two guests until he stood right in front of them, his head rising higher than Toma's himself. 'The Moșii have been many. And not all of them as stern as the ones the *Salmani* chose to listen too.'

He paused, watching as Codru became more and more intrigued by his knowledge.

'Remarkable,' he ended, with his dark, thin eyes resting on Codru's mark.

'There are rumours, as I've heard, that nobody knows where you came from either, *Jupâne*!'

It was Toma who interfered, mostly to capture the nobleman's attention and avoid Codru barking from his corner like a trapped dog.

'As long as they are loyal, that matters not,' the Boyar said, his eyes piercing the knight for a moment as he chose to return to his seat. 'Rumours don't bother me, disobedience does.'

'Tell us about the illness,' Codru urged the man.

'What's there left to tell?' he said, resting in his chair as a cupbearer approached him holding a silver tray with a golden cup on it, which the nobleman grabbed slowly with his long fingers. He sipped from it with his eyes closed, drops of the drink creeping into his long and oiled black beard.

'You have undoubtedly seen the town,' the Boyar began. 'The sick and the wretched, the miasma weighing heavily in the air, cattle rotting in ditches. Villagers feed their children the dead meat until they succumb to its poison. Enchantresses claim this disease is no ordinary ailment but a cursed one, born from deep hatred and fowl misfortune.'

'So, you believe it's a curse, then!' Toma asked, possibly holding hopes it was the same one that turned the dead into Strigoi.

'Believe it? No,' the man said, placing the goblet on the tray and waving his hand to the servant to leave his side. 'I know it to be a curse.'

'You see,' the Boyar continued. 'Not too far from here, towards the sunset, there's a grove. Woodlands where trees die of old age and grounds are untouched by man's foot. If you believe the legends, it is also where the *Iele* dwell. Cozia, they call the place.'

Codru raised his head. He heard of this place long ago. He knew of it. His heart began racing uncontrollably as his breath quivered. His ears muffled the Boyar's voice, and a pale maiden's face with brown locks took hold of his mind.

'But there is another evil creature haunting those trails. The folk call it Muma. A witch-spirit. I need you to find it and bring me its head.'

'The people say many things, Your Worship!' Toma said. 'No one has ever seen this spirit. People in your town say the same. We may not be merchants, but we do have swords. And swords can't fight phantasms, nor stories.'

Gathering his wits about him, Codru turned towards the Raven. He understood that, even if not too long ago they had faced hell hounds and Strigoi, creatures that for many were tales only old maids would carry around, it was not needed for the Boyar to know it. This way, he'd have to tell everything he knew.

'Do I look like someone who believes in legends?' the man seemed to grumble. 'Do not take me for a fool!'

He then looked at them from under his eyebrows and said in a low voice:

'The witch is as true as you and me. She crawls out of her den every night, spitting her wicked disease everywhere in her path. Turning the fields to mold and the flesh to rot. The more she destroys, the hungrier she gets.'

His words hissed through his teeth intensely until they soon faded, letting the silence rest in the sinister chamber for a short while.

'As my priests advised, I've built a grand church like no other, seeking God's favour. But he remained silent. I then turned to the devil and sacrificed all but myself. Yet even the devil gave no answer. For nearly a year, many vowed to end her cursed existence. The fortunate few gave up after weeks in the forests, returning empty-handed. The less fortunate never returned. Before long, word spread, and fear with it, until no one came to my court.'

His tone then shifted, and with a sudden raise, he spoke in a grave voice, 'Name your reward, and if you succeed in your quest, you shall have it! Gold, women, or slaves? What shall it be?'

The Raven turned to Codru, and he could read the carelessness in his eyes, because by now, even he understood that the stranger never cared for money. Money was merely the only language he ever spoke. Bloodlust has been the real reward. And since the time he was taken prisoner until now, many things have happened that have made those cravings fall somewhere in the background.

However, something in the words of this Black Boyar must have turned a key inside him, because Codru took the lead and gave the new employer the answer:

'Let us first come back from the trip, and if there's gold you need to be relieved of, we'll gladly accept it then.'

The Boyar grinned one last time and replied.

'So noble and so just—you'd made your kind proud,' he said. 'Too bad; it's also what would get you killed.'

# CHAPTER VIII

*Cozia's Groves, June 1431 (6939)*

AT FIRST, HE ONLY HEARD A THUNDERING, rhythmic noise. Then he heard chanting, ethereal voices spreading through the brushwood, entwining harmoniously with the sweet breeze. Then he felt the heat beating down on his cheek, sparks from a crackling fire whipping his skin like invisible needles. When he finally dared to open his eyes, he could only see the tall crowns of the trees losing into each other, covering the starry night's sky, and the full moon fighting to pierce the dense and dark-green curtain of the forest's dome.

He was confused, not knowing for how long he had been asleep, and his blurry vision could only discern the heat source—a great pyre swallowed by a blaze—surrounded by thin, dark shapes and silhouettes moving around. He tried wiping his eyes, trying to gain more clarity, but he realized his arms were stuck. He was a prisoner, tied to the ground, his wrists and his ankles wrapped in twisted, thick vines that had risen from the earth, capturing him. He soon found that his hunter's clothes had vanished, and he was lying there, stripped to the skin, and tied to the ground, with weeds tangled through his hair, barely able to move his head. Terrified, he yelled and began pulling his arms and legs in vain from the strong grip of the twisted ivy.

Horea's eyes began seeing more and more clearly, and he looked around for his men.

'Jupân' Mihnea,' he shouted. But no one answered.

The otherworldly songs were the only thing he could hear. And when he ceased crying out for help, his eyes turned to the figures circling around the fire. The voices resounded not only in the forest's clearing but inside his head too. It didn't take him long to understand that they were the captors. The unknown creatures which served their justice upon the unfortunate poachers. The fearless mistresses of the winds, bearers of omens, and rulers of the deep forests and animals living in them. The Iele. The Sânziene. And this was their *horă*, their sacred solstice ritual.

The woodland maidens danced unclothed around the tall campfire, with only their long, silver-gold hair covering their glowing skin. On their heads, they bore rich, lady's bedstraw crowns, with the yarn stemming from them and wrapping around the horns that adorned their delicate heads. They sang in sweet, enchanting voices and hit their hide drums uninterruptedly. As they danced, the grass under their feet was catching fire, leaving a dark circle of ash around the pyre, but without burning their white flesh. The smoke and the fireflies sparkling around the clearing and above the fire shrouded the Sânziene in a cloud, as though they had brought the sky into the heart of the grove.

Charmed by the songs, Horea left his head on its side, the grass grazing his face as he watched the phantasms floating around the fire, laughing like impish virgins out for a swim at the lake. His heart began beating slower and slower, stricken by lassitude. But before he could sink back into his slumber, he heard the woodland maidens whispering his name.

'*Horea!*' they would say, smooth-tongued. '*Do our bodies please your heart? Isn't it true that you love us? Oh, Horea, beautiful son!*' He tried speaking, asking them what they wanted with him. Where were all his comrades? Why was he pinned to the ground? But his voice didn't seem to pull through, drowning in his throat.

Out of the suite of countless maidens, one stood out brighter than the rest. The hunter recognized her. She was the same sword-bearing apparition that buried Mihnea into the hospitable blanket of moss and dirt, far away in the woods. She left her sisters behind, her bare feet carrying her towards the man. The Iele kept chanting behind her, carrying further their otherworldly songs, greedily reciting his name.

'*Oh, Horea! Are we to your liking?*' they kept giggling, their echoes spreading with the leaves and with the wind.

The closer their luminous kinswoman got to their prisoner, the clearer the man could see her. Her emerald eyes shone brightly, and her lips were ripe like sour cherries, bluntly engraved on her clear face. The deer horns broke through her mane like crooked branches, and a long, rose-coloured scar tainted her left cheekbone.

Horea could only hear the drums somewhere far away right now as the Sânziană closed in, standing right next to his body, digging her green eyes deep inside his. He was starstruck, unable to move or even breathe, looking up to the sacred being, the high woods framing her beautiful portrait. It was only when the *Zână* stepped over his body, sitting above him, that he understood why the nymphs kept him alive. As her abundant hair covered him like a blanket, his grunts turned sharper.

The same old tales of the woodland *Rusalii* always had a chosen-one; most men were fortunate, meeting their usual dark fates. Dying, being mutilated, or losing their mind. But there were a few, some less fortunate, who, once seen by the spirits, would be kept for their mating rituals during midsummer night. After all, the Iele needed men to carry on their gracious, pagan kin. But no one knew what happened to those poor souls once the maidens were done with them.

The chants continued, as did the drums and the fire. The dance and the laughter. All the sisters were quivering in tandem with the man's breaths and with the nymph's undulations. The moon and the stars seemed to him brighter, the ground softer, and the air sweeter. He felt every particle of the sky touching every fiber of his being. She grabbed his pinned hands, spreading her fingers through his, and her nails cut his palms ravenously.

Until one moment, when the forest around them seemed to have burst into solar upheaval, swept by an earthquake, he was the only one feeling. The flames in the middle cast out spears of sparks, and the drums and the songs ended, letting a pure silence and twilight take their places.

The Sânziană rose above him, leaving the man with his eyes and mouth wide open, staring into the endless sky and seemingly sinking slowly into the moss, covered by grass and swift ivy leaves. He squeezed his fists, and another cut made his blood run through his fingers. Horea turned, and he realized, even in his euphoria, that it wasn't one of the maiden's fingernails that grazed his skin—it was an arrowhead. He recognized it. It was the same one his arrows had. The same one that cut her face in the forest. She had returned his fowl shard of steel where it belonged.

He then floated into the deepest of dreams. Out there, the voices soon faded, his ears getting swallowed by the earth. Until he could only hear his own desperate voice shouting, trapped in his head, afraid of meeting his inevitable end. And yet he smiled, as his heart was oddly at peace. He knew he was going to die. And he did not care.

\*\*\*

*Cozia, March 1432 (6940)*

Upon returning to his hometown, Horea had been outcast. To him, living was a miracle; to others, it was a harbinger of bad luck. Both men and women were avoiding him as if he had been touched by demons, spreading rumours through taverns, while working in the field or around the weaver and the hearth. That the pârcălab's aide's son was a pagan coward. How could he be the only one to go scot-free, while all the other hunters were forever lost in the woods? What deal had he gotten himself into?

Horea pleaded to clear out his name. He told all of them what he went through, but no one listened. He was living in shame, away from people, locked in his father's home. But the shame was nothing compared with another, deeper feeling that has been brewing in his chest, abounding in sorrow.

From the moment he awoke in the woods, bathed in daylight, naked and alone, to his eventual return home, a growing illness consumed him. No food, drink, potion, or ointment could quell its spread because there was no cure. A weight pressed upon him, heavy and corrosive as a rusting anvil, crushing his heart. He needed her as surely as he needed breath. He felt like a piece of him, more precious than any limb, was gone forever, stuck in that clearing.

He yearned for the nymph's gaze or touch with every bone of his body. He missed her like a droughty pasture misses the weeping sky, and knowing she was gone forever made him long for her even more. He wanted to cry, but the hopelessness didn't even allow him to do that. He loved her more than he loved his father or his dead mother. He loved her more than he was ever going to love himself, and more than he knew he was able to love. He was irreversibly bound to her, for eternity, the charms of the woodland maiden, having his whole being—mind, soul, and body—captured in her lost memory.

The tales of old were, therefore, true. No, being an outcast just grazed him; the rumours held no power either, and shame was only his father's. But he was cursed to bear the memory of that creature forever. An unfortunate soul wandering the earth aimlessly until his last breath.

Month after month, he would spend his days in front of the window, in his chair, gazing out over the roofs, all the way to the horizon, where the mountains, the forest, and the sky came together. He would sometimes rub the scar he had in his palm from the arrowhead, which he now carried like a talisman, on a string around his neck. It didn't matter if it was raining, a blizzard was roaring, or if there was sun.

Food and drink were sent to him, just to be taken back, covered in mold, and eaten by maggots. He would not eat or drink. He would not bathe or sleep. His eyes were pinned towards the distance, hoping and praying that he would see a sign that she was out there. Listening to the wind and hoping for the veil to fall and show him, at least once more, her silky hair. Her eyes and her mouth. He had his heart sink more than a dozen times as his weakened, starving body made him see apparitions that weren't there.

The winter had been long and unyielding. Nights felt as if they stretched on for years. He would cry out amidst the sheets, burying his face into the pillow. On the wooden floor, he'd search for a corner where pain might allow him a moment's respite to close his eyes. He scratched at the walls, drove his head against them, and pulled at his hair. Night after night, he pleaded with God to dispatch His servant, Death, to claim him. He believed he would die, and he wanted to. The thought of feeling nothing instead of carrying this ravenous ardour in his bones sounded more and more inviting.

Spring came, and with it, townsfolk outside began celebrating it. Off his window, he could see the old and the young in their holiday clothes, ribboned with red and white strings—remains of pagan sacrificial rituals. The hunter had been waiting for a sign, and he took it as it was. And his mind cleared suddenly. He had to prey on this moment before he could sink again into the bottomless pits of despair. Before his mind was not his again for a long time.

For the first time in weeks, he removed his crumpled linen shirt, kneeled next to the window, and threw the cold, brackish water on his face and his armpits straight from the wooden bucket. He dressed in his Sunday's Mass good garments, too. His *borangic* shirt, his baize-made doublet, and his thick, woollen breeches. He even pinned a *mărțișor* on his chest, as did all the other folk. He had a stable boy prepare him the swiftest steed.

'And rope, my lad!' he asked, under his breath, handing the boy a few *bani*, so he would keep it for himself. 'The rough kind. The shortest and thickest you can find.'

He rode that horse through the mud like a bat out of hell, toward the forest where his dreams had last drawn breath. He had to, or else fear and doubt would sprout again in his heart, and the fever would grab him in its long talons. He rode like the wind, leaving the town and the spring celebrations behind. Leaving his home and his father behind. He rode with his eyes set on the groves and his hand tight on the rope hanging on the saddle. He straddled as if he were not going to return. He didn't plan to.

He knew the answer all along, hidden beneath the dreams of the charmed maiden and the countless voices swarming in his head for many moons. Because it was a frightful answer that would damn his soul, even though he believed he was already damned. He might as well just be released from the pain.

When the horse reached the forest's edges, Horea dismounted and only took the rope from its back. He smacked the animal's loins gently, urging it to return home. The horse, however, refused, shaking its mane, snuffling, and grubbing the mud with its shoe.

'*Hăis!*' Horea exclaimed. 'Off you go, *Murgule*! He knew that horses could maybe sense grief or even intentions. He cursed, pushing the horse away with his arms. He even grabbed a twig and whipped the poor animal's back. Until it gave up and bolted, leaving the hunter behind to shout like a madman.

It didn't take long for him to find the track—the old trail he has been wandering in his mind for so long. He recognized the arbours and the bushes he passed by. The fresh dew was wetting his breeches and his palm as he walked his fingers through the tall ferns, with the rope in the other hand. He recognized the tall birch-trees and the great oak when he first saw the silver deer.

Then he found his way onto the track, that he and the poachers hunted it down. Flashes of the men screaming as they were thrown in the air or swallowed by the ground ran through his head. He then stumbled on the path he had first found on his way back after he awakened from the night with the Iele. Even in his desperate scurry, his eyes and his feet memorized it. Soon, he was going to get back to that clearing. And the torture would finally end.

It was almost noon when his boots crossed the edge of the glade. It was quiet, and the air breathed swiftly through the leaves. He walked slowly, looking either towards the sky, letting the shy sun of March bathe his face, or scouting the grass for any trace of that night. To remind him that it wasn't only a dream that banished him from people and from himself. But he found no such things. The snow, the wind, and perhaps even the nymphs made it look as though that night never happened. No wonder they were only believed to be legends.

Nonetheless, he has journeyed here for one purpose, and one purpose only. This is where it all began, and this is where it would all end. He wasn't afraid, either. Not anymore.

He looked down on the rope he now held with both hands and rubbed his fingers on its dry fibres. He pulled it between his fists and nodded for himself, thinking the stable boy had done good work. He could have left him all his silver. He then looked around, measuring the trees and their branches, looking for one that would do the honours. A damned branch, like himself, sturdy enough to hold him and tall enough to not let him reach the ground. And he found it.

There it was—a beautiful beech-tree with a solid trunk, with roots sticking out like pale bones and its naked branches spreading like a bat's wings in all directions. In its prime, this tree would have grown a thick crown, full of leaves, providing shade, and perhaps housing hundreds of birds. But today, it was destined to serve as gallows.

He walked towards it, and as he did, he could hear birds chirping deep in the woods. At first, he thought he could hear a barn-owl too, a premonition of his impending end. But he did not hear it, and in a way, he felt grateful for that. He was all by himself, as sentencing oneself to hell should be.

When he reached under the tree's veiny branches, spread over like gigantic antlers, his eyes fell on one of the closest. He knew he had to climb the tree to reach it, and that was just what he was looking for. He sat there for a while, at the tree's foot. He ran the rope through his hands, making one of those bails he once made to trap rabbits with the other hunters. One of those that, once pulled and tied, would wrap around the unfortunate being like Death's claw itself, never to be unfettered.

He quivered as his glance caught the mark he had in his palm, watching it like an unforgiving eye. He made a fist, closing it, as he did not want shame to begin sprouting again in his heart. Not now, when he was so close to being released from it forevermore.

He stood up and turned to the tree, looping the rope roll on his shoulder and grabbing the arbour's husky rind with his hands. He pushed himself up, prompting his boots into it and pulling towards the wood, scratching his skin as he did. He reached out to a thin branch, then another. Until his hands took hold of the branch he had seen from below. It was cold and soft under his touch. Strong like a plough's yoke, and thick enough that he could climb on it, dragging himself towards its end. When he reached its middle, he thought it was far enough. He sat with the branch between his legs, pondering as he watched, measuring the fair distance from the ground.

He reached for the rope, bringing it down from his shoulder, and then began wrapping one of its ends around the branch. He was skilled; knots came easily to him, so it didn't take him long to tie them. He took the other end, where the noose was, and pulled it over his head. His heart was shaking, and he felt like he began choking on it as he bound the rope around his neck. It itched, and cold sweats loomed over his temples. Freedom awaited, so he gazed one last time towards the sun, let a stream of air release his trembling lips, and then closed his eyes, pushing himself off the branch.

He thought his neck would snap as the rope strung under his weight, clenching around his tender flesh like a viper around a squirrel. He felt his head pulled from his shoulders, and his heart was pumping in his ears. Blood veins burst under his eyelids, urging him to open them and witness the sin he was committing. His legs reached out to the ground instinctively, but there was no ground beneath them. His hands convulsed upwards toward the branch, but it was out of his reach. His lungs asked for air, and when they didn't get it, they shocked his whole body, triggering a spasm.

He opened his eyes, and he shouldn't have done it. He saw the forest through his teary eyes and the daylight. He suddenly wanted to be here. He was sorry, and he wanted to never have left home. He wanted to live. His bloody fingernails scratched into his skin as he pulled hopelessly at the rope, which was digging deeper into his muscle. The sound of his heart pumped its last drums, his ears muffling the world around him, where he no longer belonged. He let his hands fall around him, closing his eyes.

Then, through his last heartbeats floating in his livid head, he heard a call as sweet as heavens, thinking he had already died, and by God's mercy, He'd opened his gates for him. Then he thought it was the birds, or even his long gone sweetheart. But it was something else, much more innocent than all three—the cry of a child.

He recognized it, even if he had never heard it before. And then he knew, as sure as he knew that night in the forest, that the hunters would meet their doom. It was his child. He felt as if another, unseen hand reached out to his own, raising it to his chest. And his fingers felt the arrowhead.

With his last strength, revived by faded shards of home, he ripped the neck of his shirt, looking for the talisman. He pulled it, and with it, he began rubbing its pointy edge against the rope around the neck. He sliced the tether's fibres with it, one by one, convulsing desperately, grunting, and whispering, with spit and snot bursting on his chin. And with a violent, unexpected zing, the rope snapped, releasing Horea from its deadly grip and letting the man fall to the ground with a crushing thud.

After unwrapping the remaining thread off his neck, the hunter stood up shakingly, coughing and spitting blood, stumbling to his knees now and then. He heard the cry again, and, with his talisman in his fist, rubbing his redded neck skin, he began walking again, dragging his boots through the grass. He walked towards the middle of the clearing, where the Sânziene once danced and where the child's cry came from. And then he saw her.

A newborn girl lay there, where the pyre burned moons ago, loosely covered in a white sheet of silk, on a bed of twigs. The sun that fell on her made her glow. Horea's tears ran down his cheeks as he kneeled next to the crying baby. His heart was filling up as he recognized her mother's beauty. But that wasn't the only thing the baby inherited. A birthmark tainted her milky skin in the same place his arrow grazed her mother's. And he understood. The mark made it so that she had been rejected by her kind and abandoned there.

She took after him more than she took after her mother. She was an outcast, as he was. And she was also the one who gave him his life back.

'Hush now! Worry not, child,' he raised the baby into his arms, holding her at his chest as if she were his last breath. His tears kept dripping on the silk sheet. 'I shall raise you and love you more than I ever loved her.'

And the baby turned quiet as the man smiled peacefully.

\*\*\*

*Cozia's Groves, August 1459 (6967)*

One day and one night, that's how long it took him and the knight to reach the sinister groves the Boyar talked about. Their wagon remained back at the nobleman's stables, as they now had his protection to wander, and passing as merchants was no longer needed. The two horses only carried on their saddles their bags, their supplies, their thick sleeping mats, and their weapons.

When they left the town, Codru saw the Raven strapping to Golden-Sun's saddle both his artifacts he took from his brother's vault, but he didn't think a lot of it. The night before they arrived at the edge of the forest, while camping by the fire, he saw him, however, polishing that old mace and the iron mask. Even in the dim light of the embers, he noticed the weapon's carvings, drawn all around the mace's head, covering it in dark, mysterious cuts. All too like the ones his Damascus scimitar and his axe now bore, thanks to the master blacksmith. His old bark-skin could not reveal their meaning.

'Are you going to tell me about those one of these days?' he found himself asking while lying on his woollen sack, with his head pressed against the wooden trunk of a dead tree.

Toma didn't bother to raise his head, but he dignified the man's curiosity with an answer, while he used a small dagger's edge to remove rust off the mace's handle.

'I thought you did not care for it,' he said. 'I offered to read your hatchet before.'

'I'm used to having people stay out of my affairs, as I stay out of theirs!' Codru answered. 'But you seem to hold those iron potsherds in high regard. And if we are to join in the fight, I need to know there's a good reason why you would have a rusted mace as your weapon of choice. It's my skin at stake too.'

The Raven chuckled.

'Whatever your reason may be, wanderer...'

Then, after a pause, he stood up and approached the fire, stirring the burning wood with the mace's head. Codru could see the signs carved in it lighting up as the blaze ate at the slime freshly scooped out of them with the knight's dagger.

'Do you know why they call me the Greuthung?' he asked timidly as he looked at the relic's bulge up closely, blowing the ash off it. As Codru didn't answer anything, he continued.

'The Greuthungi appear to have been an ancient folk, roaming the northern realms long ago. Heathens, as they were praying to thunder and the mountains. Merciless, maybe even man-eating warriors.'

He returned to his sack and placed the mace next to him, then carried on:

'It's said they settled on these lands too, venturing as far as the Black Sea. They even clashed with the Râmlani. Few are aware of this, and all I know was passed down from my father, who learned it from his. My forebears believed we carried the blood of these people in our veins and took great pride in that heritage.'

'I didn't ask for your family history; why do you tell me this?' Codru interrupted.

'Because my impatient friend,' Toma said, looking at the weapon resting beside him. 'This is a mace of their making, and it bears their script, sacred letters their gods themselves conceived.'

Codru shook his head without hiding his discontent.

'A family heirloom does not make for a good defence,' he said.

The Raven sniffed.

'That's not what it is. And I believe it was forged to destroy, not to protect.'

Seeing as the wanderer frowned, he continued to reel his tale, his eyes sparkling as he looked at the campfire.

'Before you were probably even born, I used to track down ancient Dacian ruins and search them for treasures. Sándor, always good at haggling, would help me trade the trinkets for coins at the market, and then we would split the bounty like brothers. Until the Ottomans came one day over the mountains and *besieged the Citadel*. There were rumours that the siege unearthed a treasure like no other, so after the Ottomans retreated, I tracked it down. And the rumours were true. It was unlike any chest I'd ever seen, and I succumbed to its spell.'

'Csák Voivode and even the Hungarian King sent me word to bring it to the capital, promising to bury me in wealth, but I thought I had enough coin, and like a fool, I kept the treasure for myself. I hid it away in a place only I knew of.'

Toma clenched his teeth and sighed, looking at Codru over the flames as the fire crackled and his companion was still waiting for his answer.

'The strangest of things happened shortly after. One day, the sky turned dark at midday. If you looked at the skies, you'd see the night swallowing the sun with your naked eye. But then it passed, and light returned as quickly as it vanished. Some old astrologers said it was an ill-omen. But I didn't listen. I was too in love during those days. A beautiful girl—*Luna*, her parents named her. I made her my wife. I was very young, and I thought I had everything.

A few moons later, as I was returning to Härmeschtat from one of my travels, terrible news welcomed me upon arrival. Unknown outlaws, seemingly born with the 'darkening,' arrived too. No one knew where they had come from. They ransacked the town, searching for the very same treasure I had hidden away. They murdered townsmen and kidnapped their daughters. Luna was one of them.'

Codru understood where the story was going. He pitied the knight. And his words resonated with him in ways he didn't want to allow himself to.

'That's enough,' he asked. 'You mustn't carry on!'

The Raven's eyes fell on the grass as he bit his lips. But he ignored his comrade's counsel.

'I found they made their camp in the Citadels' ruins, so I gathered people and brought the treasure there, hoping they would release the women for it. We attempted to parley with these marauders. Codru, you should have seen them—these heathens were neither ordinary mercenaries nor the Akinji, as rumours had it. They were unlike any band of bandits I've ever heard of.

Towering and robust, they donned thick, horned helmets and pine-green gambesons. Their shoulders were draped in what appeared to be the flaky skin of snakes. And their faces, concealed beneath iron muzzles, left only their piercing, slithering eyes visible.'

Codru was intrigued to have recognized that description very well. He once cut the hand of a man with similar traits. Sudden waves of anguish echoed through his bones.

'They spoke in a tongue no one understood. Savages. Filthy adders! A curse that befell our realm. And their chief's eyes only looked at me, and he spoke the only word we all understood. My name. One of our people, a Moldavian, called them *Zmei*, after his elders' name given to serpents. And that's what we began calling them from then on.'

'In the end, these Zmei accepted the treasure as a tribute, peacefully. But we would soon find that the women had all already been murdered. And Luna was with a child, you see. My little, precious sun. And these monsters took them from me.

We mourned our dead, then we planned out retaliation. I was young and hurt, but fire brewed in my chest. And that criminal's gaze and words haunted me. I wanted his blood. Sándor worked tirelessly crafting our weapons. Soon, one cursed night, we surrounded and penetrated the ruins and killed them all, soothing our vengeance. When we unmasked them, we uncovered their mutilated faces. They had their noses chopped off and their tongues split in two. I murdered their leader with his own sceptre by crushing his skull to bits. We had our justice.

After that day, men hailed me for my bravery, but they were also afraid of me. They have seen a side of me I thought was never there. A heathen, as my ancestors seemed to be. But all I felt was anger, heartbreak, and shame. So, I ran away. I travelled east, over the mountains, to the place they call Luana's Lands, and buried the treasure somewhere so no one would ever have to face its curse again. Upon my return, I swore celibacy when John Hunyadi anointed me knight for rooting out the Zmei's plague.'

'The mace, the mask...' Codru mumbled. 'Those were their chief's, were they not?'

'Just so!'

'Why did you keep them?'

Toma shrugged and then looked at Codru straight, saying:

'I tell myself the mace is a symbol of my victory.'

'But that isn't the truth, is it?'

'It isn't,' Toma said. 'Wielding that sceptre in battle ignited a strength within me I never thought was there. A surge of wrath so immense, it felt as though my ancestors were joining me in the fray, endowing me with their collective might. It made me bloodthirsty and invincible. A monster, like those Zmei. And to serve vengeance, one must become a monster.'

Codru finally agreed to him, and the Raven ended his tale, saying:

'I kept the mask out of shame, to hide how much of a monster I actually became.'

\*\*\*

The red-haired stranger had finally realized that the Raven wasn't as pious as he thought of him. He has been truthful since the first day, after they defeated the Strigoi, when Toma told him that he was, too, a lost, ashamed soul, just like the monk. He did not turn to God and knighthood out of devoutness, but to silence his inner demons. To heal those old, foul wounds that fate slit on his heart, replacing vengeance with duty, and filling his losses with good deeds for the folk.

Yes, life seemed to have tamed him. But, unlike Codru, Toma let it happen. He, however, couldn't. What seemed stranger to him was that the knight took his relics from Sándor, to now sacrifice his hard-earned integrity, only to defeat a creature no one, except for the Black Boyar, believed it existed.

As they rode their horses in silence through these woods, Codru's memories continued to build up in his mind, out of bits and sounds. He felt a vague, familiar anguish was bothering him as wind-resembling voices whistled far away through the groves. He forced himself to neglect them. It has been weeks since he needed to taste that rancid poison he carried in his sack, and he hoped he didn't have to just for a bit longer.

Seeing as Toma went ahead on Golden-Sun, without asking him if he heard anything, Codru contented himself to softly touch his mark, pressing his temples to soothe himself, and pulled the merchant's mantle tighter on his shoulders, as if chills rustled through his bones. He heard Shadowfire snuffle, and he knew that his horse sensed his distress, but he didn't indulge the animal.

The riders were both seeking traces of withering vegetation, rot, and mold, as these were the only signs they knew the Muma was known to leave behind. Any hints of it would have been a blessing right now, so their search would not be as senseless as it appeared. Time was not on their side either. Through the convoluted branches grazing the sky, the sun was already following into its second half of its journey.

Codru relied on the fact that this was going to be their final fight, hoping it would end his bargain with the knights in their search for the dead coming to life. He knew, however, that the chances were slim that this witch had anything to do with it. But if she did, that would at least give him the chance to leave these lands behind, knowing that Toma and his leftover Order had their quest accomplished.

Yes, he could have left any day he pleased. He had been paid for his deeds. But something compelled him to lend them a hand regardless. It wasn't guilt. It was, perhaps, a desire for fulfilment. Some would dare say something even more selfish—a craving for that redemption the dying Ravens' captain foreseen months ago.

Shadowfire suddenly stumbled on his path, ceasing its trot, as the horse before him did the same. Toma turned in his saddle toward Codru without saying anything. But he didn't have to. In front of them, a great oak seemingly rose from the ground. Out of all the trees they had passed by since they wandered through the forest, this arbour stood out as being the only one entirely barren. There were no leaves on its dark, skeletal branches. Dense shreds of spiderweb dangled from its twigs, and rank sap leaked out of its many yeasty hollows, otherwise dry and arid. The oak was lifeless, a ghostly sentinel towering over the groves. If signs of decay were what they were after, then the two men seemed to have found their very core.

They looked around, both still quiet and sitting in their saddles, trying to find the way to go from here. Codru's temples pulsated, and the sounds he so wilfully tried to repress began to turn louder. Or, even more oddly, closer. Toma noticed his muffled struggles as the dark horse began to rustle.

'What's happening?' he asked.

But Codru couldn't answer, as what he believed were voices or the hum of the wind slowly began to become more and more clear. It was dry leaves, fallen on the ground, and footsteps. His eyes scoured the shadows between the trunks and the bushes, and just before he was about to look away, his eye corner caught a branch, shaking barely visible.

Right before he was about to warn the knight, a swift zing pierced the air, and a short, thin arrow found its way to Toma's neck, making him fall off the horse. Codru turned quickly towards the bush where that pin was released from, and another one followed, landing this time in his own neck.

He instantly felt the earth beneath him, but the fall appeared like landing in a haystack. He tried to keep his eyes open, as sleep was spreading its weave around him. Turning on the ground and dragging on his elbows, he tried to move towards Toma, who was barely moving, next to the oak. The stranger reached out to his belt, only to remember that his axe was strapped to the saddle. His ears stuffed up as his vision turned at first blurry, then the sun turned brighter, infusing colour into the leaves and the trees.

A foot on his hip turned him face up, and next to him, an apparition—their attacker—stood still and tall, hair spread like the dead oak itself, with sun rays ravelling through its black mane, and eyes turned bright white on its darkened face.

'What,' Codru maundered, quivering. 'What have you done?'

The presence didn't answer.

'What are you? Are you the witch?'

He heard a soft cackle in the sinister presence's voice when it said:

'I am not a witch!' The voice was hoarse and faint, as if dirt was covering its tongue. 'She is!'

And the phantasm's arm rose like a bough, pointing towards the strange tree. Codru followed the arm's direction, turning his head in a movement that appeared to have taken him hours to make.

As his gaze settled upon the oak, its imposing shape stood stark against a dimly lit forest backdrop, all under a suddenly dark-blue sky. The bright colours he has seen smearing like rivers on his eyes began to continue their flow on the grass around the tree's trunk. He could see deep through the ground as the oak's roots turned into fire springs, running through the earth and spreading everywhere, reaching out to other roots. All this glowing, blazing sap streamed upwards to the oak's trunk, appearing to nourish the old woman trapped inside.

'Muma!' he whispered to himself without realizing it, enchanted by the vision, grunting as he dragged himself closer to it and away from the apparition. He passed by Toma, who rolled in the grass with his sullen face turned towards the sky, moving his lips as if he were gasping for air.

Raising his head, Codru's eyes met the one the Black Boyar found responsible for the pestilence. The imposing creature's arms were the branches, swaying like snakes. Its hair was the dead oak's crown itself, pulsating a crimson and glowing vein through every wrinkle. Red, admonishing eyes found their place on its dark, emaciated visage, like the ones on the other presence. When he first looked at those two glowing charcoals, an old, well-known pain stabbed his temples, and he already knew what Muma wanted. He closed his eyes, hiding his face, but the witch's wail already resounded inside his head.

'No!' he whimpered, blundering into the grass as if it were a swamp.

'Look,' the grave whispers of his captor sounded. 'Look at her!'

When he opened his tightly squeezed eyes, the blazes of Muma's stabbed them like two burning rays, and with them, a burst of visions had Codru locked it.

As night enveloped him, the distant, mournful barking of dogs pierced the air, a sound he recognized but couldn't yet place. The moonlight sketched the familiar town's rooftops, while crows rustled and flapped on weathervanes. A tumult had broken out in the market.

Gliding like a breeze above the town, Codru moved towards the chaos. Flames devoured wooden walls and wagons, and horses were still tethered and panicking. The urgent tolling of a church bell rang out as a distress signal. Screams filled the air, their echoes carrying distorted words to his ears. People were scattered in terror.

Descending closer, Codru discerned the source of their fear. Ghastly shadows, ribcages bare and eye sockets hollow, stalked them. Lethal fangs and claws emerged from every shadow, striking down the frantic townsfolk. The accursed Strigoi.

In the square, a towering pyre spat sparks skyward. Hovering nearer, Codru saw a hulking silhouette, its head rising above the others. A girl, naked and ensnared in its iron grip, screamed for her mother. The figure, face shrouded, drained life out of her neck like a dark, ravenous wolf upon a doomed deer. Her skin paled, her voice dwindled, and only tears flowed from her lifeless eyes. The predator tore at her flesh, savouring its grisly meal.

Its manic laughter echoed as it lifted her corpse, placing it atop the pyre to be consumed by flames. Before Codru could react, a large, sickle-like grin appeared beneath the creature's dark hood. And then, the wanderer felt like a hand pulled him out of the nightmare.

He rested with his eyes wide open, his face lying in the grass, and his heart beating rapidly. He suddenly knew. In that fever dream, Muma has given him answers to questions he and the knight both had and to questions neither of them ever thought to ask. When Codru blinked, the colours washed away, and the ground under him felt solid once again.

Raising his head, he noticed the sky as he left it, daylight still washing down the forest. Although the daydream felt as if it took days, it all could have taken merely moments. He looked upwards at the oak, which returned to its grim, stone-still appearance. Before he decided to stand, he looked once again to his comrade, who lay still, lost in his mind at a stone's throw besides him.

Codru turned over, and this time, his face did not meet the ethereal presence anymore; it was that of a young woman, her wild eyes pinning him to the ground from under her thin, dark eyebrows. She stood there, barefoot, wearing layers of patched hemp rags of the leaves' colour, strangely tied in some sort of tunic, crossed by only the rugged strap of a leather pouch.

Her dirty-blonde hair was coarse, dishevelled, and adorned with crooked twigs and feathers, and in her pale-white thin arm she held a short, carved dry-wood pipe that was certainly what she used to blow out those small poisonous arrows through. Her hand, wrapped around that flute, was darkened, as if it had been sunk in ink until below the elbow, black veins spreading up faintly to her shoulder.

She kept her distance, like a feral animal, and when Codru laid eyes on her, she looked intrigued. The wanderer knew in that very moment she was not aware he had come back to his senses. She had no idea that he had had his share of mushrooms and herbs since he was a boy, so they wore off quickly on him. He would not risk giving it away, though, until he was close enough to his weapons or until the woman approached him.

'Water!' he mumbled, mimicking Toma's facial grimaces. 'Water!'

The woman squinted from her place, trying to distinguish his words. But she couldn't. She was too far, so she approached carefully, with her dark fingers wrapped tightly around the blowpipe, without losing the man in her eyes. The closer she got, the lower Codru whispered his words. When the girl got merely two steps away from him, she seemed to have understood his moans. She kneeled quickly next to him, reaching out to her pouch, probably looking for her waterskin. And that moment of kindness cost her greatly.

Codru grabbed her instantly by her ankle, swiftly winding up and pushing his other arm into the girl's chest, making her completely lose the ground from under her feet and throwing her on her back. Rabid and desperate, she tried to release another dart from her flute, but before she could do that, Codru threw himself on top of her, pinning that arm to the ground and making her drop the weapon under his strong grip. She screamed like a trapped beast, pulling away and squirming with her large eyes swallowed by fear and frustration. With her free hand, she tried her last attempt to relieve herself from under the man's clutch. Her palm grasped his face, and dirty nails sunk into his skin. Codru pulled it away and pressed her arm into the grass, taking pieces of his skin with it.

She looked at him silently, as if she waited, the man breathing heavily with his eyes piercing hers. But after a short while, her silence broke, and her eyes became madder. Her face turned towards the tree, and a heart-wrenching outcry left her yellow-teethed lips:

'Mother!'

# CHAPTER IX

*Cozia's Mountains, May 1445 (6953)*

'YOUR HAND, ALIDOR!'
The boy planted his leather-bound opinci firmly against the rock, offering his arm to the Old-Man. The master grasped it tightly, anchored his foot into the hill, and plunged his withered stick into the earth, heaving himself upward. A heavy grunt escaped through his beard, and beads of sweat swiftly appeared on his pallid temples. It was clear that the man was in his twilight years.

Although he was lean and still pale like fish meat, the boy had grown, with the Old-Man's head barely reaching his chest. The Master had him let his hair grow free, too, now passing his shoulders and fluttering in the crispy air of the mountain, as a knife would have been sacrilegious to his mane.

He was no longer the helpless orphan boy. Yet he wasn't who he was supposed to be either. Not yet. However, there were words that the Old-Man repeated to him religiously every time the boy had even the smallest attempt to talk about the past.

'Do not speak of the past,' the teacher kept telling him. 'Leave it in the depths of the mountains, or else it will stay in the way of your future. To become who the gods meant them to be, one first must lose everything they are.'

The boy now had his own stick, which the man told him to carry.

He also carried his old hemp sack, where he had his foods, his waterskin, and his scroll, and around his waist—his father's lightning-stricken hatchet. Even after all these years since the trials, he was still feeling his blood running like quicksilver when he was handling it. But, in all honesty, his blood ran quicker than the normal folk anyway, as the Master had once told him.

The hour was drawing near for him to harvest the fruits of many years' trials. Yet, before he could do so, he and his teacher embarked on one final voyage—a pilgrimage to the eight ancient gates wrought by the Sleeping-Bear within the very bedrock of the mountains. The same mystical thresholds through which the ancestors once stepped forth into other realms.

'Yes, boy... Heaven's Mouths, they called them. They're dead now, cold like an empty hearth,' the Old-Man said as they went up the hill. 'But many years ago, these were doors to the Otherworld—a realm within ours, hidden to our sight.'

The boy saw it. There was a tall, arched hole in the very wall of the mountain, through which he could see the other side of the mountain. A shortcut of sorts that, as the teacher told him, right now was only used by the shepherds and their sheep to pass through.

As they approached the short, wide tunnel, the boy felt small under its imposing appearance. He couldn't explain how the ancestors could have carved this gate and, more importantly, how they unlocked it. The man was right. It was indeed barren right now. Moss and lichens grew on its humid walls, covering dull, almost entirely faded away carvings in the rock. The folk that rarely passed by under this gate now would surely mistake it for something made by nature.

'Can we pass through?' the boy asked the master, trusting to perhaps see the Otherworld and its wonders.

'One may always pass through, as all men do at the close of their journey,' the man mumbled. 'Yet, it is the return that has been forever forbidden to us. The Sleeping-Bear was close enough to the gods that he was allowed to travel freely. And, in his righteousness, he taught others how to travel back too.'

'But now,' the teacher said. 'It's all lost in time immemorial, even to our guild. We journey three times to all eight Gates of Man during our lifetime—after we pass our trials, after our apprentice passes the trials, and when we pass our final trial—to pay our homage to the old gods, earn their favour, and replenish our strength on our long life's duty as Guardians of the Tome, as Firekeepers.'

The man took a seat on a boulder, with his stick dug in the grass and his misty-grey eyes at the Gate. He then turned to the boy, who stood before it, still awestruck by its immense grandeur.

'Go gather wood now, boy,' the man said. 'And replenish our flasks; go down the hill, to the groves, and keep towards the sunrise; you'll find a pond. We shall spend our last days of the moon here, at the Gate's foot.' Then he threw his leather pouch at the boy, gasping.

The boy carried his sack and his hatchet with him as he went down the hill that they had just climbed together, through the trees. The master wouldn't allow him to leave his burden behind, even if he had to carry back the wood and the water the man tasked him with. 'The more you carry with you, the lighter you'll be when you carry none,' he would say. All for good purpose.

He heard the leaves rustling under the smooth breeze of late spring, as his ears had been trained for years to hear noises from far away. The shadows, the crowns, and the hurst held little secrets to him, as nothing compared with the depths of the mountain. The animals, although none were in sight, were talking to him too, their whispers reaching out to his mind, sensing his presence. Their memories too.

The boy felt hungry, but the hunger wasn't his. It was of some wolf, wandering somewhere far in the groves, as he sensed the wild beasts' wants as if they were his, if he let them. It wasn't as much of a pain as it was years ago, when the Master carved the eye in his skull and inked his skin. Not since he had been bitten, either. And although the voices came and went as they pleased, he began learning how to welcome them and let them go without a fight.

Walking through the weeds, scattered thorns and twigs grazing his breeches, he drained the last mouthful of water from his flask in anticipation of the nearby pond the man told him about. Tired and with his legs tense around his knees, he followed the directions to the letter, hoping he would reach it soon. The sooner he'd find it, the sooner he'd be able to gather the brushwood too. He was looking forward to some of that girdle cake the master was so skilled at making. Pulling his rusty locks away from his face, he scouted the wild trees for any fruits, but it was too early in the year. He was in luck if he'd find any berries.

As he followed downward on what looked like a trail, a fresh one at that, he began to ignore the hunger finding its rest in his belly and follow the trail cautiously. It seemed to lead somewhere, and even more so, it coincided with his own way. He stepped carefully, straining his sharp ears, and running his eyes slowly from one tree to another, checking if there was any movement. As his feet made their way through the fallen branches, his hand was loosely resting on the hatchet's hilt.

But there was no movement. The forest was quiet and still. That was until, out of nowhere, a barely noticeable murmur made its way to his ear. He stopped for a moment and raised his head. Its source wasn't far or close, but it was hidden from his aquiline gaze for now. The almost unseen trail seemingly continued toward the noise, so he kept walking it.

The closer he got to the sound, the clearer it became. It was splatter, water being thrown into itself. 'The pond!' he thought, as his feet seemed to move quicker without his consent toward the rustle. Before him lay a mound, drawing closer, its surface cloaked in damp grass and emerging from the ferns like a small hill cradled by the forest. Atop it grew a solitary tree, encircled by bushes that rose to the boy's chest.

He reached out to one of its thin branches and peered through them with his eyes focused. And he saw it. The promised eye of water, the pond, a clear oasis in the forest's clearing, at perhaps a bit more than a stone's throw away. Silky little waves were hitting the muddy shore, chockfull of moss and burdock leaves as large as shovels' heads.

He waited in silence, breathing deeply. He knew he wasn't alone. Something, or someone, must have made the water overset and splatter. And he was right. Not too long after, as the boy was still on the mound, behind the tree and its branches, he noticed the presence. At first, only the head and the shoulders. Long, brown fringes of wet hair slithering on tender, white skin, reflecting the sun rays. Then the arms and the palms, wiping the water off the pale, washed face. As it got closer to the strand, it revealed its thin, unclothed body. Then the hips and the knees, until its feet stepped on the ground, with earth crumbs and grass straws sticking to its soles.

The boy was awestruck, unable to swallow or take his eyes off the being. A woodland spirit, no doubt, he thought. He believed that he turned to stone without realizing it, charmed by its spells. But he was wrong. Out of nowhere, he heard a muffled thud behind him.

Caught up in the subtle noise, he turned and took a step back, only to hear a twig snap crisply beneath his boot.

He glanced back at the lake, aware that the noise surely alerted the being. The lake-born creature had heard him, and its gaze shifted abruptly in his direction. In a surge of fear, the boy hid himself behind the tree, his heart pounding like a drum and his mind awash with frantic thoughts. What if it discovered him? Was there a chance he could sprint back to Heaven's Mouth, where the Master awaited? Should he have stood his ground instead and defended with the axe? What was that thud about?

When he summoned the courage to look from his hideout toward the lake once more, he discovered that the being was now gone. The lake was untouched, trembling only under the wind's sweet breeze. And it was quiet. The muffled noise didn't repeat either. He exhaled in relief, thinking it had only been another daydream.

But before his worry settled and he became ready to step out and approach the lake, his ear caught another rustle, this time dangerously close behind him. He reached out to his hatchet, unable to unhook it in due time, and turning, he was stricken violently into his chest while a blunt wave cut him down like a scythe, pulling his legs from underneath him and throwing him to the ground.

He shook his head, struggling to let air back into his lungs. A shadow was cast across his body as he lay there. When he looked up, couching and rubbing his chest, the thin, dark silhouette next to him, framed by sunlight, was holding one head of the stick that cut him down, right under his chin, ready to bite again. He raised his palms, partly covering his eyes from the sun, to see clearly and partly to admit his submission.

'Stay there,' a mellow, yet aggressive voice sounded. 'I'm not afraid to strike again!'

He nodded, biting his lower lip, but he searched for his axe with the corner of his eye just in case he could reach it quickly the moment the being ceased paying attention. It didn't happen.

'Who are you,' the creature demanded. 'Why were you skulking behind the tree like a coward?'

The boy tangled his words, stammering.

'The lake,' he finally mumbled. 'I came for water.'

'Staring at water won't make you any less thirsty,' said the being. 'Were you peeking? Perhaps enjoying the view of a helpless damsel bathing all by herself? I am not so helpless I'll have you know!'

The boy came down to only shake his head, barely understanding half of what the creature spoke in her bland tongue.

'If you don't speak, by God, I'll break your teeth!'

'I don't understand! *Damsel?*'

After a short pause, the being said in a lower voice.

'A princess, a maiden of good stock! Have you been raised in a cave?'

The apprentice shrugged indignantly, staring.

'Yes!' he answered.

'A girl!' she said.

The maiden put the stick away, taking a few steps back carefully, letting the sun fall on her as the boy was now able to see.

'You haven't seen a girl before, have you?' she almost whispered in awe, watching him as if he were the apparition the boy thought she was all along. She smirked, prompting her long stick to fall to the ground. 'We are humans, just like your lot!'

Her brown hair was still wet, but this time it was falling in damp waves over a white linen shirt embroidered with red and purple threads. She was barefoot, and her thighs were covered until her knees with a form of easy breeches of the same cloth. Her milky pale cheeks bloomed, blood rushing from the fight and from her temper, and a thin, wild rose-tinted scar seamed on her left side. Her eyes, vixen-like and alluring, were framed by dark, lustrous eyelashes, glistening further by a pair of beautifully arched brows. As she dressed up hastily, she was not a princess, yet the boy was still stunned by her beauty.

Under her vigilant watch, he dared to rise from the ground without taking his eyes from her. He could now reach for his axe, but he didn't. They looked at each other, wondering about each other's appearance. He saw her looking at his ink seal, and her eyebrows entwined.

'You have a mark, too!' she said, pointing at it, then touching her own face softly.

'Do you have a name?' she asked.

The boy wasn't sure.

'Uncheaş calls me Alidor.'

'That's an odd name,' she remarked. 'An emperor's name!'

'Names do not matter, Master says. They keep you tied where you don't belong.'

The girl chuckled.

'What does that mean?'

'He said that once you name something, you imprison it. You should let things be nameless and free.'

'Where did your master teach you that? In the womanless cave?'

The boy didn't answer. Instead, his eyes widened as another thud reached his ears. Closer than before. He saw the bushes behind the maiden shaking. Then, out of their shadows, another creature walked out slowly. A beast he only ever seen two or three times in all his years at the mountain. A dire forest lynx. Red, black-spotted fur covered its massive appearance, while a grey mane adorned its back and shoulders like a thick sheet of ashen snow. A sapphire gaze pierced him, then it turned toward the girl.

Slowly, the boy raised his finger to his lips, signalling the girl to be quiet and not startle the beast. He tried to grab his axe. The maiden frowned, and turning toward the animal, she raised her arm in a welcoming gesture. The lynx approached her hand and pushed its big head into her fingers, a soft rumbling like a distant thunder smouldering in its chest while the girl smoothed its mane. But the apprentice pulled out his axe regardless as the animal encircled her legs in a protective shield, its deep blue eyes set on the intruder.

'This is *Bruma*,' the girl said. 'She must have sensed you peeking from the bushes!'

The boy relaxed his shoulders. Bruma was a wild beast, a solitary one at that, as the teacher once said. And like all wild beasts, they wouldn't attach to people. Yet somehow, it seemed attached to the girl.

'Everything is well, love,' she spoke to the animal, trying to settle it and not let it throw itself at the apprentice. 'He's just a foolish boy! Nothing me and my stick cannot handle!'

A quick migraine rustled his head, vanishing almost instantly as his eyes met the beast's. He went into the deep woods for a few moments, feeling a strong lath around his foot. Then a girl came out of nowhere and untied him. He now felt he owed her his life.

'You saved her from a trap!' he spoke, seemingly coming to his senses and putting the axe away.

The girl turned to him, perplexed, while Bruma seemed to have calmed down, prompting itself at the girl's feet with its pale-grey face unwavering toward the boy.

'How did you know that?' she asked.

'The lynx told me.'

'Do you speak the beast's tongue?' she asked.

'I can only understand it,' he replied. 'And it's them speaking to me; I merely listen.'

He noticed a serene smile in the corner of her lips.

'It appears it's not only the skin marks we share,' she said. 'I can't understand them, but they understand me. I can command them!'

They stood there in silence for moments that seemed to have lasted ages, looking into each other's eyes as if they tried to speak in the beast's tongue to one another. They were too similar and yet too different; in ways they had no clue yet. Like the sun and the moon.

The more they stared at each other quietly, the more they understood. The apprentice only now began to realize that since her eyes pierced his, the wolfish hunger had diminished. The leaves rustling in the nearby trees did not reach him anymore. It was a warmth rushing through his veins he had never sensed before, almost nauseating, making him forget he needed air.

She dared to walk closer to him, telling him through her eyes that she was sensing it too.

'I am Ileana,' she said softly. 'Well have our paths crossed, Alidor!'

\*\*\*

*Cozia's Groves, August 1459 (6967)*

When his axe first struck, a roar sounded in the distance, as if the forest itself were lamenting under the slash. The cries were even more heartbreaking as the feral girl begged for him to end it. But he did not. The black oil gurgled out of the tree trunk's cuts like an open wound.

'Murderers!' the girl screamed; her hands entangled in her already tattered hair.

Codru indeed felt a hint of empathy for her. But, despite this, dark sap continued to splatter across his face as he did not stop his relentless chopping, striving to block out the approaching tempest, the mournful cries of the groves, and the girl's curses flung at him and the knight. His grip tightened on the axe's marked handle, his arm muscles rigid as rock, while his mind drifted almost numbly to the haunting scenes he had beheld just hours earlier.

As soon as he had restrained the savage woman, Toma came to his aid, still dazed from the vanishing poison.

'It's the Boyar,' the wanderer told him, fighting off the girl's dark talons as she was clawing at him. 'It was the Boyar all along.'

Once they tied her up to a tree, Codru recollected himself, and taking a few steps away from the imprisoned woman, he told the knight about all the visions he had while the tree talked to him and what he made of them. Completely overlooking the fact that the man told him he had been talking to a dead oak, Toma simply agreed with Codru's conclusions.

'So, the tree is the witch then,' he said, drifting in his own thoughts or maybe even remembering glimpses of his own daydreams. 'And you say the Boyar is the one raising the dead. The cause of all the nightmare the Order spent years trying to find its cradle.'

Codru still tried to make sense of all he had seen, as he wasn't entirely sure if he was right. However, something inside him told him he was. Perhaps the remnants of serpent venom that his veins tasted long ago were a giver of intuition and self-preservation.

The knight needed time to come to his senses still, and the news he had received from his comrade only made it more gruelling. But the twilight was approaching. There were unanswered questions he and the crimson-haired man needed answers to before they decided what was to be done. Or how. Before he could make up his mind, Codru had already approached the wildling woman who had been disarmed by her poisonous flute and tied to the tree.

'Who are you?' he asked her bluntly as he touched his face, tracing the wet, burning scratches oozing on his cheek.

The girl ceased squirming for a few moments, pulling away from her captor and watching him untrustingly with her dark eyes. At first, she didn't say anything, continuing to stare at him. After he repeated his question, coming closer and taking a knee in the grass, she gave in, responding but completely disregarding his curiosity. She looked at him, her thoughts clearly elsewhere.

'Why aren't you dead?' she asked bluntly.

Codru was taken aback by her out of the ordinary question, but if he picked up something from his fellow traveller during these few moons they have been on the road, it was that he could get answers easier if he haggled. As such, he humoured the wild girl.

'I don't know,' he replied, his head shaking slightly. 'I've wondered that myself for years.'

Toma approached the two, but he kept a fair distance as he understood he was not needed. The blonde, savage woman, however, wasn't satisfied with his answer.

'You should have been dead! They always die!'

'Who dies?'

'Everyone I touch.'

Codru looked at the thin, dark arms from the elbow down to her fingers. It wasn't ink, nor was it dirt. It was an illness that changed her skin colour. A disease, as rotten as the grove's core or as the town. A curse that seemed to spread up on her arms like poison veins, steadily aiming to her shoulders.

The blood he had inherited appeared to have kept him alive and shielded him from her death-giving touch. Things suddenly began to make more and more sense.

'It was you who spread the illness through town, was it not? Killing the animals...?'

The girl didn't say anything, but he could see her sombre eyes turn glassy.

'Why?'

She turned her face toward the dead oak.

'I did it for Muma!' she said.

When the girl said those words, the wind blew through the fallen leaves scattered around the trees. Without taking her eyes away, the girl continued without being asked, in a more endearing voice.

'She's hurting. The Dark-Man came and killed her daughter. He drank her blood and ate her flesh.'

'She was to be a midwife, Mother. She sometimes cast spells and prophecies to help sick babies or to see their fates. But when her daughter was murdered, she ran here to the forest and swore revenge. God was merciful and turned her into a tree to release her from pain and anger.'

'Her daughter,' Codru thought to himself. That's who the maiden in his vision was. If there was any truth to this woman's words, she must have had visions too. 'Turned to a tree...' The oak, the Forest's mother, Muma, must have spoken to her as well.

Months ago, he would have ended the talk here. Delusions of a sick, wild maiden, no doubt, he would have taken then. However, during the past few months, he has seen a few things that not only made him think twice before calling them delirious but also opened the door to other, older memories that, for a long time, he had thought of as fever dreams of a troubled childhood.

'She spoke to you,' he said in a lower voice. 'The tree.'

The feral girl turned to him and spoke in a tone matching his.

'She saved me.' Then she carried on.

'When I was a child, bad things were always happening around me. The more I grew up, the worse the things that happened were.'

'At first, it was only the magpies and the sparrowhawks preying on our birds while out. Then the rats and polecats wreaked havoc on the coops at night. After that, it was the sheep getting sick and dying. Then the cows and horses followed. My parents blamed me for having the evil-eye. They took me to the village's enchantress, who said I was a *Neînțărcată*. A *Piază-Rea*. She put spells on me. Until one day, my father fell ill too. So, they sent me away to the monastery before I would kill them.'

She paused, tears leaking down her face.

'The nuns couldn't lift the spreading curse,' she said. 'Instead, they wrapped my hands and my arms in holy water-soaked cloth and locked me in a small room in the cellar. Until the skete caught fire. And when it did, I finally ran away on my own, far from all of them, to this forest.'

'You've met Muma,' Codru said.

'I was the child she lost; she was the parent I needed!' the young woman added. 'She taught me how to survive in the forest. She protected me. She was the only one I could touch without them turning to dust.'

Then she looked at him sceptically, saying:

'Until you!'

'Why are you spreading this cursed illness?' he finally asked.

'For everything she had done for me, Muma had only one thing to ask in return. To avenge her. She had whispered to me to kill the Dark-Man... and everyone who followed him.'

The knight, who had been quiet until that moment, flared up.

'That is madness!' he said, coming closer as the wildling turned smaller, cornered at the foot of the tree she was tied up to.

'So much death,' his eyes turned fierce. 'Children!'

Codru sensed, for the first time since he had met the Raven, that he ought to be the grounded one. He understood the man's own grief and dormant rage, and he understood if he didn't stand up, coming in between him and the woman, things might have turned badly for her.

'It wasn't her fault,' he said, raising his hands in front of the wrathful knight, ready to push him back if he decided to pass. 'You surely can see that!'

Codru knew what it meant to be an orphan. He also knew how easy it was for a child's mind to be bent by someone they looked up to as their protector. The girl was sick. By the look of her arms, she was going to soon be in the ground herself. She grew up in the woods, far from other people, raised by a spirit-witch who was good at twisting minds. He knew what he had to do.

'We'll cut the oak down!' he told the knight, hoping that would settle Toma's storm. And it did.

He struck again. The tree crackled, forcefully pushed by the knight. And so, the last putrid vines keeping it to the ground snapped, letting the Forest's Mother fall with a roar, hitting the ground with a sound resembling a loud and bewailing moan. Falling to his knees, Codru let his father's hatchet, now thick with dark puss, fall into the grass.

The woman's screams ceased too, as the evening settled. Whipping off the face of the filthy sap with his sleeves, he turned to her, expecting to see her tamed by the mourning of her dead mother. However, under the young flames of the fire that Toma was starting near her, he noticed her eyes. They were still the same wild, dark eyes he first saw, but now they looked as if a mist had been lifted from her eyelashes. A fog that, up until the oak's demise, weighted on her mind.

She looked at him too. Even from the distance between them, the setting night, and his face covered in Muma's blood, he could not see hatred on her face. He could only see gratitude and hope.

\*\*\*

'It's Sunday. The evil flew to its nest,' the old woman said ominously. 'If indeed you are looking for it, that is where you'll find it.'

She walked slowly down a tight, muddy alley as the relentless drizzle creeped through the two men's mantles as they followed her. They both walked by their horses pensively, as each of them had their own fears and worries to battle with ahead of the upcoming encounter.

For the knight, finally facing not only the evil but perhaps the roots that stood at the core of his Order's creed, was a bite too great to swallow. He fought the thought of losing his life purpose, if his God had even planned for him to leave him standing once they faced the Black Boyar, the Necromancer.

Codru was righteously worried. If what Muma had told him before he cut her down was true, the foe they were now going to pursue was nothing he had ever thought he'd have to fight. This was neither a Demon nor a Paraleu. He wasn't a mindless Strigoi, answering an unheard call of the tenebrae. He was the tenebrae itself calling them. Daniil was right when he told him that the Greuthung had no chance of victory on his own. The wanderer almost believed they barely had a chance together.

On Shadowfire rode the wildling girl as Codru pulled the animal's bridle, following quietly in the old, blind woman's footsteps. She had been on the dark horse's back since they left the groves until they met once more the same blind woman, hiding from Death.

The wild woman, nurtured by the forest itself, bore the name Ilinca. It was the name her parents gave her before banishing her. She had told Codru her name when the man untied her from the tree and released her from Muma's spell. She not only followed them willingly out of the forest, but she almost begged them to take her with them, much to Toma's discontent.

'With or without the witch's poisonous whispers, there's a curse upon her! We can't take her with us into the town's heart.' He was right. It was imprudent. But Codru had something the knight didn't. Sharp, long-tempered instincts. She wasn't going to ever harm an innocent life again. He knew it.

He glanced at Ilinca as the old woman struggled to open the decaying structure she considered the gate, leading to her cottage's courtyard, with Toma lending a hand. And Ilinca met his eyes too. He reached out to her waist and helped her climb down the horse. Her dark-skinned hands intentionally caught his before he pulled them away as if something burned him, avoiding looking at her again.

'I would invite you in, my love,' the blind woman told them as a herd of cats came out of the open yard, swirling around their mistress's crooked legs. 'But I'm sure your paths have already been set to Argeș, and you don't want to lose daylight! I wonder what that worry feels like.'

She measured the men for a short while with her pale, cloudy eye sockets. Codru didn't say anything, and Toma was pleased to only mumble a grave, unnecessary gratitude for the invitation.

'Very well, then,' the woman said. 'The girl can stay here! God knows I'm in need of a diligent young lady to help around the house.'

'Your welcome at the town's edge was a godsend, auntie,' Toma said. Let the wagon we left at the Boyar's stable be the reward for your kindness. 'Here!'

He reached under his merchant's cloak and then handed the old woman a piece of scroll—the wares' deed.

'Give these to the guards there, and my apologies for not bringing them to you!'

'Save your worries for that fight, love,' she said. 'I wouldn't have survived this long if I didn't know how to. God bless your heart!'

Then she turned to Ilinca:

'Come, girl! There's work to be done!'

The wanderer agreed quietly, bending his forehead. It wasn't what the feral woman had foreseen, nor was it what she wished. Her wish was not even to follow the men. It was to follow Codru. The one who defended her against Toma's rage and unbound her from the witch's whispers. The only one in this whole wide world she was able to feel with her skin. She wanted to be close to him. She suddenly looked hopeless in each of their faces. She came closer to the wanderer, trembling timidly.

'Please, don't do this,' she whined. 'Don't leave me here!'

'It's for your own sake!' Toma said sternly while mounting Golden-Sun. She ignored him, but he then continued:

'If it were after me, I would have taken you to Härmeschtat. I know a physician there who might have taken an interest in your illness.'

Her eyes turned back to Codru, softly shaking her dirty-blonde locks, but she was unable to give any more voice to her desires.

'He is right,' he told her. 'We are lucky enough that this woman offered her roof. There's no place for you where we are going.'

'I could help you! I've hunted this monster long before you came along!'

She came closer and reached out for his hands once more.

'Please!' she said.

For the second time, Codru withdrew his hands from hers and firmly grasped her shoulders, giving her a slight shake. 'I am not your protector,' he hissed. 'You won't find what you seek here. This is what's best for you!' Then he turned to Shadowfire, mounting. Without looking back, he just kicked the horse and left the alley on his own, with Toma having to catch up to him.

By the time it took him to glance back, far away from the old woman's cottage, neither the girl nor her new caregiver were in the alley anymore.

***

The drizzle whipped his face violently as he and the knight rode towards the west, to Argeş. It was there that the Boyar had built the church to earn God's favour. Or so he had said. It appeared, however, that it was more than that. Not only that, the edifice seemed to now be the accursed noble's hideout, but it was also a place the knight himself heard strange stories about.

'It's being said that the masons who rose the church all died, buried into its walls,' Toma said from under his hood, riding besides Codru. 'I thought they were only stories, but now I tend to find them truthful.'

Codru chose to ignore his comrade's histories. It did not matter. He had already seen what they had to face, and if the Raven knew too, he wouldn't have been in the mood for reeling legends. Now, more than ever, he would rather count on Toma's past being true.

'That mace you hold so dear might come in handy today.'

Toma stopped chattering and turned as grim as the clouds gathering on the horizon.

'I have faith in God, that should be enough,' he said. 'Him and Balmut,' he ended while tapping on his great sword's hilt.

'That might not be enough this time. Faith never gets you far enough on its own. Suspicion can sometimes get you further,' Codru muttered.

'Perhaps,' Toma said. 'However, I have other plans with the Greuthungi steel.'

In the distance, Codru could see the shape of the city clearing out. Home to the Princely Court of Wallachian Voivodes up until Vlad, its history dates back perhaps to the first settlers on these lands. He could see the ruins of a church up on the hill, covered in scaffolding and fog.

'The Lady's Church!' he heard the knight saying, his eyes caught by the same ghostly brick walls.

'Lady Clara brought here Hungarian priests to convert the Wallachians to Catholicism. However, her Orthodox son, the Voivode, being at war with them, set his bombards on it and almost wrecked it. He then sent her away north, over the mountains in a bulls-pulled wagon, but she never made it to her destination. She drowned in the river where the wagon fell on the way.'

The closer their horses got, the clearer their own destination became. The white walls of a newer church towered over the landscape, like an ivory sculpture under the heavy ashen sky. Codru knew that was where the Boyar seemed to have gone to attend Sunday's ceremony. Whatever that creature thought a Sunday ceremony was. It appeared that Argeș was never meant to be a city, as there were no walls to defend it. As if they were unnecessary. It was a quiet and rather gloomy halidom, inhabited by devout people whose appearance closely resembled those in Dlăgopole.

Even if the brooding air of doom was purposefully hidden beneath a veil of grandiose Byzantine ethos, like the one Codru had seen years ago in Edirne, it still slipped through its ornamented cracks. Men and women kept their humble composure, looking away from the travellers, as the four-towered White Church rose behind them like a silent taskmaster dressed in gold and bones.

'We're here!' he heard the Raven sigh as he tried to appease his nerves. They dismounted and led their steeds to a fountain near the monastery's entrance, beautifully adorned and sheltered under a roof supported by pillars. A baptistery of sorts. They walked slowly through the fine rain, clashing against their hoods, as their hands were near their belts and their eyes were scouting vigilantly through the area, expecting guards bearing that rusty chainmail. But none were in sight. As such, they agreed by looking at each other to hitch their horses there, under the baptistery's roof.

The knight drew his sword as he led the way on the church's marble stairs to the cherry-wood tinted door, carved with biblical deities. It was only when Toma pulled the door open, with its muffled creak, that Codru reached out to his scimitar, drawing it as well with a cold slicing sound.

The same heaviness floating in the air they encountered at the Boyar's mansion hit their nostrils once again. The incense that Daniil burned when dragging the Demon out of the Strigoi was casting its sweet, smothering fumes.

The church was a mausoleum-like grand piece of jewellery. A golden bird house without any visible windows in sight. Even at a glance, anyone crossing its threshold would have felt crushed under its tall dome, depicting Christ. The ceiling was supported by thick, brown pillars, densely painted with golden and red symbols. The walls were carved with stern looking saints and angels. It was all work that must have taken years to accomplish. The warm light of the numerous candles and chandeliers lit up all corners, making the monastery shine sinisterly like the tomb of a conceited king.

'There you are!' the grave, sombre voice resounded. Codru recognized it. It was the Boyar's.

'The Salman and the Greuthung arrived,' he slithered his words in a low tone that somehow reached clearly to the newcomers' ears.

Then their gaze shifted forward, across the expansive room, towards the iconostasis. There, they saw the man kneeling with his back to them. He was clad in the same dark velvet robe, edged with black fur that encircled his shoulders like a luxurious mane, intertwining almost seamlessly with his greasy, coarse, long hair that spread over his slightly crooked back.

'Did you bring me the witch's head?' his voice slashed the smoky air.

'We did not,' Toma said. 'Turn around!'

The man turned his face quietly, but his silence was threatening.

'We had an agreement, and you did not respect it.'

The men stopped on their walk beneath the first ceiling arch, between two of the columns. Their hands were on their hilts, but the swords were aimed at the floor.

'The cursed mother you sent us hunting has been dealt with,' Codru said forthrightly.

He heard the Boyar hum as he rose from the floor.

'Ah,' he exclaimed. 'The Mother, he says. That can only mean she has spoken to you.'

He half-turned around in his circle, looking at the lefegii from beneath his tall, pale forehead.

'I should have known, Salman, that it would come to this! But I had hoped you strayed enough from your sacred vows to understand the Earth's tongue.'

He then let his head fall back with his eyes closed as his cheekbones cast shadows on his sullen face. He smirked.

'Have you then come to kill me, then? Is that why you're here?'

'Who are you,' the Raven cut him off. 'What are you?'

The same threatening silence followed Toma's question.

'I've had more names than you have hair on your head, child,' the nobleman answered. 'And what I am is a servant of Death.'

The Boyar left his place, walking tardily closer to the iconostasis. He reached out to one of the candle holders, as tall and supple as he was. He blew in the candles and grabbed the candle holder. Once he did that, he twisted its top half, and pulling it up revealed a long, sharp blade crafted in its core. A spear.

His grin turned toward the two men.

'Although I have been called many names, I was always fond of one of my oldest—Toq-Tämir. Much like this beautiful spear.'

Toma prompted Balmut in front of his chest.

'While my saintly, fearful brothers still played with bronze, I dared to forge iron.'

Codru's mind went on to his oldest memories under the mountain. The voices and the Fire-Knights. It couldn't have been possible. And a sudden migraine flooded his skull. 'Yes,' he heard the haunting Boyar's voice.

'So much potential there,' the Necromancer said this time out loud, as the headache vanished as well. 'Such a pity you'll be one with the church after today.'

He raised the spear in his long-fingered hands and rippled the floating haze with it as he passed it through the air.

'Why did you raise the dead,' Toma asked. 'You've brought a plague to these lands that can only end with you!'

The Dark-Man laughed, and his hoarse voice raised the hair on both their necks. Then, as sudden as the wind, leaving traces of dark smoke breaking out of his robe, he barked violently:

'These lands were already plagued when I first arrived, child. There was nothing here but frozen woodland and frightened creatures, such as yourselves, suffering in the dark. They turned to me to end their cursed existence. They prayed to me. They idolized me. I brought them fire. I led them in wars. Chieftains, kings, and Voivodes united, rose and fell under my command. '

Then, after a short pause, he added:

'Do not dare speak to me about these lands. I've known them since before your ancestors were born. My bloodline is at their very helm!'

He inhaled deeply.

'I bow to your valour, children,' he then said with scornful reverence, with the same large smile revealing his now yellowed fangs. 'But you should have listened to Muma's warning and not come after me!'

'I have sworn an oath to root out the poisonous vines that spread on these grounds,' said the knight. 'I intend to honour it, God willing!'

'You're facing a god now, Greuthung! And that is not my will!'

His last words reverberated through the church, hitting the embellished columns and walls. In the middle of the room, the Necromancer raised his iron spear with one hand and spat an incantation in the ancient speech. Although Codru recognized the Earth's whispers, the way the words rolled out of Toq-Tämir's tongue imbued them with venom, making them turn into a blood-chilling curse.

The floor under their feet shook, plaster shards snowed from the painted dome, and thin cracks began spreading on one of the side walls of the precious Boyar's monastery. As his words continued to resound, the cracks stretched, revealing the grout and the bricks. And then, a hand. A fleshless branch clawing at the air.

Another darkened, mummified arm emerged from the opposite wall, pushing the bricks out unwieldy. Both their ghostly, sullen heads loomed soon after. Their eyeless sockets, their fangs, and their silky, patchy whitened hair hooked to their burst off temples. Two Strigoi answered the call of their taskmaster.

'Come out, my obedient lovebirds,' the Necromancer called them. 'My precious Master Mason and his sweet, innocent wife!'

The Strigoi left their tombs, stepping on the floor, and growled as they walked, spellbound, towards the Boyar. Codru clenched his teeth and twisted both his hands on the scimitar. He knew they had to first face the Dark-Man's lieges before they even had a chance to fight him.

When the dull earthquake ceased and the Necromancer's voice dispersed, the two Strigoi now standing between the men and the Boyar turned their bony, terrifying faces at them. Their cheeks were withered and dusty, their mouths open, and they were crawling with spiders running out. It was only when the Dark-Man's spear touched the floor again that the two Strigoi ran like rabid dogs stung by horseflies, throwing themselves at Codru and Toma.

The dead woman aimed at Codru's throat, with her overgrown,

infected fingernails slashing the air. She screeched, missing her target. Codru dodged and swang his spade, its blade reflecting the warm light and missing as well. He could only glance to his side as Toma was fighting her pair, before the dead woman jumped him once more, relentlessly. His boot pushed into her chest, releasing a crack that didn't harm her.

The wanderer's scimitar roared once again, aiming at her throat. She was quick, and her mouth caught his swinging arm, plunging her filthy teeth into his sleeve. He suddenly dropped the sword and, with a twist, released his mantle, stepping to his side and violently covering her head in it, binding it around her fleshless neck.

Behind her, he shoved his shoulder into her back, crushing her between him and the column. Codru then pulled back the edges of his cloak surrounding her trapped skull and threw her to the floor. Without another thought, quivering, his foot dropped on her skull and crashed it under its weight, as one would crush a bug, leaving behind only the echoes of her last laments.

He jumped to grab his dropped sword and turn to Toma's aid, but before he could reach him, the knight's heavy spade clashed with the column, releasing sparks, and severing the Master Mason's head from his body, which dropped with an almost cluttering thud. His grimace turned to terror when his eyes met the Necromancer.

'You believe you can defeat me? How dare you?' the Boyar whirled like a dark cloud thrusting upon the knight.

Toma deflected with his sword the iron spear springing out of the grim fog. Codru ran behind it, slashing the creature's back. But his scimitar passed through him as if he were a phantasm. The Boyar turned, only his pallid face looming from the dark wave, risen high above the two men. His spear stricken like a lightning bolt, which clashed with the wanderer's blade. His hand rose from the smoke, and its back snapped across Codru's face, throwing him on his back, away from the vicious man relentlessly appearing and disappearing around the Raven, cornering him.

Codru lost his sword, and the Boyar's hit made blood burst out of his lips. The heavy blow made him lose his clarity, and waves of ache rushed through his head once again.

'Codru!' Toma yelled, a muffled gurgle joining his shout.

He turned, shaking his head, while picking himself off the floor. The Dark-Man's spear found room between the knight's ribs.

'You robbed me of my champion, Greuthung!' the Boyar barked

between his teeth as his form settled down, turning material next to the agonizing knight. He pulled his iron from Toma's side. The man gasped, coughing a thread of thick blood on his chin.

'I shall make of you my new champion,' the nobleman said, and with a sudden strike, he slashed the back of the knight's thigh, bringing him to his knees.

The Necromancer came closer to the dying man and wrapped his free hand around his throat, lifting the knight off the floor as if he were nothing and prompting him against the pillar. He clashed the spear's lower side into the floor and its head against the knight's chest.

Fighting off his violent, head-splitting pain, Codru understood that would be the end of his comrade. His hand reached to his waist, and he pulled his axe. He screamed as he released it from his arm with all his might, as if his shout would make it fly swifter.

It was only moments before the Necromancer's would impale the knight that the axe plunged into his crooked back.

The Boyar gasped, his eyes and mouth wide open, dropping the spear and casting the knight against the side wall. He turned to Codru. His long, skeletal arms vainly tried reaching for the red-haired man's weapon, deeply buried in his spine.

'It cannot be...' he quivered, his voice shaking and his exophthalmic eyes bloodshot. 'I am an eternal...'

Codru pulled away from the stumbling apparition, dragging himself over the floor in silence. Watching as the Boyar roared with his face toward the dome that cracked under his draconian yowl.

'What have you done?' he bellowed, falling to his knees. 'You thought I brought the wrath!'

'I was fighting it!'

Then a long-lasting scream abandoned his throat as the church shook down to its foundation. Cracks spread like venom across the walls and across the Boyar's face, darkness pouring out from his insides and from his mouth like a misty waterfall.

And then the same tenebrosity that carried him through the air while fighting swallowed him in its thundering embrace, crushing him to dust, sending a powerful shockwave across the whole room, and leaving the hatchet fall to the floor with a mournful tang.

## CHAPTER X

*Cozia's Mountain, May 1445 (6953)*

H E READ THE SKY AS ONE READS A MAP-riddled tome. All the candles lit in its immensity could be traced back to the golden book, resting quietly and wide open in the Chamber. All the lights had names because, unlike people, they were not as free as they appeared. They were chained to the eternal canopy. But they were so many and so old that only the Ancients could have remembered all their names.

'See there, that is the Wolf,' he said, pointing his finger at the night sky.

'It does not look like a wolf,' Ileana observed, frowning.

'No...' he sighed. 'Perhaps it does not. And those seven bright stars over there,' he continued, 'make up the Bear.'

'I can only see a wagon as one of my father's,' she said, shaking her head. 'Why did it only have to be seven?'

The boy tried to remember his lessons.

'Because seven is lucky.'

Her eyes lit up as if a great thought loomed in her mind.

'We need all the luck we can get. That should be our number! It is decided!'

'I would so love to know the Wolf and the Bear's stories,' she then said, resting her head and back against the moss-covered tree trunk behind her and turning her eyes back at the abysmal vastness.

'I don't know them,' the boy sighed hopelessly. He wished he did. 'But I can tell you one of my teacher's stories about great men turning into beasts.'

'Oh, please, tell me!'

He rested his back right next to her, shoulder to shoulder, feeling the chilling, early summer night breeze. His heart was shaking at the thought of the master looking for him. Waiting for him. But it only took him a glance at her pale face, washed in the moonlight, for those worries to vanish.

'The people who lived here many years ago, sons and daughters, would wear beast skins in battle. Some of them, the chosen few, had been given in childhood the name of a beast too, and it was their duty to live like that beast, in exile. If they bore a wolf name, they would live in packs in the forests. If they bore a bear's, they lived alone in the mountain caves. Many perished.'

The girl turned to him with a hint of realization.

'So, they were cursed.'

He paused, lost in thought, recalling the master's teachings.

'Sometimes, what appears as a curse is merely a shrouded blessing!' he repeated, as if they weren't even his words.

She didn't reply. So, he continued his story:

'Their hardship was needed for the good of many. When it was war, a few of the Beast-Men had the gift of becoming the animals they were destined to be. The animal's skin, which they were wearing on the battlefield, would become their own. They would become powerful and would obliterate the enemies, thus protecting their lands and their people.'

Ileana sat up, turning to him, as frustration could be easily seen looming on her face.

'And where are they now when our people need them so? My father always talks about the Osman's marauders crossing our southern river, plundering villages, scorching the earth, and taking children away.'

The boy shrugged. He didn't know. What he did know was that one winter night, years ago, he heard a wolf trapped in an iron claw rising from the forest grounds. He remembered the woman's cabin, where they found shelter not too long after. He remembered her many sons, the wounded boy, and the master cutting his crushed leg. And even after crippling her boy, his mother thanked and blessed his teacher, promising both help in the darkest days, if days like those would ever come.

He closed his eyes, and he could feel the stabbing warmth of the Old-Man's voice in his skull, trying to break through his thoughts. He was furious.

'*Per'skrumb!*' he whined.

Seeing him grab his head suddenly, the girl turned quiet, forgetting to ramble about the Akinji, and dared to rest her hand on his hands that were covering his temples. As soon as her warm hands touched his forehead, the stabbing murmurs lifted, like dark storm clouds pierced by the life-giving spears of sunlight.

He suddenly felt as if she was the cure for the lifetime of pain he had so far endured. His heart was shaking in joy at the thought of all that suffering being gone. She sensed it and his shivers and tried to retract her hand; afraid she was the cause. But when she did, he brought her hand back, keeping it tight between his own and his face, as if her warm skin were a poultice of pure, blessed water.

When he finally opened his eyes, he sensed the Old-Man leaving him to his fate. He turned toward her, surprised, his mouth unable to voice his gratitude. But his eyes did. And she understood, letting a suave smile arch her lips.

'I may not know as much as you about the stars, Alidor,' she said, gazing at the sky as the lights were reflecting in her dark eyes. 'But I believe that maybe fate brought them together to form these sky maps because they only have meaning if they are together. Alone, they're just flickering lights. Together, they're a wolf or a bear.'

The same warmth the boy felt seeing her at the lake was rushing through him once more.

'What if we are the same?' she asked.

'How so?'

'What if fate brought us together for the same reason? What if, by ourselves, we're no different than lights wandering without a destination on the sky map? What if we only mean something if we are together?'

He didn't reply. He didn't know what he could say either.

'They would name us Lynx! Bruma wouldn't mind,' she giggled.

Alidor only returned to Heaven's Mouth in the early morning after spending what seemed like a short night by the lake with Ileana. She told him stories about the people, the town, her home, and her father. He, in return, would reel in legends of the past, read the sky, and hear the chirping of the night birds, telling her what they said.

When he arrived, the master was meditating, kneeling silently under the wide arch of stone where they had camped. As the sun was yet to rise, anaemic coals were still lisping in the sparing embers, and broth was steaming in a cast iron bowl set on top.

'I can hear it in the way you tread upon the grass, *per'skrumb*,' the man muttered, still on his knees, without turning. 'The shame!'

The boy halted behind the teacher, dropping his knapsack. His eyes fell to the ground.

'I have not squandered my last years on this earth for nothing!' the man's voice grew heated with anger.

Suddenly, he asked as he struggled to stand, 'What have you told her?' The boy moved to help him, but the man shrugged off his arm. Turning, a tempest brewed in his cloudy eyes, beneath furrowed brows.

'Just the stories, teacher, nothing more...' the boy insisted.

'You have met this maiden for days, in secrecy, disregarding the vows you have taken,' he jawed. 'Time you were ought to spend here, paying your respects to the ancients, earning their blessing!'

'Why?' he muttered angrily.

The boy grinded his teeth.

'She takes the pain away,' he said. 'She has this gift...'

The master wallowed as he dragged himself closer to the boy, his figure sour, his stick squeezed too hard in his withered fingers.

'The pain is there for a reason, boy! It always has been,' he exhaled. 'Pain is nothing but a storm. Storms don't just appear on serene days, nor should you run from them like cowards. Welcome their rain and thunder; turn them into rich crops. Because nothing grows on a fine day; without the clouds, there's only drought.'

He continued:

'Do not forget that pain is your sister. Nor what you were born and raised to do. And above all, do not stray from the laws. Do not fail me now, young one. Not when you have become the only vessel, I laid all my eggs in. Not when my time for the Otherworld is near!'

The boy let his chin fall into his chest.

'Forgive me, Uncheaș!' he said.

The Old-Man hummed, turning away his disappointed figure, and then walked towards his rug. He grunted as he laid down on it and set his stick beside him.

'Don't ask for forgiveness; make it so you won't ever need to,' he sighed as he closed his eyes.

'There's some broth and some girdle cake left in the pot. Eat. Sleep. Tomorrow is the first day of a new moon. We will resume our journey, and gods willing, you shall never see that girl ever again.'

\*\*\*

*Braylan, September 1459 (6967)*

If there was anything useful, he believed he had learned in his early years from the one who had raised him and was still dependent on, it was his healing methods. He could heal as easily as he could kill. Much like the poisonous weeds he was so accustomed to. It had not always been that he had to use a dagger or his scimitar to earn his gold; sometimes a few drops of wolfsbane or hemlock were far more convenient and quicker.

However, it was due to this knowledge alone that Toma was now riding next to him. The journey to Braylan, the greatest port in all of Wallachia, had not been easy, and it took double the amount of time it should have.

Wounded and stabbed in his side right after their fight, the Raven had almost bled to death. After killing the Boyar, the thought of putting the man out of his misery did cross Codru's mind too. However, he brought his saddlebags inside the church, and instead of letting nature take its course, he decided that the knight was not yet done with this world.

He first patched him up the best he knew how. He had to cut through his gambeson and breeches using Toma's own daggers. He poured whatever water he had left in the flask over his wounds, then sealed them with leaves of yarrow and St. John's wort to end the bleeding. He had wrapped his leg and torso with cloth from his own shirt.

During those two nights they spent in that sinister monastery, no one bothered to come and ask of the Boyar or to pray. Codru could only believe people were quietly hopeful their nightmare had ended. And not being forced out of this shelter was something that the wanderer appreciated. Having to watch over the knight through his delirious recovery was enough of a headache. 'Luna...' he kept hearing him mumble through his wrinkled lips. 'Luna. My little sun.'

When the knight's pain and fever became frightening, Codru had to force him to swallow some of the same dark-brown poison he had been taking for years himself, as if it were his air. By the time the knight's fever broke, his sweats were fading, and the last crumbs of the poppy-mud were gone too. While the horses had rummaged through the grass growing in front of the church, the wanderer had to go out to the fountain and replenish his flask several times to keep the man out of thirst. He had to satisfy his own hunger with the communion bread he pillaged from the church.

When Toma finally opened his eyes on the third day, Codru forced him to inhale rosemary to reinvigorate.

'I thought I was done for,' the knight could barely say, exhausted and weakened. 'Thank you, wanderer!' was all he could hum, faintly.

The next day, the Greuthung could already stand, which was a shorter time than Codru had expected, given the way the man looked.

'You won't go back to your Citadel, aren't you?' Codru asked the knight while they were getting the horses ready.

'There is no knighthood if the mission is over,' Toma said. 'I have one last thing I need to do.'

'You have already accomplished your quest.'

'I have only accomplished the Order's. I haven't accomplished mine!'

'The faceless plunderers, isn't that so?' Codru asked. 'The Zmei.'

Toma nodded and said:

'I must put this to rest, too, or else I don't know when I will ever have another chance. Sándor said they were seen south, or maybe east of Braylan, a week's horse ride to the east from here. That is where I'm heading.'

Codru had to offer his shoulder for the knight to finally mount Golden-Sun.

'I'm coming with,' he felt the urge to say.

Toma sniffed. 'This is my journey alone,' he said. 'Besides, you've done more than what you were paid for. You saved my life, Codru, and from this day on, I owe it to you.'

As Codru climbed onto his horse, he replied:

'It's not just about you,' he mumbled, remembering his younger days. 'Something tells me I have unfinished affairs on that same path. And you're in no state to journey alone; you can barely sit in the saddle.'

A heartwarming smile lit up Toma's pale, weakened face. 'Be

careful now, wanderer,' he said. 'One might start to think you care about others. Some might even say you're warming up to fate itself.'

And so, they left Argeș and Dlăgopole behind.

Approaching Braylan, the large settlement they both only heard of, Codru suggested they dismount and rest before entering the city. Toma was barely breathing. He could see the wounded knight struggling to hold himself in the saddle, and after many days on horseback himself, the exhaustion was knocking him off too. Toma didn't protest. As such, they both tied their horses near a tree and sat at the road's edge, sipping from their flasks.

'What do you know of this place?' Codru decided to ask, almost as if he tried to keep the Raven spirited, a burden he did not have to carry until their fight with the Boyar.

'Not much, to be fair,' the knight said. 'Up until a hundred years ago, this place was merely a village. It only began to become the city it is now after the Ottomans swallowed Dobrotici's Domains, making this port the eastern edge of Wallachia. The great bay attracts traders from all around, who bring their wares here either on the Black Sea or along the Danube. They then travel on the Merchant's Road to Transylvania and beyond, and vice versa.'

'That seems much to me,' Codru said.

Even from afar, the two men could feel the settlement fermenting with all sorts of peddlers and wagons carrying their merchandise on the road, in and out of the city.

However, there was a caravan that stood out more than the rest—a fairly large group that seemed to have camped ahead. Some of their men even approached, scouting the place the two men halted at—a loud-mouthed herd of travellers. While they had all sorts of trinkets, wooden carved spoons, and tin pipkins strapped to the outside of their colourful wagon curtains, these people were not merchants. At least not the common ones. That much even Codru could see for himself.

As the travellers got closer, the donkeys dragging their children-riddled carts slowed down. Curiosity seemed to have been characteristic of them, and their inquiring eyes sparkled under their lambskin hats. Chatter brewed within the caravan.

'Sit, let them pass,' Toma grabbed Codru by his arm as the wanderer felt like he needed to stand up. 'If you get their attention, you'll find it damn difficult to get rid of it.'

However, it appeared the knight's strategy didn't work. It could have either been Codru's hair shade or his forehead tattoo. It could have been that the men sat at the edge of the road for no apparent reason or that the horses looked beautiful. It did not matter. Regardless of what it was, the travellers' attention had already been set on them.

Most of them halted their donkeys, maybe a few *stânjeni* further down the road, leaving their main camp behind like a dam between the newcomers and the city. And it didn't seem like they would go away too soon anywhere, as some decided to make a fire at the edge and even assemble tents, covering them in large blankets as eye-catching as their wagon curtains. Their children jumped off the carts, running naked around after each other, hitting one another with twigs, and laughing with their snot turned to crust on their chins.

Even Toma understood there was no way out of it anymore when he saw those two young boys from the group, more daring than the rest, were pairing and deciding to approach him and Codru. As such, they stood up, walking toward their horses and pretending they were getting them ready for the journey. To no avail.

'*Laćho to dés!*' one of the boys almost shouted cheerfully from a few steps away.

'*Ji kaj ʒas?*' he asked as both kept a safe distance from the men.

Codru turned, letting his ipingea's hood fall on his back and revealing his face. For once, he hoped that would scare people away. It didn't; on the contrary, it made the two young boys look at him with even more curiosity.

They turned to each other, waving their hands, and speaking their loud and colourful tongue. They were both barefoot, and the dirty, ripped rags they had as breeches barely covered their knees. Shirts from the same cloth were covering their torsos, revealing their thin and light-brown necks. The quieter of them was fidgeting with a couple of white bone pieces in his coal-stained fingers, and his fingernails darkened.

'Loli bal,' they both muttered. 'Beng, loli bal!'

Codru heard Toma chuckling faintly behind him.

'What do they want?' he asked the knight, startled.

'Your gold, perhaps. That's what they usually catch the scent of. I'm afraid these boys are now debating if it's worth it to cheat on you, as their fear may beat their curiosity.'

'They just found you a name, the Red-Haired Devil!' the knight ended.

Toma left his horse behind and approached the boys. Seeing the knight coming towards them, they took a few steps back, frowning but standing their ground.

'Karing ʒas?' the daring one asked.

'*Me na... vakărel Rromano...*' Toma tried speaking their tongue. 'Tu... vakărel Rumân?'

After a quick exchange of looks between each other, the talking boy replied, nodding:

'Aye, we do, *tiro rrajimos*! Where are you going with the Devil Man?'

'To the city, should your caravan here allow it.'

'*Te arakhel o Del*,' the boy shook his head. 'We don't want to trouble you, *tiro rrajimos*! Na, na...!'

'What is it that you want, then?' Codru approached, asking. The boys took another step back. As he looked over them, he could see a quiver full of children and folk looking at them from a distance, muttering. Men with thick, dark moustaches, holding their hats in their hands. Women in long, floral, and crumpled dresses holding babes at their bare breast.

'We're Cauldron-Smiths, you want to trade for a good cauldron? We make good, sturdy cauldrons,' the boy said frantically. 'You need many kettles and pots to eat food from. Yes, *tiro rrajimos*, you need!'

Toma reached under his cloak and revealed a gold coin, one of his last. The two boys' eyes turned big, and they bit their lower lips under checkless craving.

'Ay!'

'See this?' the Raven asked. 'We might be looking to trade indeed, but it's not for your craft, but for your knowledge.'

The boy seemed disappointed.

'*Tiro rrajimos*, I swear on my mother if I know anything!... We have willow baskets if you want!'

'We seek the faceless men clad in snakeskin,' the knight stated plainly. 'Those who take the women and vanish without a trace. Tell us what you know, and this coin—perhaps more—will be yours.'

The boys exchanged glances, their whispers growing louder in their little conflict. Eventually, the bolder one stepped forward.

'We don't know,' he said. 'But hand over that gold, and we'll lead you to someone who might. We take you to our *Bulibașă*.'

As the two men pulled their horses through the travelling tribe of Egyptians, as Codru heard these people were wrongly being called around these parts, the folk were staring at them with both fear and interest.

As each of the boys dragged the men by their free hands, they made the gold ducat worth it. They took their task seriously, finding them a smooth way through the barracks that rose like weeds, as if they were two small guides, shouting at the ones standing in their way, spitting at them, and cursing them in their language. So much that the path to their king's tent didn't last long.

When they reached there, the boys told them to wait outside and tie their horses as they went in. After a short while of standing nearby the pile of rugs covering the wooden skeleton beneath that passed at their chieftain's palace, the chattery boy returned.

'Our father will talk to you now, *tiro rrajimos*,' he said to the Raven. 'But with you only; Loli-Bal can't come in!'

'Step aside already!' Codru said, losing his patience and pushing the boy's face out of his way as he entered the tent. The knight followed, leaving the young one shouting and swearing outside.

The Egyptian king sat on more of the same rugs made of shreds of rags of all kinds of colours on the ground. His head was covered with a grey lambskin hat. His gippy face was gilded with one of the same thick moustaches his male subjects outside took pride in as well.

While more of the same poor linen or hemp clothes were covering his skinny body, he was also wearing a pair of leather and woollen opinci, unlike the rest. His back was covered in a sheepskin coat, while his thin fingers, while dirty, were adorned with thick golden rings.

Right next to him sat the younger boy, still playing around with the bone shards. To his other side, there was sitting a young girl with dark and long hair, held in two slim braids falling on her shoulders. At her neck, she had a necklace of several golden coins falling over her vibrant silk shirt.

When they entered, the king raised his dark brows and began shouting to the boy outside in his tongue, waving his hand in revolt. He calmed down as quickly as he snapped. He urged the two guests, with a hand gesture, to sit ahead of him.

'That boy needs a good slap!' he mumbled in Rumân. 'What I tell him to do, and what he does! We do not like strangers, and strangers marked by the Devil we like even less. But if it's God's will for me to deal now with the horned one, who am I to say no?'

The knight rested in front of the king, as if he almost couldn't wait to. Codru followed shortly after, his eyes dead on the Egyptian.

'We were told you might know something about the masked Akinji pillaging south from here,' Toma dared to jump to the point.

The Egyptian frowned.

'Ay, these are not marauders, but I heard stories of killing and stealing girls here, in our lands' ribs,' he said, speaking as if he were whining. 'But before that, tell me, what do you think of my daughter?'

The knight glanced at the young girl next to the king.

'I could eat your eyes at how handsome you are,' the Egyptian clapped in awe. 'And rich, no doubt! Aren't you in need of a wife? Look!' the king grabbed the girl's arm and urged her to stand up. 'Ripe, see? Not even fourteen winters! Yours for a good price!'

The girl turned around, humble, her feet stumbling in her dress' edge.

'She's a beauty,' Toma chose his words. 'But I'm a knight; my vow keeps me from taking a wife!'

'Ay, ay!' the king shook his head. 'Too bad, *tiro rrajimos*. Too bad.'

Frustrated, he told the girl to get out of the tent, smacking her bottom. She was no longer needed.

'She's my princess; I love her more than I love my life.'

Then he turned begrudgingly to Codru.

'You, Benga, don't even think of it; you hear me?'

'What can you trade?' he eventually asked, rubbing his chin, and measuring the men with his black eyes, seeing their hurry.

Toma didn't even wait for the king to finish his words. He reached out to his last pouch of gold, hidden under his cloak, and left all its gold coins to fall on the carpet in front of the Egyptian. It was less than he thought, being able to count them on his fingers.

'This is all I have with me, king! It should be more than enough for your story, I take it.'

The king shook his head and rejected the tribute with a gesture of his gold riddled hand.

'This is not good, *tiro rrajimos*!' he muttered loudly.

'We are proud people, you see. Hard working people. And so brave that the Voivode called us to war with the Turks. He promised us release from thraldom as a reward, and you come to me with a fistful of coins? Not good!'

Sitting quietly, Codru grew more impatient by the second. He plucked one of his two leather pouches he received as payment for the Strigoi deeds and dropped half of its contents on top of Toma's money. The knight remained speechless. And so did the King. His eye seemed to sparkle as his fingers began twisting the edge of his moustache.

'Take this, or we are leaving now with it!' Codru spat. 'Now speak!'

After a short pause, the Egyptian's face lightened up in a greedy smirk.

'Maybe I should have offered my daughter to the Devil after all! At least he has money,' he chuckled. 'Very well! We have a deal.'

He then spat in his hand and offered it to Codru. Glancing at Toma, he saw the knight nodding briefly, and with a final gesture, he followed the king's ritual and shook on it.

'These men you're looking for came half a year ago, south and east of Braylan, and stole a few of the peasants' daughters,' the king said while he began gathering the treasure lying in front of him.

'But they are no men,' he said, spitting down his shirt to cast the omens away. 'These are slaves to the serpent.'

Codru saw the knight clenching his jaws. The Raven then asked: 'Where can we find them?'

The Egyptian shook his head, disapproving.

'It wasn't enough that you're poor; you have bran for brain too! You don't go about seeking them out, Sire. If you ran out of luck and hear their war drums, you scamper the other way. Find yourself a fox's den, quiet your beating heart, and cross your tongue. Find them? No, they find you!'

'I thought you were a brave folk, weren't you?'

The king threw a sharp glance at Toma, humming. He took his time throwing the gold coins he gathered in the boy's lap.

'They say they dwell on the island that bears the name of their God. The Isle of Snakes. But no one in their right wits went there to ask them how their day had been. Not many know how to find the island either. They don't even paint it on the maps.'

The two men looked at each other and sighed. They had their destination.

'Do you know someone who knows?'

'I do,' the man grinned. 'But that was not part of the bargain!'

The Raven sniffed.

'That is all, then. We'll find our way on our own!' Toma said.

As they stood up, the king kept quiet, scouting them with a piercing gaze and watching them leave. As the knight pulled aside the rag that resembled the tent's door, the man mumbled behind them.

'I'll play the Devil for the name of the man who can get you there!'

'Don't!' Toma grabbed Codru by his arm as the wanderer turned.

'If I win,' the Egyptian said, rolling the bone shards he grabbed from the boy in his hand, 'then you leave the rest of that heavy pouch here. If I lose, I tell you the name!'

'So be it!' Codru turned to him, taking a knee. This time, he first spat in his hand and gave it to the king, who shook it cravingly.

He then showed the wanderer two small bone dice with dark dots carved in each side.

'We will both throw them once. Whoever throws more dots is victorious!'

And quickly, he blew in his fist as he juggled them. He threw them on the carpet and matched six dots, three on each dice. Smiling, Codru grabbed the dice, and without taking his eyes from the worried Egyptian, he cast them in front of him.

'The Devil!' he heard the man snapping and cursing as the fates had been on Codru's side. His dice showed three dots on one dice and four on the other.

'The name!' he demanded as he stood up, looking down on the king.

'Find Dobre, the one-eyed smuggler,' the Egyptian said, bowing his head in defeat.

***

The sailor was, oddly enough, a man to Codru's heart. He was getting things done and was not much of a talker. He was short, but his back and arms were thick, and although whipped by sea winds and age, his skin bore stretches that showed in his youth he had been even more brawny than he was now. The man was missing an eye, and his socket was covered with a patch. A scroungy monmouth cap was covering his bald head, and a thick white-grey beard unravelled on his tunic covered chest.

Since Codru and Toma stepped foot on his small ship, the man who answered by the name of Dobre didn't talk much to his journeyers. He was instead giving orders to the Egyptians scrubbing the deck or tying the sails, half in their tongue and half in a thick Moldavian dialect, as Toma noticed.

While they sailed the river, it had been only once or twice that he gave much attention to Codru, scouting his appearance with his unscathed right eye, and even less attention to the knight. Clearly, for a man with half vision, he has been travelling much, and he has seen more than others. Not much was new to him.

He did not seem to care much about the bargain or the destination, for that matter, even when the two men found him back at the tavern in Braylan's port and told him they needed to reach the Isle.

'*Yilan Adasi*, is that so?' he muttered.

'Indeed. We heard you are the man to get us there!' Codru remembers Toma telling him.

The wanderer sweetened the deal and laid ten silver dinars in front of the man on the counter. To which Dobre, the smuggler, sipped his last drops of brandy, wiped his mouth with his sleeve, grabbed the silver, and replied, leaving them behind: 'We set sail tomorrow.'

Planning to return, Codru had to dig once again in his own pouch for coins, leaving it to the tavern's keeper for hay and a place in his stables, where they pulled the two steeds.

It took them three days of sailing on the Danube to reach the sea, striking the sails only two times on the way. There didn't seem to be many as skilled at bargaining with the Ottomans. Codru knew how stubborn and unrelenting these people could be. Yet, dealing with them came naturally to Dobre.

They first passed their frontier garrison, which was named Isaceea, sheltered from any attention. All Codru had to do was show his gold to the crooked guards while the sailor spoke to them. After smooth sailing on at the edge of the great river, they reached the old fortress of Chilia, built on the ruins of the even older Genoese foundations of Lycostomo, as the Raven recalled. This is where the Egyptians begged their master to release them of duty, as they began crying on their knees and hitting their heads on the deck, afraid to join further toward the Isle. Dobre only booted their ragged-trousered arses and let them be.

'Leave them to their fate,' he then turned red-faced to his employers. 'If I keep them by force, they'll jump the boat before we get there. And they don't even swim.'

Codru sensed there was more than dare and bluntness to the old man, which were good enough to have as a smuggler, no doubt. And it wasn't even a disregard for his own wellbeing. It was a hidden death wish. As the old man's creaking boat prepared to leave behind the smooth stream for the stirring waves ahead under the sunless morning sky, the wanderer pondered, half-awake from his corner at the back of the ship, that months ago he wouldn't have even noticed it.

The still calmness of the purple sky before the sunrise and the breeze reminded Codru of his freedom. A feeling he wasn't letting himself hold on to, as how can one breathe in relief before the approaching doom they were warned they were travelling to?

He saw Toma lying under a pile of carpets between two barrels, sleeping. He uncovered himself from the woollen blankets he was under and stood up, walking behind the old man who was puffing in silence a pipe like Sándor's and holding the greasy helm on its course toward the upcoming sun.

'You should be getting a shut eye, *Roșcă*,' the one-eyed man said with his hoarse voice, barely glancing at Codru. 'You have your quest ahead of you, have you not?'

'I haven't seen you sleep much either.'

The man chuckled, smoke bursting off his moustache.

'My eye has been forever shut,' he said. 'Besides, there aren't many hands to spare around here anymore, as you can tell.'

After a short pause, he added.

'I wouldn't mind shooting the breeze, however.'

'I am not known for my chatter talents,' Codru answered, as his face was looming from under his hood, his eyes gazing at the shards of red forming on the waves at the horizon.

'You have other talents, I'm sure,' the man mumbled. 'You are a lefegiu, aren't you? A death-trader.'

Codru didn't turn to the smuggler, but he replied:

'You don't seem too frightened.'

'I'm not, my boy. Why should I be? Whether you trade in it or not, in the end, death buys us all,' Dobre shrugged.

'How did you know?' Codru turned.

'By the veiled burden you pretend to not carry on your shoulders. I too, carry it!'

Seeing as Codru didn't ask more of it, the sailor continued after a short silence, releasing some more smoke on his rugged beard.

'I spent my youth fighting Mircea de Wise's battles. I killed more Turks than I'm now bargaining with. After the Wallachian Voivode got old and made peace, there were many of us veterans that the war had turned into animals. Perhaps into something else entirely. And without a fight, some of us travelled north. And for a while, we earned as you earned. By spilling blood.'

The sun changed from purple to bright red in the distance, as if the sky itself was bleeding too. Glancing to his left side, just above the horizon, a wagon of almost fading lights appeared to be swallowed by fire.

'Until one day, it so happened that this young errand lad paid us to protect, not murder. He needed help to bring *Leși*'s king's daughter to the dying Moldavian's Voivode's court for an alliance marriage to one of his sons.'

'Have you?'

'We have,' the man muttered. 'And we haven't. You see, the princess arrived safely. But as it turns out, the errand was the Voivode's nephew, the son of Iuga, the Cripple-Bear, as they called him. They fell in love on the journey, so she didn't want to marry the heir any longer.'

Codru frowned as the story turned into more than the chatter he was promised.

'The sick Voivode, his uncle, offered clemency and even agreed to let this young nephew rule. Until his *postelnic* changed his mind. Under this bald looking creature's venomous words, the boy was found guilty of treason and killed in duel by this snake-tongued creature himself.'

'The vile, white skinned man even took the princess as his wife until she poisoned herself to escape. I was imprisoned for helping, as were the others. After the Voivode's death, the Cripple-Bear agreed to keep the throne warm until his nephews, his brother's rightful heirs, came of age. He found the postelnic guilty of his son's death, beheaded him, and buried him in a shallow grave.'

Stars were still flickering in the sky when the sun rose. A bird suddenly stabbed the sky, beginning to float its large, golden wings above the sails.

'I don't see your old gang anywhere around,' Codru said.

The man exhaled as he checked the herbs in his pipe. They were done for.

'You know as well as I do, Roșcă, that a life as a soldier of fortune doesn't come with restful nights or quiet lives. Two of my old comrades died in the dungeon before their release. One drank himself to death, battling inner demons. And the last one, who was also my friend, was killed in battle,' he let his words fade as he looked up at the bird.

He then left his now cold pipe fall in a pocket under his woollen coat, fit two fingers in his dry, withered mouth, and released a whistle resembling a bird's sound. The high noise not only woke the knight up from his slumber, but it reached the flying bird too. It slowly fell from the sky like an autumn leaf, spreading its large wings until it reached the man's arm, where it finally rested.

'I have this *pajură* from that friend,' he mumbled, smiling, and closing his eye as he left his forehead touch the bird's beak, as if he were listening. 'Left-Eye, its name is.'

'Beautiful creature, but far away from its home,' Codru said, looking at the bird with curiosity.

'She is far from her mountains, yes. You know your birds, of course,' Dobre smirked.

When the bird turned its face toward Codru, a stabbing pain spread instantly throughout his skull. He was suddenly pulled from the boat and flew above the sea, with wind and clear skies all around him. In the middle of all the clear landscape, there stood a patch of what could be earth, densely covered in clouds so thick that even his sun-staring eyes could not break through.

He opened his eyes, breathing heavily, as his palms and knees were on the boat's deck.

He raised his head, seeing Toma next to the smuggler, whose eye stuck silently on him.

'And here I was,' the old man said, 'thinking none of you were seasick. You'd better come to your senses now, Roșcă. There's a mist approaching.'

## CHAPTER XI

*Cozia, June 1445 (6953)*

AT FIRST, HE HEARD THEM, AS HIS EARS WERE even sharper than his eyes. The cries and the clanks. The desperate laments of the men and women praying to God, cast out into the winds, and the steel smothering them. The terror of their children being taken away from their homes and the madness of their takers.

Then he saw it, too. The smoke was fermenting far in the valley, over the trees that formed the forest beneath. Threads of dark mist reached the sky, spreading and wasting themselves in the clouds as if they were a poison tainting the rain and the sky.

His heart was beating so hard that it could break out through his ribcage. His hand was running up and down on his father's hatchet's handle, his palms itching. He clenched his jaws and crushed the dirt under his boots, pacing in the same circle for what felt like an eternity. His eyes shifted from the distant anathema unfolding on the town's outskirts to the stern man standing beside him.

'It is not our duty to determine the fate of men,' he said gravely, tearing his gaze away from the unfolding disaster.

'Why isn't it, teacher?' the boy wailed. 'Why spend our lives serving the dead? Why not use what they taught us to serve the living? What is the purpose of it all?'

'Hold your tongue now, boy!' the man turned suddenly, slapping him. His voice thundered harshly, shaking, as the apprentice staggered falling behind.

'Know your place,' his teacher raised his finger as the boy covered his face with his palm, his eyes dropped in the ground. 'Do not take the Moșii's names in vain! Think twice before letting your mouth run by itself.'

The boy puffed his nostrils, raising his eyes from the grass, and a cold metal gaze pierced right through the Old-Man's misty eyes. It was the first time in all these years he looked that way at his master.

But the Old-Man was not shaken.

'We are leaving,' he said. 'Take your sleeping rug, and we shall leave this place at once!'

The boy didn't move. His chest was, however, full of air, leaving his lungs as his eyes still flickered with fury. And the master understood that the old worry that had kept him awake at night during all these years had grounds.

The boy had reached that age when the fire burned the wildest. The blood he inherited from the Fire-Knights was now boiling through his veins. The teacher had prayed it would never come to this. He prayed that the rain and the storms would be enough to extinguish the boy's inner blaze.

In all his wisdom, he allowed himself this foolish hope, shutting his eye to the boy's bursts throughout the years, his thirst to avenge his parents, and his homesickness. His old, withered heart was now shaking, thinking at his legacy and at his heir, wasting it.

'I shall go there without you, Uncheaș.'

'Poor child,' the man's voice trembled. 'Do not dare lie to yourself; you don't want to save the people. Not that you could!'

He then said:

'It's the girl you want to save. Her womanish claws took hold of you! If it wasn't for her, you wouldn't mourn her fate now!'

The boy looked at him, his head held high, and his chin brought forward.

'I can sense they are the same men who wasted my family. I can't let her die the way my mother did. I need to go there, Uncheaș!'

A grimace soured the man's face, shadowed by unspoken grief.

'You damned fool! This isn't how you will save anyone. This is how you are killing us both.'

He came closer to the boy and grabbed his face with his old

fingers, squeezing his cheeks, ready to rip his face off. He said through his teeth:

'Don't you know you can't ever return once you pass through this gate? Have I not told you? Choose to leave now, and the oath that binds us will be forever broken. You shall never return to the Mountain.'

The boy let a tear run down his cheek, rolling over the man's wrinkled hand. He closed his eyes, letting his forehead rest on the man's forehead, and said:

'I am sorry.'

And then he pulled away like the wind, running down the hill with his hatchet in his hand and his pouch strapped to his chest. His knees were jolting as his feet were storming toward the valley, soon to be embraced by the forest lying now between him and the disaster.

He didn't turn his head back, afraid to see the man who had raised him being left on his own after all these years. He didn't look up either, knowing the weather had changed suddenly, ready to pour its tears and drown him in sorrow.

He just ran, weeds and thorns grazing his trousers, dry, thin branches scratching his face, making his way through the woodland with his axe, wielding it left and right. His chest trembled as his breaths were quivering. Why was his heart so heavy if what he was doing now was following what it wanted?

He was far from Heaven's Mouth, where his old teacher remained lost behind, when the boy finally reached the edge of the woods. He stood there, behind the last of the trees, with his breath breaking, sobbing, and his eyes in tears, gazing towards the distance in complete puzzlement.

The deafening noise of blades. The hopeless cry to the sky, praying to it to save them from the invading wrath. The fires burning the town and the staggering hoofbeats of the battle horses crushing everything beneath them. Flashes from a different life, before he had been taken away, flooded his memory. He could hear the same terrible laments in his head as he could hear them in his ears.

He had never withstood another man, and his hatchet's blade had never tasted blood.

'Stain not thy heart with deeds of killing,' the vows he had taken were now turning against him, lying heavily on his mind. 'And lead thy deeds by wisdom, not by fury.' But it was too late. They were both laws bound to be broken.

As soon as the first drizzle fell from the clouds, summoned above the plundering by unseen forces, the boy began running on the field toward the fires, leaving the forest behind, roaring as water trickled down his hair and chin. The closer he got, the louder the war cries grew.

He had seen the invaders, some on horseback, fluttering their cold, curved blades above their heads, wrapped in crimson cloth. The earth shook under his feet as the fiery steeds passed him by. A blade whooshed above his head, forcing him to throw himself onto the wounded ground, cracked and battered by the battle.

He then stood and ran as fast as he could toward a mouldering cottage with smoke blossoming from its roof, sticking himself to its wall. From his poor hideout, he saw an old man on his back on the ground, between the stables, shouting as his palms were raised in the air. The blade waving above him severed them both with a strike.

The marauder then jumped off his horse, kneeling on the frightened man's chest. He plucked a long dagger from his waist. Just before he could wet its blade, the boy forgot about himself and threw himself out of his hideout, his axe breaking through the air.

The boy's animal scream made the marauder turn, and as he did, his cheek was split open in a flash by the axe, getting stuck in the attacker's teeth and jaw. He fell with his face in the mud, eyes wide open, as blood was choking him. The boy stood there for a few long moments with his eyes bloodshot and his face drained, quaking like an aspen leaf as he watched both men die. It was only when he heard a nearby thunderstrike that he came back to his senses. He grabbed the hatchet's handle and pulled it as hard as he could, removing it from the dead man's face. He stumbled, falling back. He watched the red life oil weeping slowly off the blade, and he choked, vomit bursting out of his throat.

He stood up, drowsy, cold sweats looming on his temples, spitting and barely able to breathe as his heart was pounding in his eardrums. It was done. He knew he had irreversibly broken his oath. He had just taken a life. Gods have mercy on him.

A voice behind him broke the air. It was a disheartening cry that made him shatter and come back to life at the same time. It was her; he just knew it. Without thinking twice, he turned and ran toward it, leaving the dead bodies behind. As he ran, hay flames were spitting ashes and sparkles from both sides, hitting his face. Smoke was making his spit turn into thick sap. When he finally made it close to the cry source, he stumbled as he hid behind another wooden house's corner.

He peeped from behind it, drums smouldering in his ribcage, trying to catch his breath. He saw Ileana. The girl had thrown herself on top of the body of an older man, crying. Like a wounded animal, like the wolf he once rescued from the trap, she was roaring at the ones closing in on her, keeping them at distance with the long stick she was handling so well.

They were laughing as large, draconian smiles cracked their thin, sharp faces, showing their teeth from under their dark and dense moustaches. The boy knew the man lying there, under her desperate and vain protection, was her father. He was dead. He knew the men surrounding her had been his attackers. And he also knew their vicious duties were not going to end there.

She stood up and aimed with her stick at one of the men closing in on her like a wolf pack. Her stick dashed onto his face, making him stumble and fall onto his back, having him search for his lost teeth in the mud. The second strike missed, as the next man had seen it coming. He caught it and pulled it out of her hands, disarming her.

Another man creeped up behind her, trying to catch her arms at her back, but she hitched and turned, her nails scratching his eyes out of their sockets. In return, a back-of-the hand slap made her fall, leaving behind a red thread of blood running down her chin. While she was down, the marauder mounted her, leeching on to her embroidered shirt and ripping its neck's edges. A shard of metal flickered in the sun, dangling by a string at the girl's neck.

The rage made the boy jump out and throw himself at the attackers without thinking of his own safety. His hatchet carved the back of the first one he encountered, and before the other could sober up from the unexpected assault, the boy landed his blade in another man's neck as he was turning, leaving him fall to his knees with his hands trying to vainly catch the overflowing blood.

He screamed at the other three men as they stepped back enough to see him clearly. Blood covered his face. Hatchet, keeping them at two arms distance. He could only glance at the girl, their eyes meeting for only a moment, before the man on top of her jolted up, roaring, with his short, curved sword swishing poisonously at the boy. Freed from his hands, the girl grabbed her stick back from the ground, and before the marauder could reach the boy, its sharp head found room in the man's belly, breaking all the way through his back.

She stood up immediately, drawing the dead man's sword from his clenched fingers as she did, and came to the boy's side.

'Alidor...' she could only say, searching for his eyes.

But before he could answer anything, the other two attackers bellowed, their eyes flared by fury and their faces contorted with bloodlust. They both ran toward the young couple and slit the wind and rain with their spades.

Codru could hear sombre hoofbeats approaching from behind as one of their enemies launched his sword at him, aiming for his head. He dodged it poorly, his axe barely protecting him from its blow. With a swing, the man made him lose his grip. A kick in his chest squeezed the air out of his lungs, throwing him on his back, in the mud.

Ileana swirled the blade she captured, but the man severed it from her hand with a strong clash, hitting her chin with its own blade's hilt. He stepped over her, leaving her to his fellow as he went for the boy. Looking up at the man as he tried to catch his breath, dragging himself on the ground to escape, he saw the sword raised to the air, the flames of the burning house behind it framing it.

Then he saw the girl returning from her fallout, climbing on his back, and grabbing his face with her ravenous hands, digging her nails in his eyes. The man screamed. She reached out to the dagger dangling at his waist and plunged it without a second thought into his throat, leaving it there as she fell off his back. The man sank to his knees and pulled the blade out, while a river of blood ran over his tunic, falling face down after a few short gurgles.

Before the boy could come to himself, scouting the grounds for his father's axe, he saw the last marauder's hand plunging into Ileana's hair, dragging her down violently with his blade to her neck. He spat words in his foreign tongue as the boy grabbed the axe off the ground and ran quickly towards them. The man's blade was under her chin as tears burst out on her cheeks.

'Alidor!' she mumbled, aware this was going to be her end.

He saw the man grinning as he stepped back and dragged the girl with him. He shouted, making the young one understand that if he took another step, she would bleed her.

The horses Codru heard before approached from behind, and their storm became so loud that he had to turn. What he saw made his knees turn weak and his blood run cold in his veins. There was another gang of foes getting closer. Larger than the one that he and

Ileana had just spoiled.

At its helm, riding a steed darker than the night, stood out their leader—a mountain of man with his head covered with a large, sinister helmet that bore the great horns of a bull. His face was covered from the nose down, with only his eyes fizzling in his skull like two embers. Leather straps covered his almost naked torso, and his legs were wrapped in dark cloth. In his hand, a great, long, curved sword split through the air.

The young man turned, realizing he was caught with his back to the wall between the last of the marauders threatening Ileana's life and the doom of the upcoming wave of horsemen. Before he could do anything, he saw Ileana's captor screaming as his hand released the sword. He heard a growl, and then the jaws of a beast plunging its teeth into the man's throat. It was Bruma, the girl's faithful lynx. Ileana took the chance to draw herself from the man's arms and threw herself to the ground, reaching for his lost weapon as the man's screams were smothered by the great woodland animal ripping his face off.

Her eyes searched for the boy. Before he could turn, a truncheon's blow in the back made him lose his air once more, dragging him into the dirt face down.

'Run, Ileana!' he could only bewail, wheezing, as the riders surrounded him.

'Leave!'

Crying, the girl seemed to not be able to move. It was only when Bruma encircled her, shielding her as it hissed through its musty red muzzle at the nearby pillagers, that she finally stood up, staggering, with the sword of the last killed man in her hand. Codru saw her looking at her father's body once more, lying dead in the ashes, then wiping her tears as she gazed at the boy one last time, and finally she turned and ran in the opposite direction, away from him and the large group of men, losing herself in the distant smoke.

The horsemen completely encircled him. Their leader jumped off the horse, and the earth seemed to be shaking under his boots. He signalled two of the riders, with a wave of his thick arm, to follow Ileana while ordering the others to dismount. With his axe shaking in his hands and reeling his knees on the ground, the boy screamed like a feral animal, trying to keep them at a distance. The man caught his arm with ease and curled it violently, making him groan and drop the hatchet in the mud. Another slap made him fall with his palms on the ground and blood dripping off his lips.

The horned man took a knee quietly next to him, chuckling under his mask, pulling the boy's head up by his hair while his eyes measured his face, his forehead mark, and his red locks.

'Look at what we have found here now,' his sombre, cold voice said in a broken Rumân speech through the cloth covering his face. He removed the boy's hair from his forehead with the tip of his blade.

'What do they call you, fiery one?'

One of the marauders approached and mumbled behind the leader, waving his arms to the boy, then to the sky. The horned man stood up silently and plunged his sword into his belly, dropping the man in agony at his feet.

'Where were we?' he asked, turning back to the boy.

'Tell me your name, little fighter!' he continued. 'You don't want to follow Quadir here to Jahannam now, don't you?'

The young one didn't say a word, but his eyes could pierce his captors.' The pillager hummed under his mask.

'Very well then. From today on, you shall be Kir-Yüz,' he said. He then bent down and took the lost hatchet in his free hand, studying it briefly. The boy growled and rose from the ground, running rabidly toward the man who took his father's weapon, only to be thrown back to his knees with a kick in his stomach.

'Be nice now,' the man muttered, securing the boy's axe's handle at his waist. 'This corpse here thought you're too old, that your skin's too tainted to bring along. He wanted us to end you, Kir-Yüz...' he continued, hoisting himself onto his dark horse. 'But he couldn't see the simmering fire within you—I can. I'm certain you'll be useful to me.'

The two men who had been sent after Ileana returned without her.

'Your feisty pair seems to have escaped us this time,' the horned man said. 'I am sure there will be another occasion.'

Then he had ordered two of the marauders to dismount, and he turned his back, kicking his horse, and left him and the rest behind, continuing his deadly journey through town.

The two men grabbed the boy by his arms and shoulders, and the last thing he could see before they shut his lights off with a hit in the back of his head was the seemingly never-ending road, imagining Ileana at the end of it, running towards the woods, to safety.

\*\*\*

*Isle of Snakes, September 1459 (6967)*

'Be quiet now!' Dobre whispered, partly to himself, as he grabbed the gunwale with both hands, scouting the dense mist his ship was now navigating through.

He looked for *Ştime*, Codru was told. Creatures they said, that were swimming at the surface, with arms rising from the dark, still waters and dragging the sailors into the abyss. The man told him and the knight before the boat entered the cloud that he had heard stories from other smugglers, even if he didn't see or believe them much himself.

'There must be a reason all these people stay away from the island and its surroundings, no?' he said gravely. 'But I have *Sân-Nicoară*'s protection with me, so I don't fear much,' he ended after he revealed a small wooden cross talisman around his neck, hiding it under his shirt shortly after.

The quiet was deafening; the only sound Codru could hear was the swoosh of the grey water lapping on the ship's wooden bow. Vaguely out and about after finally he had rested, Toma seemed to remember a handful of things about the cursed island they were hopefully soon going to anchor to.

Millenia ago, he recalled, long before the Ottomans, Greeks had lived here as well as across the shore. *Axeinos* is what they called the sea at first, due to its black, savage tides and even more savage barbarians that roamed the lands nearby. It was their god of the seas himself, the knight said, who rose Leuke, the white-sanded island, from its depths. It gave people refuge from the surrounding fury. It was said they even built a temple here to bury one of their great fallen warriors.

'Look ahead!' Codru heard the smuggler saying.

He followed Dobre's raised arm towards the boat's front. Ahead, shaping out of nothingness, he could begin to see the grand, shadowy shape of a rocky shore, like a mountain top raised from the waters, spreading its cliffy edges to left and right. From the distance, he could only note there was no way the ship could anchor at its mainland. His sharp eyes could not see more than that. The waves were crashing into its sharp, great rocks violently breaking the feral silence the mist had brought.

Once Dobre dropped the sails and the anchor, helped by Codru, he first took a long, silent gaze at the horizon. Then he closed his eyes and exhaled.

'There is nothing on this forgotten land, lads,' he murmured. If there is, my eye can't see it.

He whistled, calling back his eagle from the clouds. The bird broke the mist like an arrow, coming back to its master, who welcomed it on his arm as he turned to the two men.

'This is as far as me and my boat can take you, fellows,' he said. 'You will have to swim to the shore, I'm afraid. I see you're not short of blades, but I'd say to only take one with you if you don't want to sink. I shall wait here, but I won't wait for too long. Whatever there is you need to do on this harsh patch of land, you better be done with it soon.'

Codru turned to Toma, unsure if he'd be able to swim to the land. He was wondering if it wasn't better to just turn back. If they were going to have to fight, he couldn't say wholeheartedly that the Raven was the best comrade to have right now. However, he saw him dropping Balmut and his mantle on the deck, next to a barrel. He only strapped the mace and the iron helmet to his waist. He dug his dagger into his boot. He saw Codru looking at him and said as if he knew what the red-haired man thought.

'I must do this. And I can do it.'

And Codru could understand that. He dropped his own pouch and cloak on top of Toma's together with his scimitar, saving only the hatchet, and strapped it to his belt.

'Beware of the Știme, and Sân-Nicoară may watch over you!' they heard Dobre finally saying.

Getting closer to the ship's edge, they both took another look at the sinister island ahead and the clouds swirling around it, and dove into the cold waters of the sea.

\*\*\*

'Don't even think about it!'

Codru squeezed the wet sand and gravel in his fists as the edge of a spear stung him in the back of his soaked shirt. From that position, he could only see the dark-leather boots of their captors and hear their muffled voices. A speech he had never heard before. A wild, elder speech. It appeared that only the man taming him with his blade to not move from the ground spoke the common language.

'You should not have come; you don't belong here,' the stranger told him. 'Why have you come?'

Codru didn't answer. His mind was searching for a way to turn it all in his and the knight's favour. But he knew that he wouldn't reach the axe as quickly as the man could pierce his lungs. He turned to Toma, who was resting face down on the shore, two other spears pinning him to the ground. He was puffing and blowing, his wet back raising and decreasing as he breathed heavily, drained after the swim.

The wanderer was aware they would encounter foes, but he didn't expect for it to happen right before they could barely make it to the land. As he glanced behind him, he couldn't even see Dobre's boat anymore. He wondered if he hadn't already left, abandoning them here on this rock.

He suddenly heard the boots of a sixth man, heavily grinding through the harsh, grainy, pale sand. He spoke in the same strange tongue to his fellows, as if he were giving them an order, and sure enough, soon after, he sensed his captor putting the spear away. Before he could react and grab his weapon, ready for the opportunity, Codru saw the new man taking a knee next to him and saying:

'Fights aren't necessary,' he said.

'You were expected. We have been waiting for you. Do not try to fight us, and you may stand!'

Codru could deal with that for now. He couldn't say the same for his companion.

'I need your word!' the man insisted. The wanderer nodded.

'On your feet then,' the newcomer said, standing. 'Follow me! The Priestess shall see you now.'

Codru stood up, and, toilsomely, Toma did too. The Raven's eyes, however, were the eyes of a man whose mind was wrapped in plotting. And given his past, Codru knew why. It only took him a moment to look at his captors-turned-guides to understand that these men were the ones he heard pillaging the villages on the mainland. The same ones who murdered and kidnapped virgins. The same kind of men that killed Toma's own woman and child, and the same kind he was once captured by in his early youth. Bearers of horned helmets, serpent leather patches, and grimy masks covering their faces. The Zmei.

And instead of fighting them, the two men were now following them obediently.

Their feet climbed up a damp, dark-blue hued stairway carved in the island's rock—an abrupt and slippery passageway that eventually led them to the top of the island's surface. As the two fellows were caught in the middle, the Zmei watched over them relentlessly, glancing from under their heavy helmets, making sure they obeyed and stayed on track. It wasn't only once that the last of their kind, walking behind Toma at the end of the suite, had to warn the knight to keep moving, noticing the man's unrest.

Once they reached the surface, Codru could see these people's settlement even through the sunless mist floating around. The wind was blowing, making him shiver as the damp, drying clothing was capturing the breeze in its threads.

There were neither cottages nor tents, but a plethora of barracks scraped out of wood and pelts. Instead of a village, it looked more like an untamed, temporary garrison, rashly risen, almost like the one he saw at Mehadia, the Raven's citadel, however larger, wilder, and more robust. Or even at the Egyptians they had encountered only recently.

As the Zmei led them through its midst, he could only see men, which were not many either, as some, if not the majority of these half-made kennels, seemed abandoned. They all wore masks, even though some of them did not have helmets. Leather straps and patches were the only things covering their chests, shoulders, and beefy arms. Dark cloth wraps stood for trousers. Their hair was dark blonde, long, and tallowy, soaked in salt, grease, and humidity. They watched the strangers in silence, some of them returning cheerlessly to their rugged shelters.

There was only one whose gaze followed them relentlessly until they passed his cottage, a low chieftain of some kind. And in return, Toma's blood left his cheeks, meeting his eyes, as if he had seen a ghost.

The more they walked, Codru began to see before them the towering shape of a building greater than the rest of all the barracks. Made of polished stone, the place they were guided towards had large, gargantuan columns holding the concave roof through which the sun fell, reminding him of the Mountain Heart, if it had more than one hole. He knew right then that this must have been the ancient temple the Greuthung told him about. The great warrior's tomb. It was also where the Priestess the Zmeu told him about was supposedly expecting them to be.

As they ascended the stairs, passing by towering columns, both men gazed upwards, their eyes overwhelmed by the immense size of the temple. Iron braziers flanked the entrance, where flickering flames cast a warm glow on their freezing skin. They passed through, framed by the overzealous Zmei.

The inside of the temple was warmer and brighter than the rest of the island. Dark marble walls, covered with paintings of bright red paint that told stories of an ancient war, were protecting the ones inside from the outside winds. However, the misty gloom seemed to reach even here, falling through the open roof, and making Codru wipe his eyes a few times, trying in vain to see clearer. Right at the end of the sumptuous yet saintly room, on top of three stepping stones, stood a highchair, carved in the same dark marble, from which a stern yet charming figure was watching the guest approaching. The Priestess.

She had dark, wavy hair reaching down to her round hips, beautifully framing her olive skin face. A long and loose dress of white-blue, almost translucent linen barely covered her. She wore large golden necklaces and rings. Her several bracelets matched the anklets she wore around her otherwise bare feet. Looking at her sitting larger than life on that throne, accompanied by two other young women, similarly dressed, one to her each side, Codru would have said she did not look like a priestess but a goddess.

Once they had done their deed, the Zmei, who had seen them off to her, bowed solemnly and took only a few steps back, standing in a line behind Codru and Toma without any thought of leaving the chamber.

Her dark eyes moved from the wanderer to the knight, resting with more interest on the latter.

'It has been so long since anyone came to us willingly,' her voice sounded old and loud, with an echo. 'Who knew that the one who dared to finally come would be the one we were waiting for so long?'

Toma bit his lip, his eyes looking around, perhaps for a sign of the kidnapped girls he heard about.

'Who are you? What is this place?' he snarled, unimpressed by the luxurious atmosphere or by the Priestess welcome.

She watched him as if she would have eaten him alive. She was content to only eat his words.

'I am Gunnay! Have you ever wondered who you are?' she said, ominously.

And Codru knew that the Greuthung had.

'You're a long way from home, priestess,' Codru turned to her. 'I once heard this name on the Anatolian shores.'

She told him:

'Me and my sisters arrived here from afar, yes. Our prophecy troubled people, so they killed our kind. We escaped and sailed north. And the Great Serpent offered us this land, where we could wait for his return peacefully.'

'Peacefully? You are murderers!' Toma hissed as his fists clenched. His hand rested on his mace.

The Priestess saw it, but besides resting her eyes on the Raven's weapon, she didn't react. As if she knew he wasn't going to grab it.

'Peacefully, indeed. As you can see, you have not been disarmed. And yes, our survival requires sacrifice. Ours is a merciful but demanding god.'

Codru's thoughts wandered to his own past, memories of the third trial beginning to swallow up his own mind.

'Our God promised us his return,' she said, standing up from her throne. 'Yet it wasn't him who first came to our shores. He sent his firstborn. Horned warriors wearing his offspring's skin came to us by boats.'

She approached Toma, and without any reservation, she softly touched his face, then crossed her fingers through his damp hair, removing it from his face.

'They were blonde, and their eyes were dark, like yours! Greuthungi. But they were not kind,' she said. 'Under their leader, the mace-baring one calling himself Athanar, they raped and killed us—a sacrifice we would have accepted for the Great Serpent, as this was the god they too bowed to. The men took the island for themselves, as they needed it to bury their treasures here. They needed the temple to chain a prisoner they had brought with them, shackled in gold.'

Under her touch, Toma seemed to fall under a spell, unable to move or react. He could only shake his head when the Priestess left him behind and walked this time towards Codru.

'They buried their treasures; they chained their prisoner in the island's depths. And it was only when they wanted to leave that they found out they no longer could. But the Serpent was not pleased with what they did to us, so he punished us all for it.'

She continued:

'The men then bowed to us, pleading forgiveness, and swearing obedience. They cut their noses and split their tongues, crying for the God's mercy. But the curse remained.'

Her eyes fell suddenly on Codru's tattoo, and she became more and more inquisitive the closer she got to him.

'The mist,' Codru realized. 'You are trapped here. This island is your dungeon.'

'If you only knew what kind of threshold you had crossed,' her voice faded as her black eyes pierced his.

'You're one of them!' she whispered. 'One of those with fire in their veins. I have never met them until now.'

'I can see the snakes on your skin. We serve the same God,' she whispered.

'I don't serve any god, but if it existed, it would have served me,' Codru mumbled.

She smiled.

'That is the fire-blood talking,' she said.

'Lies!' Toma barked, grabbing the mace. Codru knew that the thirst for vengeance suddenly overflowed in Toma's chest.

'You are killing people on shore; that's not what someone trapped here could do!'

Gunnay turned her head toward him.

'The prisoner has both blessed and doomed us. On this island, nothing grows, so our wombs are barren. We live in a realm of eternal youth and immortal life, yet it is a childless one.'

'We bring your people's maidens here, where they bear our men's children. Then boats carry them back to the mainland, where they give birth, and the children are being raised in our faith, hidden in the mountains. Unbound by the curse, they grow into warriors who can come and go to the island as they please, carrying on our legacy.'

'It's your own children that plunder your lands, not us!'

'Curses!' Toma shouted. 'You are a plague on this land. Your kind murdered my woman. My son. Give me a reason why I shouldn't end you all!'

The Priestess smiled as she turned and slowly walked back to her chair.

'You could try,' she said, sitting. 'But everything has already been written. What you do or don't do has already happened before and will happen again. It's fate.'

'Then fate is a prison!' Codru exclaimed.

'It is,' the Priestess replied. 'A prison with golden chains. If your family had not been sacrificed, knight, you would have never returned to us. You are the prophecy, can't you see? You are the Greuthung who has returned, bringing Athanar's mace back home, where it belongs.'

Then she turned to Codru.

'However, the prophecy had never spoken about the fire-blood. So perhaps fate can be changed!'

Her voice suddenly turned sharp, and she slurred an order to the Zmei, who had been waiting obediently behind the two men until then.

'*Kratēste!*'

Codru understood enough Greek to know what she said and grabbed his axe before the Zmei could even follow the command. But Toma did not. By the time the weakened knight turned, his hand on the mace, a blunt strike of a truncheon thrown him on his back, and two of the marauders completely restrained him, forcing him to kneel.

Codru grinded his teeth, holding his axe at arm's length while the other four men encircled him. He lost.

'I have seen a hail bringing storm in your eyes, fire-blood. A lifetime of it,' the priestess said loudly. 'But there's a warm heart under all the stone-cold ice covering it. You won't let your friend die. Fight the men, and that is what will happen.'

He turned to the Raven, who was struggling under the strong arms of his captors, his eyes heavy with rage and disappointment. Not too long ago, the wanderer would have sacrificed the man for his freedom. Not anymore.

The axe fell on the dark marble, cracking and chipping it under its sharp thud.

***

Codru was no stranger to underground dungeons, but an underground dungeon on an island, encircled by water, was a first for him.

More of the same darkened stairs had been carved ages ago in the heart of the isle, and its entrance was right under the temple. As he and the knight were forced to descend into the depths through the tight, dark passage, he thought this was the tomb where that hero had been buried. He was quiet, as Toma was too. As they followed Gunnay beneath the temple, he realized their journey had not been going well.

In one hand, she was bearing a torch to light the path, while in the other, she carried the mace that Toma held so dear until he had been disarmed. A slight headache began to loom over him. He was soon to be deprived of freedom, and that was the last thing he had always wanted.

Once they reached the bottom of the pit, he knew they were under the sea by now. He could sense it, too. The wet, roughly carved walls of the corridor had large holes in them. Dungeon iron doors. Except for one—the one at the end of the corridor, through which light seemed to pour from above.

'What will you do to us?' Toma muttered. 'Why not kill us and be done with it?'

'No one on the island wants to kill you,' she said. 'As for the one who should have not been here, I have something else prepared.'

When they reached close enough to the entrance, through which light came, she turned and gave an order to the Zmei following them. As soon as she did, two of them opened one of the iron cages and forced Toma inside, closing it as he roared, crashing himself into the bars.

'Come!' she said then to Codru in a silky tone as the Zmei pushed him forward.

It was when they finally passed the entrance that he saw it.

A chamber like the one at the Mountain, however much smaller, had been built inside this island. It was larger than the Temple of Fates, where Daniil cast the Demon back to hell. Light fell through a large round circle in the middle of the dome, spreading on the surface of a stone table that seemed to have arisen from the floor, the same as the table that held the golden Book of Light. But unlike its sister table, this one had no book on its surface. Instead, numerous other treasures surrounded it. Old, golden treasures, filled with jewels and carved with runic symbols. It was surely the same masons he was taught about who built this place.

There were no other lights, except for a few braziers like the ones at the surface. It was grim, sombre, and cold. A tomb unlike any other tomb he had ever seen, because in the middle of it, there was a tree. A great, tall tree, with its crown reaching the dome and spreading across it like a dark-green roof, covered in faded clouds.

At the foot of its trunk, there was an old, unclothed man tied to it, chained in gold. Sleeping. Light fell through the branches on his sharp, withered face as if it were made of stone. His beard and his hair grew for so long that they turned into roots. His back skin blended with the moss growing on the bark. There were snakes guarding his feet, slithering, waving their luscious bodies, and covering the ground around the arbour like a dark, lively puddle without straining from their nest.

'When we arrived here,' the Priestess said, 'we were humbled by the wonders of the white-sanded island. But it was only here, in its depths, that we discovered its true treasures.'

'We don't know who built these chambers or who planted the tree. But when we found them, we knew we were meant to arrive here. You see, this is the tree of eternal life. A cedar tree. A tree that only grows on the land we came from. It was destined for us. Our paths are forever etched by fate, and we are but ink stains upon its vast map.'

'Who is he? How is he still alive?'

'It's not who he is; it's what he is!' she said. 'His blood runs through your veins. He's one of the Ancients! One of those who bent time to his will,' she said.

'And he's alive because no one can kill time. But the warriors trapped it. Made it a prisoner. Made the time stand still, until the promised would return.'

Gunnay turned to the Zmei that followed until then and gave them an order to leave.

'You don't fear I will escape?' Codru asked, his eyes still on the prisoner.

'You have too many questions unanswered!' the Priestess replied. 'You won't go anywhere.'

She left him behind as she approached the table, where only now Codru could see a hole dug right in the middle of it. She left the torch on its surface, and with both hands, she raised the Raven's mace above her head. She closed her eyes and, holding the mace by its bulge, left its handle drop inside the hole.

The earth beneath their feet shook, and a long howl roamed

through the island's depths. Codru's sharp ears could hear a sound he had long forgotten. Creaks. Levers and pulleys. This wasn't the cavern's bottom or the Heart of the Island. Somewhere deeper, there were large, old wheels that began to turn.

As he tried to make sense of what was happening, her voice began whispering in the Old-Tongue, just as the voices from the cave or the animals did. The Earth's tongue he had long forgotten.

The snakes that until then writhed and circled in their nest at the feet of the ancient prisoner answered the call and began climbing the stone table, swirling around the mace, and reaching her. She caught one in her grip, its tail rolling around her arm, and before Codru realized what she had planned, caught up in a wave of memories, the Priestess turned. With a quick throw, she released the snake through the air towards the wanderer.

When the snake's teeth clenched in his jugular, a head splitting migraine pulsated between his temples. He grunted as he pulled the snake from his neck, with strings of blood running down his shirt. He threw the viper to the wall violently, holding his neck and staggering, feeling the venom spreading quickly and scorching through his veins.

'What have you done? What's happening.'

'You're dying!' her voice echoed. 'You were not destined to be here, fire-blood. But before the Serpent claims your soul, I will claim your flesh.'

Codru stumbled and fell to his knees. He pulled the neck of his shirt away, his throat beginning to choke and a fever suddenly spreading through his muscles.

'Time has cursed us, and we can't bear children. But your blood is older than time. I shall carry your son.'

As Codru was struggling to breathe, she took him by his shoulders and rested his head gently on the cold stone floor, raising her long dress, mounting him, and pinning his arms under her grip, which grew stronger with every moment. The venom finally reached his brain, and even if he once had been bitten, he knew that the visions were almost never lying.

At first, he felt as if her fingernails turned into talons, wrapping around his wrists, and growing like blades, slitting his skin. Her mouth grew larger, with fangs stabbing through her gums and ripping her mouth apart. On her now bare back, large, featherless wings spread to her sides, covering them both in their embrace. He stood still, his body turning to stone under the venom's trance, as Gunnay feasted on his flesh. His mind was gone, and his heart was barely beating, stuffed with thick blood, as moments appeared to last an eternity.

The Priestess suddenly screeched as a dagger slit her throat open. She fell to Codru's side, with her mouth opening for air like a fish on land, and her eyes swallowed by terror. Unable to see clearly, Codru could only make out the shape of the apparition that killed her. He heard his voice.

'*Codru...*' he murmured. He could only feel the warmth of the slaps on his numb face. 'Codru... They're coming!'

'*Codru...*'

He felt his body being dragged against the wall. He then heard more voices coming from everywhere. Roars. Threats in an unknown speech. Boots cluttering.

He couldn't do anything. He saw his saviour's shadow, covered in a red cloud, running into the light to the centre of the chamber, pulling the mace out of its restful place in the stone table. Another shadow threw itself at the saviour. He heard the crack in its skull under the terrible blow of the iron weapon. His saviour bellowed like a beast as more shadows surrounded him, as he wielded the mace around him, breaking their bones and spilling their blood mercilessly.

'*Am I dying?*' a thought sprouted in his mind as his vision turned dark and the air turned hot, only being able to hear the fight happening around him. And the more he tried to stay awake, the harder it turned, until eventually he fell into a deep, restless slumber.

\*\*\*

He opened his eyes, quivering and puffing dust as his mouth was stuck to the ground. Two strong arms turned him face up. It was Toma. On his blood-red face, he could only see the white of his eyes and the teeth, revealed by gore, dry lips.

'We need to leave; there are more of them out there!' he said, his voice trembling.

Codru stood up, feeling the chamber move. He saw the pile of dead Zmei everywhere around him. Their bodies were clawed, and their heads were crushed. He turned to the knight, who avoided his eyes, squeezing his fingers on the mace's handle and putting it away behind him.

'The prisoner,' Codru mumbled, remembering. 'We have to release him.'

'There is no time; we need to get out before they corner us in here once more!'

But Codru left him behind, stumbling as he ran towards the tree, kneeling behind it. The snakes surrounding the man's feet had all turned to stone once the Priestess gave her last breath. The Ancient one was still in deep sleep.

'Damn you, wanderer!' he heard the Raven barking as he followed his comrade, both checking for the prisoner's shackles. 'Who is he?' he asked rapidly.

Codru didn't answer. He wasn't even sure if he knew. But he knew he had to let him go if the man was still alive.

'Here!' he said as he pulled a golden chain deeply caught in the cedar's bark, as if it were almost part of it.

'Step aside!' the knight said, raising the mace above his head. With a lightning strike, he crashed into the chain. The tree itself creaked as if it moaned. But the chain did not break from the first blow. It was only in the second that it finally did, freeing the prisoner's hands, still rooted in the trunk.

'We had done what we could,' Toma said as Codru kneeled next to the old one, grabbing his inert head in his hands. The knight was right. It was no longer up to them if the man would awaken.

As such, they both left him behind and crossed the room, avoiding the Zmei corpses, as Codru glanced one last time at the Priestess, wingless and clawless, as he thought she would be, before they made their way to the dark passage.

After sprinting upward on the dark, cold stairs, they eventually reached the surface, behind the throne where Gunnay had sat not too long ago. The light fell through the roof like a translucent, golden curtain.

The other two priestesses were the first they encountered. They screamed, aware of the Raven's deeds, throwing themselves at the intruders, aiming their fingers at their eyes. Without any remorse, the knight treated the first one as he previously treated her men, now rotting at the bottom of the dungeon.

A ravenous blow to the chest made her one with the marble wall, her blood splattering on the red painting. Codru caught the second one's arms and was content to only put her to sleep with a heavy punch.

At the entrance, they had been welcomed by three horned Zmei—the last of their stock—who now covered their leather and snakeskin patches clothing with bronze plates. Their leader was the one who gazed at them earlier, as Codru and Toma were carried to the temple's entrance. They were maskless, their grotesque, mutilated faces revealing their missing noses. A familiar blade was resting in his arm.

'My axe!' Codru shouted.

The Zmeu smirked, throwing an eye at the hatchet in his hand. Toma stood in his place.

'It's you,' he hissed at their foes' leader. 'It's you who killed my family. I will split you in half!'

'I have not heard of you!' the Zmeu said in a broken speech. 'I may have; I've killed many!'

He then untied a trinket dangling from his belt. Toma's iron mask. He covered his own ugliness with it and signalled one of his men, who unstrapped his second short blade he kept at his waist. He threw it at Codru's feet.

'Pick it up!' the masked man wailed.

As soon as Codru raised the sword, the three Zmei ran towards them, roaring like the wind. And it was the first time Codru saw Toma wielding the mace in battle. As the wanderer fought two of them as skilfully as he knew, the Raven threw himself rabidly towards the masked one, crashing the walls and the columns under his heavy strikes. It was pure rage, driven by vengeance, that turned him into one of those man-beasts he heard about. It wasn't Toma anymore; it was the mace's might revealing itself through the knight's hand.

Codru's blade found room through the chain of one of the Zmei, as he dodged his fellow's spear. He heard the Raven shouting.

'Stand and fight, you coward!' he said, as the masked leader could clearly see it was no ordinary foe, the one he was now fighting. He was hiding behind the columns, trying to find a way to the knight.

Codru's spear-wavering enemy threw another strike, and the wanderer caught it under his boot, getting it stuck to the floor. He broke it in half with the other foot and raised the spear's edge. In panic, the Zmeu ran away, and with lightning speed, Codru released the half-spear into his back. The Zmeu fell to the floor, breathless.

It was almost while Toma's weapon finally grazed his foe's

bronze chest piece. But it was more than enough to throw the masked marauder to the ground, face down in the rubble, losing Codru's axe at a stone's crow away from him.

He could swear he saw a grin looming in the knight's beard.

'You are not going anywhere, cockroach!' he threatened the Zmeu as he walked behind him, watching him as he dragged himself through the rocks and dust.

'I killed you once; I'll kill you again! A thousand deaths I shall lay upon you if I must!'

He turned him face up with his boot. He raised the mace above his head, and just before he could strike, a strong wind swooped out of nowhere through the temple, killing the fires in the braziers. A hand wrapped out of a cloud of sand, materializing from nothingness, around Toma's mace wielding wrist. Next to the knight stood the Ancient one, awakened from his ages-long sleep.

The sky suddenly turned darker. Gazing through the roof, Codru could see as if the sun was being swallowed by the moon. The knight froze, unable to move his hands, his eyes bloodshot as he turned to the old prisoner, while the Zmeu watched them both in terror, dragging himself away, looking for freedom, or perhaps a way to defend himself.

*'This power is not yours to wield!'* the Ancient one thundered, as darkness befell. *'Nor wielding it will change your past!'*

The old, naked man reached for the mace and took it quietly from his stone-cold fingers.

He turned his stern figure to Codru only for a moment, meeting his eyes. The man then closed them, and within a moment, the sharp edge of a half-spear broke out through his heart. The masked Zmeu pulled it from his back hungrily, and he grabbed the mace out of the old man's hands. Dying, the Ancient could only turn, reaching out to his assassin's arm, and a heavy blast turned him and the leader to dust, releasing a shockwave of light through the temple that threw both Toma and Codru to the walls.

## CHAPTER XII

*Târgoviște, November 1459 (6967)*

'PLEASE, DON'T!'
Knocked with his back against the cold wall, the young man was frightened, and a cloud of warm air was puffing off his purple lips. He had all the reasons to be, too. The razor held under his chin, its point poking into his throttle, was one push away from piercing his skin. He had his arms held up in surrender and submitted, waiting for one of the two masked men to search his not so thick woollen coat. The man grunted, shaking his head, puzzled at the one holding the knife.

'Where's the groat?' he burst through the cloth covering his chin, pushing the blade slightly. 'Where is it, you tyke?'

'I've told you,' the young one said loudly, alarmed. 'I have none!'

The one searching for his belongings interrupted them.

'There's nothing in the bag either, Mandea! Only scrolls and feathers and other horse crap!'

'So what? Have we laid our arses on the line for nothing? Off with your boots!'

'Please,' the young man whimpered. 'It's freezing!'

'Do you want another hole in your head, boy? Off with them!'

Just when the man saw there was no way he could have gotten out of it with both his coin and his life, accepting his fate and beginning to untie his leather shoes, a shadow showed up at the end of the dark alley.

'Let him go!' it demanded.

The two muggers turned, releasing the victim from their grip and dropping him on his arse. The silhouette was nearly ten or so steps away from them, with its dark mantle framed eerily by the dirty white of the snow. Then they looked at each other.

'And who the devils are you to say so?' the razor bearer shouted.

The stranger didn't answer.

'Unless you are one of Vodă's hunters, I don't care a hang! Go chase yourself before I shave you too!'

The stranger approached unbothered by Mandea's threats while both men brought their blades forward, ready for a brawl. It was only when he got close enough that he removed his hood, revealing his crimson hair, his pale visage, and his dark and twisted sign etched in his skin.

'Gorblimey!' the searching party spat, stuttering, showing the white of his eyes, and dragging his comrade by his jerkin. 'It's the *pui-de-lele* they talk about.'

'What are you on about, Fane?'

'The Zmei-Slayer... The Muma's Headsman...'

Hearing the other mugger's frightened mumbles, the blade bearer took a couple of steps back, with his eyes frozen as if he had seen a ghost.

'We're going,' they said, dropping the young man's pouch in the puddle and taking more steps back, with their hands trembling, unable to run.

'Just leave!' the shadow snarled.

And it was all the permission the two bandits needed to turn in the blink of an eye and skedaddle, sliding their booths through the sludge. Without even thinking of turning their heads back, they soon reached the end of the alleyway and disappeared behind the corner of the wall they held the young man prisoner to up until then.

He stood right next to the young lad, watching as they vanished. He gave him his hand, which the boy grabbed and helped himself stand up.

'Thank you once again, jupân Codru!' he loudly offered his gratitude as he bent, struggling to gather his scattered and wet scrolls off the ground, fitting them back into his leather bag.

'Don't thank me, scribe!' the wanderer replied. 'Just do yourself a favour and make a stand one of these days. I won't always be around to bail you out. Now come!'

As they walked out the alleyway, traversing it, they entered one of the many, brighter main roads of the Târgoviște, the new capital of Wallachia. It was early morning, but the beginning of winter made the sky darker than usual. Apparently, besides a few fearless muggers preying silently behind some of these houses, it was otherwise quiet.

Vodă had a curfew in this city. *Vânători* trolled the streets, and watchmen trolled the towers and the walls, making sure everyone followed it. No lamps or candles were allowed to burn after sunset, either. From far outside the city, on a cloudy day or at night, only the local folk knew that the city was even there.

Codru did all he could to not draw much attention to him and Timotei, the young scribe that had been following him since shortly after his and Toma's parting in Braylan. The lad was sent to prepare the horses while he had been asking the drunkards of one of the few, if not the only, underground taverns about the Impaler's whereabouts. But since Timotei's small delay, they were now both heading quietly towards the stable they left the animals at.

'Did you find out, jupâne?' the scribe asked, doing his best to keep his voice down.

Codru brought his finger to his lips, reminding the lad to be silent while scouting the walls and the gaunt street, the thin snow squeaking under their boots.

'I did,' he eventually said. 'He appears to have left the capital weeks ago.'

'Where to? And why?'

'He told the Ottomans to shove the annual tribute demands up their arses. He killed the sultan's envoys; his men nailed their turbans to their heads. Then he ran off to a fortress, Poenari by its name.'

'So, he was here when he sent you the courtly invitation...' Timotei mumbled for himself, but Codru agreed regardless:

'It appears so! You must know where this citadel is' he then inquired, vaguely remembering its name from Sándor and the story of the boyars-turned-slaves that built it until their deaths.

Timotei's lips nearly curled into a smile.

'Oh, you have passed by its domain a couple of times!' he said. 'It is found west from here, after Dlăgopole and before Cozia's forests. Close to the mountains, watching over the cloudy waters of the Argeș river.'

Indeed, the scribe knew about his and the Raven's travels. Because instead of remaining in Kruhnen, where they had left him to set his affairs in order, the half-deaf scribe had been in their footsteps all along.

He had been in town when Codru visited the Black Boyar. He had followed them on his starveling horse to Cozia's forest, hiding as the men cut down the oak and met the feral girl. He hid at the outskirts of Argeș's Court, away from the sombre monastery, until he saw them leave and even travelled as far as Braylan, where he lost most of the coin Codru gifted him after he played dice with the Egyptians. He couldn't get a boat to the Isle of Snakes, but he waited patiently in the port for their return. Spending not more than a week in the corner of a sailors' tavern and wasting his last silver on just enough bread and broth to not be kicked out. Journaling his now-jupân's journey in his scrolls until late at night, under candlelight.

One day the young man heard some of the old ones maundering in the alehouse, spreading envious rumours, some of them even carrying plotting thoughts. They spoke of the one-eyed smuggler who had just moored his boat. They believed he had just returned from a trip to the Isle, where the Zmei seemed to have dwelled. There were two strangers with him who were looking to buy a carter's wagon. One of them, they said, bore the devil's mark, and his hair shone dark red.

As soon as he heard, the young chronicler gathered his parchments and bailed the tavern, almost running to find the newcomers. He found them right when a knight he immediately recognized was shaking a man's hand, and the red-haired one was already harnessing a pale-yellow horse to the cart they just bought.

During the evening, Timotei went as far as hiding behind the wagon when the men were loading up a mighty precious bounty in the cart, undoubtedly the island's treasure.

'Take it,' he heard one of them saying towards the end of their labour. After a pause, his fellow replied, surely accepting the first one's offer.'

'What is the meaning of it? What are you doing?'

He heard the man say, as he gasped:

'From this day on, I swear my arm to you for whenever you will need it, should you agree to do the same.'

'You were once my prisoner, then my hired sword,' Timotei heard the man continue succinctly. 'My days in the Brotherhood are over, I'm afraid, but that doesn't mean I can't have brothers.'

'Brothers?' his comrade echoed.

'You saved my life from the Boyar, and I believe I saved yours from the Priestess. What else do brothers do if they do not redeem each other?'

Timotei peeped over the wagon's edge, eaten up by curiosity and their low voices. He saw Codru slitting his palm with a knife, then shaking the other man's hand with it, who appeared to have cut his too.

*'Should the blades of our daggers one day turn to rust,*
*Then we'll know death has claimed the other of us.'*

He was close enough to jump out of his hideout and ask them once more to let him follow them. However, his heart, quiet like a mouse, wouldn't let him. He had already been turned down once. He had already been able to follow them for this long without their knowledge. So, it was given to be that way. Telling a story from afar, as a loyal witness to their odyssey, for the sake of posterity.

So, after the sun set, he ran back to the barn where his horse slept and curled up in the hay himself, sleeping with one eye open to not lose them when the men decided to leave the bay. They didn't leave the next day or the day after. He observed the knight, the red-haired man, and the sailor from a distance as they spent a couple of nights at the tavern themselves. Hunger began to eat at him, as he had already wasted the last of his coin.

There was an unknown cloak-bearing rider that arrived soon too, meeting them.

'With solemn honour, Jupân Codru received today, November 17th, 6967 Year of the World, a scroll from a man who came and went as if it never existed, under the cover of night,' he scribbled on parchment, under the last of his candle burning at the table he had already been overstaying.

'I believe we told you to stick to your letters, Timotei of John the Carpenter,' he suddenly heard a voice.

It was Codru's. He, the knight, and even the one-eyed man cornered him at the table, holding their cups and pulling their chairs next to his. The sailor spilled some wine on the table, a few drops falling on the scribe's fresh ink. The boy didn't wipe it. He froze, unable to speak or to move.

'Have you been following us all this time?' the knight asked. Timotei could only nod.

'Why?' Codru asked.

'I promised I wouldn't forget your kindness,' he braced himself, clearing his throat. 'And I didn't.'

He continued, as the men just watched him struggle:

'I have a debt to you, and I can only repay it by doing what I know—by telling your story.'

Codru frowned, and Toma's face turned sour.

'There are stories that are not worth telling, boy...' he cut him off bluntly.

'He's pale as limestone; where have you found this one?' the sailor chuckled. 'Look at him. When was the last time you ate?'

Timotei shrugged.

'And the coin we left you with?' Codru jumped him, more or less friendly, to which the chronicler shook his head as his eyes fell on the table.

'Christ!' Toma exhaled. 'You're lucky you still have your trousers, then.' He then turned, raising a hand to the maid to bring some food and some drink.

'Well, the Priestess might have been onto something, wasn't she?' the knight added, turning to Codru. 'Fate, isn't it? Bringing him to us in time of need.'

A woman brought a wooden tray with some cheese, dry sausage, and rye. She poured some wine into the young one's cup, and when she tried to take the jug away, Dobre caught her wrist gently and said:

'Now be a good lady and leave it here; less toing and froing for you!'

The knight sipped from his goblet while Timotei was stuffing his face, trying in too little time to quench his hunger.

Codru prompted a scroll on the table, on top of the ones the scribe had lying around.

'Since it appears that fate brought us together, here, have a look at this!' he demanded.

'What is this?' Timotei's voice faded, breadcrumbs rolling from his chin. Timidly, he grabbed the parchment with his greasy fingers.

'You have been under Master Lang's employment, haven't you?' the knight bothered him. 'We want to know if this scroll is forged or not.'

Timotei read the letter. It was written with the signs of St. Cyril, as on all papers. A red wax seal bore the Dragon's Order's coat of arms, which he immediately recognized. The red ink signature below read, 'I, Vlad, by the Grace of God, Ruler.' It was an invitation. Now was his chance. He had something the men needed.

'If I help you, you let me come with,' he suddenly dared to tell them.

The one-eyed sailor burst into laughter.

'Give him some food and some wine and look at him; he grows fangs!'

After a short pause, Codru nodded.

'So be it, then. It's your funeral, scribe.'

Excited, with a large and hopeful smile looming on his face, the young man recited:

'The letter is as real as it can be,' he said. 'It praises you for lifting the curse from Wallachia's heart. Vlad-Vodă himself summons you to the Princely Court for a proposition. It doesn't mention anything about the knight or the sailor.'

Codru grabbed the letter from his hand and folded it; he hid it under his mantle.

'I know what it says, I only needed to know it's real.'

'It is!'

'If I dare say,' he added in the end, 'While it may seem like a friendly-worded invitation, it doesn't look like you have a say in the matter.'

The next day, while waiting at the stables, he watched as the three men said their farewells.

The old man went his way, looking for workers on the shore, while the knight left the city with his new, chest-filled wagon. He had no clue where to.

As the light of the morning was now hitting the walls of the Târgoviște, Codru and the scribe found the stables where their horses had been left over night. The keeper was sleeping, drowsing, smothered in a holed woollen fleece, with his sheepskin hat over his ears, on a chair next to the small iron stove. It appeared that horse thieves were of no concern to the townsmen.

'Here,' Codru said to the scribe. He had revealed a dagger with a golden handle and handed it to the lad as Timotei was strapping his bag to his poor horse's saddle. 'Take it. Make use of it in the future!'

The boy shook his head. He recognized it from the promise he witnessed that night between Codru and Toma.

'I can't; it's too much... What for?' he muttered.

'Just take it!'

The man grabbed the scribe's hand forcefully and let the dagger into the palm of his glove. The boy mumbled:

'I wouldn't know what to do with it,' he said, falling on his thoughts, his eyes captured by the precious blade. It was from Zmei's treasure, he believed.

'Just point at the bandits with the sharp side,' Codru said. 'Now put it away; we need to leave the city at once!'

\*\*\*

*Poenari Citadel, November 1459 (6967)*

Even with his head wrapped in the hood, the wet, cold wind bit away at his face, roaring through the valley as it scattered anaemic snowflakes all around. Late November was a harbinger of an upcoming merciless winter. Shadowfire was breathing heavily, clouds of air leaving his puffing muzzle as its hooves were struggling and choking in the muddy, slippery ascent of the hill. The beast pulled through, however, stoically, a toughness the wanderer was aware of.

He halted, turning his head back. He couldn't say the same about the young scribe's hay burner. Or about the lad himself, for that matter. As he looked up to the misty top of the hill, he could see the shadows of the five towers of the sombre castle, swarming of crows. It was not far. But they surely needed the rest.

'We'll take a breath here!' he barked at his fellow, dismounting. 'Before your horses' knees break like twigs, that is.'

He pulled the steed under the naked crown of the tree, covering themselves partially from the dreary wind. Timotei did the same.

'It's almost as if we ought not to reach the summit, jupâne,' he whined, pulling his wheezing animal after him.

Codru could not disagree. Poenari was not a bad hideout tower; it was far from it. The tall hill was steep, and its ravines were treacherous. Surrounded by abrupt slopes and cliffs that plunged into the threatening river on three sides and shielded to the north by massive mountains towering to Codru's left, the fortress was impregnable. Small companies like theirs could barely reach it, and for an army, it would be even more daunting, if not impossible. The long, narrow path trailing from the hill behind them was the only way to approach the citadel.

If there was a place where Vodă could have chosen to both overlook any upcoming enemy and protect himself for them, he had chosen the perfect one. He was sure they had already been seen and perhaps awaited.

'I believe you and jupân Toma could have shared from the Zmei's treasure; it surely could have been more than what the Prince would promise you as a reward.'

Codru exhaled.

'There are treasures we cannot keep for ourselves,' he said vaguely, scouting the fortress from afar. 'And the Raven didn't keep it, either. He only carried it to bury somewhere...'

'...To never be found,' Timotei ended it for him. 'Yes, so you have told me, master.'

Codru looked at him and muttered as he mounted:

'Perhaps I should have buried you somewhere to never be found, too!'

He shouldn't have had him follow. As he expected, the boy proved to be more of a burden than a help. He didn't know how to cook or make a fire. Not too long ago, he almost fell into a fountain. While on the Merchants' Road, he had been relentlessly talking, loudly so he could hear himself, asking Codru to retell stories of Strigoi, Paralei, Zmei, and Demons, scribbling each of his words on parchment scraps. But at least for now, the red-haired man's last words silenced the boy.

After the long uprise on the ominous path, they finally reached the summit, where the wall of an imposing and broad square tower welcomed them. Instead of battered walls, this first corner tower had a semi-rounded lower one, strengthening it. The sole entrance, situated on its right side, was a covered iron gate set deep within the structure, flanked by red brick walls that appeared to rise directly from the hill's rock. The travellers and their horses were shielded from fierce winds only when they approached them.

Codru first noticed the presences on the neighbouring wall, moving left and right. They were guards, or perhaps archers; he couldn't tell as the thick mist was clouding even his sharp vision. He heard one of their voices cutting through the air as they issued an order. Shortly after, the gates clanked open, pulled aside by a few armoured guards.

Once the gates opened, three men stepped out of the citadel

before Codru or Timotei could even think of dismounting. Two of them had their helmets on. Dark, light gambesons covered their bodies, with chainmail falling on their shoulders and brown fur protecting their necks. They had their leathered hands resting on their hilts, ready to bring out their swords if needed. They were well prepared, by the looks of it. And if the wanderer wasn't wrong, he could sense they were even of foreign origin.

Unlike the two guardians, the man in the middle, walking forward, was not wearing nearly as much protection as them. Besides a black cowl falling on his shoulders and a hood covering his head, there was nothing else keeping the cold wind away, either. The tall man wore a long mantle that reminded Codru of monks he had seen in Scodra years ago. But this man was no man of God, for sure, and the short blade he bore at his waist was proof of it.

His face loomed from beneath the hood as he got closer to the horses.

'If you will, travellers, dismount and state your affairs!' his velvety voice resounded, somehow covering nature's howls.

Codru agreed. He got off his horse and signalled his companion to do the same. He then stood his ground without approaching, searching under his cloak, and revealing the scroll he had. He showed it vaguely to the strange welcoming party as he waited for the tall man to come and take it out of his hand.

'Read this,' he said as the man reached out slowly and took the parchment of Codru's glove with his thin, long, and waxy fingers. 'Your Prince summoned me to the capital, then left the city.'

The man lifted his eyes from the scroll, glancing at Codru from under the hood with a piercing silence.

'Urgent times call for urgent decisions!' he eventually said.

'It appears, however, that you had no difficulty in locating His Highness. Please spare us the baseless complaints.'

Codru sniffed, biting his tongue, as the man finished reading the scroll. Rolling it back and putting it away under his own cloak, he spun on his boots' heels and called Codru and the scribe to follow with a hand gesture.

'I am Dragomir, His Highness' sword bearer and councillor,' he said. 'Welcome to Poenari Citadel, Zmei-Slayer. Follow me; you are expected, although I can't vouch for the boy here. Leave the horses; they will be looked after.'

Followed by the two guards as they passed the iron gates and walked slightly upwards, Codru passed through a rather narrow passage, sided by the walls of the large, multiple levelled square tower to the left and the fortress wall itself to the right. Not too long after, they entered what looked like the courtyard—longer rather than wider.

Codru glanced around. Besides the tower they had just left behind, where guards peered through holes to scout the newcomers, Codru could see four more towers tied together by the fortress walls. Two of these towers were to his right, on the southern side, and another stood on the opposite wall. However, the largest tower was at the end of the courtyard, slightly oriented to the south, making room for the keep beside it, which was only half as tall. The closer they got to the towered keep, the larger the courtyard became, leaving behind the barracks, the stables, and even what appeared like a small chapel, that framed the first half of it.

Poenari was only what its masons—the dead boyars—built it to be, the wanderer noted. A hideout. Nothing more than what was necessary to live had been brought here, nor less than what was needed to keep the foes away. Two more guards, like the ones walking in guests' footsteps, were quietly waiting at the framed door's keep. Turning, Dragomir dismissed the previous two men, and then, returning to the door, commanded the other two to open the door.

There was no sumptuous hall expecting them inside. After passing through a rather small and bleak hallway, they entered the main room. Even the dimly lit chamber he once walked into at the Black Boyar's mansion had a more grandiose atmosphere than the Prince's castle.

Burning braziers were hanging from the tall ceiling, providing some warmth and light. A long, brown tinted carpet was stretching over the red-brick, cold floor. The dull, bleary carpets, embroidered with silver, hung from the stone walls. As Codru followed the sword bearer across the room, on his left, small, iron-grated eyes covered with blurry, thick glass stood for windows, while on the right wall, breaking the tapestries, there was an open door with a staircase leading up, most likely to the larger tower.

There were dark-clothed guards that surrounded the chamber, silently moving slowly alongside the walls, while two of them stood at the end of the room, where the wooden throne was, without a podium underneath, framing the man sitting on it. The Prince,

Codru figured. In the corner behind the throne, a wooden staircase led to the next level of the keep.

When it suited him, and the guests were now close enough, he stood from the tall-backed chair and raised his arm. On his signal, Dragomir let his hood fall on his back, revealing a pale, hairless scalp. Not shaven. Instead, it rather looked as if hair had never grown on it. He turned to the travellers and waved for them to cease walking. As he moved back to his side, scraping a bow, he delivered a short yet grave introduction:

'In the name of God almighty, Vlad-Voivode, Lord and Ruler of all Wallachia, and Duke of Amlaș and Făgăraș, welcomes you to the Citadel!'

Codru saw Timotei bowing during the introduction speech, yet before he could think of doing the same, he heard the Prince saying, barely letting his councillor finish his discourse.

'Welcome, indeed, friends!'

His arms were loosely stretched to his sides, as if he embraced his guests from a distance. He was neither short nor tall, but he had broad shoulders, draped in a brownish mantle edged with fur of the same hue. His long, dark hair cascaded in waves over it. Under the medium-length mantle, he wore a scarlet tunic, thick and adorned with braided golden threads fastening across his wide chest. At his thick belt hung a scabbard, which swayed above his breeches, stuffed into his dark leather boots.

He walked slowly towards his visitors, thudding over the thin rug. As he approached, his black eyes gazed inquisitively at Codru from under a pair of raven-dark brows. His nose was bony, as were his cheekbones. His lips were thin and hidden under a moustache matching his eyebrows.

'Please accept my apologies for having you make the journey in this awful weather and on such short notice,' he carefully chose his words. His voice was low and cold, yet blunt.

'I am at a precipice,' he continued, only side-glancing at Codru's tattoo. 'There are difficult times weighing on my lands and storms brewing at my doorsteps. I am not proud of it, but I was forced to hastily leave my home, my wife, and my children and come here. I trust you will forgive my lack of tact?'

By the way he hung his last words in the air, he expected an answer, so Codru thought he could at least give him that.

'I am sure we can put this past us! I have been taught to not hold grudges.'

The Prince smiled vaguely under his moustache.

'Praise be, I am overjoyed to hear that,' he exhaled, as if someone lifted the weight of his chest, bringing his hands together in sort of a praying gesture.

After that, he left his arms down, joining them behind him, and looking into the floor, he began walking in a small circle in front of his guests.

'Of course, you understand why it picked up my interest when I heard the rumours of not one but two merchants from the north wandering through my country and hunting down creatures I only heard of in our old maid stories.'

Codru began to understand that, under the humble veil of his words, the Prince was not quite amiable. Codru wasn't a stranger to Vlad's stories of cruelty. He was a wise, cunning man, as Toma once described him. Skilled in the arts of courtly intrigue. The red-haired man suddenly became aware that the guards waiting obediently in the shadows were His Highness's most trusting men, bought with gold. Perhaps they were even the ones who put iron bolts in the Ottomans' envoys heads.

The wanderer kept what he knew or did to himself, although he felt the quiet scribe to his right, staring up to him.

'Some might believe these men are some sort of redeemers, see? Lifting curses and curing plagues left and right... Clearing the far corners of the domain of vile pillagers... Putting the dead back to their graves.'

The Prince chuckled.

'It makes for a beautiful legacy, Zmei-Slayer! May I call you that?'

'I prefer Codru, Sire!'

'Codru...' Vlad echoed him. 'What an unusual and yet very Wallachian name! Even though you have travelled to foreign lands, by your speech, if my ear doesn't trick me.'

He stopped in his walk and turned to Codru, briefly looking down at Timotei, who kept his chin in his chest.

'Well, Codru,' the Voivode said calmly. 'If one day someone you don't know nor have ever heard of comes to your home and begins swiping your floor, you would at least want to know who they are and why they suddenly began doing your chores, wouldn't you agree?'

The wanderer didn't lose the man in his eyes and remained silent.

'Perhaps, from the outside, others might think that I do not know how to clean my own house. My mutts would turn on me, confused, not knowing who their master is, forgetting the scent of my hand that fed them all these years.'

'So,' he finally asked in a demanding manner. 'Who are you, Codru, the Zmei-Slayer. What is it that you are doing in my house, shaking out my carpets?'

The chronicler was right. This seemed less and less like an invitation and more like an ambush. But Codru didn't lose himself. If the Prince had any idea how much of those old maid stories he put in the ground, it would be Vlad losing it. The men surrounding the place were trained, no doubt, but he faced worse odds. His axe's blade would bleed them enough to find himself a way out.

In the doorway on his right, suddenly, a young woman showed up. He only turned his head when he noticed the movement, and Vlad didn't turn at all. She was brown-skinned and beautiful. And, if he wasn't mistaken, based on her floral dress, her gold rings wrapped around her forearms, and her ebony black hair, she was of Egyptian origin, same as the slaves.

'I was taken from these lands by the Ottomans when I was younger than my fellow here,' the wanderer said, turning to Timotei. 'I returned because I believed the past wasn't done with me. But I was mistaken. The past doesn't give a damn—it was I who wasn't done with it. So, I was ready to leave.'

Prince Vlad looked at him as if he had absorbed each of his guest's words.

'Why did you stay behind?'

Codru would have lied to himself if he denied he ever wondered.

'Perhaps I was hunting down a purpose, not monsters,' he said, realizing it as the words were leaving his mouth. 'A monk once told me that the only way to rest with the past is not by running from it or confronting it. We can't do either. Repenting for it is all we can do.'

Vlad slightly bowed his head, seemingly falling into his own thoughts.

'I will have to admit, I was not expecting such candour from you,' he said, raising his head with a forced smile under his moustache. 'But I am thankful for it. It may have just saved your lives and spared me good company.'

'Now I am sure you are weary and hungry after the journey,' he continued. 'Servants will prepare your chamber in the tower to bathe. Then we shall dine at my table.'

He waved his hand, and the Egyptian young woman approached, leaving her place in the doorway.

'My faithful servant Luladija will show you to your rooms. Rest. I have matters of the utmost importance I want to discuss with you after, Zmei-Slayer.'

***

Warm, silky water was trickling down his coarse, long hair. He couldn't lie; Luladija's warm hands running through it as she washed it were soothing. The Egyptian woman insisted on letting her pour water from the jug onto his head, as it was her duty. He protested at first. But now, sitting in the wooden tub, with steam filling the rather small, bedded chamber the Prince had been so kind to offer, he was quietly glad he accepted her offer.

After many moons in the saddle, sleeping under the sky, or washing himself now and again in the springs, this was a godsend. He was so tranquil, as if charms had been put on him. And the Egyptian woman was aware.

'You know, traveller,' she said, taking the chance, 'I can do more to help you cast the worries away.'

Her hands ran onto his scarred shoulder, reaching to his chest.

'When all my other potions fail, this sometimes helps His Highness too, with his head aches, lifting the weights off his shoulders.'

With his head pressed on the edge of the tub, Codru opened his eyes and caught her hand.

'No!' he said, then he released her hand. She slowly retracted it, continuing to pour water from her jug.

'That's a shame,' she whispered and smiled. 'There's an icefloe around that withered heart of yours; it could have melted at least for a while.'

She then reached out, turned his palm up, and rubbed her thumb softly in it, looking into it. He pulled it and turned to her.

'What are you trying to do?'

'Not a lot,' she said, leaving the jug on a short wooden stool as she rose off the floor, where she had kneeled until then. 'Only read what has already been done.'

She then sat on the edge of the wooden tub, watching Codru, her contoured, dark eyes falling into his.

'I have seen your past and your future, love, long before you arrived.'

'My cards say you are a strong man, but not strong enough. You are longing. Your yearning for deliverance and a lasting legacy binds you. Like all men, these desires are your weaknesses.'

She continued:

'You have lost much, but you will not reap the power that had been destined for you. Not yet. You still have much to lose before you become who you are meant to be.'

Codru grunted as the soothing state he had been in until then suddenly vanished. He once heard empty words such as these from the teacher, and he had no patience for the Egyptian's riddles. His mind wandered without his will to his parents, whom he couldn't remember, to the Old-Man he abandoned at the mountain, and to Ileana, the girl he was taken away from.

'Destiny, I've found recently, is only a trick that Time plays on us. And you know nothing of me; I have already lost everything.'

He stood up from the waters, grabbing a long linen rag he wrapped around his waist. She stood up as well.

'Not everything, wanderer.'

'And what else is there to lose?'

'Everything you're yet to have. That is your prophecy.'

She then said this as she walked towards the door:

'You and the Prince share more than your eyes let you see. And it was destiny that led you to him. He is a strong man too, but the same as yourself, eaten up by demons and trapped by human frailties. We are helping him achieve the power he was born to wield.'

Codru began to see that she was more than what she let others know.

'And I can help you too, if you are willing to make the sacrifice.'

'Who are you? You are not a servant.'

'I am not the servant you believe I am, but I do serve the Prince.'

A knock on the door interrupted them, and Luladija opened it. The councillor stood in the doorway, his pale, bald figure looking at her, then turning to Codru:

'Dinner will be served, and His Highness invites you to join him in his chamber the soonest possible.'

***

'Where is the boy I came with?' Codru asked as he followed Dragomir down the circular stairs of the tower. The tall, bald man leading him carried a brass candle holder as darkness kicked in through the tower's small windows.

'The young man had already been fed and had been invited to browse through our humble library in the Midnight-Tower,' he answered with almost no inflexion in his voice. 'His Highness will only discuss his affairs with you.'

'And with you, I presume. You will be there too, won't you?'

After a short moment, Dragomir answered.

'I am the councillor; it is part of my duty.'

As they passed the Prince's hall, Codru followed the man up the wooden stairs in the corner behind the throne. It led right into Vlad's thalamus, one of his private chambers, where two quiet servants were placing their last silver chalices onto a rather large wooden table.

The table was covered in red cloth, and there was meat, rye, and long-neck silver jugs spread out all over it and lit up by candles. As they entered through the room's corner, there was a stone chimney on the immediate left wall, close to the opposite corner. The Prince was sitting on a chair at the head of the table, facing the right, far wall. Two of the same round, small glass covered windows were poked in the wall in front of the guests. The standing braziers in the corner did not give much light, so that not so tall chamber seemed still cold, with all the fire sources burning around.

'Please, come,' the Voivode said at the sight of Codru and his sword-bearer, prompted with the back in his chair and slightly waving a gesture with his golden rings-covered left hand to the servants to leave the room. With their heads bowed, they passed by the visitors and disappeared down the wooden staircase.

'Thank you for honouring me with your presence, Codru,' Vlad said. 'The bath and the chamber are to your liking, I hope.'

Codru's mind thought about the strange encounter he had not too long ago with Luladija. The Prince's eyes scouted him inquisitively over the flickering candles, casting shadows over his prominent cheekbones.

'Certainly, better than a cave,' he was content to reply.

The Prince stood from his chair, inviting him with his arms to join him at the table.

'Please, sit!' he doubled it with a soft but blunt invitation. To which the wanderer agreed, walking toward the first chair he noticed, on the side of the table, toward the middle.

He saw Dragomir leaving his side without sitting, but instead circling the table and prompting himself behind his master, not too close nor too far, shadowed in the back of the room, where another wooden staircase could be seen in the corner, perhaps leading to the Prince's bedding.

As the servants had been sent away, Vlad took it upon himself to do the honours. Leaving his chair's area, he poured some liquor out of one of the silver jugs in the goblet closest to Codru, with his free arm behind him.

'Now tell me,' he dared, as he filled Codru's cup with wine and placed the jugs back. 'How many of the stories are true, Zmei-Slayer?' His voice was calm, and he seemed truly interested.

The traveller wasn't sure if the truth would be the right answer.

'People say many things, Sire,' he said. 'I am sure much of what I've heard about Your Highness is not true either.'

The Prince hummed, walking toward the top of the table, reaching for his own goblet.

'By the way you look, perhaps it was but a matter of time until people began threading legends about you,' Vlad said, briefly measuring Codru's hair and forehead mark, with the cup in his hand. He raised it, and the wanderer followed his way.

'To our health!' he uttered as he sipped the wine, sitting back in his chair. Codru did the same.

'I have been told many things about you. At first, I believed you were an Ottoman spy. Rumour has it you had also earned your living with your blade, not too long ago.'

Codru sighed. He wasn't completely surprised. The Prince had eyes and ears in many places. Maybe even outside his domain. But he felt a slight distress upon hearing him mention it. As if he did not want to be known for his past anymore.

'If at least half of what I heard is true,' Vlad continued, 'I would very much like to hire your sword for a very important task.'

Codru bit his lower lip, then said:

'What is the quest?'

Vlad sat back in his chair, and with an inexpressive face, he answered, unexpectedly bluntly:

'I want you to travel to Istanbul and kill the Sultan.'

The room turned quiet. Codru grinded his teeth. It was now, when he began to believe that the past did not care to follow, that it decided to prove him wrong. He had his answer, and his answer had been decided years ago.

'This dinner will be short,' he mumbled. 'Because, Sire, I won't accept the task.'

Vlad remained quiet, no emotion showing on his shadowed face.

'On what grounds?' he only asked.

Codru could have spent hours giving the Prince a tome-full of reasons. But he didn't.

'It cannot be done, and I refuse to be the one failing!'

He heard Vlad puffing softly, taking his eyes off him, and beginning to gather some pieces of meat, laying them on the plate in front of him.

'It pains me to hear that, Codru, and I'm rather disappointed you believe it, too,' he said. 'But indulge me in telling you a short story.'

He then cleared his throat without taking his eyes off the table, continuing to slowly pick his food as carefully as he chose to pick his words.

'Since the beginning, it has been my family's blood that has united these lands. My lineage's cursed yet strong blood. But some of my forefathers were weak and spineless. Unworthy. They let our heritage fall into the fangs of the Ottoman Crescent, which sucked our country dry of its youth and its riches.'

'When I was young,' he continued, 'My father left me and my younger brother as a warranty to the Sultan. A promise he wouldn't ever dare revolt. Until he and my older brother were slain mercilessly like dogs by those he considered allies, only to be replaced by usurpers more to their liking.'

He paused as he bit into a pork piece, a thread of grease rolling down his chin. He wiped it with the back of his hand, then continued.

'Not only was I held hostage by the Ottomans, but I convinced them to give me an army. Like you, I returned. I came back to free my country. I dethroned and defeated the fool who sat at its helm. I was shortly betrayed—that is true—and forced into exile for years. But, against all odds, I once again arose and took my land back for the second time.'

The Prince fell on his thoughts for a moment as he used a piece of cloth to wipe off his hands, chewing. Once he swallowed his nibble, he raised his eyes and stared at Codru.

'If you are daring enough, you can forge and bend the odds in your favour,' he said. 'Anything can be done!'

The wanderer admitted the Prince was a man of great passion. And he began to see why the Egyptian fortune-teller said they had a great deal in common. He had been the same. He, too, was a prisoner of the Turks. He, too, had his family slaughtered. The Prince talked about his family's cursed blood, and what else was it, if not his own blood that had haunted him all his life?

He was now pondering how much more he shared with the Voivode and, even more dauntingly, how much of what Luladija said was true. Even the knight once told him that he and the Prince might have shared a great deal of traits. Regardless, he knew what the quest Vlad wanted him to undertake entailed, and he would not change his mind.

'I cannot accept the task, and this is my final word on it.'

Vlad nodded barely visible, then half-turned his head to his councillor.

'Leave us, Dragomir!'

'Very well, Your Highness!' the bald man bowed, then left the room, glancing coldly at the guest as he passed.

Once he vanished down the staircase, Vlad rose again from his chair. He walked toward the wall behind Codru. Turning, the wanderer saw a large tapestry he hadn't noticed when he entered. Threaded with silver, just like the ones in the hall downstairs, it showed a great tree with many branches and letters embroidered on them. Under the tapestry, there was a wooden cabinet with a candle holder lying on it, casting a gloomy light on the wall carpet, making the tree's branches and trunk spark like snow under a clear moon.

'I know what that sign you bare on your face means, Codru,' Vlad said as he stood in front of the tree, gazing at it with his arms behind his back. 'When I was a child, my father spoke about the Salmans—the smoke-threaders, the cloud-walkers. He hasn't always spoken in the kindest way, true, and he believed they were even a threat to our lineage.'

He opened a drawer in the cabinet, and Codru heard him poking around through scrolls and trinkets.

'But I always believed our kinds were so much alike. Yours and mine. After all, we share common ancestors. If only we could have become allies, what great things we could have achieved! Unfortunately, while your sort fell to the ravages of time, mine succumbed to the lure of power and vice.'

He turned. In his hand, he held a strange heirloom in his fist—a string of blonde hair tied in a silk ribbon—that he brought to his face, inhaling as he closed his eyes and rubbed his temples with his other hand. Soothing himself.

'I despise my bloodline, and I despise everyone that surrounds me, Codru, because I need their coin and their men to rule,' he said as if he were merely talking to himself, passing by the guest, and walking toward the chimney. He gazed in the fire, prompting his elbow on its stone and continuing to keep his face fallen in the heirloom-holding hand.

'But if gold is what keeps them loyal, they're not your allies, and an ally is what I am in need of.'

Codru left his chair.

'What makes you believe I can be it?'

'Because I already know what drives you. It's not gold you seek, but peace,' he said, opening his eyes and gazing at the golden lock lying in his hand, reflecting the warm fire. 'Perhaps love,' he added.

'Even if I could do the deed, you would not be able to offer any of those.'

The Prince awakened from his thoughts and scouted his guest with his dark eyes.

'You would be surprised at the things I can offer you.'

'A very dear ally of mine recently died, Codru,' he said, changing his tone and turning graver than before. 'One whose power had the odds to turn the balance in my favour. By helping me build an army so fierce, the Empire would have trembled in its sight. But now, with the ally gone, I was sent back on my quest to destroy the snake's nest and to defend my lands. I need a new ally.'

Walking across the room and leaving the fireplace behind, he let the heirloom drop back into the drawer, closing it. With his hands brought back once more, he puffed his chest and said:

'Do not answer me now. Sleep on it, Zmei-Slayer,' he said in a final attempt to convince Codru, although they both knew the answer already. 'Help me sever the snake's head, and I can at least vouch that, by the grace of God, I will offer you a life in the heart of the lands we could redeem together. As brothers.'

# CHAPTER XIII

*Poenari Citadel, November 1459 (6967)*

THE ONLY SOUNDS WERE THE WIND HOWLING, hitting the walls, and their boots and horseshoes screeching on the snow. The morning sun was yet to gift the sky with its light. Codru was almost sure the guards had been instructed to not open the gates, but regardless, he didn't care to wait. He knew he had to leave the Citadel. Behind the hospitable veil of dinners and chambers, his gut was telling him the Prince was no friend of his, that was certain.

Pulling the other horse behind him, Timotei stumbled, still drowsy after having been dragged out of bed before the rooster's song.

'Would you keep it down?' Codru snapped at him, whispering, as he pulled Shadowfire reins after him towards the sloped and slippery passage leading to the iron entrance. The scribe recovered his footing and nodded without saying anything. As he turned his face to the top of the wall, the guards were standing silently, watching them as they approached.

When they finally reached the gate, Codru didn't wait for an invitation. He went straight up to one of the two armoured men and said:

'We are leaving; open the gates!'

The men looked at each other silently, unbothered, then replied: 'His Highness had left word to not let anyone out.'

Codru expected this much, but he wanted to make sure they were indeed prisoners.

'What is the meaning of this?' Codru cut him off, clenching his teeth. 'We are His Highness' guests, not his prisoners. Open the gates, I say!'

The guardian shook his head slowly as he rested his hand on his sword.

'We mean no trouble, traveller, but if that is what you seek, then you shall find it; worry not,' he said calmly. 'Unless Lord Dragomir or Vodă himself wakes up and orders me to let you go, I will have to kindly ask you to go back to your chambers at once.'

Codru knew they were outnumbered, and this was the only way in or out, but he was short-tempered, so when he saw the man reaching for his sword, his own palms itched for his axe too. Fortunately, or unfortunately, before he could have made a decision that got him and the chronicler killed, a silky, grave voice broke the early morning crisp air, reaching to his ears from behind.

'These men would give their lives and their souls to their master, traveller!' the voice said.

Codru and Timotei turned. The tall, dark hooded man stood behind them, merely a few steps away. Dragomir. His white, sunken cheeks could be seen even through the morning blackness. His hands were brought together, covered in the other's arm sleeve. He stood there, watching them silently. The wanderer was both frustrated and surprised, as his sharp ears did not get a hold of the councillor's steps on the snow.

'We are leaving the fortress; tell your men to open the gates,' he told the sword-bearer.

'So soon?' Dragomir asked. 'I am taking you did not agree with His Highness terms then.'

Codru left his dark steed's side for a moment, walking towards the man, who did not step back.

'I have given my answer to your Prince. Twice. He is consumed by delusion, and I refuse to be dragged into it.'

Dragomir watched him with his flickering eyes as the red-haired man spoke.

'Besides,' Codru said, 'unless we are being kept against our will, we can leave when we please. So, the gates!'

'I have to say, Zmei-Slayer,' Dragomir said, 'I would have expected more courtesy from you. You had been welcomed honourably to the Citadel. The Prince holds you in high regard. However, you choose to leave thievishly, under the cover of darkness, without bidding your host neither thanks nor a farewell.'

Then, in a lower tone, as he sighed, he added:

'Disappointing!'

Codru knew that the way he had chosen to leave the fortress wouldn't sit well with the Voivode, but he felt he had not been given a choice. He knew that his and the scribe's next destination, if by any chance they could have left the walls, would be north, over the mountains; there was a blacksmith where they could have rested for some time before he sorted out his next destination.

But he also knew the Voivode did not take a no for an answer. So, he chose to leave before he was going to refuse him once more.

A blade showed its icy teeth from under the sword-bearer's sleeves. Codru spun around abruptly as a gust of wind brushed past his side. It was the scribe. He saw Timotei, who clearly sensed the threat too, running towards Dragomir, and in that moment, he knew what was going to happen. Before a word could leave his lips to make him cease his foolish attack, the young man sneaked behind the councillor, his arm wrapped around his head, uncovering his bald scalp. The other hand held a dagger at his throat. Its gold handle could be seen tightly squeezed in his hand, as its blade was pressing on the man's pale skin, revealing a great ashen scar around his neck.

'Give the order!' the boy shouted, his voice trembling.

Codru's and Dragomir's eyes met. The man's eyes were wide open, surprised by the young man's attack.

'No!' was the only word the wanderer could summon before reaching out to his hatchet.

In less than a moment, the sword-bearer's face grimaced, his lips stretched on his teeth, and, parting his arms until then kept hidden in each-other's sleeve, he revealed his own blade, its cold reflection slitting the shadows. With a strong grip, he removed the boy's knife, twisting his arm as Timotei dropped the golden dagger in the dirty snow. As he brought his short-time captor to his knees, the councillor slid his knife under the scribe's chin, towering behind him.

Desperately, he did all he could to cover back his scarred neck, wrapping his head in the hood, as if the young man had just shamed him. Then his long and thin fingers plunged like a claw into the chronicler's shoulder, keeping him to his knees with the blade at his throat, ready to end him.

Timotei looked up to Codru, begging him with his eyes.

'Don't even let that thought cross your mind, traveller!' Dragomir hissed, gasping as Codru pulled the axe, ready to step forward and strike him, hoping to free his comrade. 'Drop it, or I'll carve a pocket in your fellow's neck!'

'Drop the axe!' Dragomir urged him, pressing the long knife in Timotei's skin as he pulled his head back by his hair. 'Now!'

Codru clenched his fists. He had been once again cornered in a place he loathed to be. He had no choice.

'Curses!' he barked as he threw the hatchet, its head sticking in the snow-covered earth.

'Why?' he mumbled, asking the trapped boy.

'He was a foe, jupâne, wasn't he? I had to point the sharp edge at him!'

In that moment, Codru didn't know what he despised more—himself or the young one. Timotei had in him the same fire he had, which was now diminishing. The young man was willing to sacrifice for others, just as he had done before. He served as a living reminder of what the wanderer had long lost—naive, selfless innocence.

'Seize him!' the sword-bearer demanded. In an instant, the two guardians behind Codru stepped forward and pulled his arms to the side, wrapping their gloves around his forearms and pressing down on his shoulder until, forced by his arms' twist, Codru had to bend the knee. He bit his lip, his blood boiling in his veins, steam coming out of his chin.

He didn't even realize the light came out, the sky turning from dark to heavy grey as the anaemic morning loomed over the walls. He first heard the clank. Then, across the long courtyard, he saw the keep's doors opening as the shadows of its inhabitants made their appearance. Dragomir first turned his head in their direction, then turned to Codru while his hand was still tight in Timotei's hair.

'I hope you did not think that His Highness had not already been told of your transgression, traveller, nor that he did not foresee it!'

Then, turning back to the ones approaching from the opposite direction, he bellowed:

'His young comrade dared to swing his blade at me, Sire!'

Codru saw the wrathful Voivode getting closer. His mantle was fluttering in the cold air as his dark-red tunic was loosely open. He had a sceptre he used as a crutch so his black, heavy boots wouldn't slide on the frost. He was surrounded by men in dark and grey light armour, with their mouths covered in black cloth. Codru had seen them all around the Prince's hall. To his left side walked Luladija, the Egyptian, her black, silky hair covered with a red hood of her own, emerging like a bloodstain on the black walls behind her, while her eyes were set on the kneeling wanderer.

'Take the boy to the dungeon!' he hissed at the sword-bearer, then he turned to the wanderer as Dragomir dragged Timotei after him.

'It pains me, Codru,' Vlad's voice then sounded luringly, 'To see that after welcoming you into my home and breaking bread together, you have chosen to leave the walls like rat.'

Codru raised his head, shaking the hair off his face.

'Running away from what I thought was a thorn we both shared grievances about!' the Voivode waved at the ones following him to wait there, behind him, as he came closer to the captured man. 'What have you to say for yourself? Talk!'

He shook his chin at Codru's captors to raise him to his feet, so they both now faced each other, piercing each other's eyes.

'You are a man who takes what he desires, and my answer did not soothe your questions!' Codru muttered. 'You gave me no choice.'

'I take what I'm owed, not what I desire!' the Prince snapped, taking his eyes away from him and turning his back. 'But you're right,' he said, speaking in a lower tone. 'You had no choice; truth be told, I never intended to give you any!'

Vlad walked around him and the two guards, measuring Codru. He was grunting, his fists were clenched, and his dark hair was fluttering in the cold morning wind.

'You may or may not know this, Zmei-Slayer, but you and the other man you've done your heroic deeds with have both cost me a great deal, crippling me in my fight! Blinding and deafening me!'

Codru turned his head, pulling from the guardian's arms, trying to see if he had any room for opportunity. He had none.

'I have purged your lands of things you only heard stories about, Sire.'

'Careful, now... You should hold your tongue!' Vlad thundered, storming up to him. He grabbed Codru's face with such ferocity that his eyes blazed, almost as if he were about to bite his face. 'Don't you dare tell me of the things I heard or saw!'

He pushed Codru's face out of his sight as he turned away from him.

'Is it a reward you desire? How dare you? The reward for your achievements is every breath you still draw; for that all of them pale in comparison to the damage you also caused!'

Codru didn't say anything. His mind wandered, digging deeply for a few moments, taking advantage of Vlad's simmering silence.

'Blinded you... Your eyes and ears...!' he finally understood. Then he raised his head, his eyes meeting Vlad's once more. 'I've killed the Black Boyar. He meant something to you. He was important to you...'

His voice faded, while his mind was spiralling, reaching depths so murky he was yet unable to swim in. The Voivode's heavy silence was all the assurance he needed.

'He was essential,' Vlad said, lifting any shade of doubt. 'He was going to grant me an army, as I have told you.'

Codru's mind was racing. For some reason, it swept back in time to his first encounter with creatures in the Cioclovina woods. To Toma, the Raven's Order, and their mission. To the rotten prisoner whose body was inhabited by the Demon. To the dead digging their way out of their graves—the Strigoi.

It had never been a plague. It had never been a curse; it had been wretched recruitment. An unholy call to arms.

'The Necromancer! It was you that he was calling up the dead for!'

Vlad stared at him, choking with frustration, barely able to hide the anger smouldering in his chest.

'It wasn't enough that Hunyadi had my family slaughtered; his plagued arms now reach out from beyond his grave, crushing everything I am building. He made it a dying wish to set his obedient acolytes, his bloody Ravens, on finding my unseen weapon.'

Then he shouted, as his mouth contorted in a strange way and his eyes turned darker, as if tar had been poured into them.

'I should have you flayed! I should run a pike through your guts!' he said, turning away, and hiding his face as he struggled to calm himself. 'I never cared for John's hypocritical mob of redeemed, God-fearing rogues, rapists, and scavengers until you came around. Until you helped them find my living forefather and destroyed him, and with him, every hope of victory I had in the war to come.'

It was the blood Vlad shared with the Black Boyar, the cursed blood the Prince had spoken about during their supper. Vlad's ignorance of the nightmares lurking in his domain's shadows was merely a facade. He was all too aware of them, for he was one of them—a rabid, blood-hungry hound, ready to sacrifice innocent lives as fodder to the awakened dead and to the Dark-Man. All this in his quest to embrace the lands promised by the shameful ancestry coursing through his veins.

Vlad turned quiet, like a thunderstorm that had just passed.

'It was never a question when I asked of you to bring me the Sultan's head,' he then said, turning back to Codru, his face regaining his sharp features and clear eyes. 'It was me claiming the debt you owe me.'

'A bloody shame,' the Prince eventually said. 'We could have done great things, you and I. But no matter. I have few other tricks up my sleeve.'

As his voice faded, his eyes turned willingly to his side, from where Luladija was still staring at Codru. She was of great importance to the Prince, he thought.

'Her aid once helped me meet my ancestor; she could reach beyond the veil once more if needed be. The costs are great, but the rewards are made to measure.'

Closing in on Codru, he said:

'You think you have seen everything there is to see in the shadows, but you merely grazed their walls. There are things greater than me or you out there than our eyes can see. We could have shared their power, but now, I have no use for you!'

Vlad looked around at his men behind him and at the ones holding Codru trapped in their grasp.

'These men are the finest princely guards that gold can buy. My faithful Hounds of Sebasteia, dogs that never bite the hand that feeds. Each would fall on their sword at my command, but today, it is your blood their swords will taste.'

'Send this Salman to his cowardly ancestors!'

Codru was mad at himself. While he expected it would come to this, his last few months spent in Wallachia numbed his senses, and he dared to hope he was wrong. But now he knew he should have never let his guard down.

He did not wait for the Voivode to say his last words. Before his execution was ordered, he twisted his right arm the strongest he could, and his elbow met the Hound's stomach. He dodged the other one's short blade that howled above him, and with his shoulder pushed into the one he hit, he threw him to the ground. He caught the second one's arm as his blade bit at the air between them. His boot met his calf with a crack, breaking his knee and exposing the bone through the breeches as the guardian belched in his foreign tongue.

He threw himself to the ground, recovering the axe he dropped in the snow, as he rolled back on his feet, facing the enemies as they came from both sides. As soon as he stood, he took a quick look around, splitting the air with the hatchet and keeping the Hounds at a distance. Besides the two guardians he freed himself from on his left, there were four more that came with Vlad on his right.

The Prince had already left the area, followed by the woman, standing now near the keep's tower, watching the fight from a distance. A falchion whirred from Codru's right side, which he could barely meet in time with his axe. The Hound twisted it, deflecting the wanderer's defence, and with an almost unhuman lunge, a short and thin blade sprang out his other arm, aiming to his chest, which Codru shifted away from, although he felt its point cutting his shirt. He stumbled and awakened. He realized Vlad was not lying when he said they were worth their gold.

He dropped his cloak in the snow and drew his scimitar from his scabbard with his left hand. He had to give more. It didn't take more than a moment, and his sword met another, the spade of the guardian to his left, as he plunged through the air with both hands on his hilt, above his head. Codru kicked a Hound in his chest to his right, keeping him away, and while he rejected the guardian's sword with his scimitar, his right hand wielded the axe towards the now-shook man, severing his jaw. Codru yelled. A long cut dragged on his thigh, splitting his breeches and the skin under them.

'Curses!' he grunted, turning his back to the two defeated guardians, and throwing his axe at the closest Hound running at him at full speed. The hatchet clashed into the man's light chest piece, throwing him onto his back without breath.

A bolt whirred by his ear, it's cold arrowhead nearly splitting his cheek. Codru dashed backwards, throwing himself at the guardian with the broken knee. The man gave his last breath when the wanderer used him as a shield against the slithering wave of arrows spat out by one of the hounds' crossbows. Fortunately, the crossbow's bearer wasn't the first to charge at Codru, who was shielded by the corpse.

The falchion of the mercenary that followed fell like an axe above him, and Codru wheezed as his scimitar caught it above him. He could see the robust men's fiery eyes above his face cloth. With a skilful swirl, Codru left his clench, which made the man stumble over the dead body as the traveller rolled in the snow to his side.

He felt the stingy pain in his thigh as he jumped up, leaving a trail of blood behind. Too much of it. Before the man could stand, Codru's lightning and merciless scimitar strike left him without a head, and at almost the same time, a crossbow bolt pierced the wanderer's left shoulder. Making him fall on his back in agonizing pain. He dragged himself in the snow on his back, weaving his sword with his unharmed arm to keep the upcoming three marauders away.

'End him!' he heard the Voivode's ruthless command. As he lied on his back, another bolt missed Codru, and the great sword of his closest foe fell next to him as he rolled. He tried counter striking with his scimitar, but the Hound's hand caught his wrist, and a heavy, sword bearing fist hit him like a hammer in the face as he lost his own blade.

He gasped, reeling himself away on his belly from the next hit, which might have as well been his last. He felt the man's boot on his calf, ready to plunge his sword in his back, but at the same time a golden spark, reflecting the daylight, appeared in the snow—the dagger Timotei had dropped. He reached out to it, grabbing it desperately, and without a shade of thought, he swirled and threw the dagger at will. It hit its mark, stuck in the man's forehead. As the foe dropped on his back, Codru knew that had been his last chance. The crossbow bearer was already stringing the bolt that would send him to the gods.

In pain and exhausted after the fight, knowing the unavoidable ending, he exhaled as he dropped to his back, his eyes in the sky. And then he saw a spear flying above him, framed by the grey and heavy sky. He heard a muffled gasp and a bolt flying randomly in the air. He raised his head and saw the last Hound with the large pike stuck in his chest, falling on his back.

Codru turned his head towards the back, to the gate area, from where a horse-riding party appeared to have just come through. He heard the Prince cursing as he stormed toward the riders. Their light armoured leader, the helmet bearer, dismounted. While the Prince continued his slurs, the leader's hidden face was turned towards Codru. Abandoning Vlad, the rider approached the last of the mercenaries first and recovered the spear from his chest, continuing to walk towards Codru.

The wanderer thought it was to finish the job. But instead, the rider prompted the bloody pike in the snow and took a knee next to him. He bent above him, roughly wiping the blood and the mud off his forehead. At the same time, the pain in his shoulder and thigh suddenly began to fade away. A necklace emerged from around the rider's neck, dangling above Codru's face. A metal shard. An arrowhead. Codru's lungs were unable to fill with air, as he knew in that moment who the rider was.

The rider removed the helmet, revealing a long, silky, and brown mane, loosely tied behind. Framing the white cheeks turned red from the cold and effort. The glistening eyes, shaded by dark lashes.

'Ileana,' he softly said before the darkness cornered his eyes, falling into an empty, dreamless sleep.

✷✷✷

When he woke up, he first saw a warm, blurred light surrounded by a fading dark frame. He blinked a few times as he tried to get a clearer sense of his environment. It was a fireplace, and a figure was close to it, fanning the embers with an iron poke. He moved his head, prompted by a pillow, and gasped as he tried to sit up, wiping his dried-out eyes. The figure above the fire turned suddenly.

'Take it easy; you've lost blood,' she said as she came closer to the bed, resting her hands on his shoulders and gently urging him to lie back.

Codru looked at his bare chest and at his shoulder, wrapped in a white linen cloth. He winced. The pain was raw. Under the woollen blanket, he sensed his thigh had been similarly patched. He accepted her guidance and sat back on the feather pillow. Not that he had much of a choice. His head was killing him, and his mouth was spongy.

'Here, drink this!' her voice sounded as she lifted a small wooden bowl under his chin and let its soothing liquid flow between his peeled lips. The potion was lukewarm and bitter. He recognized it. Mugwort tea. He drank it obediently, as thirst was already burning his throat. He must have been out quite some time.

'Ileana!' he whispered as he looked at her once she let the bowl on the bedside table and sat on the bed, gazing at him. He had so many questions. A familiar warmth embraced him.

She was as beautiful as he remembered, though it had been years since she was the innocent yet spirited maiden he first encountered by the lake. Her chin had become narrower, and her cheekbones were more pronounced. The sour-cherry tinted scar on her left cheek had not faded away. Yet her hawk-like eyes remained as piercing as ever beneath those dark, slender brows. Her lips were faded, as withered wild rose hips. Instead of her white, embroidered clothes, she now donned a loose, earth-toned shirt, cinched at the waist with a wide leather belt, and her legs were clad in thick man breeches. It was a far cry from what the other maidens wore.

'Where are we?' he first asked, as he had to begin somewhere. He began suddenly remembering flashes and bits of the Voivode's ambush.

'We haven't left the Citadel,' she answered. 'The Prince offered this chamber so you could recover.'

'The Prince tried to have me killed... My weapons... My axe...' he mumbled. 'We've butchered his Dogs. How are we not in the dungeons? How are we alive?'

She didn't answer right away. She sighed softly as she rose off the bed, moving towards the fire.

'Your belongings are here; worry not. And he didn't have you killed,' she said. 'If he wanted you dead, you would be dead.' Then, as she turned, crossing her arms, and prompting her back against the fireplace's wall, she said:

'It was a trial, not an ambush.'

'A trial for what?'

'To see for himself if you're fit for the quest.'

'His quest?' Codru grunted as he remembered Voivode's proposal. 'Throwing his own men to perdition only for him to see how skilled I am in battle? For a mission I had already refused?'

She smiled.

'He got carried away, I agree... But I believe you know by now Vlad is not too shy to sacrifice men for the greater good, nor too understanding when he is being refused.'

Codru's frown deepened as it dawned on him that she had arrived at the Citadel on horseback, freely and accompanied by other riders, possibly soldiers. She had saved him from the last of the Voivode's mercenaries, and she was still walking his tower freely.

'How are you here?' he suddenly asked her. 'You are no prisoner, are you?' he asked.

She turned, watching the fire with her arms still folded on her chest. She seemed to have fallen into her own thoughts.

'Me and the Prince have an understanding,' then she looked at Codru, and a gentle mocking smile loomed on her lips. 'Why the wolf-cub gaze? Don't look so disappointed. It has been a long time since we were counting stars on the night sky. Things have happened since. Things changed.'

'You've changed,' his voice faded. It was neither pity nor disappointment. What he felt was a shock.

'Years haven't been easy for me after that battle, and I can see they haven't been easy for you.' She walked back toward the bed and sat on its edge, with a leg beneath her as she faced him.

'I have. And so have you.' Then she continued: 'After the Ottomans killed my father and caught you, I wandered for a while, until an old woman found me, hungry and terrified. Helpless. She took me in and raised me. She also told me things about my past that my father had kept for himself, thinking he could protect me. Things about where I come from and who I am. Things that could have protected me more if I knew them.'

She noticed Codru's inquisitive look.

'I always felt different,' she added. 'But it wasn't until I met Mother Wednesday that I found out why. I learned it all about the Iele, the Sânziene... Woodland maidens I come from. Until the Ottomans returned.'

Codru remembered her ability to command the woodland beasts.

'What happened?'

She hesitated to say it immediately, or she was looking to find the right way to say it, not knowing if she was willing to talk about the past.

'They scorched the earth once more,' she agreed to say. 'I fought them away the best I could when they broke through our cottage. The woman who took me in had her eyes gouged out, and I was one step away from being dishonoured.'

Codru jaw clenched at its own will.

'But then Vlad appeared. Those were his men, but he couldn't tolerate their misdeeds. He first ensured they received a fitting punishment, and afterward, he confided in me. He said he only needed those devils until he reclaimed his throne. Once in power, he would require skilled fighters, like me. Allies of his own choosing. Men and women who share his love for the Empire.'

'It was my chance to avenge my father's death. So, I agreed. Now I'm leading one of his strongest companies. Keeping his *Bashibazouks* at bay.'

Hearing those last words made his nightmares of his time spent in their nest come to life. She had always been his beacon of light in the darkest times—a guiding luminescent rock in the cavern labyrinth of his life, his North Star, a lighthouse amidst the storms. He never thought he would see her again, yet now that he did, the Old-Man's words echoed in his weary mind; revenge was indeed poison.

He had been blind to its corrupting influence on his spirit, but now, seeing Ileana's hardened demeanour and pondering the path she had chosen, fighting the men he had run away from, all he could sense was a profound ache. His stone heart began to crack. He felt a sudden urge to grab her hand, and when he did it, she didn't retract it.

'Why have you arrived at the Citadel now,' he was almost afraid to ask.

'Can't it be that I wanted to see you?' she smiled.

'I don't believe that, how could you have known I was here?'

'You are free to believe what you will.' She paused, then rose from the bed, standing next to it. 'You were never going to travel there by yourself if you had accepted the mission. You would have joined me!'

'It was you then, who asked Vlad to have me summoned, wasn't it?'

She nodded.

'Once I heard about the red-haired man bearing the devil's mark on his face, I just knew it was you. The Prince agreed that you could help us. Now, it appears I was wrong.'

The thought of her in the heart of that snake pit was something he never thought would come to realization, even in his nightmares. 'She has no place there!' a thought crossed his mind. She was going to get herself murdered trying to chase the ghosts of her past. He felt his chest squeezing in.

'There's nothing for you there,' he said, reaching out to her hand and catching it in his. She didn't retract it. 'Don't make the journey.'

'Perhaps you haven't changed as much as I thought, after all,' she said, leaving his bedside. 'To this day, you still wrongly believe I am a damsel.'

***

'Sire!' Codru heard Dragomir say to the Voivode, sitting on his highchair. The councillor noticed him, and Ileana having just left the tower entrance and arriving in the princely hall and alerted his master of their appearance.

Before Vlad and his faithful sinister servant stood what looked like three soldiers. By their attire, they were not Wallachian's, Codru realized. And he was right. As he followed Ileana alongside the wall, he could hear them and the Prince discussing fervently, and he recognized their language, as he had heard it many times in Härmeschtat. They spoke Sándor's language. And they were errands, not soldiers.

The Voivode had a parchment in his hand and rested on his knees as his other arm's elbow was prompted on the chair's handle, his hand keeping his chin. He was pensive, his eyes moving, only to awaken from his thoughts when Dragomir made him aware of the Zmei-Slayer presence.

'You may go!' he dismissed the errands in Rumân, while Dragomir repeated the command in Hungarian. 'And let my dear friend Szilágyi know that, by the grace of God, he shall have every man I can spare!'

Once the councillor informed the men of the Voivode's promise, they showed great reverence and turned, walking across the hall, where two guards opened the door as they disappeared behind them.

'Ileana, the Sânziana of Cozia!' Vlad pronounced, handing the scroll to Dragomir, and standing from his chair, approaching her and Codru. 'And of course, the Salman, the Zmei-Slayer, Codru!' he seemed to almost mock. 'I am pleased to see you rejuvenated!'

Codru did all he could to contain his discontent, but he was sure he was not doing nearly half of the good job he thought he was doing. Regardless, the subtle smirk the Prince had on his face was proof he did not care much for his resentfulness. He then looked at the councillor, towards whom he had even more, may it be unexplainable, resentment.

'I was going to summon you, captain,' Vlad said to Ileana. 'The men that just left were bearers of unfortunate news. It appears our enemy's army, led by Ali Bey, turned bolder but was defeated on their way to Banat by our ally, Michael Szilágyi.'

'If that is the case, they won't turn back for long, I'm afraid!' Ileana said as Vlad walked with his arms behind his back towards the throne. 'They always return once they regather their strengths.'

'You speak the truth,' he said. 'This is why he asked us for help, to send a company while they're on the run to the Iron Gates, before the enemy regroups.'

'Sire,' Dragomir interfered. 'I would not do my deed if I wouldn't advise you against it. I'm afraid you never had men to spare.' Turning his bald head to Codru, he continued: 'And after the courtyard blood bath that transpired, you have even less.'

'That was necessary!' the Prince shouted suddenly, as his temper became shorter and shorter. 'Then what am I to do, Dragomir? I don't have the snotty Hungarian child-king's support, and I can't lose my only neighbouring ally. How am I to count on his help if I don't lend my arm when he too needs it? You are to counsel me, so Christ give me strength, counsel!'

The chamber turned quiet as Vlad let himself fall in his chair, as pensive as he had been until then.

'My lord,' the man dared to speak after a while. 'We could turn this in our favour. While the Ottomans have their eyes set on the West, we could plan a march South.'

'South? To what purpose?'

'Perhaps we could regain Giurgiu, the river-fortress they nested in a year ago, on the Danube. We may not have the men, but we do have the arquebuses and the devil-powder-eating bombards for it. That would cripple their armies crossing the river and it could be a great victory for us, Your Highness.'

Codru saw the Voivode raise his head in awe at the idea. A hopeful green rose on his face.

'Why compromise, though?' he mumbled.

'Sire?'

'Why not plot our way on both fronts? They would never expect it!'

He stood back from the chair and approached Ileana.

'My faithful captain, gather a hundred of the men under your command and march towards the sunset to Szilágyi's aid!'

Ileana frowned.

'Your Highness,' she said in a worrisome tone, almost stuttering as she stepped forward. 'You have given me your word that I shall have my revenge. You must let me go South! I plead of you!'

'I'm sorry, Ileana,' he said. 'Not this time. This is more important now than putting past demons to sleep. You shall travel West the soonest possible.'

Codru found himself abruptly torn between a desire for Ileana to fulfil her long-overdue wish of avenging her father and relief at the thought of her not having to descend into the hellish depths he had barely escaped and vowed never to return to.

'So be it!' he then spoke for the first time since they entered the hall. 'I'll journey South and kill the Sultan for you.'

All the eyes turned to him while silence weighted on the room. He saw Ileana's face looking up to him, a vague air of wonder looming on her face; he saw the Prince's black eyes squinting with satisfaction; and he saw Dragomir's face scouting him intriguingly from his place beside the throne.

'Ah, there it is!' the Voivode said, smiling, and looking at Ileana, then turning back to the wanderer. 'I was right all along about what drives you. Worry not, Zmei-Slayer; your secret is safe with me.'

Codru replied in a defying tone, dismissing Vlad's remarks:

'But the boy I came with walks free right this moment. And once I complete the task, you free me from your lands too!'

'The boy stays.' Vlad said. 'Your scribe has been sent back to the capital while you were pinned to your bed. I will also travel there after today to plan our march south. At most, I can send him your regards.'

'What did you do with him? Where is he?'

'I sent him to the capital to do what he knows how to do. It was either that or a dungeon at Chindia Tower. You see, your word alone isn't anymore a warranty that you will go south if I'm to release you out of these walls. Unfortunately for you, you seem to care about the chronicler. And that's how I know you will stick to your word.'

'You are no different than the men that held you prisoner, Sire!' Codru snarled.

'You had me robbed of six good warriors,' Vlad answered. 'Let's call it even!'

## CHAPTER XIV

*Edirne, September 1445 (6953)*

THE VEINS ON HIS NECK AND HIS TEMPLES FELT as if blood were turning solid. The pain was excruciating, reminding him of the day he had been lying chained to the stone under the bare sky and the hollow eyes of the Sphynx. Trapped in this hog pen reminded him of his darkest days beneath the mountain. But their burdensome memories weren't what made his head feel as if it had cracked. The chains and the iron bars around the top of the filthy walls of this barn, halfway deep into the ground did. The screams of the boys closed in there with him, crying for their homes. Dirty, scared. The hopeless, terrified whines of the ones being dragged outside, whipped by the hands of the people that took them from their families' bosom. It was the missing freedom.

Through the short grate he could only reach by standing up, he could see the boots of his kidnappers. The dust brought inside by droughty winds covered his already teary eyes, smothering him. He was thirsty and starving. He screamed, pushing his face into the iron while grabbing the bars with his wounded hands and asking anyone passing to bring water. He tried to reach out, pulling at the men's trousers, but his arms had been severely punished with whips as a result, so his only hope now was that they would soon show mercy.

What a mistake he had made! He should have stayed on the path with the Old-Man. He missed the poor hemp rag he had to carry day and night with him. What was his teacher doing now? A painful knot got stuck in his throat, chocking him with yearning and remorse. Was he looking for him? Would he know if he was taken away from his lands or if he was dead? Would he care for it?

He thought his mind could reach him. But either the pain or the distance made it seem as if he had been stripped of all the things he was taught to do. The birds and the winds turned quiet, and if they spoke, they did so in tongues he could not hear nor understand. The horned man snatched his father's hatchet from him. The others shared the rest of the bounty of his knapsack; his precious bark scroll was surely eaten by these murderers' campfires by now.

'There is no one coming,' he heard a faded voice that spoke to him in Rumân. 'So, you might as well save your strengths and sleep.'

He thought it was his delirious mind playing on him. But he turned toward the voice.

Out of the group of half-naked, frightened, mucky boys, most of them much younger than he was, there was another closer to him. A quiet boy, no older than thirteen winters or so, with his blonde hair darkened by earth and his face reddened and cracked by sun. He was sitting behind him, propped with his back towards the wall. His body was only covered with a pair of dirty trousers. No shirt was covering his skinny, scarred body, and his feet were bare, with his soles calloused. He had been here longer than him.

'The men come once a day and throw water through the roof. Some hogwashes for food, rotten fruit, or bones if we are lucky. But that will be tomorrow now. So go to sleep' he said, then, turning to the other few boys in the pen, he shouted half in his tongue and half in the foreign one.

'Close your mouths and cease crying! What are you crying for?' He turned to the apprentice: 'Well, sleep if you can!'

'They miss their home and their families!' the red-haired one said. 'Let them be!'

'Worry not. Half of them will be dead by the week's end. It will be quieter soon.'

Alidor left his hands off the iron bars. The boy was right; it was in vain. And he was so weak that he could barely stand. So, he turned away from the grate and almost fell into the wall, letting his back drag down on the harsh and cracked earth-made surface. Sitting, he held his head between his hands as if he tried to split in two, his eyes tightly squeezed. He mumbled a few words in the Old-Tongue, an incantation he once learned from the master to sooth himself.

'You will survive the labours; you're not like these other ones,' he heard the boy saying as he was sitting now across the pen, next to the other wall.

'Labours, what labours?' Alidor moaned. 'Leave me be!'

'The labours the 'bazouks have for us, you will see after they feed us.'

'Survive...' the apprentice said for himself. All he did since he could remember was survive. He survived his family's murder by the same people he was now a slave to. He survived the mountain, the marking, and the snake. He no longer wanted to survive; he wanted to live. And the men who left him an orphan had now been the same men who took that away too. His weary mind suddenly flew to Ileana. And somehow, the headache began to break. He didn't know if it was the incantation or the thought of the lake maiden.

'What do they call you?' he asked the boy.

'I have no memory of my given name; I was too young when I was taken. But who's to say we can't choose our own names? In a few years, should I survive, I will pick a fitting one.'

'What do they want from us?'

The boy shrugged.

'To survive, grow, and become like them. These men were once slaves like us, in pens like this one, taken away from their homes,' he said, looking around their hole, his eyes fixed on the door trap.

'I won't become like them!' said Alidor, grinding his teeth and clenching his jaw.

'Then you will perish, like the other ones who came before you. And if you perish, you will not have your chance.'

'What chance?'

'To kill them!'

The apprentice's eyes fell to the ground silently.

'To defeat them, you must become like them. You must join their pack. You can't fight the wolves in your sheep's clothing. One day,' the boy continued, 'I will grow just like them. And when they think I am one of them and they trust me with their sword, I will kill them in their sleep. And Hultan will be the one to die first!'

'Hultan?'

'The man with horns. The Bashi-bazouks' chieftain.'

Alidor understood who the boy was talking about. The eyes and the hidden face of the same man leading the riders that took his axe were plaguing his mind too.

'Hultan...' he whispered to himself. And he agreed. If he had the chance, that man would be the one he would go after too.

As Alidor's new friend promised, the hay and brushwood trap door opened in the morning. As soon as it did, the herd of child-slaves gathered under it like famished dogs. It was their loud shouting and yelling that woke him up from his corner. The boys had their hands up, as if they were praying. The younger one that talked to him the day before, until he fell asleep, was part of the group too.

A long wooden ladle was dropped into the pit, bearing water with it. One by one, the boys were grabbing it, spilling half of the liquid over their chests as they tried to drink from it. They fought for it, with half of the prisoners being dragged under the feet of the rest. Alidor saw his nameless friend trying to lift some of them up so they would have a chance to drink before the marauders closed the trap.

'Come, red-haired one, before it's too late!' he heard him.

Alidor listened. He walked toward the herd, stumbling, drained of strength and tongue dry, waiting for his turn.

The boys drank, some washing their faces with the muddy water, others grabbing the ladle with their hands, which were shortly and severely blessed with a whip or a ladle strike over their heads. The men above cursed in their tongues and laughed as the victims would fall to the ground or run to their corners to lick their wounds, many giving up on the life-giving potion.

'Come, quickly,' the boy said, dragging Alidor by his arm. 'They're leaving; come!'

Pushed almost without his will under the trap, the last mouthful of water hit his chin, as he was taller than the rest. Just when his lips touched the wooden, soaked edge of the scoop, the task master holding it pulled it away. The other boy grabbed it before it could disappear, struggling with all his might to keep it closer to Alidor's face as a few drops of the liquid creeped in between his cracked lips.

A whiplash swished the rotten air, and its braided leather left a blood mark on the boy's hand, making him drop the ladle and fall to the ground in agony. Awoken, Alidor screamed at the punisher and dragged the ladle owner inside by it. The man grunted as he fell over the pack of boys, and Alidor jumped him. Before the marauder could sober up, the apprentice's knuckles met the man's chin and cheekbones as he mounted him. Alidor screamed as his hands were digging into the man's face, until another whiplash carved his back.

When he felt it, his trousers turned wet, and cold sweat rolled instantly on his temples. He threw himself away from the ladle-bearer and dragged himself to his corner. As he stood up, the man jumped next to him. The kick in his stomach made Alidor's first hit seem numb by comparison. The next one left him breathless and squirming on the ground until long after the man was dragged out of the pit by his kind, closing the trap behind them.

'The animals!' the other boy screamed as he rolled, bruising his knees as he did, returning to the wall he was normally sleeping by. As Alidor pressed his palms on the ground, trying to lift himself up, he spat blood. He was trembling, agonizing in his filth, as he began to slowly catch his breath.

'Do not worry, friend,' the boy told him as he licked the blood off the back of his swelling, peeled off hand. 'One day we will have our chance. Just wait and see. Try to stay awake; they'll bring us food soon.'

But Alidor heard his friend's last words fading through a dream as he fell deep into the painful yet liberating slumber.

He felt a slap across his face that woke him up. It was the boy. He felt as if he had slept for days, but it couldn't have been more than an hour. Another slap woke him from his thoughts too.

'I am awake, I'm awake!' he mumbled.

'I told you not to fall asleep. They came and threw away their leftovers. What a good day! They had chicken bones! You missed it!'

Alidor didn't care for it.

'Leave me be...' he curled, trying to turn his back as he rolled on the sandy ground. 'Go away!'

The boy grabbed his shoulder, keeping him from turning.

'Here, I saved an apple stub for you.'

'I don't want it; go!' Alidor snapped, summoning all the energy he had to push the boy away.

The younger one fell on his back as the withered piece of apple rolled in the dirt. He became quiet and dragged himself to his wall, leaving Alidor alone, as he desired. He fainted again, sucked in the whirl of his own mind.

Time passed as he became delirious. He heard the children shouting outside. He felt his mouth being open and warm, sweet matter being pushed into his mouth forcefully. He heard the men muttering and clamping their boots above the pit. But he couldn't wake up.

When he did, it was in the evening. The sun didn't burn as much through the grates. He wasn't as drowsy, although his thirst was there, and so was the migraine. He looked around the pen, and he saw, through the shadows, that some of the boys were no longer there. He pushed himself off the floor, gasping, as he let his back fall on the wall behind him. He quivered, remembering the burst skin on his back. His friend was watching him, with a half-proud grin on his dirty face.

'Where is the rest?' Alidor dared to ask, his voice dry and hoarse.

'Not with us anymore. They met their families in the Otherworld.'

Alidor looked at the remaining ones. They were not sleeping, but they lay on the ground like fish on a dry shore. Some had their backs covered in bloody cuts, like his.

'What happened to them?' he asked the boy.

'Some were fed the mud. The others were fed the whip!'

'Fed...' Alidor said. 'It was you who fed me.'

'I had to chew the apple for you,' the other one answered.

He thought of himself being taken care of by this boy younger than him and felt ashamed. He thanked him with his eyes, then looked back to the ones lying motionless.

'What of this mud you speak about?'

The boy sighed as his eyes looked out the grates.

'You will find out tomorrow; I think it will be your turn.'

The next day, they were fed again. Alidor grabbed the pieces of mouldy bread and the bones they threw in the pit with both hands. Before that, he made sure to not touch the ladle with anything else other than his lips. By this time, his thirst knew no bounds, and those drops of liquor could barely begin to help, but it was more than what his tongue touched in days. His hands were full of leftovers, which he brought with himself to his corner, where the other boy joined him with his own share. They feasted together on the garbage the men gave them. He was so famished that he could barely breathe.

'Slow now!' the dirty-faced boy giggled. 'A bone might get stuck in your throat.'

He gasped, shivering, as the apprentice began to chew the bitter, sticky rye and slurp the marrow off a pale, naked divvy.

'What will happen?' he asked the boy, thinking this could prepare him for what was to come.

The boy sighed, chewing his own nibble, with his eyes saddening, turning to the earth beneath them.

'They turn us into animals and make us fight each other until one of us falls. The victorious one lives another day; maybe gets some meat.'

Alidor felt a chill on his spine.

'I won't do their bidding. I won't fight for them. We can't let them have us kill each other.'

'You have to,' he said. 'If you don't, they tie you up to the pole and whip you until you soil yourself.'

His mind went abruptly to the slash he felt on his back the other day, and he coughed as a bit of crushed chicken bone went the wrong way. The boy hit his back until he spat.

'Haven't I told you to slow down? That bit could have been in your stomach and not on the ground now.'

Alidor looked at the phlegm, then turned to the boy. He just remembered that he said he had been here a long time. Yet, he was still alive.

'You fought, haven't you,' he mumbled as he pulled away. 'You fought for them; you killed the others.'

The boy frowned as he licked his dirty fingers, gazing at Alidor's face quietly for a few moments. He said:

'I did. How am I going to survive until they trust me if I don't? How else am I going to reach the horned man? And you will too if you want the same.'

The trap door opened, and a man jumped inside, dressed in large, dark trousers and a green shirt, open across his chest, revealing his grimy skin. He wore a crimson turban around his head. Bending his head so he would fit standing, he showed his whip, grinning from under his thick moustache, as the boys knew that it was better to stay away and not dare do anything reckless. He grabbed one of them by his shoulder and brought him into the light, as several hands from above took the boy by his arms and pulled him out. He grabbed another one. And another one. He then turned to the corner, where Alidor and his friend were finishing their meal.

'*Sen!*' he said, raising his arm. '*Sen, Buraya!*'

Alidor looked at the boy, whose head was down, as if he had avoided being noticed.

'Go with him' he whispered. 'Go!'

The young man stood up and dropped whatever food scraps he had left in his lap. Before he could reach the taskmaster, the man reached out and grabbed him violently by the neck of his shirt and pulled him under the open trap, as he did with the first three boys. Arms plunged from above, some tediously pulling him up by his already ripped clothes and some by his hair, until he was finally out.

They dropped him on the dry ground. Still on his knees, Alidor struggled to open his eyes, blinded by the heat and daylight. But before he could come to his senses, a hand bit at the back of his neck, forcing him to stand up and urging him to walk, as several men, dressed as the one who jumped in the pit, followed him.

He looked around disoriented, with his eyes in tears, as the wind was covering his face in dust. The hole he had been thrown into wasn't the only one. A dozen just like his was surrounding what looked like a courtyard where tents and barracks were stacked here and there, propped against each other, perhaps where these wicked men were sleeping. But they weren't sleeping now. Many of them were out, yelling and laughing. Wagering. Some were trying to reach out to him, catching the strings of his red hair, spitting at him, and cursing him as the group that accompanied the boys tried to make their way through the crowd, guiding them towards the centre of the courtyard.

When they arrived, he first noticed the large wooden pole stuck in the ground, with chains dangling off it, close to the middle. The other three boys were lined up, shaking as a man he already knew well and haunted his last few nights was standing in front of them, towering like a monster he was. His horns were larger than any bull the apprentice had ever seen, and his back was almost as wide as theirs. A long mane of blonde-grey, dirty hair was falling on his almost bare and tanned back, covered with leather straps and scars. Hultan was his name, as the boy in the underground prison said.

Hultan turned when the last of his men were bringing Alidor over, straightening him in line with the others. His eyes squinted, yet under his mask, the young man knew he was smiling.

'Oh, Kir-Yüz! I remember you!' his muffled, grave voice said, as he prompted in front of him. 'Let us see what you are made of, boy!'

He grabbed his face with his hands and then ran one of them over his forehead, looking at the seal again.

'Who did this to you?'

Alidor pulled his face away and spat in the dirt. The back of

Hultan's slap made his face turn and spit blood, very near the boot of a man approaching and carrying on his palm an unwrapped piece of oily parchment.

'You will learn to behave!' he said. 'Now take this; open your mouth!'

Hultan pinched a piece of the dark matter revealed from the parchment between his dirty fingers and then forced it up Alidor's mouth, as the man kept it open with a grip of his other hand.

'Chew. Swallow. It will take some of the pain away, to not faint, and some of the guilt away, to not cry!'

As he kept his nose and mouth covered, the apprentice's only choice was to swallow the bitter mud.

'Very good! That should keep you docile for now!' the man giggled and patted his cheek in a friendly way.

He heard him issue an order to the others as he turned his back, taking distance from them. One of his marauders passed by the boys, grabbed their arms, and handed them each a pointy, grey rock.

'Take these rocks and use them to break your chains, *devşirme* children,' the man shouted as he raised his arms, as if he welcomed him. 'Three of you will soon see your families. The one left will be closer to serving the Great *Ebū'l-feth*, Mehmet.'

The man's voice began to slow down and disappear somewhere far away as Alidor was losing his sight. He shook his head, but it was in vain. It was the mud; he was sure of it. It did lift the pain; his head was as light as it had never been before. He looked at the sky, and it looked yellow and red. He felt he could touch it if only he could move his arms at will. He heard the men laughing. He looked at them as their faces fell off their skulls. He turned to the horned man as his helmet bore two trees with red leaves growing above his eyes. He could hear his breathing. He looked at the rock in his hand. And he remembered.

'I won't fight for you,' he thought and tried to say. Maybe he did. He squeezed the rock and threw it toward Hultan.

He only heard his voice thundering, and two sets of arms lifted him off the ground, pulling him closer to what looked like a column brought to the surface from the depths of the Hollow Mountain.

'Don't...' he whispered. 'Please, don't!'

They chained him in those shackles and ripped the shirt off his back.

'No...!'

The men left him there. He tried turning his head. He saw one of them behind him with a snake wrapped around his arm, unravelling.

'No, please!'

He heard him shouting, as Alidor knew what was going to happen. He turned his face away, closed his eyes tight, and clenched his jaws. And when the first venomous whiplash stroke occurred, his knees turned into nothing, the sky turned dark, the earth returned under his feet, and his throat released a roar that he thought belonged to someone else. Another strike followed, and he fell to his knees. The mud was not helping.

Since that cursed day on, the men came and took the boys one by one from the pit, and day after day, less and less of them returned. The ones who did had their hands covered in blood and their eyes sunken. Whenever he saw his friend leaving the pit, he returned and fell next to his wall, crying himself to sleep. Whenever he was called out, he returned carried by the men, with blood running off his back and thrown to his corner.

No, his head didn't ache anymore. He had long dreams where the men did not exist. When he was being punished for not fighting the other children, his mind was leaving his body and wandering somewhere far, nearby a green everglade, where a young maiden stood on the shore, her white face reflecting the sun. When he suffered from long, feverish nights, he would count stars on the dirty ceiling.

Days turned to weeks, but he had long lost track of time. Until one day, when it was only him and the other boy left in the pit. The time had come that they were both dragged out of there and thrown in the courtyard. For the first time, they were not given any of that brown poison. For the first time, the wooden pole had no chains on it. And for the first time, instead of a rock, they were given each a short and dull blade. Alidor's first thought was to pull himself from the man holding his arm and run towards Hultan, who was watching them. But he was too far away. He turned to his friend silently, who returned the gaze, as they both knew what it meant. They both knew this day would come.

'There will be no whip today, nor return to your hole,' the horned man said. 'There will be only one standing, or none. Either of you refuses to fight, and you're both dead.'

'I am sorry, friend,' the boy suddenly said softly to the apprentice. 'But I've come a long way.'

And before Alidor could answer, the blade whirred by his face, barely able to step back and avoid it. He lost his sword and dragged himself to reach it, only to be blocked by his friend's sword, almost cutting his hand. He turned face up and kicked the boy in the chest, throwing him on his back, letting him recover the great knife.

By the time he turned, the boy was running towards him, screaming, with his face gripped by both bloodlust and fear. Their blades clanked and clanked again. All Alidor could do was block the ravenous swings of his now-foe, whose spirit was swallowed by frenzy. He deflected his last blow, then, aided by his fist, he hit the boy, making him stumble and step back, whipping his chin. His friend was fiery, but Alidor was older.

'Wait, please!' Alidor tried to say, but the boy plunged toward him once again, relentlessly. Until he blessed the apprentice's arm with a swift cut. He felt the sharp pain across all his body. But it woke him up. And when the next swing was close to cutting through his flesh once more, Alidor dodged it, his own blade slicing now through the boy's arm, and with another fist, he threw him on the ground.

He felt the anger flowing through his veins when he jumped on top of his friend. Fury for what the men were making him do and for what they did to him. He dropped his blade, and his fists began hitting the younger one after the other. He crushed his own teeth as his mind was away, gripped by hatred and revenge he would one day inflict on his captors while his fists were turning red.

'No,' the boy cried, choking. But Alidor didn't cease the storm until the boy was barely moving under him, twitching. He gasped as he rolled over him.

'End him, Kir-Yüz!' he heard Hultan. 'And the reward will be yours. You'll be raised to serve the Emperor as one of us!'

He didn't have the heart to turn or to hear the boy. He grabbed the blade of the ground as his eyes were out there, looking at the horned man, and he would have given anything to be a few steps closer.

'End him!'

He braced himself and turned to his friend, with his skin cracked and swollen on his face, shivering, barely able to move his eyes to watch Alidor. He saw him moving his fingers, trying to raise his hand, and calling the apprentice to come closer. He understood, and he bent over the boy's body, and the only words he could make out of were:

'Promise you'll make him pay.'

Alidor began crying as he was kneeling next to him, holding his hand. He nodded. The boy closed his eyes, and with a heavy stroke, the apprentice stabbed him in the chest.

\*\*\*

*Edirne, September 1450 (6958)*

'After sundown, I set sails, with or without you!' the merchant said definitively as he walked at fast pace from the gang where he had been cornered.

The Florentin peddler did not give him much choice, nor was he offering what he desired. He wasn't travelling north, where he so wanted to return. Instead, his boat was going to follow the river that led them south-west. But he was in no position to refuse. Anywhere would have been better than here.

The young Janissary stumbled upon Bruno, the merchant, by chance while patrolling in the company of another member of his guild. He overheard the foreign merchant giving a command in Rumân to one of his boat workers. Alidor had to leave his comrade under the pretext of taking a leak and almost desperately approached the merchant, cornering him behind a stall in the market. Alidor's first question was if perhaps he could find a place on the boat for him as he planned on leaving.

'I am not going to risk my neck for you, Janissary,' the man dismissed him.

'Helping a member of the Sultan's guard commit treason won't sit well with the young Mehmet; people have been sawed in half for less! And I came here to earn my bread, not lose my head.

'I'll pay plenty!' Alidor grabbed him by the arm immediately, hissing, as the men tried to bail.

Bruno rubbed his chin as he frowned, grimacing. The Janissary had been putting aside his coin for many moons since Hultan sent him to the palace.

'I can give two thousand *akçes*.'

The merchant shook his head.

'Are you mad? That's not enough to cover the stake,' the man pulled his arm, ready to leave the market hideout.

'Three thousand,' Alidor almost shouted. 'It's almost all I have gathered!'

The merchant poked his cheek with his tongue, measuring the man.

'Make it three thousand and a half, two of them upfront,' he eventually said. 'And change your clothes—it's a long way on *nell'Evros* until the *Archipelago*. I would very much like to not be seen with a Janissary on my deck.'

'I'll get you all the coin you require, but you are wrong to think I carry all that silver on me while patrolling. It's back, at the garrison,' Alidor said, biting his lip as he was going to giveaway all his silver.

'Then no deal!'

Alidor lost his patience and shoved the man by his neck into the dusty wall behind him. He threw his head over the corner, scouting for the other Janissary, who began looking for him through the port bazaar.

'Listen to me, you scoundrel!' he said impatiently. 'You know who I am and what I can do. Should I and my friend come aboard? Are you sure your papers are all in order?'

The man gulped.

'Very well,' he said, his mouth getting dry. 'Bring the coin when joining the crew, then. But you must make it tonight!'

He almost heard the man as through a dream, the last of Bruno's words hitting him like a hammer. It had to be today. The chances were that out of all days, it was this day that Hultan, the man who trained him, tormented him, and turned him into a tormentor, was also in the city. He was in audience with the Sultan, at the Palace. His axe was with him. And more so, Alidor had a promise to fulfil.

For the four years he had been under this man's yoke, he thought of countless ways he would make him pay for what he had done to him and what he made him do. He turned him, as a boy once foreseen, slowly and systematically into one of those marauders he promised himself not to become.

Alidor had tortured and murdered innocent children under his eyes and at his command, leaving wounds he never thought the hands of a man could inflict on another. Every night, for so many moons he lost track of, he grieved under the fever of nightmares in his barrack, the man he could have become if only he didn't abandon the teacher.

The only release he could find was in the wretched, brown poison he was trapped to since, which granted him sleep and numbed the screams of his victims as he his mind lifted his body toward the pale face of the maiden he began to forget.

One day, the young Sultan visited the barracks to see his captain, one of the most efficient taskmasters at work, and Alidor's appearance and his fire during fighting caught his eye. Mehmet was about the same age as the boy he was forced to end years ago. He ordered Hultan to have Alidor sent to the capital, to be schooled, and to make him one of his guards.

'He is not ready, great *Padishah*,' Hultan said. 'He is a savage, and he holds hatred for the Empire. I'm afraid he will try to kill you in your sleep.'

'Worry not. He will be schooled and disciplined, Doğan,' Mehmet said. 'I believe we can become friends.'

And the Sultan was almost right. Once Alidor had been given the teachings of their God and the gift of their language, he was tamed. So much so that Mehmet often would spend time with his now most cherished guard, fencing in the gardens.

'I want you to teach me to fight as fearless as you do, with fire and storm, like your people,' he once told Alidor. 'Not prudent and stealthy as these old men taught me to.'

One day, in one of his chambers, Mehmet guided him through his collection of artifacts, telling stories of his own father and of the past that his teachers had told him. He shared his dreams of conquering the old Râmlan fortress and restoring its glory under his seal, as if it were his destiny. He showed him an old, open book, written by a woman—a bounty from one of his father's conquests.

'A story of the northern barbarians and a dying empire!' the young Sultan said.

It was then that he handed him a gift, in appreciation for helping him improve his sword wielding skills. A scroll he had kept in this chamber as an artifact for years. When he saw it, Alidor felt like the earth was taken from under his feet. Touching the old piece of bark sent him back in time, to memories buried under the dense haze of the mud and beatings.

'I know this once belonged to you,' Mehmet said. 'You have been faithful and are deserving of its return, as a symbol of our camaraderie.'

Alidor and the other Janissary soon approached the palace. The red-haired man, accompanied by the other one, walked through the vibrant and colourful city, traversing the tight, boisterous, and convoluted bazaar where the stallholders laid their wares under the bright sun. And his heart was pumping in his ears as he walked up the stairs and came through the door.

And, of course, the man was there, in the Sultan's large hall. His helmet was not suitable for the palace, so instead, his long and ashen-grey hair unravelled over the thick, dark green tunic that covered his large back. He kept his shameful mask on, mostly for the sake of the civilised meeting, but Alidor saw his face and knew very well the snake that hid underneath. He bore a long scimitar to the wide belt wrapped around his waist on his right side. On his left, Alidor saw the old weapon the man had used since his capture to cleave people, staining his father's only inheritance with innocent blood.

Alidor and his fellow guard passed by him on the way to Mehmet's throne, making their customary reverences. A glance was enough for Hultan to notice him, but he did not interrupt while the two guards reported to their master. It wasn't until later, once the audience ended and the Sultan returned to his chambers, that the apprentice himself had been tasked with escorting his old captor to the room the servants had prepared for him at the Saray.

'If it isn't my boy himself!' Hultan finally let go of the forged politeness he took on the meeting with the Emperor. They had just arrived at the door of the man's soon-to-be room. Alidor nodded to the other guard so that he could return, letting him alone with the man.

'I was told this is where you shall sleep tonight. There's a bath and servants had been spared to see to your needs.'

'Look at you,' the man dared to rough him up, smacking him with a friendly slap over his cheek. 'Right-down an elite guard, isn't it? A year under our young *Hünkâr*'s wing and you cleaned up nicely, one would believe!'

The young man remained quiet, as he wanted to leave. He only looked at Hultan dead in the eye, keeping his feelings at bay, but the storm was gathering in his veins. And the horned man sensed it.

'But you are not fooling me, Kir-Yüz,' he said, waving his finger. 'I know you are only waiting for the right time to slaughter the men that burned your home and broke your spirit, like I taught you to slaughter. And I will make your protector see it too. I've been watching you; you know. I have eyes all-over. Mehmet has eyes and allies all over. You'll show your teeth soon enough, and when you do, I will see to finish the work I had begun on you!'

He grinned under his mask, while Alidor clenched his fists. Alidor knew that tonight, it was either the man or himself that would die. He then turned, ready to leave, as the man raised his voice frustratingly behind him.

'What would your countrymen say of you if they knew how many of their offspring you put in the ground? Our work isn't done yet! You will return to the pit, you hear me?'

The remainder of his duty passed as slowly as an hourglass filled with wet sand. Once it did and the other guard took his place, he hurried to the small tower where he and the rest of his comrades had their beds. Once he entered his tight room, he grabbed one of the pillows and screamed into it so hard that he felt his lungs breaking in his throat. As he sat at the side of the small bed, his heart was racing, and cold sweats were rolling on his temples.

Pain was gathering in his skull, and, shivering, he opened the small drawer to his nightstand, where a small packet of oily parchment laid at the bottom. He unravelled it hungrily, ready to take a piece, but then, as his eyes were caught by the red sunset visible through his round window, he stopped. He needed his wits tonight. His eyes fell on the bark scroll he also had in the drawer. He grinded his teeth and grabbed the scroll, and plunging across the room, he took a leather bag where he threw in both the mud and the scroll. He pulled the bed aside, and from under it, he lifted one of the floor's polished brown stones where his silver was hidden. He took, one by one, all four pouches he had and let them fall into the same bag.

He spent the last couple of hours recovering his senses as he watched the bloody red clouds slowly turn grey in the distance, then disappear as the sun fell under the horizon. He let the scarlet Janissary robe fall on the floor, and instead he threw on his back a hooded robe of a darker but similar tone, under which he kept his dagger and the leather pouch. He breathed in deeply and left the room, and soon after, the tower.

He had been at the Saray long enough to know the hidden corners and paths not walked by the guards, so passing through the palace unnoticed was no hard task. He knew what he needed to do, and he was going to do it.

Once he reached Hultan's door, he first placed his ear on the wood. There was a faded noise coming from within. Odalisks, or courtesans, were sent by the Sultan to keep his captain in good spirits. If they were there, they had certainly brought the narghile. Which meant the man was dream-walking by now. Alidor wanted him aware of when he'd send him into the underworld, and he didn't expect witnesses either. But he had to work with what he had been given.

He slowly pushed the door and entered the room, sneaking quickly behind the *mashrabiya* from where he could freely see everything. He noticed the numerous large pillows and shawls that were embraced in a cloud of smoke, swirling around, and covering the half-naked and wavy bodies of the two women. There were candles placed in their holders and a minstrel playing the *oud* in a corner as he and another man, with his back toward the door, sat right on the floor, covered in sheets and blankets.

Alidor reached for his dagger and pulled it softly out of its scabbard. With his fist tight on the hilt, he mustered up his courage and approached the man sitting with the back to him, lying in his velvet pillows in a haze of opium. He pressed his finger on his lips and his eyes on the dancers before they were ready to shout. They didn't. However, the minstrel ceased playing his tune.

Almost immediately, as if he had woken up, the man tried to turn, but Alidor plunged his hand in his hair and swiftly slid his blade under his chin, keeping him down in his place. He heard a sombre titter in the man's chest as he stood still.

'Is that you then, Kir-Yüz?'

Alidor didn't answer.

'Oh, it sure is! I can smell your treachery...' Hultan smirked, holding tight under the young man's grip. 'I knew I was right about you all along. A murderer right down to your marrow!'

'Don't speak!' Alidor muttered as he pressed his dagger against the man's neck, shading blood, and watched the witnesses, who were horrified, pressing their backs against the front wall.

'What are you going to do now, boy? If you kill me, you will have to kill them too. Or else they'll sound the alarm, and you get caught before you reach the Saray's door!'

'I don't have to! They're slaves, just like I am.'

The minstrel was walking backwards slowly, trying to avoid the middle of the room, his eyes on the door. Alidor said towards them:

'I won't hurt you; I swear! My quarrel is with this man! Don't run!'

Hultan laughed.

'You think they will understand? Look at them! You will have to kill them, boy, and quickly, just as I taught you. You will have to show your true nature once more!'

The minstrel suddenly threw the oud as a diversion and made a run towards the door. Taking advantage of Alidor's loss of focus, Hultan grabbed his wrist and disarmed him with a violent punch, standing up from the floor and turning as the young man fell on his back. Immediately, while the women were screaming in their corner, Hultan ran to the bed, where his clothes and weapons lay freely. Alidor reached the floor, recovering his dagger, and with a throw, he chose to aim at the minstrel, the blade piercing his back right before he could open the door. The man fell to the floor without breath.

He had no time to express his regret. The marauder's heavy scimitar hit the floor as he dodged it. He jumped back to his feet with no weapon, keeping a safe distance from his foe, who was now walking slowly through the room, laughing.

'Was that all your plan, boy? You thought that was all it took to defeat me? I'm a man of the Isle! We are like rocks; we don't break that easily.'

Alidor was in a deadlock. The sword whirred to his side, hitting a standing candle holder, and scattering flames all over the carpets. The fire and smoke began spreading quickly through the chamber as Hultan dominated its centre and Alidor circled the room. He saw his axe on the bed with the man's clothes.

'Is that what you want?' the captain shouted. 'Go on then, take it! I swear I'll let you, the way you swore to let that poor bastard go, and now there he lies, with a dagger in his spine!'

As the man yelled his words, Alidor jumped and reached out to the hatchet, rolling off the bed with it in his hand as the man's scimitar sliced through his cloak. Once on the floor, he squeezed its hilt as if it had been missing. And he raised it with force, blocking his old taskmaster's next attack.

'Go!' he turned and yelled at the women as the fire began surrounding them.

They didn't wait for another invitation, running behind his back as they reached the door and left it. It was too late for him, he thought. The fire will soon set the alarm on its own. He'd be executed. But Hultan had to die first. So, he grabbed one of the flaming pillows on the floor and threw it in his foe's face as he was getting ready for the next sword attack. The blaze immediately spread to his hair and face, making him lose his focus just enough for Alidor to strike back with his axe, only slashing the skin of the man's chest.

It didn't wound him much, but it made him stumble, and with all his strength, Alidor threw himself at him, pushing him on his back. The man tried to handle the sword, raising it to defend himself, but the young Janissary barred it, and pinning it to the floor, he let his hatchet fall with all its might right on the man's forearm, severing it from its owner.

Hultan roared as blood splattered in the fire overtaking the room. He knew he was done. In agony, with his face burning and bleeding like a pig, he pushed Alidor off himself and ran screaming towards the window, throwing himself through the glass.

Alidor took the scimitar off the man's dead hand and ran towards the window, ready to jump after him. But he didn't. He saw him lying on the ground, face down. He was dead; he had to be. Before the fire could swallow him too, he decided to make a run through the door instead. Under the danger of fire taking over the Saray and the Sultan himself, no one would run after him. His way to the river port was waiting.

\*\*\*

*Târgoviște, February 1460 (6968)*

'Wait, you *giaour*! By the mercy of your gods and my gods, I beg of you, wait!'

The rope tied around his wrists pulled the man into the cold mud. Without any free hands, he dived face first. Codru had to rein in his horse. He looked back at the man, who was unable to stand up, so he dismounted to set him back on track. He grabbed him by the shoulders.

'There,' he said, looking at the short man, with the mud leaking off his moustache and turban. 'You are all better now. You should keep up.'

Then he turned to Shadowfire, grabbing the saddle horn, ready to resume his journey.

'Wait!' the man said. 'Wait... Have you thought of what I told you? Cut me loose; you have everything you need. Please!

He whimpered, aware of his fate if the captor reached the end of his journey.

Codru didn't say anything. He glanced at him for a moment, then mounted the horse. He kicked it softly, continuing his journey at a trot, as the man began crying as he walked and slid through the mud.

The wanderer also knew the future that lay in front of the deserter, even a grimmer one for an Ottoman.

On his way south, about one or two days away from the great river, Codru stumbled upon an ad-hoc peasant revolt. Men and women armed with pitchforks, truncheons, and pieces of wooden planks were gathered in a peasant revolt against a man, tied up hand and foot, gagged, and stuffed in a burlap sack at the edge of the river. The men were wearing cloaks like his own, given to him in Kruhnen by Toma. The one who looked like the mayor of the village was reading to the forlorn from the Bible.

Codru wanted to initially pass by, as he did not care to get involved, nor did he have the time. But as he passed, the peasants noted him and his appearance. Their revolt was misguided towards him too.

'Where do you think you are going, grimalkin?' a group of three men, armed, cut the horse's way. Their fists itched and their faces were not the friendliest.

Codru didn't need to, but it seemed the easiest way to get them off his back so he could be on his way.

'I'm on duty from Vlad-Voivode, are you sure you want to stay in my way?' he said.

The men paled immediately and backed off.

'Pray forgive us, young master,' one said. 'With all the Egyptian bandits and Turkish deserters at our doorstep, we wanted to make sure you weren't one of them.'

Codru was now interested.

'What deserter?' he asked. The men turned almost simultaneously towards the moving sack next to the mayor.

'Like that one we caught this morning sleeping in the shed; poor him, he was too tired from all the running from the battle, I'm taking!' one of the men said.

The wanderer's mind instantly thought of the one Ileana had been sent to. If these villagers were not wrong, the only battle close enough for this prisoner to have run from was that one. He needed to see it for himself.

'Open the sack; I want to see him!

The men hesitated.

'If you want to pass him the time of the day, you are welcome to. But one way or another, off to the river he goes by noon!'

Codru dismounted and made his way through the crowd, pushing them aside as he reached the sack.

'Open it!' he demanded.

Half-heartedly, the men nearby opened it. The face of the man, with his mouth tied up and a turban fit on his head, showed up. The women in the crowd began crossing themselves as their faces turned into such a surprise, as if they'd seen the devil. And Codru understood why. He had been living long enough among the Ottomans to know this prisoner wasn't one.

'Who is this man?' he asked.

The mayor answered, his voice shaking.

'This is Voinea, the village's cow-herder.'

He couldn't understand how the cow-herder ended up in the sack, but as he turned, scouting at the peasants' crowd, Codru's eye looked around for the one dressed like one. The trickster surely traded clothes with his victim.

And then his eyes laid on a man with a lambskin hat and large sheepskin coat, trying to backtrack and lose himself amongst the people, hiding his face.

'There's your true prisoner!' he pointed, and as if they just woke up, the man surrounded the intruder and seized him, putting him to the ground and stripping him of the disguise.

'Don't kill me, giaours!' he whined in a broken Rumân speech, holding his hands up in surrender. Codru approached, squatting next to him.

'Where do you come from? What fight did you run from?'

'Bazias, master! Please, have mercy!'

'Why did you run?'

'The Impaler's men arrived! I know what the Devil's Voivode does to his prisoners. I didn't wait around to risk becoming one!'

'Did you see a woman there, on the battlefield?'

'A woman, master?'

Codru didn't repeat his question. He stood up and nodded to the peasants.

'He's all yours!'

As he turned to leave, the man shouted behind him.

'Wait, young giaour! Wait! I have news for your Voivode! There is a plot against him... There's a traitor who helped the Sultan!'

Codru halted on his way; he turned in his place silently.

'I tell you all I know, I swear!' the Turk said. 'Spare me from this mob, and I'll sing like a nightingale.'

To the crowd's grief, Codru agreed.

The man said his name was Pakalin. Once Codru released him from the furious mob, he questioned him in detail. By the end of the story the deserter had to say, he knew that the plan to cross the River and do his work on the Sultan was no longer possible. It no longer mattered. Someone had already told Mehmet about it, and he had since taken measures. Not only that, but he also had plans of his own, aimed at the Prince himself. So instead of journeying back to the snake pit he escaped from years ago, Codru had to turn back and take this prisoner to the Wallachian capital.

Soon, as the sun was setting, they reached the town he and Timotei left four moons ago. The scribe was to be here now, the wanderer thought. And for everyone's sake, he ought to be in one piece. The city was no longer hiding, a sign of sudden bravery or perhaps a subtle war declaration. From outside the Wallachian capital's walls, he could now see the fire tower of Chindia that Vlad built to keep both his treasures and his prisoners. One could see that as an irony, but if the Prince prized his prisoners so much, then Pakalin de deserter was soon going to be a true gem.

Unlike the northern towns over the mountain, the Prince's bleak capital could barely pass as one. It was nothing but a *târg* after all, as its name had it, but with a throne, as the chronicler described it on their first visit. At its heart stood the Princely Court, around which the rest of it had been built without a plan. The stone and wood houses and shops belonged to boyars and some craftsmen that arrived here from other greater towns. Old churches and scarcely paved roads were brought together only by the outer wall surrounding the settlement.

The townsmen watched him and the Turk with disdain through the windows and door frames, closing the shutters and doors as they passed. The wanderer followed the path through the city freely, guided by the fire tower, as he had Vlad's benefit of safe conduct, until he and his prisoner reached the Princely Court.

The area was strengthened by walls itself and surrounded by a large moat. There was a small, retractable wooden log bridge crossing it, and at the end of it, unusually, an open gate tower, from which the guards had already been alerted of Codru and his prisoner's arrival.

'Dismount!' two Wallachian torch-bearing guards demanded by raising their arms as soon as the two men passed the gate.

'Who's this man, Zmei-Slayer?'

Codru pierced the guard with his eyes, making him understand he did not appreciate the name. Glancing at Pakalin, he said, as he got off Shadowfire and while the Turk continued to whimper, praying in his language:

'He's my prisoner, as one could clearly tell by the rope. He has some important things to say to your Prince.'

'His Highness is in a meeting with his Sfat, it will have to wait!' the guard replied snarkily, holding perhaps grudges against Codru for his deeds against his comrades at Poenari.

The wanderer, however, did not care for it.

'You will take me to the Voivode now, or I'll make my own way. I don't have time to waste, and neither does he. I don't think he will appreciate the delay in hearing what this man has to say.'

The guard pondered for a long moment, exchanging looks with his fellow, then sucked on his teeth, and with a taunting wave of his hand, he turned and took the lead as a guide.

'Hold your horses now, devil! Follow me, then.'

As Codru passed through the large, stone-paved courtyard, holding, and pulling the prisoner's rope, he could only see the shape of the palace, which, in all fairness, while large and strengthened by wide walls, wasn't by far a castle but an overgrown mansion. By comparison, the fire tower to his far left peeked from behind the palace's roof, like a watchful protector. The mast of a church, with its iron cross scarring the dark-blue sky behind, could be seen forward, behind the palace's peak too.

When they reached the large entrance, the torch-bearing guide approached and spoke to the Hound standing there. He didn't say anything, but he did open the door and waved to Codru and the deserter to follow through a tall and narrow passageway that led straight to the main chamber.

The tall, but not so wide room was lit by standing iron candle holders in each of the corners and braziers hanging from the flat ceiling. A large, burning fireplace faced the door, while a long, brown carpet filled the space between the two as it unravelled over the cold, stone floor. Boyars and councilmen stood in their long, rich robes all over the tall room, most of them gathered on the right side around a large wooden table. Their heated chatter ended when the guard, accompanied by the two visitors, entered the room, as their eyes scouted them sanctimoniously.

Codru met the Voivode's eyes as he sat on the chair at the head of the table, with Dragomir standing by his side with a sour expression on his pallid face. As it was expected, the wanderer could see the Prince's surprise and discontent. He stood up from his chair slowly, circling the table without moving his eyes from his new guests, until he reached the fireplace, letting the fire behind him frame his posture—an omen of his true feelings for the visit.

'What is the meaning of this?' his first words were. 'Why have you returned so soon, Codru, without bringing me the Sultan's head?'

Codru opened his mouth to answer, but he was immediately shut off with a wave of Vlad's finger.

'Not only I have lost my only ally, taken to Istanbul, tortured and cut to pieces,' he muttered as he slowly stepped forward, without taking his eyes from him, 'but I now have to endure another failure at the hands of a man I have put all my trust in accomplishing the task he had been given.'

'Sire...'

'You surely have something to say for yourself, Zmei-Slayer, bringing a filthy Ottoman to my court, and for your sake and your scribe's sake, it better be very good, because if I find it isn't, by the Almighty, I will unleash God's wrath upon you!'

Codru paused as he watched the stern, cold face of the Prince, with subtle blue-hued veins pulsating on his temples and neck, as his eyes fell on Pakalin.

'He's a deserter from the battle you sent your men as aid. I found him south, close to the river.'

'And what lies had this rat filled your head with?'

'I believe he speaks the truth,' Codru answered. 'He was terrified of meeting Your Highness, and yet, knowing what fate would have waited for him if he stuck to the same story until the end of our journey, he did it nonetheless.'

Then he turned to the cowardly prisoner, his head deeply entrenched between his shoulders.

'Tell the Voivode what you have told me.'

The Turk did his best to find the few words he knew in the language and said through the stutters:

'You have been betrayed, Hünkâr! The Sultan knows of all your plots. Have mercy, I beg you!'

Pakalin fell to his knees as his feet turned numb.

'What plots are you talking of?' Vlad demanded.

'The letters, the alliance you secretly made with the young Hungarian King against him, your plans for war... The plans to send an assassin to his Saray... All of it, Hünkâr.'

'He had been exchanging red ink letters with a man at your court!'

As the deserter cried, Codru could hear murmurs among the boyars. His eyes were already piercing the crowd. The Prince was silent and brooding, his eyes watching the Turk at his feet, but his mind was gone elsewhere.

'Tell His Highness about the Sultan's plans,' Codru urged Pakalin.

'I don't know much of it...'

'Say it!' Vlad demanded.

Through sobbing and hiccups, the Ottoman continued:

'Mehmet will soon send an envoy to your court, summoning you to Istanbul to make a truce. But you shouldn't go, Hünkâr; you shouldn't. The Bey Hamza, south of the River, had been given orders to capture you as soon as you set foot on Ottoman ground.'

'The Sultan wants to torture and kill you. He wants your head. He wants to turn you into a warning to his other enemies!'

'How do you know all of this, Turk? Why should I believe any of your poisonous words?' Vlad asked.

'I served as an errand to Mehmet's court before I was, to my horror, sent to war. I've seen much!'

'Have you ever seen this traitor?'

'He had only once come to the Saray, and he always hid his face. I only saw the back of his head as he joined the Sultan in one of his bath chambers. He had no hair on it and there was a thick, grey scar on the back of his neck.'

In that moment, out of the group of councilmen, Codru singled out Dragomir, the Voivode's faithful sword-bearer. He was slowly moving backwards as he hid his skull under his hood, trying to take advantage of the growing chatter and vanish through the back door. Codru's mind wandered immediately to an old story of betrayal told by Dobre the smuggler and the bald 'postelnic' who had been beheaded as punishment. It couldn't be him, could it?

'Don't even dare!' Vlad shouted without turning, as the voices of his boyars were reduced to silence and Dragomir turned to stone.

Vlad then turned his face towards the table and demanded, as anger began filling his voice.

'Have you betrayed me, Dragomir? Is this true?'

Codru saw the councillor exhale as his tall shoulders fell.

'It is!' he hissed. 'But I didn't do any of it to betray you; I did it for my own sake!'

'Why, Dragomir?'

As the noblemen watched in awe and distrust, they pulled away from the sword-bearer, gathering on one side of the table. Codru's hand slowly moved to his belt, resting his fingers on the sword's hilt.

Dragomir walked almost freely and boldly toward the fireplace.

'Where should I begin?' he asked himself as the fire light hit his now revealed silky skin.

'You are a weak ruler who disowned his bloodline and heritage, seeing it as a curse and not a blessing. A pharisee who denied himself who he is and the power he can wield for the sake of pretending who he is not and submitting willingly to how others perceive him.'

He continued as he revealed two long daggers hidden in his sleeves:

'Instead of honouring the return of your forefather, whom the witch made possible, and bowing to his greatness, you trapped him in that hole in the earth to do your bidding, using his powers for your narrow, human dreams. You are a shame, content with nothing but scraps, forcing me and others to follow your way of forged piety.'

'Curse you, wretched scum!' Vlad shouted as he drew his sword from under his mantle.

'You never allowed me to be more than your servant, keeping me docile and hungry! The Sultan knows who I am and didn't look away. He let me hone my strength. Fed me. If only once you tasted it, Prince, and you would know!'

'The witch knew of your misdeeds, you maggot?'

Dragomir laughed, and when he did, his eyes turned dark, and Codru noticed, for the first time, the fangs hidden under his thin and pale lips. He drew his scimitar as Pakalin ran to the right corner, praying.

'She was never told!' the bald councillor said, grinning. 'But she can foresee what things are to come, Prince, yet she never said anything. What does that tell you?'

The Prince roared as he plunged towards Dragomir with his sword in both hands, to the horrified screams of the councilmen, rushing towards the entrance. With a humanly impossible quick dodge, Dragomir's blade stuck one of his sharp blades in his stomach, making him scream in pain. Codru ran towards the middle of the chamber, as now the councilman stood right between him and the Prince. His scimitar's strike met the tall man's remaining blade. Swinging it, he deflected the wanderer's spade, making him step back. Codru could only ponder for a moment, bewildered by the man's strength.

'What are you?' he muttered, scouting the bald man's sullen face and the fangs growing on his jaws, as to an animal's.

'You have fought the mutts until now, Zmei-Slayer!' Dragomir barked. 'You are now facing the wolf!'

Codru pulled his axe, and with a strong throw, he cast it towards his foe. As if he just vanished, leaving the hatchet fall aimlessly into the opposite wall, Dragomir showed up immediately across the room, with his talon-like fingers wrapped around Pakalin's shoulder. His mouth widened, letting his head fall on his back for a moment, and then, with ravenous hunger, he dug his fangs into the terrified man's neck as he was squirming and bellowing under the dark robe of his predator.

Dragomir revealed his face, covered in red, and his chin drenched in thick, fresh blood. He roared, leaving the Turk's still body behind as his eyes turned to the remaining boyars screaming in the doorway. Wounded, the Prince ran after him before he could reach them, swinging his great sword, but all he could do was disarm Dragomir, his long dagger falling to the floor. A back of his hand crossed the Voivode's face, and Vlad was thrown on his back, with his sword clanking on the stone floor. But it was enough to let the men find their escape.

Dragomir walked towards the Prince as he was dragging on his back. He watched him struggle and pressed his boot on his chest.

'Weak! I will save you for last!'

His eyes turned to Codru, whose scimitar was now serving as a shield. A useless one, at that. As if he were crashed by a ruthless wave of wind, he was dashed into the wall behind him. He felt both creature's claws wrapped around his neck, strangling him. His boots no longer touched the floor, being dragged upwards and lifted in the air by the long arms of the councillor.

'I have longed to feast on you, Salman, since the day I first laid eyes on you!'

Codru's hands tried scraping the man's face, but to no avail. He was strong, and his hands turned numb as he could hear his heartbeat in his ears and the light pale from his own eyes. Dragomir opened his mouth wide, bending his head backwards, ready to bite. And that's when the tip of a sharp blade grew from his mouth, breaking his fangs and making the creature drop his arms and fall to the floor, choking and gurgling.

Behind him remained the Prince, who released the sword's hilt as the Councillor fell to the floor. He could only briefly exchange a faint look with the wanderer before he himself fell to his knees, barely breathing and wounded, and stepped away from his own death.

'Cut him to pieces and throw his head in the River,' he sighed as he fell to the floor, face down.

# CHAPTER XV

*Transylvania, April 1439 (6947)*

THE APPRENTICE WATCHED HIS FACE IN THE clear, small eye of water he just drank from. For the first time, he could see his master's work forever etched in his skin, and he was in awe at its sight. The eye carved in his forehead, with three long lashes upwards and three downwards, encircled the middle dot where his skull had been chipped. The two circle halves—snakes that trailed after each other without ever meeting.

He touched it curiously. But even though it had been drawn on his skin for many moons and the scar covered the missing shard of bone, it was still raw to touch. This was a wound that time would never heal. 'Many wounds heal. But there are some that never do, and there are a few that never should,' he remembered the Old-Man's words.

As he thought of the teacher, next to his own reflection in the water appeared the figure of the very man who brought him here, to this eye of water. The man stood there quietly, watching over the boy.

'What does it mean, Uncheaş?' Alidor asked as he ran his fingers softly over the ink seal.

'The sleepless eye that lets you see the unseen.'

'It will always be awake, even when you're sleeping,' he

continued. 'A *zila'ditas*. A flower of life.'

'And what of the broken circle?'

'Right now, it shall mean patience, as you need it before finding out. All in due time!'

After a pause, the Old-Man turned, and as he did, the boy turned away from the lake, following him. He took off the knapsack he had propped next to a rock on the shore. It had only been two days since he left the old-man's den on the mountain, following him toward the sunset. At the end of this journey, he was told he would receive the last of his labours—the final trial he had been told he had to go through.

Besides his crooked old stick, the Elder was now carrying with him a birch bark hamper too, which he left in the grass while they halted. The boy asked him when they left the mountain what it was that he carried, but he did not receive an answer.

'You will find out all in due time,' he was then told as well.

Once they left behind the eye of the water and the steep meadows that followed, the two reached a more bizarre, treacherous path. There was an untamed river on their right side, with its waters roaring as they crashed into the rocks. The trail, almost untouched by man's foot, could not fit two men side by side, and there was nothing between the path and the waters.

As the Old-Man slowly advanced, burdened by the hamper and his large rags tangling around his feet, the path appeared to steepen upward. His and his follower's only crutch was the enormous wall of the mountain on their right side that they both would lie towards to avoid falling off the rising edge.

'Best you will remember the way; it will come a time you will have to return. And when you do, I may not be around,' the man grunted his stories in his beard, barely audible from the sound of water.

Bits of ground and small rocks were falling off the path's edge, rustled by the feet of the two travellers. As the stones rolled off the cliff, they then vanished, taken by the rushing current, as the wind seemed to bring back the voices. Although they were different than the ones at the bottom of the mountain.

'You hear them?' the man asked.

'I don't know what I hear,' the boy answered.

'It's them, Alidor; we are getting closer to the tunnels they dwell in.'

'Who, teacher?'

'The *Vântoase*, my boy. The ones who walk through the *Mare's Nest*—one of the many Heaven's Gates!'

Soon after, a dark hole opened in the mountain's wall. A tall, doorless pathway through which the wind came and went. Closing in on it, the boy could not see its end, but it's where the trail went further. He dropped the knapsack on the ground, as he already knew what he had to do. Out of it, he brought up one of the glowing rocks from beneath the Hollow Mountain, to the Old-Man's unexpressed delight. With the sack back on his shoulder, he raised his arm before the strange cavern, as the wind was reaching out to his ears and whispering. Calling him inside.

'Men who venture in this chain of tunnels with no purpose lose themselves here, prey to the calls of these maids' carneys,' the Old-Man said. 'But you are on a path; no harm will befall you.'

Encouraged by the master's words, he stepped into the tunnel, taking the lead. He guided the man through the shadowy passage, casting the dim light of the crystal shard onto the tuberose walls. Listening to the haunting whistle, he could sense the sweet breeze reaching out to them, perhaps from beyond the Otherworld, however hidden from their eyes.

By the time the sun began falling into its second half of the sky, the two travellers traversed this passage and the others that followed on their trail, eventually reaching a portion of forest, from where the apprentice could hear once more the water lapping onto the stones. An abrupt path through the woods, fit for his age but less agreeable with the Old-Man's knees, soon began to shape up ahead, leading, as the boy thought, right to the precipice.

Before they headed on their way down, the Old-Man handed over to his protégé the hamper he had been carrying until then. Alidor could hear a subtle lisp in it, but he no longer asked about what it was. He knew he would soon see it for himself, and the man avoided letting him know. As they walked down the sloping, brittle ground, the boy supported his teacher's hand on his shoulder, as he himself was holding on to the trees with his free hand to not slide on his leather opinci. Until they fell back on a path like the one before, with the mountain on one side and the far below river on the other.

Urged by the teacher, Alidor led the way through the final stretch of the trail, buoyed by the promise that they would soon reach a lake, which, as he understood, was their destination.

When they finally reached it, his heart sank as he stood on the edge of the large, echo-engulfing pit. A half-covered cavern lake, as if the mountain wall to his left had stood a giant, toothless mouth, opened before them. Its waters were blue green to the edges and purple dark toward the middle—a sign of the endless bottom.

'Behold!' the man said. 'One of the last whirls of earth the elders called Sorb. Remnants of the Earth's very creation, when the grounds fell into themselves and swallowed the surrounding seas, thus birthing the mountains and the lands you now see around you.'

'But it's only here, in the womb of these deep waters, that your given Storm-Gatherer will hatch and grow, with the Vântoase as its nursemaids. And in seven winters, you shall return and set it loose, from the Earth's belly to the Sky's embracing hands.'

He told the boy to let the birchbark hamper on the ground, and as Alidor followed the word, the master gazed to the clear, sunset sky, raising his crooked stick and his empty arm toward it. He closed his eyes and murmured a prayer in the Old-Tongue, and as the winds howled in the distance, strings of rain-bearing clouds began to gather. And as lightning smouldered on the horizon, thundering in the sky's bosom, Alidor had, for the first time and for only a blink of an eye, glimpsed at the dark shadow swirling in the clouds like a nest. The shadow vanished as quickly as it showed its presence, never to be seen again.

'Uncheaș,' he whispered, his eyes pinned and widened at the sudden grey sky.

'Ay!' the man hummed. 'The Fire-Knights were sky riders too, mounting cloud dwelling beasts and moving the storms. As Salmans, we have never been as worthy, nor do we bring rain on our own. But we have been blessed enough to learn to tame these beasts, the Storm-Gatherers, from far away, by blood tie. Commanding the mighty, sky dwelling *Balaur* that is bound to us for life, from the day it laid its first bite to our last on this earth's night. My Storm-Gatherer had now been summoned, as you have seen; it shall witness the birth of the one to come.'

The boy felt the warm rain on his face as the man turned to him and removed the wet hair from his forehead, tracing the broken circle he had drawn on his face.

'It's been cast in your skin long before today. The two serpents that follow yet never reach each other's tails. Because once you release your Storm-Gatherer from the pit, our Book says you'll never see it again, but instead, you will journey through life bound by the same path. The Balaur will serve you with loyalty and answer your calls from above, bringing rain, storms or casting them away to your will.'

He demanded the boy uncover the birchbark basket lying between them. Alidor kneeled next to it without complaining, with water trickling off his red locks. He removed the cover, and there it was.

It's pale-grey and dark scales shimmered as rain rolled over its long, wreathed body, ending in a pale-red tail. Its flat and wide, pale-yellow head bore a short, pointy horn where its nose was to be. A frightening snake was rolling silently in the shadows of the basket. He turned away, covering the basket, scared at the sight of the venomous reptile.

'Master?'

'Fear not, boy!'

The man left his stick on the ground, opened the hamper, and lifted the snake out of it, bringing it to light in his hands. He whispered to it as he walked closer to Alidor, giving it orders in the Earth-Tongue not to dare bite him.

'This is an *aspidă*,' the Old-Man said. 'Its venomous bite is deadly to common folk. But to us, it only gives us a glimpse into the Otherworld.'

'You shall let it do what it's in his nature to do. Bite you. And then we shall cast it into the depths of the lake. Once it bites, you will become one and the same. And one day, you shall return and release it to the sky's light, for it is only within your power to free it.'

'Because, in the end,' the man said, as he was getting closer. 'it is only you who can set yourself free.'

Alidor looked at the snake as the man approached, with it unrolling off his arm and raising the horned, hissing muzzle towards the young one.

'Go on!' the Elder urged him. 'Roll up your sleeve!'

Trembling and shivering, Alidor followed the order. He raised his head once more toward the man.

'What if I never return?'

The Elder gazed at him; his brows riddled with discontent.

'Fail in your mission and your vows, and the rain shall turn to stone,' he grunted. 'For there are few things as wild and frightening as an untamed and imprisoned Balaur.'

With a quick strike, the snake sprang from the Old-Man's grip, and its teeth sank deep into Alidor's forearm's flesh, down to the bone. The apprentice screamed, his whole body gripped by a severe and wrenching pain, as the venom began to spread through his veins and entwine with his fiery blood. The man grasped the snake's head, forcefully unclenching its jaws off the boy's arm, blood trickling down his skin, and threw the reptile into the lake with a howling incantation.

Alidor heard the thunder in the distance as the snake plashed in the water, and he fell on his back under the heavy warmth that gathered in his flesh like a fever.

\*\*\*

*Târgoviște, March 1460 (6968)*

'I need your sword here, Codru,' the Prince said. 'There is nothing you will find there. They had taken hold of the Severino Fortress, and the whole area swarms with their scouts. If she and the rest of the men are alive, I trust they will find their way home.

Codru didn't say this to Vlad, but little did he care for the Voivode's war preparations. By handing over the Ottoman deserter, now dead, and ultimately uncovering the pagan traitor that nested in the Wallachian's Princely Court, his duty to the Prince, if there was ever any, was fully paid.

He only agreed to make the journey to the new Mehmet's home for the sake of bringing peace to Ileana's old grievances and keeping the scribe away from Chindia's dungeons. Timotei was now safe, but even though the defeated, remaining Wallachian soldiers returned to Târgoviște, the Maid of Cozia was not among them. And nothing was going to keep him from finding her. Much less the Prince.

As he was preparing his horse at the Court's stables, Vlad cornered him. Even he was acknowledging that he owed the Zmei-Slayer for the exposed betrayal, so he was not going to force him to stay and fight by his side in the battles to come. But he also thought he owed it to himself to try to change the wanderer's mind.

'I do not know what sort of vicious, sickening curse lies here at your court, Sire,' Codru let him know, 'but I have had my share of curses lately, and I won't be part of any more of them.'

He was surely referring to Dragomir, the bald creature that

almost had him killed in the palace weeks ago.

'The sword bearer was right,' the Prince almost disregarded Codru's last words, standing next to him as he gazed somewhere far over the walls of his fortress, with his arms behind.

'I am unwilling to accept who I am because I want to believe I can break the curse that my family has been plagued with for generations. Maybe it would just be easier to embrace the devil we are. Maybe this is something we both have in common.'

Then, turning to him, he continued:

'But Dragomir had been dealt with; he had been torn to pieces and each of his limbs given to riders sent to scatter and bury his remains in all corners of Wallachia. He won't be a problem anymore.'

'As for the Egyptian witch, I have no knowledge of her whereabouts, but the Hounds have been sent after her.'

'So, you believe the sword Your Highness split his head with was not enough,' Codru interrupted as he tied the harness to Shadowfire.

'There is no sword that can kill a *Moroi*, at least not one that I know of. I always knew who Dragomir was, and he was right; I starved him. I hoped that if he could go against his nature, I could go against mine. But I was wrong. He and the likes of him are an unnatural breed of both man and Strigoi, damned with a deathless life and blood thirst. Word of advice—better stay clear of these hairless, slippery demons.'

Eventually Vlad turned his back and stepped away from his mercenary, as he understood no promise of reward would stray the man from his already decided path. He grimaced, subtly patting himself where the Moroi's dagger pierced him.

'What will you do then, Sire?' Codru asked as he mounted the steed.

'For now, I shall send my lady and my sons to Poenari, away from the city. I will fall behind; there is much to do, and every hand counts. If you reconsider offering your axe to help your countrymen, send a raven to the Court.'

Then, as he left the stables, Vlad turned once more.

'And worry not of your chronicler—he'll be cared for. Every story has a right to be told. Not telling them is sacrilege. And without people to tell our stories, our pursuit of a legacy is worthless.'

The weather was sweetening as the spring loomed over the hills and the mountains on Codru's far right. The ground was wet, glistening under the early daylight as the melting snow revealed patches of mud and frostbitten, withered grass that were dug and drowned under the dark horse's galloping hooves. There were snowdrop flowers and hyacinths refreshing the air.

He had travelled the same path a few times until now. Leaving the Impaler's town behind, however, Codru had just realized it was the first time he was doing it alone. But never with a plan to travel as far as the western Wallachian edge. Coincidentally, it was also close to where he had first arrived in the realm beyond the forests, where it all began. The almost prophetic words of fate and destiny of Gunnay, the serpent priestess, whirled through his mind, but he let them slide away as they came. His mind was set on the matter at hand.

After the fight with Dragomir, while Vlad was still pinned to bed, he tracked and questioned thoroughly every able or disabled survivor he had encountered and had been part of Sânziana's company.

'What happened to your captain?' he was roughing them up. 'Why isn't she here? Why was she left behind?'

All he could sum up from every lead he could pull out of these frightened men was that after their captain sounded the retreat and the Hungarian Szilágyi had fallen prisoner, they encountered another foe on their way back to the capital. An unseen foe lurked around the Locvei Mountains, very near the Citadel where the Ravens' Order itself dwelled.

It seemed that a group, led by Ileana, ventured to explore an area known to the villagers as the Devil's Lake. They said the lake itself had awakened, grinded by anger and hunger, and was now preying on those who dared to cross it. But the group, and the maiden included, never returned. And they never sent more men after them.

'We haven't survived the war, only to be killed by whichever demon harbours in there,' some were arguing.

'If any of what the folk say is true, then both the men and their captain are long gone to kingdom come.'

They were not exactly deserters, but Codru thought they deserved a deserter's fate. But he wouldn't take their word for it. She couldn't have been gone. Not now, when he had just found her. He had to go look for her.

So, as he was now travelling once more towards the lands he had first seen upon his return to the country, with both the heaviness of Ileana's disappearance and the awareness that these lands were the very same he had spent most of his years in the Old-Man's company on—a domain close to the very place he wanted to return to almost a year ago: the Hollow Mountain.

Shadowfire could not gallop faster than it already was, and Codru would only rarely halt, just enough to let the steed rummage through whatever fresh knotgrass or sorrel bushes it could scout before he would once again mount it and ride hell for leather towards the west.

It took him less than two days to arrive, by nightfall, close to a town they called Strehaia. Both he and the horse were exhausted, but Codru saw no reason to enter the town as he knew he would have to go north, towards the mountains.

The night was cold, but tempered enough that he could camp outside. He found a patch of dry land, not too far from the road nor too secluded, at the town's outskirts, where he reined in and hitched the horse. Shielded by the bald tree trunks, he made a small fire and unrolled the mat to rest without planning to fall asleep, as he had to be watchful. But he did.

As if he sensed danger, confused, and frustrated that he had dozed, Codru opened his eyes suddenly before the cockcrow. Although the sun hadn't hit the horizon yet, the sky was not as dark as before, and with only the light of the fizzling campfire embers, his eyes could not distinguish much. But he heard noises. Soft, muffled thumps on the damp grass and sear leaves. Footsteps.

He stealthily slid one of his arms under his cloak, preparing to reach for any of his weapons, and pushed the ground with the other so he could jump straight. Before he could do any of that, he noticed the intruders' shadows, framed by the dark blue sky. And with no other warning, an aching, blunt strike in the back of his neck made him lose any sense of his surroundings, sending him to a well-deserved sleep he had denied himself before.

When he woke up from his blackout, his head was killing him. He squinted his eyes from the pain and from the apparently blinding daylight. It was only when he tried to reach for his face and forehead that he realized, even before he could distinguish any of his camp, that he was tied up with string at the base of a tree trunk. Much like how he and the knight once tied Ilinca, the grief-howling maiden, in the forest. He tried jolting and puffing up his arms in a vain attempt to break the sturdy rope rolled around him, barely letting him breathe in.

A few blurred out silhouettes took shape in his vicinity. The fire he let die had been relit, and smoke and steam from a tin cauldron were coming from it as something was cooking. His captors really made a home in his camp.

'Let go of me,' Codru mumbled. 'Let me out!'

'Not so fast!' he then heard a female voice, which he did not expect. She came closer, standing a step away from his boots and keeping a safe distance.

As Codru began to gain clarity, he distinguished his kidnapper's appearance. A not too old, not too young woman with her head wrapped in a loose headdress of the deep-grass tone. Strings of dark hair were coming from under it, running over a linen shawl of the same colour, covering her brown tunic's shoulders. She wore male breeches, like Ileana's, and leather boots. She was sipping, most likely, some broth from a wooden bowl she kept close to her chin with her hands covered in strange tattoos.

'You can squirm all you wish,' she said, watching him vigilantly.

'That's a threefold birchbark rope around you, stranger. Made to keep an ox in heat away from the poor cows.' And she carried on slurping from the brewage.

Codru gasped, ceasing his struggle. She was right; there was no way to break that. The clearer his sight became, the better he could look at his new companions. There were both men and women of different ages, dressed in attire like the one who spoke to him. Some of them had their mouths covered and their eyes set on him; some were wearing sheepskin coats; and some even had mantles like his.

'Who are you?' he turned to the chatty woman, fighting off his migraine.

'I was going to ask you the same thing,' she replied.

'You are obviously a scout of sorts, but for the life of me, I could not figure who you are scouting for.'

Codru sighed, looking away.

'I am no scout, and I could not care less about your affairs.' He fittingly remembered the Old-Man's counsel to stay out of the people's duties.

The woman ignored him as she continued.

'You wear a Wallachian-made coat, you have an axe with Székelys engravings, an Ottoman scimitar... The heathen forehead tattoo and your hair colour are even more intriguing. And you speak our tongue.'

Codru understood that they had searched through his belongings. He turned to where he remembered having tied his horse. Shadowfire was still there, unharmed, and with the saddlebags apparently untouched.

'Your beautiful horse is safe,' she eventually said, turning and letting her bowl fall on the grass, close to the fire. 'I can't say the same for you if you do not begin chirping. And soon!'

Codru was angry. He had no time to waste. He had to find Ileana as soon as possible. He made the journey from Târgovişte all in a breath for this very reason. So, he agreed that he did not have many choices. The truth might have hopefully been enough for this odd boodle to set him free. And by their appearances and speech, freely wandering these domains, these men and women surely weren't foes of His Highness.

'I'm travelling from Târgovişte, where I helped the Voivode with certain matters,' he said. 'I was heading north-west tracing the men who never made home after the battle, not too far from here.'

As the woman listened, her eyebrows entwined. After a very short pause, she said, in a sceptical tone:

'Is that so?' Then she continued as she squinted, her hand revealing a small dagger. 'Here's how I know you are lying. If you had any touch with the Voivode, you would have known he doesn't give a rat's arse about the men he loses on the field. They're fodder. He wouldn't spare more of them searching for the lost ones. And even if he did care hill of beans for them, a single man searching for a whole company sounds plain reckless.'

Codru pierced her eyes as he clenched his jaw. She was clear-eyed, he could see it. Brave too, no doubt. So, he gave in.

'I never said he sent me!' he replied.

She smiled.

'You want to find the missing soldiers out of kindness, is that it?'

'I have my own reasons!'

She nodded pensively.

'That isn't enough, stranger! So be it.'

Behind the woman showed up another, younger one, dressed similarly, except for the headdress, which was missing, revealing, as such, her chestnut hair loosely tied behind her back. She was shorter and younger, and her eye shape matched the dark-haired one's. She approached her comrade and whispered something over her shoulder, as his sharp captor didn't lose him in her eyes.

When the other woman finished what she had to say, both their eyes looked at him strangely, as if they suddenly realized something.

'My sister Ana here told me something very odd. She reminded me of a story we both heard not too long ago, of a man with crimson hair and his forehead inked with symbols. He cut through the crowd, leaving behind his fellow, to save the honour of a young woman from the Pillar of Infamy in Kruhnen Square.'

Codru raised his eyes towards them, remembering the blonde woman with child, tied, and mocked by the townsmen. He never got to rescue her, but her eyes, when unchained and taken away from the pole by her father, met his long enough to recognize gratitude.

'Yes,' he muttered. 'I was there; I remember her.'

The women looked at each other for a moment before the older one put her dagger away as she stood back up.

'That was our dear cousin, Katharina!' she said. 'She remembers of you too!'

Ana, the red-haired maid, touched her sister's arm and spoke softly.

'Maybe we should free him, Stana. He was going to do the same for our *Lăptița.*'

'Not until I know his name and his true purpose!' the dark-haired one said decisively, her eyes set on the stranger once more.

Codru was still surprised by the sudden turn of the situation. But he realized she was right. His only way out was through pure truth, and nothing less.

'I go by Codru,' he said. 'I was born on these lands, but I have since travelled a lot, so I picked up a few items on the way. And I have been in Vlad's service, but now I am on a path of my own.'

'You aren't looking for his missing soldiers, then?'

'I am not; I am looking for the maiden that led them.'

The women turned once again to each other.

Stana, the older sister, circled around his legs, reaching behind the tree where Codru was tied up too. She untangled his rope and pulled it away, releasing him as she rolled the twine carefully around her elbow, with a vague smile on her face and his eyes to him.

'Then, Codru the pathfinder, you better hurry up and eat some of Ana's borscht before we depart. We share the same purpose, you see. We are looking for Ileana too!'

\*\*\*

*Locvei Mountains, March 1460 (6968)*

The sun was still up, yet the further into the gorges the riders went, the clearer and colder the air turned. The path through the ascending hill covered with trees barely let two horses side by side, so the group advanced slowly and tediously.

At the end of the cortege, Codru was following it silently, as he oddly began to believe it was a more than fortunate coincidence having met them. He was thinking of what Stana, who led these scouts, told him on the way here while they were passing by from afar, a port close to the Danube's Iron Gates he heard of.

She and the others were offering their resistance aid, when fate allowed it, to Wallachian soldiers, such as the ones of Vlad. They would sipe on the enemy's camp and either lynch them in their sleep or cause damage to their armoury, vanishing before the Ottomans had had a chance to make them. However, they were not doing it for Prince's sake; Stana had no soft spot for the Impaler, not at all. She despised that her cousin bore the Devil's Voivode's twin bastards, making her suffer on his account. She was doing it for the people.

'I know why my men are looking for the missing soldiers and for Ileana,' she said just a while ago, riding next to Shadowfire as Codru's eyes gazed to his far right, noticing the walls and the tower of the Raven's Citadel they were then passing by.

'She's like a sister to us, you see. She spent some time at our home years ago. I taught her how to fight, no less. But she was different and stronger. She soon outlearned me and then went on to lead the Voivode's army, as she was promised it would help her one day revenge her father's death.'

'What I do not know is why you are looking for her. What's the Maiden of Cozia to you?' she then asked.

He didn't reply, as he wasn't sure of the reason himself. However, flashes and memories that transpired since he had set foot on his native land kept recurring. From the words of the first Raven that died in his arms, to Toma and Daniil, to the vague prophecies of the Zmei's Priestess and Luladija, and even to the confessions of the Wallachian Voivode, there was something that cast its light over his path all along. Something the beggar and the old teacher at the mountain spoke of too. A mission. A purpose. Maybe the girl he once met at the lake—the shieldmaiden she had become—was it.

Stana noticed his silence.

'It is love, isn't it?' she sniffed. 'That's what guides your steps towards her. She has her hand wrapped around your heart.'

He had no clue. He did not know it.

'I have lived in pain for a very long time. All I know,' he said out of nowhere, in a low and sombre voice, 'Is that when I'm around her, that pain goes away. She has a gift.'

To that, the scouts' leader did not say anything more for some time.

'Does that pain have to do anything with that strange ink on your face?' she asked after, vaguely curious.

She was right to think that, but Codru didn't feel the need to confirm it. His eyes noticed once more the markings the woman bore on the back of her palms, surely all the way up to her elbows. Now that he was closer to them, he could see crosses, trees, and flowers.

'Those seem to have been painful to carve too,' he said, pointing his chin at her hands wrapped around her horse's reins.

'They were, but they surely spared me from greater pain.'

'What's their meaning?'

'Only a trick our elder women learned from their sisters over the Great River. Their young ones are marked to not be taken away when the Turks come for their blood tribute. They have no love for tainted skin.'

He sniffed. It did not save him. Yet, her words reminded him of one Turk who met Hultan's blade for this reason when he lodged a protest against taking Codru with them.

Later, when Codru asked her how she was so sure the missing soldiers were on this trail, she answered:

'The villagers talk of a devil that lurked for many years, deep in the gorges. It only recently seems to have awakened and fuelled their nightmares. People who never returned to their homes. Some have said that as they were on their way to the capital, Ileana gathered a few men and went in to search for them, just like we do now. If there is anywhere the soldiers and their captain could be, then that is the place.'

Her voice sounded at a halt. Shortly after their path narrowed and the walls of rock became more and more abrupt, he heard her signal, now at the helm of the party.

'Arm yourself and hitch your horses; from here on, we'll go on foot.'

Codru dismounted and pulled his dark steed off the path, beneath a pine's shadow. Looking around, at the trail he left behind and at the abrupt clearing ahead, he began to sense he had been here before, the same as when he had a familiar feeling while he was being held prisoner in the Ravens' jail wagon, as it roamed through the forest before the Strigoi ambushed them. The same earthy scent of pine and juniper reached out to his nostrils. It wasn't until sometime later, as the pathfinders continued their upward hike, that his ears became aware of it too.

The fresh water rippled, embracing the edgy rocks. The tall, almost vertical walls of stone loomed through the trees' crowns ahead. He knew now that he had been here before, once, many years ago. Codru felt a faint, sudden urge to rub his hands. He long forgot about what happened here and about his vow and his duty to return. And as he continued to walk on the ascending edge of the river, with his heart beginning to race, a familiar ache sprouted between his temples, different from the one the scouts' truncheon gave him. His feet followed the group closely, as if not to be left behind. But if Codru closed his eyes, he knew his legs would find the way on their own.

Walking, with his cloak fluttering in the hastening wind, he ran his hand on the cold rock wall he had touched before, gazing at the rising edge of the cliff as the river lowered. The whistling noise of the biting air soothed him, but it did not make the ache go away. Instead, it reminded him of the creatures the Old-Man talked of— the same ones this very wind was premonitory of—the Vântoase.

So, when Stana halted in front of the tunnel's entrance Codru was sure they would eventually stumble upon, he pushed the rest of the scouts out of his way in a hurry, reaching out to the beginning of the cortege and joining the two sisters. His head turned towards the deep and tall entrance in the mountain, and he told them:

'You will have to find another way further; it isn't safe.'

Stana eyed the cave.

'There isn't another; this is the only way to the lake.'

'Why?' Ana, the ginger-haired maid asked Codru. 'What's in there?'

The wanderer paused as he remembered the Old-Man's warnings.

'Nothing any of us would be glad to encounter.'

He only now realized what happened to the missing villagers Stana spoke about. There was no devil wasting them; it was the wind, Iele, preying on the lost travellers. The serpent's nursemaids protecting their whelp and keeping the meddling intruders at bay. He knew right then and there that his companions had wasted their time.

'Your missing soldiers are gone; I'm now certain of it!' he said, turning to the sisters. 'You may as well turn back.'

Stana laughed.

'I have yet to live the day I will be ordered around by a man!' she said. 'We haven't come all this way to turn around now.'

'You don't understand; you have no reason to be here. You'll get yourself killed in there, as the ones before you did.'

'Would you turn back?' Stana asked him angrily, closing in on him and piercing him with her sharp eyes.

'I wouldn't; I ought to find her.'

'And what makes you so sure she isn't already gone too?'

He knew she wasn't gone, as sure as he knew the sun rises in the east. How could she have been? At the end of the day, if what Ileana learned from Mother Wednesday was true, she was, after all, one and the same blood as the wind maidens. He didn't say anything.

Seeing as he turned quiet, Stana eventually replied:

'If having a reason is this cave's tribute, then it should know we have as much of one as you do. You forget we care for her too. And if she's already dead, it's our duty to at least look for her body.'

He gave up arguing. It was time he could rather use to cross the passageways. The reason they had for being here was nowhere near as great as the one he had and began to remember. He not only cared for her in ways they could barely begin to comprehend, but the lake had been waiting for him. And his return was years overdue. He wasn't safe; he was expected.

It was only after the scouts brought up torches and traversed the chain of grottos that he began admitting he might have been wrong. No wind phantasm appeared to snatch them into the Otherworld. The Elder might have only told old stories, which he also heard from his own elders.

The wind was there; however, the flames of the torches were barely able to keep up. And as he walked through the maze, the headache worsened. So much so that his feet would not listen to him, making him wobble and having to hold on to the walls. The cramped passageway, like any other prison he had been into—the Raven's dungeon, their jail waggon, the caverns beneath Zmei's temple—all stripped him of clarity and caused him headache. He had wounds he had been gifted with since many years ago, when he had been trapped in the Bashi-bazouks' pit and lacked freedom.

When Codru and his companions safely emerged from the maze beneath the mountain, his migraine gave way to the familiar voices he recalled from the Heart of the Mountain. Voices he would not understand. The sisters noticed as he held on to the trees in the abrupt valley that followed their path to not fall under the overwhelming weight of the whispers suddenly rustling through his head.

His heart raced, and his worry grew that he would have no other choice but to touch the dark poison wrapped at the bottom of the leather pouch he carried. So much so that as the sun began descending, he ceased his walking and took a knee next to one of the trees and unbuckled the pouch, digging with his hands through it, searching for the parchment packet.

When he found it, he held it in his hand without taking it out of the sack. He looked up at the sky, grazed by the trees' branches, as he rested his head on the trunk, unable to follow the others. He closed his eyes, trying to navigate the pain, but all he was doing was letting it take over as his temples pulsated with agony.

Then something unexpected happened. The overwhelming chatter turned rapidly quiet as, one by one, the voices he was once told belonged to the ancestors were silenced. Except for one. A grave voice, as of a man. A voice that wasn't angry nor kind. A whisper sounded like an echo as the headache dissipated as well. At first, he heard it from far away, but soon, as if it came closer to his ears, it turned clearer and louder. It spoke in a language he thought was lost on him. The Earth-Tongue.

'*You have finally arrived, brethren!*' it said.

And Codru opened his eyes, his breath quivering as he dropped the dark matter back in his pouch and stood up, ready to grab his axe. The men and women before him ceased their hike as well, noting their follower's sudden disquiet. The sisters returned so much as to even get closer to him, confused and worried about his struggle, which scared their people.

'What's the matter,' Stana asked.

But Codru didn't answer. His head was turning from one tree to another, trying to find the source of the voice, even though he was aware it didn't come from outside but from within.

'*Come!*' the voice tranced him. '*Come, I have been so lonely! But I am not alone anymore! Come, brethren!*'

'The lake!' Codru moved the people out of his way without justifying himself, as he grabbed his hatchet and began running down the slope towards the lake that he noticed through the tree trunks.

'Wait!' the pathfinders' leader shouted behind him. But he cared not for it. He knew now what it was, and he knew that if Ileana was alive, she was there. A bait to make him return to the forgotten earth's whirl.

He saw the lake down the valley, and an abrupt patch of treeless ground lay between him and the waters. As he went down the last patch of naked earth, letting his boots slide on it and hanging from the old roots and vines sticking out, he heard a sound in his head as if the eerie voice kept itself from laughing.

His feet reached the lake's edge, his legs sinking knees deep in it, and he looked at the vast eye of green to purple water unfold before him, like the open mouth of a hungry mountain. All around, the water was surrounded by the tall walls of the mountain. To his far left, as he looked up, he could see the cliff where he left himself to get bitten when he was young. And right across the lake, he could see the opposite shore, engulfed in the dark and wide mouth of a cave.

And at that dark cave's edge, on the other shore, he saw the fire. A small campfire. And someone standing next to it by themselves. From the distance, he could not see who they were, but his heart knew. He turned his head back, looking up at the scouts who did not follow down to the lake, but they noticed the same fire as their faces looked towards it too.

Both him and Stana's troopers knew what that meant, even though none of them were saying it. The only way to the other side was through the water. And if it could have been done, the one over there wouldn't have needed rescue. They could have swum, so why haven't they?

As Codru looked around the lake, measuring and trying to find a way other than through the water, he sensed the deep quiet that lay over the group. The air turned heavy as winds were no longer flowing. It was like this for moments that seemed to drag forever, the only sounds being the ones of his boots lapping through the sunken mud and the mutters of the men and women behind him, with their bows and short swords at the ready, unsure of the next steps but expecting nothing good out of this timeless trap. And their worries had been fruitful.

*'Welcome!'*

At first, a long and deep howl was born in the earth's belly. A thundering growl that made the scouts' blood freeze in their veins. Then the ground beneath their feet began to tremble, shaking rapidly and cracking, releasing fumes, dust, and steam from its core. A sour, chocking miasma that seemed to spout straight from the depths of the underworld. The until then mirror-clear surface of the otherworldly lake trembled too in its womb, countless strings and wafts spreading across all corners.

He heard the men lamenting, as they were sure the Devil had awakened, and Hell was opening its gates. But they did not run. With her daggers out, commanding her men to retreat behind the cover of the trees, Stana shouted to Codru from the top of the small hill to get out of the waters and climb back to join them, but he ignored her. His eyes were pinned on the waters that had lost their colour, turning from blue and green to a muddy, earthen swamp.

Out of nowhere, as the earthquake hastened and the underwater sludge began to swallow his feet, Codru then felt the sharp winds passing by from all directions, like presences, unseen by eyes but felt by his spirit. The wave of air was so harsh and sudden that it made him stumble on his back under its reaping blast, like a scythe. Arrows began to whirr from the men's bows, and blades began to slash the air. Then a despairing lament, almost like a chorus of all the poor souls up on the hill, echoed from between the trees.

'God have mercy!' Codru could only hear them.

Before he could even get back on his feet, trying to return to offer his arm and leave the waters behind, Codru saw the waters rising, splashing waves violently into the shores, covering him from head to toe. He grabbed the fresh mud with his free arm, gasping and dragging himself away from the lake as quickly as he could, before he heard another sombre whisper in his mind, covering the pathfinders' yelling and the winds smothering them.

*'Do not dare leave me again!'*

He turned, squeezing the axe's handle in his fist. And then he saw it. From the middle of the lake appeared what looked like a gigantic, ashen white tail, striking towards the sky like a monumental column.

Just above the water, it was as big as the great furnace in the Hollow Mountain, narrowing towards the top that rose like molten iron, as high as the peaks around the lake. Covered in great, luscious scales as wide as a horse.

Pinned on the ground as his eyes stuck on the incredible and extraordinary sight, Codru had no time to react. He froze. The great serpent tail fell like a lightning strike on the lake's water, whipping it with a deafening and echoing blast, throwing deadly tides to its sides. Massive rocks cracked from the walls, rolling over the mountains and falling with a moaning tang into the lake. The shore Codru was stuck on began to break down, one chunk of land at a time.

He had seen things he never would have thought he would see, but this creature was beyond everything he would have ever imagined. He dragged over the caving ground beneath, striking the hill's ground with the axe to not fall and grabbing every putrid root that unravelled from the wounded ground. But the colossal tail fell once more with a powerful strike, dangerously close to him. The ground under him, which he so desperately tried to hold on to, fell into itself, and as if seized by unseen claws, Codru found himself being dragged into the abyss of the lake.

The complete silence of the lake flooded his ears, the lake embracing him whole in its cold grip. Floating. Drifting in the deep-blue nothingness. From the distancing above, the anaemic light almost failed to stab through the water. And the quietude was comforting and almost tempting. As he sank into the bottomless mere, his mind agreed. He had fought all his life, and now he could allow himself to rest. It was so much easier. He kept his hand on the axe for so long without losing it, but he could just let go of it, letting it float away.

But then, the same long tail loomed in the waters around him, taunting him. Encircling him.

'*You aren't to receive the sweet release of death you so much desire,*' he heard the voice as clear as day in his skull. '*Not now, when you are to grant me freedom.*'

Codru turned and, swimming, tried to strike the tail through the treacherous waters, keeping it away from him. The voice laughed as the pale monster avoided the aimless hit.

And then, right in front of him, from the tenebrae loomed a gigantic head, as big as the Black Boyar's mansion. A great, albino, sun deprived snake's head, lighted by the wavy green light coming from the surface. A great, rock-like horn was pinned on its huge muzzle, right above the unnaturally large mouth, and two deep, dark-green eyes were carved in its solid, scaly, and wide skull. The Serpent. His Storm-Gatherer. His long promised and abandoned Balaur.

Both were floating and facing each other. Codru felt both hatred and love for this creature. He wanted to fight it and embrace it all at once. If he had the might, he would have both sunk it in the abyss and unchained it from the blood spell it had been trapped in for all these years.

He then suddenly felt as though his air was almost gone, and his heart pumped slower and slower. He was drowning, and as it did, flashes of Ileana's visage returned to his mind over the murmurs of the Balaur's. And suddenly, he no longer wanted to let go of his axe.

He tried to swim upwards and away from the serpent, with his arms numb and the lake's surface getting farther with each pull, as if a rock hung to his feet. The monster waved next to him, and the whirls it created made Codru's escape impossible, pulling him into their undulations as if he were a speck of dust in the immensity.

Until, out of nowhere, from above, a long and thick noose dropped, sinking in the waters. It was a rope thrown in by someone—a birchbark rope. He swam towards it with all the strength he had left and at the same time tried keeping the scaly tail at a distance with his hatchet, as if that would have helped. Darkness began to encircle his vision, and his free, heavy arm could barely reach the floating rope's end. And just before his fist grabbed it, he heard a 'no!' roar in his head. And the rope pulled Codru from the depths.

He spat and coughed on the ground as Stana's and Ana's arms pulled him away from the water. He could only see they were the only ones in sight before the lake awakened once more with greater fury, and this time, the very head of the serpent sprang out from the lake.

Somehow, Codru felt both its anger and its hopelessness. Then the creature's mouth plunged into the shore, reaching out hungrily to the two rescuers who had deprived it of its saviour. And the wanderer knew they were going to die if he didn't do anything. He pushed them out of the way, bracing himself for the next plunge of the Balaur.

His eye glanced to his side, where the birchbark rope lay in the mud. He hung his axe quickly to his waist so he would free both his hands, and then he threw himself over the rope, rolling it behind his arms. And when the monster's mouth opened violently, ready for the next bite, Codru threw the noose around its horn and pulled. Stana came to his aid, but it was not enough. The serpent only jerked his head once, and she lost her grip. Codru didn't. And although he pulled as much as he could, trying to reach the rope's end at the closest tree, he was no match for the Balaur.

'*You are to free me, not ensnare me!*'

The Balaur rose entirely from the lake, and Codru's feet left the ground with a hitch, his left arm entangled painfully in the rope now pinned to the creature's horn. After years of lurking in the waters, the serpent was leaving its nest behind. The limbless monster reeled itself upwards on the rocky walls, rolling over to its sides, squirming, and breaking trees and earth under its desperate attempt to free itself of Codru's unwanted presence.

'*You have forsaken me, doomed me to this filthy pit for years, and forgot to return!*'

The wanderer screamed as his arm was pinned between the rope and the monster's cold, rocky skin. He took the axe out and struck between the monster's neck scales to prevent him from falling. The serpent roared, and lightning struck in the distance, more violently than Codru had heard before. To evade the piercing broken tree branches and avoid being crushed between the Balaur's body and the cliffs, Codru struggled and gasped for breath. Desperately, he used his axe, embedded in the monster's skin, to pull himself up. He climbed the Balaur's solid, pointy scales as if scaling a ladder.

'*You have broken your oaths, and you have broken our bound—there is nothing tying me to you now; release me!*' the Balaur's voice resounded in his head.

As the monster crushed his body against the mountain and the hills like an untamed mare, Codru mounted the serpent's head right at the base of its skull, and his boots were anchored deep beneath the scales. Not only did he free his arm, but he also used the other one to strengthen the grip. And then he pulled with all his might, releasing a roar from his throat. He pulled as one pulls the reins of a war horse. The creature bellowed and stumbled on its destructive path as its head bent up towards the sky. And as it did, the rest of its enormous body followed the head.

'*Do not dare you mount me, godless one! I have so much anger; I have lived in the depths and dreamed of all the atrocities you committed.*'

Codru could hear everything the Balaur was shouting with grief and rage inside his head. Little did he know he could answer. And when he realized it, he gave the scared and wounded monster an answer.

'I was lost,' he could only say, as this had always been true to him.

'*Lost, you say?*' the voice replied as the serpent broke through one of the mountain peaks and scales broke off its belly.

'*Yes, I know you have been lost. Through the years, I have felt every pain you endured, as we were once one and the same.*'

Its voice faded as, in the endless struggle, Codru could see the blood coming off the Balaur's grazed skin. Yet he held on to the reins. He had too, if he didn't want to fall off its back and crush against the abrupt and high mountain the monster climbed.

'I am here now; I have returned!' Codru said.

'*Too late now, brethren, you have turned me into a feral, godless monster that knows no master, like yourself. All I know now is wrath! Say the words! You know them! Free me, or we'll both find our end in this aimless fight!*'

Then, without being able to change his mind, the words the serpent was looking for escaped Codru's memory.

'*Rebo'ditas!*' the teacher's words resounded.

Suddenly, a jolt ran through the creature's body, immediately followed by an unexpected clap of thunder in the sky. Rain clashed with the man's face, and then, instead of water, stones fell from the sky. Ice shards and rocks suddenly broke from the deeply grey clouds, grazing the serpent's scales. A rain of stones as he had never seen before, nor had he ever seen the Master bringing, but he heard him speaking of. Hail.

After the strong shake, Codru's arms snapped off the reins. As an untamed horse prances and throws one of its back, the wanderer was severely cast off the serpent's neck, losing the reins completely. He was going to fall from the mountain's peak into the chasm beneath, all the way to his unavoidable perdition. He shouted as he rolled over and felt the emptiness of the height in his stomach.

The voice left his mind as he was falling. He closed his eyes, bracing for his inevitable end. And then, with a sudden move, he felt the scaly back of the hail bringing Balaur sliding under his falling body.

'*Take those reins, godless one. I will let you go to the lake, as you have freed me. Then my debt for freeing me shall be paid, and we will part ways.*'

The sky cleared. As Codru followed the serpent's advice, the

Hailbringer ended as he slid, this time smoothly, into the valley, reaching out to the lake he had arisen from:

'*You are no longer lost, just as I am no longer trapped. You have returned, even if only for your maiden. Yes, the maiden you seek has appeared in my dreams as well. You did not return for me, but I knew you would come searching for her. Even I, a monster, can understand that you cannot truly come back unless there is something—or someone—to return to, just as you cannot be free unless someone sets you free.*'

From afar, Codru could see Ileana and the two sisters joined on the shore of the abandoned and broken cave.

# CHAPTER XVI

*Härmeschtat, March 1462 (6970)*

HER LIPS ON HIS FOREHEAD FELT LIKE WATER on a hot stove. Soothing. Safe. A sweet dream in a lifetime of nightmares. He smiled before, while his eyes were still closed, afraid that it might have indeed been a dream and that opening them would cast it away. But it wasn't, and it didn't. Her warm hand covered his cheek, her thumb running softly over the eye carved in his skin. And he then summoned the courage to open his eyes.

When he did, Ileana was sitting at the bedside. She wore a loose, unadorned linen shirt that reached until her knees but did not cover her arms. Her brown hair flowed like dark silk over her shoulders. Her sour-cherry-tinted lips bore a peaceful smile as she watched Codru, removing his hair from his face. Today she had awakened earlier than before, so Codru could already hear the fire crackling in the small fireplace of this inn's room.

'We need to prepare,' her voice sounded softly.

He sighed without taking his eyes from her, catching her hand on his face, and holding it there.

'We don't have to...' he said. 'We can stay here for a while longer.' She didn't reply, but he knew her answer as he continued: 'We've grown to mean something now, haven't we?'

She pulled her hand swiftly from under his and left the bed. On the wooden chair close to the door, there was his cloak, hanging on its back. Walking barefoot on the wooden plank floor, she reached for the mantle and pulled it over her shoulders as she headed towards the small and crooked window, looking over the cloudy morning.

'You know I can't!' she said. 'Time is running out, and there are others depending on me. On us. You agreed to follow...'

He got off the bed and stretched, vaguely uneased. As he walked in her footsteps, the cold floor touching his soles sent chilling shivers up his legs and spine. He embraced her over the cloak as his chin fell on her head, gazing as well through the bleary glass of the window.

The roof eyes on the building around the inn were ever watchful, and a thin drizzle washed the stone alley next to it. The warm scent of Ileana's hair covering his face was enough to make him see the stillness of the town in a peaceful way. Peace was all he ever yearned for, and although perhaps it had been short-lived, this moment here was more than he ever dreamed of.

'You know I would follow you to the edge of the world,' his voice faded.

Two winters have passed since he rescued her from the Balaur's den, releasing the frightful brute from the spell bound. He hasn't seen it since. Ileana was, as he expected, the only survivor of the missing soldiers, as the Serpent only needed her as bait, and half of Stana's pathfinders found their horrifying end at the hands of the vengeful wind nymph while he was battling their monstruous offspring.

He and the Maiden of Cozia reunited, and since then, she has been on a long journey throughout the lands, searching for allies while Vlad was planning his war. He first impaled the Akinji, who, since his refusal to send the blood tribute to the Crescent, began taking it on their own.

The word was that the plot against him that the deserter had spoken about turned out to be true as well. Mehmet did send envoys, inviting the Prince to Constantinople for a supposed truce. Vlad promised them he would come to pay his long overdue tribute and renew his pledge of loyalty if the Sultan would send a man in his stead to keep the throne warm.

When Mehmet sent Hamza Bey, Vlad's Hounds ambushed the company at Giurgiu with fire-breathing hand gunners, then had them impaled, giving the highest stake to Hamza himself. After that, he went on a rampage and purged the southern towns, villages, and even fortresses near the Great River. He listened to Dragomir's advice, after all, and even took hold of Giurgiu's Keep.

But it was only when he heard that the angered Sultan was raising an army as great as the one that conquered Constantinople to respond to this war declaration, that the Prince realized the cataclysm he unleashed. Since then, he has been sending letters and envoys to all his neighbours. And Ileana was one of them.

The two sisters have been the first to join her since the beginning, promising they and their men would stand by her side regardless of whoever sits on the throne. She had been travelling as an envoy herself to some of the richest Wallachian boyars all over the country, carrying Vlad's word and plea for their men and gold in the coming war, which many declined. The Hungarian King, son of Ravens' Order's founder, although he initially promised his arm, was another one that turned the Voivode down personally.

For more than twenty moons that passed as if they never existed, Codru always followed Ileana in her travels, although she never demanded it, in hopes that he could make her see that the fate of the man she served was already decided. He held hope that she would eventually leave the Prince and the coming doom behind. He had hoped her thirst for vengeance would fade away. Yet, deep down, he always knew it wouldn't—just as his own never had.

When he followed Ileana to her old home, where she wanted to pay her respects to the woman who raised her after her father's death, he was surprised to find that Mother Wednesday and the blind woman hiding from Death were one and the same. The woman who told Ileana of her unearthly origins was the same woman who now had Muma's adopted daughter in her care.

The town had changed for the better since the Dark-Man's ending. The cart he and Toma left behind was now pulled into the courtyard and empty. The blind woman welcomed both Codru and Ileana, not at all stunned that they had arrived together in her modest, cat-riddled cottage.

They dined, and later that day, Ilinca returned home too from her familiar forest, where the old lady was sending her for potion herbs and mushrooms. Codru noticed she wasn't entirely tamed, as some would have believed, although she was clean now and her hair was tidied under a dark headdress. The curse appeared to have ceased spreading further than her shoulders, yet her arms were wrapped, down to her fingertips, in thin linen cloth. Her and Codru exchanged a look, and the forest's daughter gazed at the maiden next to him. Then she left the room quietly, tending to her herb-filled hamper.

'Don't fret!' Mother Wednesday excused her on her behalf. 'She had been an outdoor cat for a long while, but she's hardworking and deserving of kindness and shelter, just like all of us.'

Although Ileana was in a hurry, the blind woman insisted they would spend the night there, rest, and leave in the morning. The Sânziană told her of her duty and time being of the essence, but the old one wouldn't budge. Overhearing, Ilinca showed up once more, completely ignoring Codru. She asked Ileana if she could serve.

'I know remedies, and I can tend to the wounded if you will have me,' the young woman said. 'I cannot undo the harm I have caused in the past, but I can at least help lessen the harm others will cause from now on.'

In that moment, Codru learned two things. First, he understood now, just as he understood when he helped keep the wounded knight alive, that poison can also be a cure. And so, even if Ilinca's touch was deadly, she grew into a healer. And secondly, he found that everyone sought deliverance, and although more than two years ago he denied her that, this time he did not oppose. Ileana didn't have the luxury to do so either, as every man or woman counted. So, she agreed, letting the girl know she may travel to the capital and announce to the Prince that she had been sent by her.

Meanwhile, Codru wanted to help Ileana for the same reason Stana did. If she wasn't going to give up, he might as well give her the best fighting chance. His arm already belonged to her, but he also had a sworn brother he hadn't seen since their return from the Isle of Snakes that he believed he would help. While he did not know his whereabouts, he was acquainted with someone who might have known. So, he asked Ileana to follow him to Härmeschtat to pay a visit to a certain blacksmith.

Eventually the sun broke through the clouds, and as soon as it did, they left the inn, went down to the stables, and readied their horses. Shadowfire was waiting patiently next to Ileana's pale mare, but Codru chuckled when his eyes met the horse's as the steed's unruly thoughts rustled through the man's otherwise oddly clear head.

The Red Fortress was rustling and bustling with townsmen coming all over the streets, from here to the square and back. Yet, when they arrived, the Master Blacksmith's workshop was closed.

Codru dismounted near the back entrance, and while Ileana remained behind in the saddle, he traversed the low roof with wooden beams supporting it, knocking in the solid door. He knew Sándor was not going to welcome him with open arms, even if Codru sent word he would arrive, but the workshop might have made good coin on such a day if it remained open.

He knocked in the door and called him out, but after not too long, a young man showed up in the doorframe, barely cracking the door open, wearing his dirty leather apron and a hammer in his left hand. His face and hands were greased and stained with coal.

'*Uram!*' he said, opening the door wider. 'Welcome back! The master said you would come.'

'Where's Sándor, István?' he asked the blacksmith's apprentice.

'Oh, he's drowning his sorrows upstairs! Please enter; I'll let him know you're here!'

Codru turned to Ileana, who was dismounting as well, pulling her white horse by its reins. The boy dropped the hammer, and while wiping the dirt off his hands with an even dirtier rag, he came to her aid.

'Beautiful mare, milady!' he exclaimed as he admired Ileana's horse. 'Does she have a name?'

'*Floare-de-Colţ*,' she said, smoothing down the horse's mane and handing over the reins.

'Floare-de-Colţ, indeed,' the apprentice echoed for himself. 'Fitting!'

No waiting had been necessary. While István brought both horses into the blacksmith's stable, Codru and Ileana entered the workshop on their own, and a dark-haired man welcomed them from the top of the staircase leading to his chamber above, behind him. He seemed oddly jolly to see Codru. From his doorframe, without coming downstairs, he opened his brawny forearms and said:

'Ha! If it isn't the Devil in the flesh—my new brother from another mother!'

Codru frowned sceptically as he looked up at their host. Glancing at the maiden by his side, he could see her grinning, overwhelmed by the brotherly spirit in the room.

'Sándor!' Codru greeted him with a nod.

The man eyed Ileana with a tacit, joking smirk, then turned back to the wanderer.

'Come on up; I was afraid I'd finish the wine by myself!' then he withdrew to his room, leaving the door open, just about the same time the apprentice returned and locked the workshop behind him.

Once Ileana and Codru climbed the wooden, creaking staircase, they entered the room. It has been a while since the wanderer was last here, but nothing has changed. He saw the same crooked windows toward the alleyway, which Sándor was now covering with the drapes as he cursed through his teeth. The same low ceiling almost made him bend his knee. The thick wooden table surrounded by small chairs, and the same lanky carpets covering the creaking plank floor.

Once he rested a bottle of wine on the table, he returned to his visitors with a wide smile on his blowzy face. Stumbling, he made sort of a reverence towards Ileana, grabbing her fingers in his rough-skinned hand and blessing them with a respectful kiss, he introduced himself. She revealed her name, and after he nodded, he turned to Codru, almost jumping him as he wrapped his strong arms around his whole body, seemingly forgetting that once they threatened each other. He reeked of liquor, Codru noticed, but at least he didn't bare any ill will towards him anymore.

'How's the axe holding up?' the blacksmith asked. 'I've been told those runes helped sending a certain Boyar back to the wretched hell he spawned from, hadn't they?'

Sándor peeked.

'Resting there safely, I see,' he smiled proudly. 'Yet never sleeping, am I right?'

He turned towards the table as he pulled a chair for Ileana, inviting her silently to sit with a hand gesture. Distracted by an overjoyed outdoor whoop, he let the chair go and muttered a barely audible curse towards the window wall.

'These celebrations are not to your liking?' Ileana smiled as she sat at the table.

'I beg your pardon, milady...' he said with a sigh. 'Them youngsters and their *Dragobete*, they made me lay siege to my cellar.' Then, with a suspicious eye turned to both the Sânziană and the wanderer, who was taking a seat next to her, he added, giggling:

'I hold hope you two aren't going to run around the chamber like dogs in heat while I'm around. Wait at least until the wine sends me to sleep.'

It was only when the blacksmith began pouring the liquor into the glasses that Codru realized there were four of them. He raised his head, ready to ask why, but before he had the time to do so, he heard a familiar voice from the room's corner, where the stairs to the attic were.

'Let Hanna and her four little boyar's spawns to themselves, Sándor!'

It was Toma making his way towards the table as Codru stood up. The Raven wore this time only a light grey tunic, breeches, and leather boots. His long blonde-grey hair was tied behind him, and no weapons were seen hanging from his belt.

'Good to see you again, brother!' he said, shaking Codru's arm strongly. 'And that you are all well nonetheless,' he smiled kindly as he gazed at the maiden.

'You must be the brave Ileana, Vlad's trusting captain I have heard of. I'm Toma.'

'Greetings, Raven,' she said, shaking his hand. 'I've heard a great deal of you as well!'

'Not much of a knight anymore, I'm afraid, milady. But just as honourable, one can hope.'

As he sat across from the two guests, Sándor went searching for his apprentice, demanding that he hit the pantry and gather some goods for dinner.

'I was counting on the fact there were still some men left at Mehadia,' Codru told Toma. 'And that without the late Captain and having cleared the Strigoi's curse, you might have a great word in their affairs.'

'Regretfully, whatever men were left there, they scattered soon after word of our forest ambush reached the Citadel,' Toma said.

'Besides, I wouldn't count that all the Strigoi are all gone, just as I wouldn't count all the Zmei are gone. We got rid of the roots, but their stems are out there, somewhere. As scattered and headless as the Order. It's just a matter of time until they show their heads once again.'

As the half-drunk blacksmith returned to his table next to the shelves with a bunch of sausages and cheeses, Codru was exchanging looks with Ileana. They might have made the journey for nothing. Alas, he thought it would be best to stray from the conversation.

'What of the treasure?' he asked. 'Have you had any troubles burying it?'

'Ha!' he heard Sándor exclaiming as he overheard the question, cutting and munching on sausage ends. 'Let's just say the Earth itself doesn't want that cursed Greuthungi gold; isn't that right, Toma?'

'It is safe for now, I believe; I broke it in smaller chests and buried them in many different places,' the Raven added as he sipped wine, vaguely irritated by his brother. 'Though once I did, flames began lighting up above their grounds, like beacons.'

Sándor laughed with his back towards them, while Ileana could not hold a smile either.

'Instead of hiding the treasure,' the knight continued, amused, 'I ended up drawing a fire trail, a map to where the Zmei's gold rests.'

'Aren't you afraid they'll find it?' the maiden asked, curious.

'Not at all, milady,' Toma said. 'The priests in the area already called it a sign from God, sacred lands, eternal fire, and other befitting names that will safeguard it for a long time.'

In the silence that followed, interrupted only by the blacksmith's knife on the cutting board, the Raven lay back in his chair with his mind wandering, his hand resting on the wine glass, and his eyes studying his companions.

'I know you are in need of men, and I wish I could have offered the Order's reins in your war. But for what it's worth, you should know you have my sword, milady, as I have promised it to my sworn brother here.'

'You have my gratitude, great knight!' she answered humbled.

Then Toma continued:

'Further on, I have sent a letter north to a certain monk that found his way around the throne of the young, yet hard-bitten Moldavian Voivode, Stephen. I am sure he will answer my summon to Târgoviște.'

Codru remembered Daniil, the exorcist, last seen on his way towards midnight, with the hell Paralei in his tail.

'If God wills it, he won't come alone. You see, Vlad and Stephen are blood too. He could spare some men if our priest puts in a good word, I reckon.'

Soon, Sándor returned unsteadily, holding a platter with meats and cheeses for his guests, which he then left on the table. While he was refilling the glasses, Toma turned to Codru:

'Speaking of sworn brotherhood and blood ties—what of the gold handle dagger I gave you?'

Codru did not have it. Once he killed the Hound, it remained behind, most likely stuck in his chest, buried somewhere in the ground with the corpse.

'I went to look for it with Ileana, but I lost its trace long ago. It's probably rusting somewhere in a shallow grave with its last victim.'

'That's a shame,' Toma answered, falling on his own thought. 'But at least it would explain why its sister's blade began to lose its shine of late.'

And calmly, he revealed his own dagger from behind and left it on the table, between them. Rust was beginning to show its teeth on the once mirror-clear iron.

\*\*\*

*Târgoviște, June 1462 (6970)*

In Vlad's tent, the silence was heavier and sharper than the Janissaries' scimitars. Having just ridden from the battle, depleted and hopeless, he sat in his chair, with his elbows resting on his knees and his cap in his bloodied hands. They were shaking. His eyes were wide and sunken in his skull, overshadowed by dark locks of hair. The muscles on his jaw pulsated, and sweat riddled his skin, rolling off his temples and dripping down.

He stared at the ground as Timotei was next to a map riddled wooden table in the middle, holding unrolled letters. Answers brought by ravens that weren't bearing good news. From his corner, exhausted himself, Codru could see it. It was fear. He knew, as all the other people in the tent knew, that they were going to lose the war. And they were all going to die.

'Burn those letters, scribe!' Vlad said, his voice shaking. Then he stood up, approaching the table, propping his arms into the wood, and crushing the maps and parchments under his grip.

'They have thrown us to the wolves. They have all abandoned us, the caitiffs. I swear on my forefathers' graves; so help me, God, if I live through this, I will gut them all and their offspring, one by one, and feast on their innards while they watch!'

Vlad's slow words were crushed between his teeth, full of anger and slough. With a sudden burst of wrath, he pushed everything off the table, throwing them to the tent's walls, howling ragefully like a wounded animal. But that was wishful thinking, Codru thought, just as unimpressed by the burst as the rest of the people. He wasn't going to live, as none of them were going to survive this war. Looking around, at all the ones present at this last supper council, he was aware they would soon be buried deep under the wayward hooves of the Ottoman's horses, crushed, and burned under their oil-soaked catapult stones, or eviscerated by their slaying blades.

His and Ileana's eyes met, and without talking, he understood from her gaze that she agreed she made a mistake by not leaving with him when they had the chance. But it was too late now; they knew. She let her eyes fall to the ground, and without excusing herself, she left the tent, holding tears in, leaving him, the Prince, the scribe, his advisers, and all the rest behind.

It has been over a week since the first masts and flagpoles grazed ominously on the Black Sea's horizon. When they appeared, people turned silent, thunderstruck at the sight of the frightful incoming vessels. A death-bringing fleet, as far as their eyes could see.

Before the ships could reach the shore, they first fell to their knees, praying, crushed under the weight of the coming, unstoppable doom. They then gathered their children and their elders, threw their lifetime-worth of work savings in their wagons and boats, and began running towards Braylan to escape.

When the terrible, blood-chilling news of the enemy crawling all over the Danube from both south and east, like the gutsy jaw of a monster, reached the Voivode's ears, Codru, Ileana, and Toma were already at the Princely Court of Târgoviște with him.

The Raven was right. When Daniil, the devil-taming priest, arrived as well, he did not come alone. Moldavian soldiers, not more than two hundred strong, have been sent to Vlad's aid, which added to the rest of thirty thousand soldiers the Voivode could gather, made of Viteji, Sluji, Hounds, mercenaries, and Egyptian slaves. He went as far as recruiting women and children that could barely hold a sword and even gathering the lepers and the plagued for a sacrificial army.

Codru met the monk when they were preparing to ride in different directions. He realized Daniil had never returned to his oath of silence. They did not exchange many words, as the urgency of war preparation did not allow it, but there was one thing Daniil said that stuck with him, just as the omen of Toma's dagger did:

'You should not be here, wanderer. This isn't your path.'

'I am where I'm needed. Isn't that purposeful enough?'

'It isn't if the purpose isn't yours,' the monk replied. 'Before the end is near, I will want to share the dreams of you I had, Codru.'

The Maiden of Cozia's regiment, as well as some others, have been tasked with greeting Mehmet's army to Braylan, while the majority of the Voivode's army has been sent towards midday, stretching too thinly over the vast lands of southern fortresses. Codru followed her to battle, and so did the knight and Stana's men.

But all they could do was shield the crowds of people desperately retreating towards the mountains, as Mehmet's foul army was tenfold theirs. The Ottomans had brought devastating, devil's powder-eating, bronze bombards that Codru's hatchet or Toma's sword were no match for. It was simply not enough.

Retreating, they had to fight blood and nail to not fall under the fiery, corpse swallowing waves of crushed earth, eviscerated by the cataclysm the marching Turkish riders were bringing with them. Codru had no love for them, yet as he was slashing through their shields and chest pieces, the anger that fuelled his murderous fight sprang straight from his rage against the Voivode himself, who was submitting his own people to a carnage impossible to stand against. And the words of Stana sounded as clear as day. They were fodder.

'We need to fall back!' he advised the Sânziană, as she was commanding her men to stand their ground against the impending purge, driven by her own hunger for the Sultan's blood. She only relented when most of the villagers, elders, women, and newborns had been freed and secured a clear path, as her ranks were broken, and her small army stripped to the bones.

It was then that, in the Braylan blood bath, a man stood out on the battlefield. Dressed in an old Wallachian gambeson, his unscathed eye was rolling from one foe to another, withstanding several on his own as he was wetting his sword's blade with their blood and defending his town.

'Dobre!' Codru came to his aid. 'We are retreating towards the capital. We are defeated here!'

At the behest of the Voivode, the remaining soldiers burned and salted the earth behind them as they retreated. They poisoned the fountains and dug into the brooks, letting water flood the lands and turning them into horse and wagon-eating marshes.

When they reached the outskirts of Târgoviște, one of the few last standing great camps, Codru heard that most of the southern bastions had fallen, prey to the grinding yoke of Mehmet's war ram. Distracted by the soldiers' bravery, the mercenaries' bloodlust, and the slaves' dreams of freedom, Codru didn't realize until later, when he heard the screams of the wounded and cripples echoing in the camp, that it was a lost cause. The sky appeared to agree, as rain was pouring from it as if the clouds had raptured.

Walking the mud filled encampment on his own, where the tents had been raised to shield the anaemic campfires and the mutilated, terrorised men and women and to give the forged impression of safety and respite for a while longer, Codru was witnessing the last days of the Wallachian resistance.

He saw Ilinca out there, under a makeshift barrack, screaming at two men standing beside her to hold another still and pinned to his soon-to-be death bed, while she was trying to saw his leg off with a chipped iron blade.

'Move!' Codru went in, joining the soldiers in keeping the man down. As she looked at him quietly, with rain, tears, and sweat rolling on her face, the wanderer forcefully stuffed a wooden shard in the poor man's mouth and touched his face, murmuring, almost unwillingly, words in the Old-Tongue, words that he never knew what they meant. The poor soldier's bone cracked, and he blacked out as blood was flowing into the mud.

'Give him this if he ever wakes up!' he told her as he let his last bits of dark matter, wrapped in parchment, fall in her blood-soaked, cloth-wrapped hand.

'I'm afraid,' she told Codru before he left the tent, shivering, 'He'll kill us all. He is sending the sick out there to spread the illness.'

The errand soldier Vlad sent to bring him to the Princely tent found him lost in the lamenting crowd as the rain clouds lifted, the red sky of the sunset blooming through the cracks. A clear sky was not a good sign. It only meant a clear path for the enemy to continue its march towards the city.

When he arrived, Vlad was wiping blood from his hands, his dark mantle dragging through the barely dried out ground that was to be the floor. Ileana was already there, as were Daniil and a few other loyal, steel plate-wearing boyars. The maiden noticed his entrance but turned away from him quickly as Codru remained in the corner near the tent exit, waiting to see what the Voivode wanted with him.

'We ought to surrender, Your Highness!' the men were saying. 'We are worth more to the Sultan than the earth beneath our feet. He surely can see that butchering our people means no tribute.'

'We will not surrender, steward!' the Prince barked, a light flashing through his cold eyes. 'Counsel me of that once more, and I'll have your tongue!'

'I will not bend the knee! I swear I will turn these lands into an inhabitable Purgatory before I let it fall.'

He was proud—too proud, Codru thought—but he was right. There was no turning back. He himself knew Mehmet well enough to know that the Sultan was proud too. The Voivode's resistance and stealthy attacks from last year were an affront to him. He raised one of the greatest armies with one purpose only—to wipe Wallachia off the map. He would never stand back, nor would he accept the surrender.

'What do you propose, Sire?' the monk said, sitting solemnly with his arms on the long pike, propped into the ground.

After a not too long pause, hesitantly, Vlad spoke, letting himself rest in the chair.

'I am still waiting for some ravens, but I can sense what news they will bring. We cannot count on any of them to send help. We are on our own...'

'Your Highness?'

'Our only choice is to do what we should have done years ago. Severe the serpent's head.'

And the Prince's eyes turned to Codru, while the rest of the men and women in the tent followed.

'I need you, Zmei-Slayer, to break into their camp tonight and slaughter Mehmet in his sleep. There isn't, nor will ever be, a better chance than this one to accomplish this quest.' Then he added: 'And you are our only hope.'

And so it happened that the past, which he had tried to run away from when he returned to the country, was once again catching up to him. Nothing of what he had done during the last more than a couple of years could erase it or keep it away. They all looked at him and saw in him what he had fought to not be—a death-trader. An assassin. A murderer.

Before he could answer, the young scribe broke into the tent, disrupting the council meeting. He had a scroll in his hand, and he pushed the men out of his way to reach the Voivode to hand it over.

In the rabid outburst of the Prince that followed, Codru took advantage and followed Ileana outside, though he sensed that after the battles and after that meeting, she was probably looking for a moment of quiet as she headed towards one of the wooden, roofless watchtowers built at the corners of their camp.

Walking in her footsteps, he passed by Toma, with his cloth wrapped around his arm, and Dobre, both sitting around a campfire with other men, eating perhaps one of their final meals, laughing at one of the smuggler's unsavoury jokes, as the old veteran let his faithful Left-Eye nibble the meat of a bone.

He saw Stana, Ana, and a handful of her scouts helping strengthen the palisades. He saw the healer, Ilinca, throwing water from a wooden bucket around her barrack, vainly trying to wash away the redness that stained the earth around it.

With his heart oddly heavy, he climbed the ladder after the Sânziană.

'Go feed yourself; I have this covered for now,' she excused the sentinel, who seemed both startled and grateful, and left the structure as soon as Codru ended his climb.

She knew he followed her, but she didn't turn. Instead, she gazed in the distance as the darkness lay heavily and the sun fizzled behind the horizon. He came closer to her and admired her face, contoured by the dying light.

'Look at all those fires, lighting up in the dark,' her voice sounded faintly, as from afar. 'Like the countless eyes of a lurking creature, preparing for a great feast.'

Codru saw them too. They were the Ottomans' camp, shaping up in the distance. Foreboding. Silent. Threatening. They were too many. As bold as it was, Vlad's last resort to an attack had no odds of success.

'I know you have your duties, Ileana,' he muttered, covering her hand resting on the rail with his. 'And I know the unsatiated justice that weighs in your stomach and heart. I have lived with them too. But you have given it all. This is beyond any of us now.'

She didn't say anything.

'Let's leave now,' he continued. 'Before it's too late. We could go anywhere and spend the rest of our years peacefully somewhere away from blood, revenge, and sorrow. The fight is over; let's just live.'

She turned to him.

'Where could we go, Alidor? Where could we run so that the pain and hatred I feel smouldering in my chest would not burn anymore?'

'I don't care where,' he said. 'Somewhere far. I will scour the end of the world to find a cure that would soothe you and I will make a vow to keep the blaze away from your heart until the end of time.'

Even through the falling night, he could still see a hopeful smile looming on her pale face. She then turned and let herself fall, propped with her back on the rail surrounding the edge of the tower and with her eyes towards the stars. She pulled him gently by his hand next to her, and then she laid her head on his shoulder, as they were both sitting and gazing at the night sky.

'Alidor,' she said softly. 'Will you tell me once more the story of the Wolf and the Bear?'

# CHAPTER XVII

*Târgoviște, June 1462 (6970)*

AT FIRST, HE HEARD THE SCREAMS, THEN HE felt the earth shaking under the thunders of the fire-breathing bronze beasts. He opened his eyes as he thought it to be a nightmare, as he had napped without wanting to. But it wasn't. He turned to his side, and Ileana was no longer there. He jumped to the rail, and in the distance, what not too long ago were only blinks of fire in a sea of darkness, turned into hell on earth. A tempest of battle under the cover of the night, with clouds of ash and lightnings of amber effervescing on the grounds. His stomach dropped; he had to find her.

He climbed down the tower in one breath and pulled his heavy feet through the overly agitated crowd of disoriented soldiers as they ran in all directions, lamenting, praying, and cursing, grabbing their swords and shields, and whipping their already frightened horses. They were leaderless, like headless animals running towards their fateful end. Codru pushed them violently out of his way, running towards the Princely tent with his hatchet at the ready as he glanced over the palisades and the mounds surrounding the camp, the distant fires flickering in his eyes.

He found that the tent was empty, and his heart began sinking as air seemed to not find its way towards his lungs. He felt a hand creeping up on his shoulder, and he turned ferociously, with his axe ready to smite, and pushed the unknown intruder against the nearby barrack. It was Toma, with his arms up.

'Where have you been? They broke into their camp, brother,' he muttered. 'They went for the snake's head.'

Codru felt his throat choking.

'No, no!' he left the knight off his grip, turning away from him with his eyes pinned to the ongoing battle. 'Who, Greuthung? Who went there?'

The knight shook his head.

'I don't know, Codru?' he said. 'Vlad gathered his men and they disappeared into the night on foot.'

'Where is she? Where is Ileana?'

Toma shrugged.

'What are we doing? We are sitting ducks here. The men are running.'

'Then don't let them!' he shouted, and then left the knight behind, running towards the entrance.

From there, he could see the torches and the ranks of the generals left behind gathering their men and horses and preparing to march towards their deaths too.

'Wanderer!' he heard a voice running towards him. It was Daniil.

'What is it, monk? Have you seen Ileana?'

The priest disregarded his question.

'You ought to stay behind, Codru,' he told him, his breath quivering and grabbing him by the arm. 'There's nothing for you there! Take a horse and leave this war at once?'

Codru pulled his arm from his grip and ignored his omens. He had no time for them.

'I care not for your riddles, monk! I must find her!'

He ran away from him, leaving Daniil behind, as he was shouting after him. But Codru did not listen, nor did he turn back. As he squeezed himself between the soldiers and their steeds, he reached the front line, where one of their leaders was issuing final orders, trying to nerve the panicked men. He saw Dobre right next to this man, with his arm up towards the dark sky. The eagle landed on his arm from the night sky. And the smuggler listened.

'Sailor!' Codru shouted out of the crowd, walking hot-headedly towards the captain and the one-eyed veteran.

The leader attempted to put himself between him and the Old-

Man, raising his arm and shouting a command, as one tries to stand between the predator and its prey. Codru grabbed his arm and twisted it violently, then knocked the man out with his fist, where his axe was tightly squeezed in.

'Dobre!' he then said. 'What is happening?'

'I have failed them...' the man almost whispered, his eyes falling to the ground. 'I've sent them to their deaths!'

'Speak, smuggler!' Codru roared, grabbing the man by the throat as the bird fluttered away, distressed. 'Talk, or your head falls first!'

The man turned up to Codru, and in the light of the fires crashing closer and closer to them, like burning rocks falling from the heavens, he could see a tear rolling on his wrinkled cheek and into his beard.

'The Prince asked me to scout their camp and find Sultan's tent. I was so sure of my Left-Eye...'

'What happened?'

'They went where I told them to. Him, the Hounds, the pathfinders. The warrior maiden... They went after the Sultan. But it was the wrong tent.'

'No...!'

His ears flooded as if someone held his head under water. He released the man off his arm and dragged his feet away, gasping, facing the battle. Off the distant clouds of smoke, he heard the shouts and the hoofbeats, getting closer and closer. He could see enemy riders running away from the massacre, coming towards the Wallachian camp.

Codru couldn't move his feet, but he could brace himself against them. His fury was greater than his fear of death. He drew his scimitar from under his mantle, and his fingers squeezed tightly on its hilt and on the hatchet's handle. Then, as the riders were approaching, he heard the Wallachians shouting behind him.

'It's the Voivode!' they said.

They were right. Leading the men towards the camp was Vlad's horse. The closer he and his followers rode, the clearer Codru could see they were not enemies; they were only dressed as them, and he realized it had been a disguise to confuse the Ottomans during their attack. With no foe to strike, Codru's anger grew even more. He jumped in front of the Prince's steed, which pranced, neighing, almost throwing its master off the saddle.

'Get out of the way, Zmei-Slayer, before I trample over you!'

'What have you done?' Codru shouted, standing his ground, as if he were ready to drag the Prince off his horse.

He turned his head around frantically, looking at the survivors that were riding from both sides, returning behind the safety of the ranks. Wounded. Scared.

'I did what you haven't got the guts to do! Move, I say!'

'Where is the rest of your men?' Codru asked, dismissing the orders.

'We were sent on the wrong path, don't you see? They were butchered! The scouts, the sisters... They're all dead! Curse you, Codru, for bringing the blind old man to us. Curse you!'

Codru's arms fell beside him, his chest tightening. Vlad's horse passed him by at a trot, and turning his head towards the fires behind him, he muttered:

'This has cost us the war. The captain was captured; last I saw her, she was circled by Janissaries. If there is any god you believe in, you should pray to them that she's dead.'

Then he kicked his horse, screaming orders to his generals to retreat.

Codru jumped in front of one of the last men returning and then pulled the wounded soldier off the saddle, turning the agitated horse in the other direction. He eagerly kicked the animal and whipped it violently with its own reins, grazing the already battered earth beneath its hooves and riding towards the battle embers with no care for himself. Nothing mattered. Let Vlad and his soldiers run, then, he thought. All the others were going to die soon at the hands of the Ottomans, and he had no patience to wait.

With the first fading lights of morning breaking through the sky, far away behind the coals of the simmering Turkish camp, he ran like the wind. Air fluttered through his hair and through his cloak as he broke it like a ravenous storm, clenching his fists on the reins and cursing the beast for not racing fast enough.

From a distance, the shadows of soldiers and horses lining up, framed by giant fires, began to form. By the time he reached the outskirts of the camp, enough that the dark morning breeze brought with it sparkles and ashes to him, he saw the horsemen forming ranks and standing ready like an impenetrable wall between him and the camp, as if they were waiting for his arrival. Very soon, he found out it was exactly what they were doing.

Riding more cautiously, aware of the suspicious trap that was setting ahead, his eyes pierced the smoke clouds and the air rippled by heat, scouting the disquiet forming between the large line of prepared soldiers. A path was formed through the ranks, pushing towards the front, as if an unseen force were pulling apart the sea of men. It was only when it reached the end of the crowd that he saw it. And when he did, his stomach dropped, and he pulled the horse to cease its gallop with such strength that the earth under its feet cracked, almost throwing him to the ground.

He saw the horns, their shadows carving ominously into the air. The helmet that bore them. The solid appearance of a man almost as tall as the horses. Chainmail and heavy plates covered his body, and a sharp, threatening blade was embedded into the stump that was once his arm. Hultan came forward in front of the rest of the soldiers and waited there at their helm, gazing towards Codru from a distance.

It couldn't be. He was supposed to be dead. He saw him dead, crushed from the fall, burned by the fires, and bloodless from the amputation. Codru's blood turned thick, freezing in his veins, and a great, sudden migraine began scratching inside his skull. At the sight of the ghost of his tormentor, he remained still in the saddle, unable to move or speak. Through the undulating air, he saw the man uncovering his face with a pull and dropping his wretched helmet to the ground. A grin showed on his disfigured face. He recognized the wanderer too.

He heard him howling an order in Ottoman, and out of the crowd, two Janissaries brought forward a prisoner with their arms tied behind their back and a sack dragged over their head. Codru's heartbeat in his eardrums as his throat tightened. He dismounted and left the horse to itself as he walked, staggering, with his hatchet almost dropping from his hand.

'Kir-Yüz!' he heard the man yelling, and Codru stopped on his walk. 'What a sight for sore eyes you are! I should have expected to find you here, fraternizing with your traitor of a prince; after all, birds of a feather flock together!'

Codru continued to hold his tongue, on purpose, as his temples pulsated and his eyes, unable to stray from the prisoner, held tightly in the soldiers' grip. Hultan smirked once more, walking towards them.

'I believe you didn't ride all this way just to see me,' he said. 'I believe you came for her!'

And with a violent pull, he dragged the sack off the prisoner's head, revealing Ileana.

'No!' Codru tried speaking, but the words got stuck in his jaw.

Even in the hazing light of the blooming morning, he could see the string of dried blood on her chin and the bruises on her already scarred cheek. She was weak, and she had been beaten. If it wasn't for the soldiers keeping her on her feet, she would have dropped to the ground.

'Ileana!' Codru bellowed. 'Ileana!'

Her eyes met his from a distance.

'Alidor...' she mumbled.

'Oh my!' Hultan came behind her, resting his arm on her shoulder and gently removing her hair off her face. He yelled: 'The maiden that escaped my riders years ago, isn't she, Kir-Yüz? Haven't I promised I will one day find her?'

'Get your hand off her! Release her!'

The Zmeu laughed.

'But you see, boy, you freed me of my hand, remember?'

'What is it that you want?'

'One would say justice, but that isn't me. I merely want you to suffer.'

Codru dropped his axe, its head getting stuck in the ground next to his feet. He then let his scimitar fall too. He stepped forward, his arms wide open.

'Then take me! This is between the two of us! Break my body; do with me whatever you see fit! But don't hurt her.'

'I beg of you,' he ended. 'Let he go!'

Hultan pulled her head back by her hair with his unscathed hand and slid his blade under her chin. Codru clenched his fists and his jaws, hearing the maiden gasp as her eyes begged him from a distance.

'Why should I waste time breaking your body when breaking your soul is so much sweeter?' the marauder said.

Unexpectedly, a haunting growl scattered to their side, at about the mid distance between the wanderer and the horned man. Out of the morning mist, a creature took shape, as grey as the air around it. A lynx. Before any of the men could realize what was happening or what the phantasm was, Bruma raced out of nowhere, right towards the men holding Ileana hostage.

The beast's claws pushed the earth and left it behind as its jaws stuck in one of the two Janissaries' faces, feasting on it and drowning the man's helpless screams in blood as he hit the ground. In an instant, the lynx jumped like an unearthly apparition to the other captor, its claw brutally slashing his throat.

Before the animal could turn to continue its rampage, a coward's blade went through its side as the marauder pinned the ferocious animal to the ground with a deadly blow, releasing a cry out of its chest.

Codru heard Ileana scream her old-friend's name. As if time had ceased flowing, he saw her trying to run towards Bruma, then stumbling to the ground, face down, hindered by the ropes wrapped around her wrists. With all the strength she had left in her, she raised her head off the ground, and her eyes met Codru's, who remained stuck in time.

The silence crushed him, and he couldn't see anything else for moments that dragged like ages, but her. And then the silence broke as Hultan arose behind her, grabbed her shoulder with his hand, and plunged his nefarious, bloodied spade into her back.

'You aren't running away again, milady,' he smirked.

A woeful, unhuman roar that he never believed it could unleash from his throat, spread across the field, entwining with a sudden flash of lightning and an ethereal thunderstrike that shook the sky's very foundation. After he howled, Codru fell to his knees, crushing the ground under him and wrapping his hand around the hatchet, now suddenly burning with sizzling white lights that began cracking through its blade's runes and through the once-dark veins left on the wood.

And as his heart shattered at the sight of Ileana's body lying motionless on the field, a storm began to gather in the heavy, crackling clouds. Codru's eyes, brewing with tempest and rage, turned to Hultan.

\*\*\*

After ordering the attack, Hultan mounted his horse and let himself fall back, soon swallowed by the mass of the army. Codru had to reach Ileana before she was trampled and buried under the Janissary steeds, but he was too far. He ran desperately, screaming rabidly, letting his scimitar behind him, and slashing the air with the furious hatchet. He was going to stand against an immense horde of enemies, but his bloodlust made him blind to it.

His axe first bitten the side of a horse running towards him, and it appeared as if the sky's own wrath flowed through its blade, searing the animal's wound with a white blaze, severing its owner's leg entirely, and casting them both to the ground. More of the same lightning struck at will through the army, falling from above. He glanced at his weapon as its blazing light veins spread all over his arm with an agonizing jolt, rendering him unable to drop it. But the pain he felt was nothing compared to his sorrow. He struck again, barking with a beast-like hunger, to crumple up the army in his path.

The flood erupted from the yellowed, thick clouds. Codru wielded the axe like a scythe, obliterating the riders and their steeds, thunder resounding in the vastness with each strike he landed.

He looked for her, but in the haunting vociferation, he lost her from his sight. The thought of her being now broken under these murderous army feet made him scream and plunge his weapon into the ground, as if he wanted to eviscerate Mother Earth itself. The ground cracked with a lamenting cry released from the depths, the large spreading scars oozing with light and swallowing the foes into their stretching abyss, dividing the attackers, and laying destruction on their continuous paths.

He struck again, releasing a blast of power that clashed like an invisible wall into the ranks and throwing them back, making them crash into the hungry sea of mud that was beginning to form.

Even with this unexpected blessing from his ancestors, Codru knew they were too many, and he was only one. And the strength that this force flowing now through his veins took to wield was draining. He was afraid he had lost her.

But then, through the storm and the wind whirring by his ears, he heard a chorus of familiar growls from behind. And the ground shook, foreboding of a great ally coming to his aid. Turning only for a moment, with his face covered in blood and his eyes flashing fire, he saw a herd of dark, fire-breathing beasts galloping towards the Ottomans and mud turning to ashes beneath their claws. Paralei.

And leading them, racing a grey horse, was the priest, handling his bifurcated pike as if it were the staff the devil creatures listened to. A deal he had surely made, promising them enough souls to kill their insatiable hunger. Only a few hundred Wallachians followed, and the Prince was not with them. But with the monk rode a few others—people that he now knew would stand by his side until the end.

He felt the earth trembling as the massive, fiery hounds passed by him, setting on the Ottoman's soldiers, who cried for help from their God, astounded at the unholy Wallachian summoning. The beasts' claws and long fangs shattered with their victims, ripping their throats and hearts out. Decimating them.

Falling behind, hopelessly, Codru saw the one-eyed Dobre, following on the clear path the hell hounds made, killing off the remaining foes, as its loyal eagle plunged from the whirling sky to his aid, gouging their eyes out and slashing their faces with its talons. He saw the knight, Toma, cutting through the enemy like an icebreaker, his Balmut mauling the men under its heavy blows. He even saw the healer, Ilinca, riding and casting her poisonous bolts off her wooden flute. When she fell off the horse, losing her only weapon, he saw her removing her arms' wraps and plunging savagely with her darkened hands towards the enemies' faces. Grabbing them and letting their heads rot and turn to dust under her very eyes.

He then saw her drop to her knees, digging with her hands through the mud. She turned to him and called out his name from a distance. In his heart, he knew what it was she discovered. Ilinca found her. The call and his renewed urge made him run towards the maiden in one breath. And then he saw Ileana, turned face up, with her head in Ilinca's lap. Her eyes were open, and blood was dripping from her chin. Next to her, the mud was red. Ilinca kept her hand over her chest, the Sânziană's life-oil flowing over her black fingers.

He fell next to her, dropping the axe and grabbing her face in his dirty hands, with a painful knot stuck in his throat, unable to speak. But his eyes said everything.

'Alidor!' she said faintly. 'I should have listened to you.' She coughed up blood. 'We should have left!'

'Ileana...' he muttered. 'It will be alright!'

'Find the one that wasted me, Alidor.'

He turned to Ilinca, who said before he even asked:

'I will do everything I can. Go!'

He took Ileana's hand in both hands and kissed it feverishly. He then reached out for his hatchet once more and stood up. He turned towards the battle, where his allies, the Wallachians, and the hellhounds made a wide whole in the enemies' ranks. The rain hastened and the thunder began rustling in the heaven's once more as his hand trembled under the strings of lighting swirling through his veins.

In the fire of the fight, the marauder's horns soon stood out. Codru went to smite the first Janissary he encountered, breaking him off his steed and mounting it in his stead. Hultan saw him from afar, too, on his own horse. His grin was long gone, perhaps stunned by his old apprentice's newly discovered powers. He was on his own horse, and when their eyes met, he turned the horse around, trying to lose himself behind the lines. He was running. And Codru was not going to let him disappear again, and he will make sure he stays dead.

Before setting the horse on his path, a long howl reverberated on the far, distant smoke battered by rain. The shadow of another creature walked on the field, greater than even the rabid Paralei under the exorcist's command. A dire wolf, missing one of his back paws. He walked on the field slowly, with his head bowed down, snarling as the first men to see scattered in all directions away from it. The beast stared at the wanderer, and when their eyes met, he remembered the wolf cub from the forest, with the iron teeth around its foot. Then the animal turned towards the running marauder, catching up speed and Codru knew the wolf was on the coward Zmeu's path.

The wanderer kicked the horse and began galloping, his way and the wolf's soon converging, racing side by side through the storm and the battle, through the blood and the mud, through the howling infernal creatures, the men torn to shreds under their claws, and the bronze, fire-breathing bombards that crushed through the Wallachian's lines. Breaking and widening the way the horned one was making through his own army as he desperately tried to escape.

When close enough, Codru heard the wolf's chest thundering as he threw himself in the air, and his large muzzle clashed into the wicked man's back, throwing him off his horse as if he were nothing and falling on its feet behind him. The fallen horse squirmed in the swamp under it, and when it found its way up, it bolted through the soldiers, crushing the ones in its way under its legs.

The rest of the men parted at the sight of the grand wolf that snarled and encircled the marauder, but the noose he and the wolf began to tighten around Hultan was severely crushed when the blast of the Ottoman's fire-beasts fell right next to them, carving a crater where the wolf stood and throwing the others to the ground, leaving an ear-screeching echo with it.

In the immediate aftermath, Hultan rose to his knees, disoriented without his helmet, wiping the dirt off his face. Codru stood up, staggering, unwilling to let him escape again. His eyes turned to a naked man missing a foot, face down in the wounded ground behind the Zmeu. The wolf-man's eyes were open but lifeless, and a peaceful smile was frozen on his face. The same as his ancestors, who laughed in the face of death. He was gone.

The marauder grinned like a madman as he propped his sword in the ground, helping himself stand up and watching the wanderer dismount.

'I haven't broken you enough, I see; you were full of secrets all along. Killing me won't bring your maiden back; it will only, once again, reveal to everyone who you truly are and have always been— a death-trader, just like me.'

As he laughed, the rain froze, and the drops began turning to stone. Hurt and with painful chunks of strength pumping through his veins, Codru lifted his empty palm, and the shards of ice bounced off it.

*'My cold heart breaks for you, brethren!'*

He turned to the sky as the unnatural ice grazed his face.

*'Your loss is my loss, for we are one and the same.'*

The lightning erupted in the sky's belly, revealing a terrifying, enormous shadow lurking in the clouds' nest.

*'Raise your axe, Hailbringer, and reap your vengeance!'*

Codru listened to the voice, and with his last strength, he followed its words. When he raised his father's hatchet, the winds and the hail rummaged through the battlefield, slashing skin, and grazing shields. A long roar stirred the heavens like never before, and the fields trembled under their fury. From the immense leaven whirl of clouds, lightning struck the blade of the axe, its glow trickling through the engravings and through the handle's black veins, grinding down his arm and making Codru kneel under its weight as he screamed, unable to pull his arm away.

*'Where to now, brethren?'*

With all his power, he unclenched the axe from the lightning's grip, and like a heavenly whip, the light broke through the fighters, laying a rampant siege to the men and their bronze beasts. And that is when the great Balaur plunged stoutly from the sky too, at his command, faithfully following the whip's guidance, bringing the tempest with it and scything everything the light left standing in its sight, making it all one with the earth.

At the sight of the Storm-Gatherer, the Paralei vanished themselves, having had their fill of soul and bone. They retreated, leaving the enemy prey to the sky beast, swirling like a scally, ashen cloud through the field and levelling it to nothingness. Similarly, the Serpent left the marauder to Codru, and as for the rest of his allies, they stood back, frightened at the sight of the wanderer's unknown might and the creature he had summoned. Hultan stood up, and his deformed face grimaced with terror as he saw Codru walking towards him with his blazing white axe in his hand, the forehead's ancestral eye lit up by unknown forces, and the piercing tempest embracing him, surrounding him like a cloud as he walked the earth.

The Zmeu tried to run, sliding desperately through the bloodied swamp. When he did, the Hailbringer threw the hatchet with a godly scream, and the weapon's sizzling blade plunged into the Zmeu's back, casting him back in the mud. Codru stood next to him, and with his boot, he turned the man face up, the sky ice crashing against his skin. He tried to raise his blade, gasping with fear, but Codru stepped on it, crashing his stump under his heavy foot. Then he mounted the man silently as the ice turned back to rain, his red hair soaking.

'You are...' Hultan began to say through his bleeding, defiant sneer, but before he could finish his filthy threats, Codru's fist landed on his face with thunder. The man laughed. Another fist silenced him. And then another broke his teeth like a hammer. The next one broke his jaw. Codru landed his knuckles like shattering mauls into his skull, one after the other, faster, and faster, as he screamed the heartbreaking rage out of his chest, unable to see anything but red. And when the last of his echoes dispersed, he stood there, above the dead, headless tormentor, shivering, with his bloodied hands trembling.

As the Serpent was now slowly swirling through the fresh nest it had made in what was left of the Ottoman's camp, Codru walked away. He returned, drained of strength, and dragged his feet to where he remembered Ilinca had remained behind to tend to the Maiden of Cozia. Numb, his eyes empty, and his hatchet dangling in his arm, he walked, ignoring the men that moved out of his way with both fear and curiosity.

On the way to Ileana, he saw Toma with a long cut across his face, bleeding. He saw Daniil sitting on a rock, behind the crowd, with his pike in the ground. And he saw Dobre, stuck on the field with a spear in his chest, lying amongst the dead. '*At least he joined his old comrades now...*' Codru could only think, pondering the old man's sacrifice.

He then saw Ileana, her eyes closed, lying on the ground. The woodland-girl was next to her, on her knees, with her hands now covered once more.

'Is she...?' he mumbled.

'Not yet, but she will be!' the young woman answered. 'I am sorry; no herbs or potions can repair a pierced heart back together.'

Codru kneeled next to Ileana, removing the hair from her pale forehead with his red hand. If she had a drop of life in her, she wasn't lost, he thought. He promised her he would keep her heart safe, and he failed. He knew what he had to do.

He hitched his axe to his belt and lifted Ileana's still body into his arms. He closed his eyes, and out of its nest, the Serpent answered to his summoning once more, dragging its great, massive body close to where he and Ileana were.

As the men watched in awe, Codru rested her body, almost as if it were a ritual, on the creature's neck, helped by the Storm-Gatherer which let its head rest on the ground. Then, the red-haired Salman climbed the rock-solid scales of the creature next to her, holding the maiden covered under his grip.

'*Take me to the Hollow-Mountain, brother!*' Codru said in his head. '*Take me to the Old-Man.*'

And as soon as the serpent had its command, it lifted its head and then its long body off the ground, flying towards the scattering clouds in search of his lost home.

✷✷✷

*Hollow Mountain, June 1462 (6970)*

The Old-Man's den was as he remembered it; poor, bleak, and narrow. Dried herbs hanged from the low, cavernous ceiling and wooden jars, with ointments and dust hanging in the walls' holes. Its entrance was covered only by a thick hemp curtain to shield him from the mountain's winds. Yet the man was different. He was smaller and thinner. His skin was leathery, and the remaining strings of hair turned whiter than snow. He was old. Older than the man himself ever believed he would have to be. The smoke was filling the den. The same smoke kept Codru numb when he was gifted the eye. And a wax candle cast their trembling shadows on the walls.

The teacher had kneeled next to the inert woman on the floor, spreading smoke over her from a stone scoop and reciting his ancient spells. As the master was trying to heal Ileana, Codru kept quiet, sitting in the corner without taking his eyes off her. If he knew for certain that there were any gods listening, he would have long since begun praying. But instead, all he could do was hope.

Soon, however, the Old-Man ended his incantations and left the smoke die, shredding the herbs ashes between his fingers. He saw him touch his tongue, then dip the finger in the ash. He then used it to draw a small, barely visible sun over her forehead. A sun with six sunrays coming from it, much like his own. He raised his haggard face to Codru without leaving the maiden's side, and the hailbringer understood. The words of his teacher resounded between his temples as clear as day.

'She is beyond my healing powers, *per'skrumb*. There is not enough blood oil to keep the flame flickering, and her heart is torn to shreds. She's ready for her final journey.'

The Old-Man had been his last hope, but deep down, he knew that even the Elder could not have brought her back from her endless sleep. Coming down to his knees and facing the teacher, the Hailbringer's eyes fell on Ileana's beautiful face, and a cold tear rolled down his cheekbone. He slid his arms under her and stood up. He quietly and slowly stepped out of the den without taking his eyes off her and letting the warm light of the candle scatter out through the moonlit night.

He looked up to the stars, his tears beginning to flow from his eyes as never before, sobbing and shaking as his chest appeared to have held in it decades of uncured, heavy sorrow. He had only recently found his peace, hope, and purpose, and now he was being stripped from all of them once more.

'Alidor...' her voice sounded as if it were a dream. She had her eyes closed.

'Ileana,' he gasped. 'I thought I lost you again.' 'Ileana!' he insisted, shaking his arms. 'I am here; you are safe now.'

He turned to the Old-Man, who was standing at the cave's entrance.

'She's awake; help me, teacher. It's not all lost; it can't be!'

But the man remained silent, without moving.

As he continued to shake her to wake up, repeating her name relentlessly, the mountain's winds began blowing. Warm, sweet winds, bringing with them floating flower petals and leaves. The voices that came with them were alluring and soothing. Codru left Ileana to rest on the grass, ready to reach for his ever-faithful weapon. But one of the ancient voices, louder than the rest, stopped him.

'You won't need that, sky-rider!' the unseen maiden said. 'We are coming in peace. We are coming for our own.'

A light flashed in the air, just before him and Ileana. So bright that he had to shield his eyes with his arm. The light began to stretch vertically, as if an unseen hand were slicing the ether, and the mountain seemed to be shaking under its apparition. When the vibrant, pulsating light became tall enough, it began to widen to the sides too, forming a strange doorway. The sight was so astounding that even the Old-Man left his den, approaching behind Codru in awe of the wondrous heaven's mouth.

The winds ceased, and from the ethereal, green and purple aurora, bathing in light, the shapes of three unclothed tall, young, and radiant women stepped onto the grass, turning the grass to ash under their feet. Their luminous bodies were only covered in their long, floating silver-gold hair, reaching their ankles. Their skin was as pure as milk, yet the phantasm in the middle had a long scar on her left cheek, just like Ileana.

The Old-Man kneeled as he saw them, and in their presence, Ileana gained enough strength to open her eyes.

'We have come to take you home, child...' the grave, yet melodious voices of the maidens sounded as if they were one.

'Who are you?' Codru asked, his heart racing.

'We have many names, brave one,' they said. 'But your kind calls us all Iele.'

'You are her mother...' he said, faintly, for himself.

They didn't reply. The one in the middle kneeled next to Ileana and touched her face softly, and it appeared to relieve her from all the pain.

'Can you help her?' Codru dropped next to Ileana, facing her mother.

Suddenly, a white, small bird with long feathers in its tail flew through the doorway of pulsating light. When he heard its endearing song, Codru felt as if an arrow went through his heart. A dirge. The bird floated above Ileana for a short time, then it landed at her feet, its golden beak twinkling in the blinding rays.

'The *calandrinon* has already sang its song,' the Mother said. 'Our daughter's time with you and your kind has ended; it is now her time to come home.'

'No!' Codru denied, throwing himself over Ileana. 'I won't let you take her from me!'

The unearthly, beautiful, and wise eyes of the nymph looked deeply into Codru's, then she said, without looking away:

'Tell me then, mortal. Would you let her die only to have her here with you? Or would you rather let her live and prosper away from you, even if you'll never see her again?'

Codru had been reduced to silence. He understood now that it was a sacrifice that was required. To endure, she had to be away from him forever. He cherished her more than he cherished himself, and if not ever seeing her again meant that she would live peacefully alongside these maidens, then it wasn't a choice; it was the only path.

'My time is running out, Alidor,' Ileana said, raising her arm and caressing his face. 'I can feel it. You must let me go.'

After a short pause, he nodded, holding her hand next to his face and kissing her warm palm.

'I know.'

He turned to her Mother.

'Where are you taking her?'

'Somewhere where mortals can never go. To *Youth-Eternal, Life-Everlasting*!' she answered.

'She is a rare breed, one of the few *Drăgaice*, the sword-bearing Iele. She will be taught our ways. She will live happily.'

Ileana then reached to her neck, pulled her talisman from the string, and left it in his hand.

'To remember me by... And to remember that, only because our time flew by as swiftly as an arrow, it doesn't mean what we had did not matter.'

Codru looked into her eyes for the last time and then kissed her pale lips until she, the Iele, the bird, and the light doorway vanished into nothingness, as if they never existed.

# *EPILOGUE*

Codru's eyes were stuck on the flames, but he was merely looking through them. The rain was drizzling, but not enough to end the pyre that was crackling on the mountain peak. The wind was flowing through his cloak, but it wasn't cold. And if it was, he wasn't sure he felt it. He was numb. He remembered the guilt that washed over him weeks ago, after Ileana disappeared into her kind's realm. But the Old-Man helped him with it.

'It was supposed to be me breaking into that camp,' Codru cried his heart out in the den. 'All the omens were saying I was supposed to die—the knight's dagger, the priest's dream... And now I am alive, and she's gone because of me.'

'But you did die, Alidor, when that murderer stabbed her in the back,' the Old-Man said. 'Or at least, the last part of your old self did. It died with her.'

Through the coughs, the man struggled to continue:

'It appears I was wrong, dear child. All those years I have given you nothing but suffering, as myself I was given; it only held you back from your true self. It wasn't mere pain you had to endure, but heartbreak, the greatest pain of all. It wasn't a mere loss you had to face, but a loss of love. It was only then that you unleashed a power that no other Salman has ever unleashed. Bringing the sky and the earth together, bringing the gods' wrath on earth through hail, riding the Balaur, wielding the thunder and the lightning at will. You are the truest of our kind and the first of yours. As great and powerful as your ancestors...' The Old-Man rested on his back, gasping. 'And you had to lose everything to become it. I was only holding you back from your true purpose.'

Codru thought vaguely of the prophecy the Egyptian maiden made some time ago. '*You have to first lose everything you're yet to have before you become who you are destined to be.*'

'Here, teacher, drink this!' Codru said, kneeling next to the man's sleeping rag and bringing a wooden cup close to his lips, holding his head up with the other hand. Then, after the man drank, he rested his head back as the teacher seemed to settle, quivering.

'You haven't held me back; without you, I would not be alive today. And without you, I wouldn't have caught the running Zmeu.'

He thought of the wolf, which Codru found out was sent to his aid by the Old-Man himself.

'His mother and his other seven brothers never accepted him after that night, my boy. He was a cripple, unfit for the pack. They outcast him. And he always remembered you, saving him from that trap. I gave him a purpose, and he accepted it wholeheartedly, knowing of the danger. He died in battle, like his ancestors. Laughing at Death as it reaped him.'

'I won't tell you what needs to be done from now on,' the Old-Man said before he died. 'But you should know, *per'skrumb*, that the path you have forged for yourself, with or without my aid, was the good path to take, the only path. Regardless of the hardships of life you have endured or will endure, rest assured that you will always stumble upon the path that is meant for you. No one ever loses their way; they're always right at the time and place they are ought to be.'

'I am proud of you, and I am at peace with you carrying on my legacy. I am now ready to meet my forefathers.'

He wanted to be burned and let the winds and the rain he reined for a hundred years carry his ashes and his spirit to the clouds he never had the chance to wander, for at least in the Otherworld, he could ride the serpent side by side with the Fire-Knights.

As the pyre burned and the master's ashes were scattering to the sky, the hailbringer stood on the mountain peak, gazing over the flames, towards the vast horizon. A silent lightning flashed, a sign of the teacher's spirit reaching the Gods. And in the nesting clouds, the shadow of a Storm-Gatherer shaped in its midst, then vanished as if it were never there.

# GLOSSARY

**akçes** – Ottoman silver coin
**Akinji** – Light Ottoman cavalrymen who conducted raids
**archipelago** – Refers to the Aegean Sea, the 'Sea of Islands'
**axeinos** – 'Inhospitable' in Ancient Greek
**aspidă** (*as-pee-duh*) – Legendary snake; viper
**balaur(i)** (*ba-la-oor*) – Serpent-like creature like the dragon from other mythologies
**bashi-bazouks** – Fierce, irregular, undisciplined Ottoman soldiers; marauders
**ban(i)** (*ba-nee*) – Silver coins
**'...besieged the Citadel'** – Refers to Râşnov Fortress in Kruhnen, besieged by the Ottomans in 1421
**bogdaproste** (*bog-da-pros-te*) – Thanks addressed to someone who gives something as charity, usually in honour of someone who died
**borangic** (*bo-ran-jik*) – Silk
**brimstone** – Sulfur
**bruma** (*broo-ma*) – 'Hoarfrost' in Romanian
**bulibaşă** (*boo-lee-ba-sha*) – Gypsy chieftain
**buris'rouka, visa'kapura** – 'Plentiful rain for fertile lands' in the Old-Tongue
**burgher** (*bur-ger*) – Citizen; here more in the 'noble man' sense
**calandrinon** (*ka-lan-dree-non*) – Romanian mythological bird often seen as a harbinger of death
**dacian** – Native people living where is today Romania
**devşirme** (*dev-sheer-me*) – Blood tribute
**dinar** (*dee-nar*) – Silver coin
**doină** (*doy-na*) – Old song of yearning
**dragobete** (*dra-go-beh-teh*) – A traditional Romanian holiday celebrating love and spring
**drăgaică / drăgaice** (*druh-guy-ka / drah-guy-che*) – Sword-bearing Iele
**earth-tongue** – In the book, synonymous to the proto-Indo-European language
**falcă** (*fal-ka*) – In Romanian, it means 'jaw'; Dacian people used a weapon called 'falx' that fits the same description
**floare-de-colţ** – Lion's-paw, or Edelweiss, a white, star-shaped

flower specific to the Alps and Carpathian regions, is coincidentally celebrated in Romania, where it is considered a natural monument, on March 5th

**giaour** – 'Infidel' in Turkish

**greuthung(i)** (*gre-oo-tung*) – Gothic tribes name living during the 3rd and 4th centuries in Central Europe

**hăis!** (*hah-ees*) – Command given to a horse to go, to start

**horă** (*ho-ra*) – Traditional Romanian dance where dancers hold each other's hands, forming a spinning circle

**hünkâr** – 'Highness,' in Ottoman-Turkish

**ie** (*ee-eh*) – Traditional women's linen or silk shirt

**iele** (*ee-e-leh*) – Romanian correspondent for the woodland female nymphs

**ipingea** (*ee-pin-gea*) – Woollen or cloth mantles adorned with chenilles

**iţari** (*ee-tsar-ee*) – Linen or woollen breeches

**ji kaj ʒas?** – 'Where are you going?' in Rromani

**judeţ** (*joo-detz*) - Mayor, magistrate, judge

**jupân** (*zhoo-pahn*) – Master, Sir, Lord

**krátēste!** – 'Seize (them, him)!' in Ancient Greek

**laćho to děs** – 'Good day to you!' in Rromani

**lefegiu** (*le-fe-joo*) – Killer for hire, mercenary; death-trader

**leşi** (*le-she*) – Polish people

**luna** (*loo-na*) – 'Moon'

**lăptiţa** (*lup-tee-tsah*) – Term of endearment which could translate as 'Milk-like'

**magna mortalis** – Latin for 'Great Death,' as the plague was called during Middle Ages

**mashrabiya** - Wooden interior latticed screens used in Oriental style rooms for privacy

**'me na vakărel Rromano...'** - Incorrect way of saying 'I don't speak Rromani' in Rromani

**michiduţă** (*mee-key-doo-tsa*) – Name given to the devil

**moarte-neagră** (mwar-te-nee-ag-rah) – Romanian for 'the plague'

**moroi** (*mo-roy*) – Vampire in Romanian mythology

**moşi(i)** (*mo-shee*) – The Ancients, The Elders; Ancestral deities

**muma** (*moo-mah*) – Archaic Romanian form of the word 'Mother'

**murgule** (*moor-goo-leh*) – Appellative for a horse; chestnut horse

**mărţişor** (*mar-tsee-shor*) – Red-white ribbon talisman

**necurat** (*ne-koo-rat*) – One of the many names given to the Devil

**nell'Evros** – Refers to the river Maritza in Italian
**neînțărcată** (*neh-yn-tzar-ca-tah*) – 'Unweaned,' an infant or young animal that has not yet been weaned off its mother's milk
**old-tongue** – in the book, the Dacian language, spoken by the native tribes living where is today Romania
**oltenian** – Name given to the folk living in the south-western part of Wallachia, from the river Olt
**opinci** (*o-pin-che*) – Hardened leather and wool shoes
**oud** – A lute-like stringed instrument
**padishah** – 'Master King' in Ottoman-Turkish
**pajură** (*pa-zhoo-ra*) – Golden eagle
**palincă** (*pa-leen-ka* – Fruit brandy specific to the Carpathian Mountains area
**paraleu/paralei** (*pa-ra-leh-oo / pa-ra-ley*) – spawns of the Underworld, similar to hellhounds
**pârcălab** (*par-kah-lab*) – Governor or commander of a fortress or town
**per'skrumb** – 'Son of the Ashes,' or 'The one born from the ashes' in the Old-Tongue
**piază-rea** (*pya-za re-a*) – 'Calamity-Howler,' someone who often predicts or attracts disaster
**polistai** – 'Founders of cities' in Greek
**postelnic** (*pos-tel-nik*) – Closest councillor to the Voivode
**pui-de-lele** (*pwee de le-le*) – Whoreson
**rebo'ditas** – 'Flow towards the light,' in the Old-Tongue
**roșcă** (*rosh-ka*) – Archaic Romanian slang for red-headed person
**rock-wood** – Fossilized driftwood washed in by ancient underground rivers
**râmlan(i)** (*rym-la-nee*) – Name for 'Romans' in old Romanian
**rumân** (*roo-mahn*) – Archaic way of saying 'Romanian language'
**salman(i)** (*sal-ma-nee*) – Name given by the Wallachians to the members of Codru's caste; *solomonar*
**samian astrologer** – Pythagoras (of Samos)
**sarmizegetusa** (*sar-mee-ze-ge-too-sa*) – Capital of the ancient Dacia
**sântandrei** (*sun-tahn-dray*) – Archaic way of saying 'Sfântul Andrei' or Saint Andrew, patron of the wolves
**sân-nicoară** (*sun-nee-ko-a-ra*) – Saint Nicholas, patron of sailors
**sânziană/sânziene** (*sun-zee-ah-nuh / sun-zee-eh-neh*) – Iele, woodland nymphs
**scimitar** – Curved, single-edged Ottoman sword

**scodra** – Or Shkodra, a Venetian city. It also means 'forested hill'
**secui** (se-koo-ee) – Székely people, ethnic group
**sen!** – 'Hey, you there!' in Ottoman
**sen, Buraya!** – '(Come) over here!' in Ottoman
**sfat** (*sfat*) – Council
**sluji** (*sloo-jee*) – 'The Small Army' or the 'Voivode's Guard,' made of boyars and servants
**stânjen(i)** (*stuhn-je-nee*) - A traditional unit of length measurement in Romania, historically used especially in rural areas
**strigoi** (*stree-goy*) – In Romanian, 'striga' means 'to shout'
**ştimă/ştime** (*shtee-muh / shtee-meh*) – water nymphs, similar to the mermaids
**târg** (*targ*) – Market
**târgovişte** (tar-go-vish-te) – Wallachian capital
**te arakhel o Del** – 'God forbid!' in Rromani
**the otherworld** – *Tărâmul-Celălalt*, or the Afterlife
**the youth-eternal, life-everlasting** – *Tinereţe-fără-Bătrâneţe şi Viaţă-fără-de-Morte*, a realm from Romanian folklore, different than the Otherworld
**tiro rrajimos** – 'Good sir!'
**the beyond-the-forests' land** – Transylvania
**uncheaş** (*oon-key-ash*) – Old-Man, Old-Father, Uncle
**uriaş(i)** (*oo-ree-ash*) - Giants
**vânători** (*va-nah-to-ree*) – Literally meaning 'hunters,' although they acted as a militia
**vântoasă/vântoase** (*vun-toe-ah-suh / vun-toe-ah-seh*) – Female spirits that can cause winds and storms
**vodă** (*vo-da*) – Short version of 'Voivode'
**viteji** (*vee-tej*) – A military contingent composed of battlefield-proven farmers; 'The Great Army,' mostly made of peasants and farmers
**yilan adasi** – The name Ottomans gave to the island of snakes
**zalmos** – Name given to Zalmoxis/Zamolxis, the supreme Dacian god; 'zalmos' also means 'animal pelt, fur' in Thracian language
**zână(e)** (*zy-nuh*) – Synonymous to 'Iele', 'Sânziene', 'Rusalii'
**zila'ditas** (zee-la-dee-tas) – Could be translated as 'flower of light' in Dacian
**zmeu/zmei** (*zmeh-oo / zmeh-y*) – A type of fantastic creature in Romanian folklore, usually human-like, with reptilian features
**zwingers** – Inner belt walls in a fortress

# THANK YOU FOR READING!

Please consider adding a review and rate the book on Amazon and do let me know what you thought of it. Amazon reviews are very helpful for self-published authors, so I would appreciate you for taking the time to support me and my work. Feel free to share your review on social media with the hashtags *#hailbringer* and *#hailbringer_novel* to encourage others to read the story too.

## DON'T FORGET TO SIGN UP FOR MY AUTHOR NEWSLETTER

Be the first to know about Daniel Alexandrescu's new releases and receive exclusive content! By signing up for the newsletter, you can also receive special offers, giveaways, discounts, and other bonuses.

www.hailbringer.com

# ACKNOWLEDGMENTS

I'd like to thank a few people who supported me throughout this writing journey. A big thank you to my sister, Cristina, a published author, for being an inspiration. Thanks to Camellia, whose help was crucial after I lost my initial draft and who has been there since day one. I'm grateful to Nico and Baldo, the family I chose, for their unrelenting moral support. My friends Maricar, Charis, and Panagiotis deserve thanks for encouraging me and being there for me these past few months. Thanks to Annamaria, who taught me an important lesson: art is about transformation, not perfection. Thanks to my younger siblings, Roxana, Andrei, and Alex, for reminding me of myself at their age, and to my parents for their unexpected thumbs up to continue writing the book, even if only to get it out of my system. Lastly, thank you to everyone who followed my journey on social media, to my Patreon supporters and to all who sent me heartfelt encouragement through DMs. Publishing a novel has always been a dream of mine, but without every one of you, it wouldn't have become a reality. So, cheers!

## ABOUT THE AUTHOR

***Daniel Alexandrescu*** is a 33-year-old Romanian self-published author currently residing in Cyprus, where he relocated 10 years ago. His writing journey began at the age of 12 with short stories, and by 14 he started drafting a fantasy novel that remained unfinished. During his college years, Daniel had an opportunity to publish a volume of poetry, but the project was not completed. With a bachelor's in philosophy and a mix of technical skills due to various jobs he worked at. Daniel has been engaged in writing for about 20 years, both for personal projects or blogging and as a freelance journalist, content writer and copywriter. In 2014, he co-founded CVLTARTES, an unconventional culture webzine. The idea for a fantasy novel drawing inspiration from Romanian folktales emerged in 2020. Despite several interruptions, Daniel committed fully to this project in September 2023, leaving his last job to focus on the novel. This debut book represents the fruition of his longstanding passion for writing and storytelling. Hobbies: hiking, cinema, photography, bouldering, mythology, Norse culture.

Website: www.hailbringer.com
Instagram: @daniel.alec.zander

Made in the USA
Columbia, SC
17 July 2024